WHO WAITS
BEHIND THE DOOR?

THOMAS MAINWARING: a medical mind as advanced as it is abnormal. Convinced he's found the cure for cancer, he kills more often than he heals.

■   ■   ■

SHANE COVINGTON: a beautiful lesbian with dangerously hypnotic eyes. Young girls reject her on pain of death—a slow, slicing death.

■   ■

PAUL ST. DENIS: textbooks call him a homicidal paranoid. Now he moves through society with all the attributes of a normal personality, until somebody pulls his trigger.

■   ■   ■

JOHN HUGHES: the rare addict who doesn't lose his sexual desires on drugs. On heroin he's the most personable man you'll ever see. On PCP he becomes a killing machine.

■   ■   ■

TINA DUCHIN: wife of one of the richest men in the country. She's a fanatically devoted satanist. With a special fondness for human sacrifice.

■   ■   ■

In this hospital
of horrors,
who is crazy?
who is sane?
You may die before
you find out...

BEHIND THE DOOR

A NOVEL BY
FRANK LAMBIRTH

POPULAR LIBRARY

An Imprint of Warner Books, Inc.

A Warner Communications Company

PROLOGUE

Madeleine Turner reeled off a few choice obscenities as the car swerved again toward the shoulder of the road. The headlights showed a roadway alive with wind-driven sprays of leaves, dried weeds, and even occasional newspapers skidding across the blacktop. She looked down at the clock on the dash—two A.M. Her hard-earned new friends would think she was scatterbrained if they could see her now.

If it hadn't been for the argument with Benton that afternoon over the expense of renovating the old farmhouse, she would be asleep in her bed. Her husband had ducked out of the fracas, off on a business trip to Kansas City. Madeleine sighed. He was on the road much of the time, leaving her to make friends in the staid, clannish community.

But now after renting an apartment in town for the first year, they had bought a farmhouse and she had been working feverishly to get it in condition to move into. Planning a surprise housewarming party, Madeleine had decided to tell none of their friends until they had set a date for the party.

She glanced at the rearview mirror. The headlights were still behind her—the only sign of life she had seen on the otherwise deserted road. The other car had swung out behind her from a side road just outside town. It was probably someone coming home late from a party, but still she was nervous, remembering the horrible crimes that had terrorized the Stoneville area for the last year and a half.

With a sense of relief she spotted a shiny new aluminum mailbox that marked the lane leading to their new house.

Madeleine had gone perhaps fifty yards on the gravel lane when for the first time in her life she suffered a moment of utter terror. The welcome darkness in her rearview mirror was shattered by the ominous twin circles of light. This was a private road, and no one had any business on it. For a foolish second she wanted to believe that Benton had somehow returned and was following her, but the idea was ridiculous. Thoroughly frightened, fighting the urge to floorboard the accelerator and rush down the dead-end lane, she tried to think of what she should do.

The rifle! Of course. If she could reach the farmhouse, she would have the gun. Benton had brought the .22 out day before yesterday to use on the horde of rabbits that infested the place.

Despite her efforts to control herself, she started to drive faster. The car was bouncing hard on the rutted lane. Her pursuer had to know she was aware of him.

As the car sped across the top of the dam that formed the big bass pond, she risked another look into the rearview mirror and an enormous feeling of relief overwhelmed her. She braked to a stop and shut off the motor, conscious in the resulting quietness of the wind-driven waves lapping against the rip-rap of the dam. Torn between relief and anger that she had been unnecessarily frightened, she rolled down the window as he leaned over to peer into the car.

"Thank God it's you. I was scared to death. But why didn't you . . . ?"

"Sorry ma'am. My fault. When I saw you turn off into the Terlin place, I thought maybe you were lost. After all, nobody's lived here since Edgar died last year."

Madeleine laughed. "Oh, what an idiot I am! I should have told *you*. Nobody's supposed to know we bought the place. We wanted to surprise our friends. I have been working day and night, getting it ready for the big move. I couldn't sleep, so I thought I might as well get up and drive out here to work on the floors for a while."

He straightened up, his fingers drumming on the car's roof, and glanced around ostentatiously. His voice had developed an edge. "Aren't you worried about being on the roads late at night after all the stories in the newspapers? It's pretty lonely around here, especially on a night like this. Doesn't your husband object to an attractive young lady like you taking chances this way?"

Madeleine did attract attention with both her face and form, and when she blushed guiltily as she was doing now, she was especially pretty. "He doesn't know I'm here. He left on a business trip to Kansas City this afternoon. Benton wouldn't much care, anyway. We had a row over carpet costs for the house."

He stared at her thoughtfully for an uncomfortably long time. A full minute must have dragged by, and he said nothing. Something was wrong—very wrong. He abruptly stepped back and nodded. "Okay. I'm sorry I frightened you. When I saw you turn in here and then noticed that back tire, I thought . . ."

Without thinking, she opened the door and slid out of the car. "Oh, God, more trouble. What's wrong with the tire?"

Madeleine hurried around to the back of the car and looked. It seemed perfectly all right. She looked up, startled to find him standing so close beside her, drawing on a pair of leather gloves that looked black in the headlights. "What do you mean? I don't see anything wrong with the tires."

He ignored her question and asked one of his own. Nodding toward the farmhouse, ghostly white in the uncertain light of the cloudy night, he asked, "There's a light on in there. Maybe I had better go in and check it out?"

She laughed uneasily, her nerves on a raw edge. He was standing so close, staring down at her, his body rigid, pounding his gloved fist into the leather-clad palm of the other hand. "Oh, no, I . . . I left it on deliberately. We have some heaters going to dry out the new plaster. I was coming out very early in the morning to turn them off, so I left the light on."

"Not someone waiting for your arrival, then?"

She stared at him, growing indignant. "What do you mean?"

He nodded toward the dwelling again. "There's a pickup parked out in front. Sure you don't have a little late-evening company?"

Her voice broke in her anger. "That's Chad's truck—the plasterer's. It broke down and I gave him a ride back to town this morning. Besides, what business is it of—"

"You filthy bitch!"

His fist exploded into her midsection, and she had no breath to scream. She reeled backward against the car and he followed her, his shoulder pinning her against the vehicle as he drove his fists time after time into her body. The only sounds were those of his grunting and hard breathing and the soft thud of his fists landing. It was only when he stepped back to rain blows on her face that her limp body was free to slide down onto the graveled surface.

For a moment she regained consciousness and mumbled "Why?" through the ruin of her lips, and then he sprawled atop her, clutching her by the hair and slamming her head sideways into the steel rim of the wheel with insane fury.

When, at last, exhaustion forced him to stop, he rolled away from the body, down on all fours in the lane, head sagging, dry-heaving as he fought to catch his breath. When he regained his feet, he staggered across to Madeleine's car. Starting the engine, he lifted her body and slid it into the front seat. He slipped the gear lever into neutral and turned the wheels hard toward the steep front slope of the dam. Straining, he threw his weight against the rear of the car. The effort was back-breaking against the drag of the soft ground until one front wheel slipped over the edge of the dam facing—and then the car tipped sideways, plunging downward to disappear with an enormous splash into the pond, leaving little sign of its passage on the rock rip-rap of the dam. It was perhaps thirty seconds before it sank out of sight in a maelstrom of whirlpools and exploding bubbles.

Soon the only sound competing with the steadily rising wind was the diminishing whine of an automatic transmission as the second car backed down the lane. At the pond, an occasional outburst of bubbles still rose noisily to pop on the wind-roughened waves.

Madeleine Turner was to lie in her watery grave for eight days.

CHAPTER 1 _____

T he small plane seemed to hang motionless in the blue sky that stretched over it like a great dome. Beneath the plane a roiling blanket of sun-etched clouds stretched on a broad front from Michigan to Texas. The storm was hurling silvery needles of cold rain against the limbs of bare trees in the Ozark country of Missouri and Arkansas.

Gavin Thorne lowered his gaze from the jet's window to his watch and turned toward his companions. Elizabeth Shea snapped out of her reverie, aware that Gavin was talking to them. "What did you say?"

"I said, 'We must be getting close. The plane is losing altitude.'"

He was right. The billowing sea of white was nearer now, and the jet engines had changed their pitch. The pilot's voice burst from the loudspeaker. "Mr. Thorne, we will be making our final approach in four minutes. That soup below us is plenty thick. We're going to be in it for a while, but don't worry. There is a nine-hundred-foot ceiling. No problem at all. And don't forget those seat belts."

As they dipped into the heavy cloud cover, Meredith said,

"Damn it, I always hate this. I hate not being able to see where I'm headed."

The clouds closed around the plane, and the interior of the cabin darkened abruptly. The mist around them was so thick that Elizabeth could barely make out the wingtips.

Meredith Thorne exploded, "Damn it to hell! What is that stupid son of a bitch doing? Has he leveled off in the middle of this stuff? For God's sake!"

Scott leaned toward her. "Hey, no problem, Meredith. He said the cloud cover was thick. We'll be out in a minute. Why don't you—"

"Shut it up, Scott! Just shut it up. I don't need any sermonette from you. If I—"

Gavin Thorne's voice was sharp. "Meredith, control yourself! We'll be in the clear in a second."

He was as good as his word. Before he could finish the sentence, the plane burst out of the clouds into a dim, grayish world. The land, flashing by beneath the wingtips, was monochromatic, the color sucked from it by the strangely lit sky. They had plunged from a world of light to one of darkness.

The speaker came to life again. "One minute to touch-down."

There was a hard jolt, and the plane raced along the ground. The small jet rushed past a row of low buildings through whose windows the lights shone brightly in the bleak afternoon.

As the plane taxied slowly back toward the largest of the buildings, Elizabeth could feel the aircraft being buffeted by a howling gale. Fifty yards from the terminal, the plane halted on the gleaming asphalt apron.

The door to the pilot's compartment opened, and a rakish young man leaned through the opening.

"I'll give you people a minute to get your coats on before I open the hatch. It's storming like hell outside. Never mind about your bags. The airport has a man who will take care of them."

"How about the rental car?" asked Gavin. "Is it here?"

The pilot shook his head, smiling. "Sorry, I couldn't say.

The airport has nothing to do with that. You'll have to ask after you get inside."

Elizabeth slipped into her raincoat and was struggling to free her makeup case from under the seat when the pilot opened the hatch. The sounds of the raging wind filled the cabin.

Afraid that she would be left behind, Elizabeth hastily buttoned the collar of her raincoat and sidled down the aisle. As she stepped through the small opening on to the step, a gust of wind caught her, opening her coat like a sail, blowing her backwards into the plane. She felt two arms close on her and twisted around in sudden panic to find the young pilot's laughing face bare inches from hers.

"Hey, sweet lady, you'd better button that coat or you're going to take off like a hang glider."

She started to say something, then blushed, aware that she was still leaning back into his arms. She pulled herself upright, buttoned her coat, and stepped down into the wild maelstrom of the storm.

She felt like a fool, not even acknowledging his help. Would she ever be at ease around men again?

The pilot remained in the hatch, watching his attractive passenger struggling across the windswept concrete. Elizabeth was in her late twenties, tall—about five-eight, and no more than one hundred and twenty-five pounds.

Buffeted by the air blasts that sent her light brown hair whipping across her face, alternately revealing and concealing the gold earrings that complemented her deeply tanned skin, she reeled toward the terminal building, passing an elderly black man in a yellow rain suit pushing a luggage cart.

When she reached the terminal, she tugged futilely at the heavy glass door, unable to overcome the pressure of the wind against it. Only when Scott Sutherlin hurried to her assistance was she able to lurch into the small waiting room.

He winked. "I like your new hairdo, kiddo. I will use it in my next horror movie."

She looked at her reflected image in the door. "Oh, Jesus! What a wreck! I need a major repair job in the little girls' room."

"Meredith's in there, doing her own reconstruction. She took one look at her reflection in the door, burst out crying, and ran for the ladies' room." His face grew serious. "Listen, Elizabeth, I wonder . . ."

She knew what was coming—more questions about Meredith—and wanted no part of it. She interrupted him to declare that she was off to repair herself.

It wasn't that she didn't want to help Scott. Elizabeth liked him as she might have liked a great, overgrown puppy. He was twenty-seven, six-four, and always eager to please —a straight shooter. Scott was nice looking—maybe not attractive—but appealing to the maternal type. His features were neat except for his oversized ears, which peered through his brown hair, worn with an old-fashioned part on the side. His only weakness was Meredith Thorne. He was crazy about her, and his sun rose and set on her moods.

When Elizabeth entered the small restroom, it appeared empty. She had expected to see Meredith standing at the lavatory mirrors. She was puzzled until she heard an odd sound behind her and glanced toward the enclosed toilet stalls. She could see hose-clad legs standing in the near stall and recognized Meredith's shoes.

Satisfied, she dug a comb into her tangled tresses, gritting her teeth in pain, pausing as a sniffling sound came from the stall. Scott had been right. Not only had Meredith been crying, but she still sounded upset.

"Meredith, are you okay?"

Meredith's voice was odd, but certainly not emotion-choked. "Yeah, I'm okay, Elizabeth. I'll be out in a minute."

"Are you crying? Scott said you were upset."

"Oh, no. You know Scott. The cold air gave me the sniffles. I'm okay now."

When Meredith left the stall, a puzzled Elizabeth saw no trace of tears. The look of fatigue and the paleness that Elizabeth had noticed on the plane were gone. Her eyes were sparkling, and her face glowed. When she was at her best, as she was now, Meredith was a focus of male attention. From her mother she had inherited the lovely white skin that contrasted magnificently with her thick, coal-black hair and flashing dark brown eyes. She always dressed to accentuate her trim legs and petite body, with its pert, pointed breasts.

Meredith giggled. "My God, Elizabeth, you look like a witch. The windblown look is definitely not your hairstyle. Excuse me. I'd better go assure dear Scott that I'm all right before he worries himself to death."

Dissolving into a fit of giggles, Meredith bounced out of the restroom, leaving a thoughtful Elizabeth to stare after her. Luckily, it wasn't one of her secretarial tasks to tell Gavin he should keep a close eye on his daughter.

When Elizabeth joined her companions in the waiting room, she found an enraged Gavin Thorne shouting into Scott's face, "Okay, Scott, you get those sons of bitches on the telephone. By God, I told them to have a car here by one-thirty. Tell them I'll sue their asses if I don't have a car in fifteen minutes."

While Scott was thumbing through the phone book, a suit-clad man in a plastic raincoat burst through the door. He stopped, surveyed the tenants of the room, and headed toward Gavin.

Before the newcomer could identify himself, Gavin, recognizing his prey, shouted, "You must be the car man. Do you realize how long you've kept me waiting?"

Whatever poise the man had vanished, and he sputtered, "Ah . . . gee, I'm sorry, Mr. Thorne. It's the weather—it's terrible for driving."

"Never mind the crap, buster. Just give me the keys."

The man sputtered a last apology and fled as Gavin whirled toward Scott. "Okay, Scott, get the bags in the trunk so we can get out of this burg."

Since Meredith had brought three suitcases, Scott had to make two trips to the Cadillac parked at the far end of the parking lot. By the time the car was ready, he was soaked from head to toe.

At the last moment, while the others waited in the car, Gavin decided to call his chief accountant to tell him they were on their way. The accountant, Aaron Blomfeld, had spent the last week at Gavin's vacation lodge getting the books in shape for the lender's examination. From the airport at Poplar Bluff, Missouri, they were driving to Bull

Shoals, halfway across Missouri in the Ozarks to rendezvous with Blomfeld. Gavin intended to drive on to Hot Springs with the financial records. He needed to borrow three million and forestall a bank foreclosure. If he failed, Thorne Construction was down the drain and he would be walking the streets of Chicago, a fifty-five-year-old loser. And rather than risk that, Gavin was willing to meet a less than reputable lender in Hot Springs and make a secret deal. The others had no real idea of just how shady this business was, accepting his story that he wanted it kept quiet so rivals would not learn that he was in trouble.

Breathing hard, he barked, "Okay, Scott, let's get this show on the road."

Gavin reclined his seat as far as it would go and tried to nap. A few miles outside Poplar Bluff, the road narrowed and began to rise. The woods were growing thicker. The bare branches of the deciduous trees were dark and shiny in the gray light.

The wind—strong enough to push the heavy car across the center line where the road crossed the gentle rises— made driving difficult. The rain was growing heavier.

The straight stretches became less frequent, and the curves grew sharper with less banking. The road's surface was treacherous, especially where loose gravel was washed onto the pavement.

Gavin's mood darkened as it became evident that they were not going to reach Bull Shoals before midnight. He was growing angry, making comments when the wind shoved the car out of its lane. Elizabeth knew he was looking for a target for his frustration. He found his target in the outskirts of Doniphan when Scott glanced at the gas gauge.

"We either have a gas leak or they didn't give us a full tank of gas."

"Why, those cheap sons of bitches!" Gavin exploded. "Okay, let's fill up in this burg. God knows when we'll find another filling station open." They pulled into Doniphan's one open station. While the ancient gasoline pump slowly filled the tank, Gavin paced back and forth in the driving rain. It did not help his mood when the toothless geezer pumping the gas called to him, "Mister, you ought to settle down. The way you're carrying on, a man could end up dead of a heart attack."

Startled, Gavin glared at him. "I'd say you're a good deal closer to that point than I am, old-timer."

The old-timer cackled. "Don't you believe it. You could be spending your last day on earth, mister."

Gavin stalked away and stood in the doorway of the station until the tank was filled. He resolutely ignored the old man's queries about their destination while he signed the credit card slip.

As they pulled away from the pumps, the elderly man watched them out of sight, shaking his head.

Full darkness found them still far from Bull Shoals Lake. The driving conditions, bad as they had been during the afternoon, grew monstrous after dark. Elizabeth felt relieved when she saw, at last, the Welcome to Arkansas sign, barely visible through the falling rain.

They had gone only a few miles farther when Gavin shouted, "Okay, slow down, Scott. It's not far to the turn-off."

Fifteen minutes later, the Cadillac halted before a large house of peeled logs with floodlights illuminating the graveled parking area. The wind had dropped, but the rain continued to drum against the metal roof of the car.

A huge fire was burning in the living room fireplace. The accountant pointed them toward the couches and, moments later, returned, carrying four steaming cups of coffee. He looked at Gavin, a faint smile playing across his face. "I must admit, I was getting a bit worried. It isn't much of an evening to be driving through the Ozarks. I should have known, though, that a bullheaded bastard like you would make it."

Gavin grumbled, "I was on that road two years ago, and I don't remember it being that bad."

Elizabeth settled back, enjoying the warmth of the coffee, and watched Gavin unwinding. It was a short break, though. He took a last swallow of coffee and set the cup on the coffee table.

Blomfeld stood. "I'm afraid I'm not being a very good

host. You people must be starved. I'm not much of a cook, but I can fix a few things besides coffee."

Gavin shook his head. "Don't bother, Aaron. We don't have time, not with this weather. I think you'd better brief me on the report and let us be on our way. Show Meredith and Elizabeth what you have for sandwiches.

"Scott, the wood in the bin is getting low. Grab a parka off the rack and bring some more wood in while we're working. I imagine Aaron will stay the rest of the weekend, and he is going to need a warm fire."

Scott choked back an angry retort.

Just as Elizabeth was putting the bread away, an angry Scott, his shoes sodden, joined them in the kitchen. He grabbed a plate of sandwiches, filled a mug with coffee, and sat down next to Meredith. He started talking to her, his voice little more than a whisper.

Embarrassed by the implied intimacy, Elizabeth took a sandwich, refilled her cup, and went out to sit by the fireplace. She settled on the sofa, watching the fire and shuddering delicately from time to time when the rain splattered against the dark windows.

An hour later, Meredith came into the room, looking angry, and slumped down into a chair. She was silent for a time and then, without preamble, announced, "I don't know how to convince Scott that I want nothing to do with him. Maybe if I invite him in for a chat sometime when I'm balling someone, he'll get the idea."

Rather than offer platitudes—for she had no wish to get involved—Elizabeth grabbed her coat and, to no one in particular, said, "I need a breath of fresh air."

She stepped out onto the front porch and felt her way across its dark width. The air felt bitterly cold. She had been there only a minute or so when the door opened and Scott, clutching two attache cases, hurried out to the car.

Before he could return to the house Meredith stepped out onto the porch. She grabbed his arm as he tried to brush past. She sounded angry, but the rain and the muffled beat of the waves masked her words. Abruptly, her voice rose. "I'm warning you, Scott! Keep your mouth shut! You're acting like a fool . . . jeopardizing my future."

His voice was louder, too. "I know what you have in your purse, Meredith. Can't you see that I'm—"

"You just open your mouth, and I'll shaft you good. That's a promise."

She ran back into the house and he followed, calling her name.

Before Elizabeth could move, Gavin came out the door, his raincoat on. Obviously the meeting was over. As Blomfeld tried to suggest an alternate route, Gavin interrupted, "Hell, you're acting like an old woman. I can't take a grand tour of Arkansas. It'll be three or four in the morning, as it is, before we get to Hot Springs. I don't want the lender to decide we're not interested and drop the deal. I—er had difficulty setting it up, you know."

Scott sounded interested. "What route do you suggest, Mr. Blomfeld?"

"Go down to Mountain Home, turn west on 62, pick up 65, take it to where it runs into Interstate 40, bypass Little Rock, and take Interstate 30 right into Hot Springs."

Gavin snorted. "Hell, that's sixty–sixty-five miles out of the way."

"I am not saying it isn't, but the state roads will have water standing on them. For all I know, some of them may be closed. It's rained hard since early afternoon."

"Yeah, but the weather reports say the worst is over," Gavin protested. "The roads should be clear long before we get there. We're going to chance it."

When Meredith joined them, they headed for the car. Gavin paused at the bottom of the steps. "Now, Aaron, you'll be back in Chicago when we return. I'm staying here until I know about the loan—either way it will be my last chance to relax for a while. If anyone at the office wants something you have the information—take care of it yourself. I don't want to hear a peep from anyone until next Wednesday."

As the Caddy eased out of the driveway, Gavin was at the wheel.

Scott looked over his shoulder. "Okay, folks," he said with a nervous laugh, "get these seat belts on. I bet the captain won't promise a smooth ride tonight."

Elizabeth reached for her seat belt but Gavin retorted, "Damn it, Scott, you are an old woman—I've been driving for forty years without those damned things and I'm sure not starting now."

Meredith's seat belt snapped shut. Elizabeth wormed her way into the corner, drowsy in the warm car. Soon she closed her eyes but remained awake, listening to the whine of the tires against the wet pavement. From time to time washes of gravel crunched beneath the tires. Gavin dropped into low gear several times to plow through pools of water masking the pavement, but immediately brought the car back up to speed.

When they reached Mountain Home, it was after midnight and the rain had ceased. Elizabeth looked at the road with renewed interest. It was quite narrow, with inadequate muddy shoulders and no center line, only dots of paint on the pavement. The land grew steeper, and they climbed lengthy grades with abrupt switchbacks. Meredith muttered, "Jesus Christ!" as the car dived around an abrupt turn, pitching her across the backseat.

Elizabeth found herself growing queasy. She folded a sweater between her head and the cold glass of the window, and leaned back, determined to rest. Meredith unbuckled her seat belt and curled up on the backseat, her head resting against Elizabeth's thigh.

Elizabeth was nearly asleep when she heard Gavin shout, "Oh, shit!"

The car swung wildly to the left, and she could feel the back wheels break free of the pavement, sliding sideways across it. There was a sudden jolt, and a hard shower of gravel and dirt crashed into the underside of the car. Her eyes flew open, and she saw him fighting the wheel. The car came back onto the road, crossed it, and almost crashed into the bank on the uphill side before Gavin could control it. Gravel and mud continued to pepper the underside as Gavin snarled, "Son of a bitch! Don't these crackers put curve signs on their damned roads?"

"Hey, there was one back there," Scott protested.

"Then, by God, they ought to make them big enough to see."

Meredith came upright. "Damn it! What are you trying to do—kill us?"

Gavin ignored his daughter, staring fixedly at the dark roadway.

The car surged forward as the angry Gavin slammed his foot against the accelerator. Elizabeth was growing concerned. He was far too tense to be fighting a backwoods Arkansas road on a rainy night.

Scott had reached the same conclusion. "Hey, Mr. Thorne, why don't you let me take over? We're not going to make good time, anyway. Besides, you ought to be fresh for your meeting tomorrow."

Gavin Thorne, not a stupid man, saw through Scott's concern. "Go to hell, kid. If you don't like it, I'll let you out right here."

Even in the darkness, Elizabeth could sense the loneliness of the land around them. Shortly after leaving Mountain Home, they had passed through two tiny hamlets. Since then, the countryside had been empty. Even the muddy lanes leading from the road had become scarce.

They thundered off one particularly tortuous section of pavement onto an arrow-straight stretch across a small plateau. The car was moving so fast that Elizabeth was not sure she actually saw the man beside the road.

Gavin's words confirmed her own startled perception. "My God, Scott, did you see that poor son of a bitch standing out in the ass end of nowhere at one o'clock in the morning?"

They raced along for three or four minutes at eighty miles an hour as Gavin took advantage of the unusually straight stretch before Scott shouted, "Watch out!"

Gavin only had time for a startled "What—?" before the tires screamed as he slammed on the brakes.

Elizabeth saw the road drop from view at the same instant Gavin did. There was nothing ahead but a thick stand of bare-limbed hardwoods. At the last second, she saw that the road dipped sharply downward to the left.

A panic-stricken Gavin fought the steering wheel as the heavy vehicle skidded into the curve. He did the only thing he could. He hit the accelerator, trying to regain traction.

The Cadillac, almost airborne, sliding broadside across the road, skidded onto the shoulder with the right wheels sinking into the mushy earth. There was a sudden blow as the car's side hit the embankment and rebounded onto the pavement.

They were still going too fast as they thundered toward the second leg of the S-curve, a sharp dip to the right. The vehicle's momentum was carrying it toward the left shoulder. They shot into the curve, and Gavin yanked the wheel to the right. The front end began to turn downslope, but inertia was hurling it straight ahead. The right-side wheels lifted into the air, and the Cadillac started to roll onto its side as it sailed over the road's edge.

It was the last thing Elizabeth remembered. The screams —hers and the others—went unheard as the car rolled over again and again before crashing into the side of a giant maple.

When Elizabeth regained consciousness, she was aware of the odor of gasoline. She kicked at the door, but it would not open. She expected the car to burst into flames at any moment. Twisting around, she tried to reach the other door. An unmoving body, wedged against her, blocked her efforts.

She blinked. A faint pinpoint of light was approaching the car.

CHAPTER 2

The ancient stepside pickup moved so slowly that its laboring motor protested loudly at being held in high gear. Its dim headlights barely illuminated the road ahead.

John Carpenter turned toward his twelve-year-old son, who was peering anxiously out the side window into the gloom. "Keep your eyes open, Billy Joe. If we drive by that old cow without you seeing her, I'm gonna whip your bottom."

The boy protested, "Daddy, it wasn't my fault. I told you that tree came down in the wind and tore out that section of fence."

"Don't smart-talk your daddy, boy. There that S-curve is up ahead. I'll go on through the curve to Mr. Miller's driveway, but if we ain't found her by then, you're gonna have to walk after her. That heifer won't stray far off the road. The woods are too thick for her."

With the straining motor threatening to stall, John Carpenter shifted into second. As he swung into the turn, his son shouted, "Stop, Daddy!"

The worn-out brakes squealed, and Carpenter looked toward his son. "Thank God! Hop out there and get a rope on her, Billy Joe."

"I didn't see Pearlie," the boy protested. "It's the paddle markers on the shoulder. Somebody's gone off the road."

"Well, dadgum it, boy! That coulda happened anytime today. In this weather, folks is always skidding off this curve."

"They were okay when I came by on the school bus before dark, Daddy."

Carpenter was becoming angry. "Billy Joe, do what your daddy says. Look for the dadgummed cow! I ain't in no mood for you sassing me."

Before he could restart the stalled motor, the boy had rolled down his window and was aiming a flashlight into the darkness. "Daddy, wait a minute! There's a car over there, and . . . somebody's in it."

"Let me see, boy."

The farmer leaned across the cab to stare past his son's shoulder.

"By golly, I believe you're right. But that car is just parked there. Those darned fools got that thing over there somehow, and they're bedded down for the night. The heck with them!"

"Wait, Daddy. Look! There's mud all over it, and it's banged up. It's been rolled. And look at the ground in front of it, all torn up this way. Besides, that man is bent up all funny."

"Tell you what. Slide down the bank and see if they are okay."

"I don't want to. They might be dead. That man in there ain't moved none."

John Carpenter reached over and opened the door. "Boy, get your little tail to moving."

Reluctantly, the boy slid from the truck and clambered down the muddy bank. He worked his way across the soggy ground, anxious to be done with it and back in the safety of the pickup.

Relief flooded through Elizabeth as she realized that the pinpoint of light was growing. Someone was coming to help. She was half off the seat, with one foot caught under it, her legs pinned by Meredith's unmoving body lying across them.

"Is everybody okay?" she called. "Mr. Thorne . . . Mr. Thorne?"

She heard a groan from the front seat.

"Scott, are you okay? Scott? Answer me!"

A muffled voice called from outside the car. "Hey, is any of you folks hurt in there?"

The light caught her in the face. Blinded, she motioned toward the front seat. "Help! Please get help. People are hurt. I can't move. I . . ."

The bearer of the flashlight jumped away as if he was frightened. After a silence, the youngster called, "It's okay, ma'am. I'm gonna get my daddy. He's up on the road."

Terrified at being abandoned, Elizabeth begged, "Wait! Get us out! The car's going to catch fire!"

Her pleas went unheeded. She could see the light bobbing up and down as it receded in the distance. Car headlights flared to life. With a sinking heart, she saw the headlights moving off up the road.

The flashlight bearer returned to announce, "Daddy's gonna turn around up at Millers' so he can get the truck off on the shoulder. He'll be right back."

Near the breaking point, Elizabeth shouted, "For God's sake! We don't need your daddy. We need medical help. Call an ambulance."

Moments later, she sensed that someone had joined the boy. The flashlight's rays lanced into the front and then the backseat, resting on each of them for a moment.

Another voice, more mature and twangy, called, "Ma'am, can't you move? Are you hurt?"

"For God's sake, open the door."

"They're jammed, and I'm afraid to break the glass, with all you people in there."

There was a moment's silence while John Carpenter decided what he would do. "Ma'am, the others look like they need help bad. The nearest phone is about four miles down the road. I'll leave my boy with you. Ain't nothing he can do, but maybe he'll be a comfort."

She heard the boy's sudden objection.

"Shut up, Billy Joe! Your daddy will be back in twenty minutes."

Scott moaned and muttered something about his arm, but when she called to him, he didn't answer. Only his incoherent rambling disturbed the awful silence in the car. The cooling engine continued to pop, and an occasional gust of wind dropped a shower of water from the trees onto the metal top.

She started to cry, softly at first, and then in great sobs. She was beginning to feel cold, deadly cold, and she was shivering. Her teeth were chattering so loudly that she almost missed the distant howl of a siren.

Its banshee cry grew louder, and soon she saw headlights through the trees. A car with a flashing red light atop it burst into view. It slowed to a stop, and she could hear the slamming of doors and see flashlights bobbing down the slope.

A splash of light from a stronger flashlight hit her face, and a male voice called, "Take it easy, ma'am. I'm a deputy sheriff. We'll have you out of there in a jiffy."

Another flashlight was playing over the unmoving bodies of Gavin and Scott. A second voice softly commented, "They had better shake a leg. That one guy doesn't look so hot."

The first voice spoke again, different, more stilted. Elizabeth recognized that he was talking over the radio. "County dispatch, Henry one."

"Henry one, go ahead."

"Millie, has Cobb left yet?"

"That's negative, Henry one. At least, I don't think so."

"Then tell him to bring the Hurst tool with him. It looks like we may have trouble getting them out of the front."

The deputy struck the window again with his flashlight. "Ma'am, I'm gonna break this window out. Work that cloth over your face if you can. I don't think the glass will fly that far, but I can't be sure."

The door didn't yield without a struggle. The three men labored over its sprung metal for five minutes before it surrendered with a shriek.

"Thank God," Elizabeth muttered.

Scott's voice, weak and slurred, asked, "Elizabeth, is that you? Are you two okay? We must have had a wreck."

"Oh, we did, Scott. How badly are you hurt?"

"I . . . I don't know. My arm hurts like hell, and my head. I must have hit the windshield. How . . . how's Meredith? Meredith, are you okay? Meredith? Meredith!"

His voice was rising. Before she could reassure him, a new voice imposed itself. In the dim light, she could see a man wearing a white jacket lean into the car. She sighed. The ambulance had arrived.

The Johnson brothers, owners and operators of Beauregard County's only ambulance, swung into action. Once Elizabeth was freed, she was given a cursory examination. Meanwhile, Meredith, still unconscious, was carried up the muddy slope to the waiting ambulance. When the front door proved impossible to open, Scott was slipped out through the window and borne away on a stretcher. The two medics, Otis and Chester Johnson, remained in the car with Gavin.

While Elizabeth watched with mounting concern, they worked feverishly over his still form. One of them slid across the seat and put his head out the window, listening. "I hear a siren, thank God. That must be Cobb."

Moments later, another police car joined the string of vehicles along the road, and a man wearing a western-style hat appeared beside the car.

Otis Johnson straightened up from Gavin's unmoving body. "Cobb, hurry up and get this thing open. It's touch and go."

The newcomer and a deputy attacked the car's metal frame with what looked like a giant pair of shears attached to a battery. The car banged repeatedly against the big maple it rested against as they worked with the device. The front door, squealing like a live thing, finally broke loose.

One of the ambulance men yelled into the darkness. "Boys, bring that other gurney down here . . . and shake a leg."

As they were lowering Gavin onto the gurney, one of the medics leaned over, looked closely at him, and with a startled "Damn it!" frantically began to apply cardiopulmonary massage. The second medic looked up at the hat-clad figure above them.

"Cobb, this fellow isn't going to last until we get to the county hospital. I think we'd better see if they will take him at Skystone."

"Skystone! Are you crazy? Why shouldn't he take his chances like everyone else?"

The medic looked at his partner, laboring over the still figure. "Look at that car and the clothes this man is wearing. These aren't Ozark dirt farmers." His voice dropped. "Besides, one of these people is going to remember about that curve sign, and this county's ass is going to be in a sling."

"What do you mean about a sign, Chester?"

"You know my brother-in-law Archie, who works for the road department? Well, the sign at the top of the curve got knocked down the other day, and they didn't have any more S-curve signs, so they figured they wouldn't put anything up until they got some new ones. Archie was worried about it."

The hat-clad officer cursed softly. "What the hell could they do for him at Skystone?"

"This man's heart needs stabilizing. We can't keep it beating. God knows, they ought to have had enough experience with that at Skystone."

The man thought for a moment. "Okay, but needing to get in and getting in are two different things. I'll notify the sheriff. You men get him in the ambulance and be ready to roll if we have a go-ahead."

He turned away, raising his portable to his mouth. "County dispatcher, Henry X."

There was a burst of static, and an elderly woman replied, "Henry X, county dispatcher."

"Millie, get hold of Toby as quick as you can and have him contact me. It's an emergency."

Millie's voice lost its bored quality. "What's the trouble? Something wrong with that wreck?"

"Damn it, Millie. Do what I tell you. 10-4."

He turned to one of the deputies. "Tip, take Ed and Charlie with you and make a physical plot of the skid marks. I want those measurements accurate. This may get a little sticky before it's over."

Elizabeth remained by the car, seemingly forgotten. Only a single officer was still there, removing their personal effects. She was afraid that she was going to be left, but before she could call out, the tall, hat-clad officer materialized beside her.

"Ma'am, I'm Cobb Kendall, the night-shift sergeant."

Before he could say more, a querulous baritone voice burst from his portable. "Henry X, this is County one."

"Henry X."

"Cobb, what in the hell do you want? By God, I had just dropped off to sleep. This had better be good."

"Sheriff, we have a kid-glover here—an accident with four people injured. I have a man of about sixty experiencing cardiac difficulties. The Johnson boys say he'll never make it to county hospital. I think, under the circumstances, you'd better call Skystone and see if they'll let us admit this patient for emergency treatment. 10-4."

The voice sputtered. "Damn it, Cobb, speaking of kid gloves, what do you think Skystone is? They're not exactly the friendliest folks on earth. Aren't you aware of that? 10-4."

"Sheriff, I think you'd better put yourself in debt if you have to. I can't talk now, but we have egg on our face."

"Okay, boy, but it's your ass for it if old Toby ends up in trouble. I'll get back to you as soon as I can."

The man started questioning Elizabeth as if he had not been interrupted, scribbling her answers in his notebook. When he was through, he asked her if she wanted relatives notified.

"There's no one to tell. Mr. Thorne isn't in touch with his ex-wife, and Scott Sutherlin is an orphan. Mr. Throne was supposed to be away from his office for ten days, so they don't need to be notified immediately."

"Okay, ma'am, that covers everything for now. Oh, I suppose one of these purses is yours?" He reached into the backseat and handed her the purse she indicated, but before she could thank him, the radio came to life.

"Henry X, County one."

"Henry X."

"That was the God-damnedest conversation I've ever had,

Cobb. The damned man said yes and no a half-dozen times. I hung up on him the last time he sounded agreeable. Tell the ambulance boys there will be a man at the gates in ten minutes. I hope to hell you know what you're doing. As soon as you get back to town, call me. I'll be waiting. 10-4."

The man turned toward the road and yelled, "Hey, Chester, head for Skystone. There will be a man at the gate. I'll have the boys run this lady up there."

The ambulance pulled away, its lights flashing. It disappeared almost immediately around the sharp turn of the S-curve.

Elizabeth looked after it in panic. "I have to go with them. I must see that they're okay."

"Don't worry, little lady. One of our units will run you up there. I need to stay here and finish my report."

Taking her hand, he escorted her toward the road.

She stopped again. "What is this Skystone? Is it a hospital? I didn't understand why you were talking about getting permission to go up there."

Gently he pulled at her elbow to keep her walking. "You passed it, but you probably didn't notice it in the dark, especially as fast as your Mr. Thorne appears to have been driving. It's three miles back up the road, along McKinstry Flat. It's a convalescent hospital, but not just your ordinary rest home. It has its own airstrip. I guess it's one of the fanciest places of its kind in the country. The patients are from wealthy families. Skystone has very little to do with the people in this county. We operate on a live-and-let-live basis down here.

"Now, don't you worry. Your friends are in good hands. I think it's time you headed for the hospital. You should have a checkup yourself."

Elizabeth allowed herself to be led across the churned-up muck to the highway. It took the sergeant's assistance to make it up the slope. By the time she reached the asphalt surface, both her hands and slacks were muddy, and she was somewhat upset with the unintentional intimacy of the sergeant's hands.

In the glow from the headlights, she could see that he was grinning. "You're a big girl, Mrs. Shea. I thought for a minute there we were going to have to rope you and haul you up."

He shouted toward the distant flashlights, "Ed, you and Charlie run this little lady up to Skystone. Then get back here on the double . . . okay?"

The distant voice answered, "Okay, Cobb, we're on our way."

Cobb reached through the window and lifted the hand mike. "County Medic, Henry X."

There was a burst of static, and a voice answered faintly, "Henry X, County Medic."

"County Medic, are you 10-97?"

"10-97. We're waiting at the gate. I can see somebody coming down the drive now. Everything's 10-4."

"County Medic, tell the man at the gate to remain there. I'm sending the last victim, code-3."

"Negative on that, Cobb. They probably don't want their patients disturbed with sirens. We'll tell the man to wait until they get here. Okay?"

"10-4."

The sergeant turned to Elizabeth. "Mrs. Shea, the deputies will run you up to Skystone. I'll be out there in the morning to see how you're doing."

He opened the back door for her. "Okay, boys, code 2. Drop her off, and tell the Johnsons to get back to town as quick as they can. With these wet roads, I wouldn't be surprised if we didn't have another 11-79 before the night's over."

CHAPTER 3 _____

T he ride was short. The deputy drove fast with the red light flashing, but with a control that Elizabeth had not felt with Gavin at the wheel of the Cadillac.

The car swerved left off the highway onto a graveled driveway and stopped, its way blocked by a massive iron gate. There was enough light from the headlights to see, above it, in letters of the same wrought iron, the name SKYSTONE. On each side of the gate, twelve-feet-high stone walls paralleled the road as far as she could see. A heavyset young man in a white tunic appeared out of the dark, bearing a flashlight. He pulled back the gates, and the sheriff's car moved slowly through the opening. But as they drew abreast of the man, the deputy stopped the vehicle.

"Hey, where's Ike?" he called. "Isn't he still grounds-keeper?"

For an instant it appeared that the man was not going to reply, but then he shrugged, answering with a brisk Eastern accent: "You'll have to ask the doctor. I'm not supposed to say."

There was another confrontational silence before the deputy asked, "What's your name?"

The man looked down at the ground, his face masked by the shadows. He seemed angry. "You can call me Joe."

The deputy nodded, his gaze on the man's averted face. "Okay, whatever you say . . . Joe."

Slowly the patrol car moved up the narrow drive, leaving the sullen tunic-clad figure in the darkness behind them. Swinging to their left, they drove under a porte cochere and stopped next to the ambulance, parked with its rear doors open.

Elizabeth had but a moment to view Skystone. It was a single-storied building with white walls of pre-cast concrete panels. No light was visible in any of the windows. The only illumination was from widely spaced outdoor fixtures mounted on the walls, spilling fans of light down the facade.

As they stepped out of the car, one of the deputies said, "We're sure not causing much excitement. There's not a light on up at the Hall."

Elizabeth looked at him. "The hall? What's that?"

"This used to be a large private estate. It belonged to the Albritton family. Their home was called the Hall. It's used now, so they say, by the employees at Skystone."

While he was talking, the double doors leading onto the porte cochere opened, and a nurse stepped out.

"Officer, you can talk about the good old days some other time. We are waiting for the young lady you have with you."

The deputy smiled ruefully. "Yes, ma'am,"

They followed the woman inside. Directly facing them across a tiny, dimly lit entry hall was a second set of doors. She pushed them open, and Elizabeth and the deputies trailed after her into a brightly lit room that was crowded with people.

Two examination tables were centered under powerful lights. On one of them lay Gavin Thorne, terribly pale, his eyes shut. It was so quiet in the room that Elizabeth could hear his quick, shallow breathing. His clothes had been removed, and a sheet covered his lower body.

A tall man in a doctor's smock leaned over the inert Thorne, and a pudgy, red-haired woman in her late fifties stood next to him. The doctor had an extraordinarily craggy face with a pointed, jutting chin and high cheekbones, across which the skin was tightly stretched. He was a man in his late fifties, his auburn hair laced with gray, shading to full gray at the temples. His eyebrows were amazingly heavy, with the hair in them so long that it swept far past his eyes toward his temples. It was the most striking face Elizabeth had ever seen.

Meredith was stretched out on the other table. She had a sheet pulled up to her chin, but it was apparent that she still wore her blouse, since her arms rested across her chest outside the sheet. To Elizabeth's intense relief, Meredith's eyes were open. A tall, slender nurse, her hair escaping from her nurse's cap in a silvery shower, stood next to Meredith, taking her pulse and staring intently into her eyes.

Scott was sitting in a chair along one wall, watching as one of the medics used scissors to cut away his sports jacket and dress shirt. The second medic was sitting beside Scott, talking to him in a low voice.

As Elizabeth entered the room, Scott called to her, his words slurred, "Thank God you got here, Elizabeth. I was worried."

He was so heavily drugged that he wore a foolish grin. His unfocused eyes sought the table where Meredith lay, and he called, "It's okay, Meredith. Everything's going to be okay."

Then his face crumpled as a wave of pain broke through the defenses of the drugs.

A second doctor was standing beyond the examination tables. As Elizabeth entered the room, he was glancing from table to table, worry lines etched on his face. He was, perhaps, no older than the other doctor, but his hair was a luminescent silver. He was small, with perfect features, a man who was quite distinguished looking—even handsome—in his older years.

Behind him, against the wall, leaned a third nurse, her eyes in constant motion as she watched the scene before her. She was in her early forties, wearing a uniform a bit too tight on her, displaying a still youthful and lush figure. There was about her face the same attractive, if overdone, quality her body had: full, ripe lips; dark eyes; eyelashes that seemed too long to be true; and a glowing dark-rose complexion that added to her exotic looks. Her face was without expression, and her arms were folded across her chest, with a pink cardigan draped over them.

As Elizabeth turned away from Scott, the short doctor bounded forward, his hand extended. "Well, you must be the last of our visitors. I'm Thomas Mainwaring—Dr. Thomas Mainwaring."

His offer to shake hands caught Elizabeth off guard, and there was an awkward moment before she extended her hand. "I'm Elizabeth Shea, doctor. How are they? How's Mr. Thorne?"

"They're doing splendidly, Mrs. Shea. You can see that the other young lady has regained consciousness. The young man has a broken arm—a rather bad break, I'm afraid. We're doing everything we can for the other gentleman, but there's time for that later. I want you to sit down and let me take a look at you."

He grasped her arm but was interrupted by the older medic, Otis Johnson, a short, pugnacious individual with a sour look on his face. "Dr. Mainwaring, I think you should do something for this fellow first. That arm of his is really busted up, and he keeps threatening to go into shock."

Mainwaring released Elizabeth's arm and glared at the medic. Annoyance sharpened his voice. "Dr. Caudill, check the young man. I'm sure that Mrs. Farmington can keep an eye on your patient for a few moments."

The craggy-faced doctor whirled toward the speaker, his face reddening before he nodded abruptly. "Let me know, Lena, if there is any change in his heart action."

The deputies took advantage of the sudden awkward silence to excuse themselves. The older of the two said, "Folks, it looks like you're in good hands, so I think we'd better hit the road. We have a lot of calls stacked up out there."

He smiled at Elizabeth. "I'm sure your friends will be all right now, Mrs. Shea. Somebody from the office will be by in the morning to check on you."

As they disappeared through the swinging doors, the pugnacious medic, Otis, rose to follow them. Dr. Mainwaring's voice stopped him in midstride. "Wait a minute. This isn't a

public emergency ward, you know. I want a written statement detailing the circumstances that brought you to Skystone. We will need it for our records."

Otis flushed. "Don't worry; I'll sign your paper in a minute. I just want to talk with the deputy. Something funny—"

"Listen. You'll sit here and write that report now, or you
can load these people back into your ambulance and leave.
We're doing this as a favor to everybody concerned, and we
aren't assuming any liability."

The second medic, Chester, who was assisting the
craggy-faced doctor as he worked over Scott's arm, looked
up. "Cool it, Otis. The doctor is right. This isn't a public
hospital, after all."

The sound of the sheriff's car backing out of the porte
cochere was barely audible in the brightly lit room. Mainwaring came to his feet and disappeared into the hall, returning a few minutes later with a clipboard and paper. He
pushed them at the still upset Otis Johnson.

"And now, sir, if you'll jot down the names of the patients, the circumstances under which you encountered
them, and why you brought them to Skystone, that will be
all that is necessary. Both of you sign it, and you can be on
your way."

He turned back to Elizabeth. "Okay, my dear, if you'll sit
down, I'll check you over."

As he hovered over her, peering into her eyes with a penlight and checking her reflexes, the swinging doors opened
and the heavyset man that had opened the gate for them
walked in. He was in his mid-twenties, about six feet tall,
and packed some two hundred and twenty pounds on his
heavy frame. He had an olive complexion and black hair. As
he came through the doors, he grinned at Dr. Mainwaring.
"Surprised, doc?"

Mainwaring frowned at him. "I want you to help Nurse
Boulanger get Miss Thorne into bed."

He looked at the other doctor who was working over the
moaning Scott. "Dr. Caudill, do you agree? Go ahead and
put Miss Thorne to bed?"

Dr. Caudill looked up. "She appears to be okay—a slight
concussion—but she will have to be watched. She should be

checked regularly for the next twelve hours." Immediately he transferred his attention back to Scott.

Dr. Mainwaring nodded at the beefy orderly. "Joe, go get the gurney."

"Gurney?"

"Yes, the gurney. Don't be so dense. We're going to move Miss Thorne to a room. Place her in number eight. Nurse Boulanger will help you."

The orderly hurried from the room, and Dr. Mainwaring, accompanied by the young nurse, soon followed. The three of them reappeared in a few moments and, lifting Meredith onto the gurney, rolled her through the double doors.

When the trio returned, Dr. Caudill was again standing over Gavin Thorne. He looked at Mainwaring and then nodded toward Scott. Scott was slumped in the chair, his plaster-encased arm suspended in a sling. His eyes were closed.

"I had to shoot him up quite heavily. He's pretty much out of it, but if you get a wheelchair, I think he can be put to bed easily enough. He should sleep like a baby until noon."

Nurse Boulanger and the orderly vanished again. When they reentered the room they were pushing a wheelchair. Not until Dr. Mainwaring angrily instructed Joe to help did they succeed in placing the half-conscious Scott in the chair. The silver-blond nurse rolled him out through the doors, followed by the increasingly sullen orderly.

Otis Johnson, who had been doggedly writing the accident report, slapped the paper down onto the seat. "Okay, here's what you want, I hope. I'm sure the hell not writing it again."

His brother protested, but Otis was having none of it. He looked toward Elizabeth apologetically. "I'm sorry, ma'am. I know I shouldn't be carrying on like this—especially with your friend so badly hurt—but, by God . . ."

Chester Johnson hurriedly signed the paper and, grabbing his brother by the arm, hustled him toward the door. "Shut up, Otis, and let's get out of here."

He turned toward the room's occupants. "I'm sorry about this. Otis is a little tired. . . . It's been a hard night. It was nice of you to take these people in, I'm sure. Good night."

Dr. Caudill, who had been studying them intently, said, "Don't worry about it. We'll take care of everything here."

Mainwaring's voice was sharp. "Wait a minute, gentlemen. I want you to understand that I didn't mean to hassle you. Our insurance company insists on this sort of thing . . . liability, you know."

He turned as the orderly hurried back into the room. "Joe, go out and help these fellows get turned around. After you take care of them, walk down and lock the gate. Better be safe than sorry."

Nodding, the burly young man grinned at the two medics. "Hey, fellows, mind giving me a ride to the gate? It would save me a few steps."

Chester shrugged. "Why not?"

As the three of them disappeared, the black-haired nurse, who had been standing all this time against the back wall, sat down on a chair.

Dr. Mainwaring turned to Elizabeth with a smile. "Okay, my dear, at last it's your turn. Let's get you into bed."

She rose, was dizzy for a second, and then walked out the door ahead of him.

The treatment room, which had served as an emergency ward, discharged into a long, tenebrous hall. At the far end of the corridor, where a large ice machine rested, Elizabeth could see a glow of fluorescent light spilling across the passage. They passed, on the left, a massive steel door painted a brilliant red.

"What on earth is in there?" Elizabeth asked.

The doctor chuckled. "Nothing to concern yourself about. It's the emergency exit."

At the end of the hall, they encountered the nurses' station. Elizabeth realized that the building was L-shaped, with another corridor stretching away at a right angle. The nurses' station sat in the angle of the L. Nurse Boulanger leaned against the counter next to a small, very pretty girl. The petite girl was younger—she didn't look eighteen—and had a lovely face that still held a bit of baby fat. Her face was framed by masses of curly, medium brown hair. Her uniform was not like the others. She wore a nurse's cap, but her white uniform was a jumper with a pale blue blouse under it.

Dr. Mainwaring introduced her as Molly, but Elizabeth's attention was taken by the woman sitting at a desk on which rested two heart monitors. She was a girl who would have been noticed anywhere. Like the others, she wore a nurse's uniform. All Elizabeth noticed at first was her face. She had golden blond hair drawn back into a bun, with her nurse's cap resting jauntily atop it. Her eyes were so stunning that it was hard to notice much else. In a face that was pure Caucasian, she had the sloe-eyed look of the Far East. Her eyes were the most incredible jade green that Elizabeth had ever seen. They seemed incandescent, literally glowing, with a light behind them. Elizabeth stood, transfixed. When the girl realized how she had captured Elizabeth's attention, she laughed—a low, feline laugh—and her hands automatically went to her hair. Lazily she came to her feet and stretched, preening before her audience.

She studied Elizabeth, then looked at the doctor. "Well, this is the last of the lot, eh? And where do we put this one?"

Dr. Mainwaring frowned. "This is Mrs. Shea—Elizabeth Shea. She was fortunate enough to escape serious injury. I think room two. Is that room free?"

The girl with the incredible eyes laughed. "Yes, Dr. Mainwaring. Luckily that one's free."

Her expression hardened, and she looked toward the silvery-haired nurse, "Boulanger, why don't you help the doctor get Mrs. Shea into bed?"

At the door to room 2, the doctor flipped on the light switch. She stared in amazement. It was like no hospital room she had ever seen before.

There was a standard hospital bed, but there the resemblance stopped. The lighting was discreet, hidden behind valances. The room was large, its walls wood-paneled and hung with several original if not worthwhile oils. The same tile flooring as in the corridor covered the area around the bed, but the rest of the room was richly carpeted. The furnishings included leather chairs, a coffee table, and floor lamps. Suspended above the foot of the bed was a color television, with impressive speakers mounted on the walls facing the bed. The bedside table, a massive, permanent console, contained a built-in panel of television, stereo, and bed controls.

"What is this? I've never seen a hospital room like this in my life."

The doctor smiled. "I believe you could say that's the whole idea, Mrs. Shea—to make these appear as much like ordinary bedrooms as possible. This is a convalescent hospital. The families of our patients are willing to pay whatever is necessary to make their loved ones comfortable. Skystone's rooms are probably as luxurious as any in the country."

Gently he nudged her into the room. "Nurse Boulanger will help you get ready for bed. You'll be happy to know that we offer some choice of bed wear here. You won't have to run around with your rear end exposed."

To her surprise, the doctor did not leave while the tall nurse was helping her. Instead, he sat in a chair and stared ostentatiously toward the ceiling while the nurse helped her into a gown and then washed the mud from her face, hands, and legs. When she was through, the doctor rose and— herding the nurse ahead of him—said, "I'll be back in a few moments, Mrs. Shea."

Stretched out on the bed, Elizabeth realized that she was more bruised than she had thought—nothing bad, but she was going to be plenty sore come morning.

Her eyes popped open, and she was startled to find the doctor standing by the bed, placing a small metal tray on the console. He had entered the room as quietly as a stalking cat.

"Now, Mrs. Shea. There doesn't seem to be much wrong with you except for a few bumps and bruises, but we always worry a little when somebody has lost consciousness. I'm going to give you a shot to help you sleep, and we'll check you in the morning."

A flicker of fear ran through her at the idea of being rendered unconscious among strangers in this isolated, unfamiliar place. She tried to stall him.

"But, doctor . . . uh . . ." She could not think of his name.

He frowned, regarding her steadily. "Dr. Mainwaring, my dear, Dr. Mainwaring."

"But, doctor, how is Mr. Thorne? Does he have a chance?"

He raised a small vial, slipped the syringe needle through its rubber nipple, and drew out its contents—all before he answered her.

"I'll be honest with you, Mrs. Shea. I don't know. Now let me have your arm."

The sharp prick of the needle stung her. It bounced off her arm, and then the pain hit a second time and she felt the needle sliding into her flesh.

"Sorry," he muttered as he pulled the needle away and dabbed at her arm with the alcohol-soaked cotton. "Now, you sleep well, my dear. I don't think you have anything to worry about."

CHAPTER 4

While Elizabeth could still hear his footsteps in the corridor, the drug rushed through her with a startling suddenness. Panicked, she reached for the buzzer, but then felt so incredibly relaxed that she sank back on the bed, yielding to the sensation. She lay, staring at the ceiling, illuminated by a streak of light coming through the crack in the door. Sleep rolled over her like a giant breaker.

Sometime later she became aware that she was lying flat on a bed that was too hard to be hers. Startled, she opened her eyes and peered about the unfamiliar surroundings, trying to remember where she was.

Her attempts to reason, to remember, were being overwhelmed by a breathtaking physical awareness of herself. The sheet and light blanket were gripping her in a tight embrace, clinging to her, pressing her against the bed. Grunting with the effort, she raised her heavy arm, aware of the thick air flowing around it. The muscles of her arm glided smoothly over one another. It was incredible.

She did not want to move. Her body was so alive and pulsating. She reveled in her enjoyment of it, not worrying that she was in a strange bed.

Unbidden, an uneasiness stirred in Elizabeth. Something

about the bed triggered an awareness that she was in a hospital. As quickly, the memory of the accident flashed into her mind. Her recall was vivid and immediate—the wild chaos inside the Cadillac as it rolled over and over, her body wrenching at her seat belt, her head bouncing against the unyielding window. She thought of Scott moaning in the quiet car and of Meredith's weight pinning her. The thought of the gravely injured Gavin Thorne came into her mind, and she thought she should summon a nurse to find out if he was still alive.

But before she could act, something jarred against the corridor wall outside the room. She recognized the sound as one she had heard before in the shadowland of sleep. It was what had awakened her.

The sounds of a struggle, muffled but distinct, floated through the partly open door. Elizabeth could hear labored breathing, and then a female voice gasped, "No, Shane, don't!"

Silence followed, a long, provocative silence broken suddenly by more heavy breathing. The same female voice begged, "Shane, don't! It ain't natural."

There was another outbreak of scuffling and a heavy thud against the wall that made the picture frames rattle. The voice sounded surprised, "Oh!" and then alarmed: "Please, Shane, you're going to tear my uniform. Stop!"

It was quiet again until the voice moaned, "You're hurting me."

Another female voice, harsher, commanded, "Kiss me again."

This time the silence lasted longer, dissolving into another struggle, but shorter this time. The scuffing feet moved away from the wall.

The softer voice pleaded, "No . . . no. Where are you taking me? Shane, let me go! No. What are you doing to me?"

She heard a door opening, and abruptly the footsteps ceased. It was quiet again.

Elizabeth pushed herself upright in bed. She wondered if her mind could be playing tricks on her. Could what she heard have been Meredith begging for help?

The effort to think exhausted her, and she fell heavily onto her back. Why did Meredith sound so different? It had to be some quirk of Elizabeth's mind . . . some confusion caused by the accident.

She raised herself again. The room spun slowly before her eyes, and she found it hard to tell where the light-outlined door was. Carefully she swung her legs over the side of the bed and held on grimly as it rocked under her. Gradually it steadied.

She gasped in surprise. She was huge. Her head was an immense distance from her hips. She felt powerful, able to grapple with whatever threatened Meredith.

Sliding forward, Elizabeth lowered her feet to the floor. The agony of the frigid tiles shot through her legs. Taking a step forward, she struggled to maintain her equilibrium. Her head, tremendously heavy, was pitching forward, while her feet, feather light, threatened to float upward. As she floundered about, trying to keep her feet on the ground, the bed crashed into the back of her legs and she tumbled backwards onto it.

The room tilted, swaying gently for several moments. Again, Elizabeth stood, more cautious now, and carefully extended a foot. Gingerly, she tested her balance before she dared move again. She took two reeling steps and staggered into the wall, almost falling. Her knees buckled, and she grabbed the door frame. For long moments she clung to it in desperation, but all at once she felt perfectly all right. She laughed aloud.

Elizabeth thought of returning to bed. She remembered Meredith—that somewhere in the quiet hall Meredith was struggling with some enemy.

The corridor was dimly lit. Cautiously she leaned through the doorway to examine the passage. To her left, it was lined with doors on both sides and was lighted by small illuminated glass panels located along the baseboards. Light showed from a single open doorway across the hall.

Turning, Elizabeth glanced toward the nurses' station. The harsh fluorescent lights revealed an empty corridor, but as she watched, they dimmed. The hall began filling with mist, a mist that grew ever thicker, threatening to render her sightless. She slipped slowly to her knees, gripping the door frame with all her strength. Closing her eyes, she huddled there for several minutes. When she risked opening them again, the mist was clearing and the nurses' station was emerging like a developing photograph.

She pushed herself upright. Immediately the hall began to rock, a slow, sickening swing, and she clung to the door frame until the floor steadied. While she stood there, trying to understand what was happening to her, a soft breeze was gently stroking her face and molding her gown to the curves of her body. The nipples of her breasts hardened under the silky caress of the fabric. Embarrassed, she looked toward the nurses' station to see if anyone was watching. The corridor was still empty.

Her hearing was terribly acute, and she could hear the sound of the air rushing through the vents in a never-ending whisper. Another noise, more human, floated down the empty passageway. A long-held moan, a living thread of sound, stretched long and thin as it trailed past her ears.

Sighs, breathy and thrilling, followed . . . dark, misty streamers flowing from the half-closed door of that one lighted room across the corridor.

Elizabeth stepped into the hallway, lifting her arms to balance herself. She knew it was unnecessary . . . that she could lift her feet and float wherever she wanted, like a white puffball sailing on the wind. She was so delighted with herself that she barely stopped in time to avoid crashing into the wall.

She stared, bewildered. There was the door in front of her, but it was closed. There was no light around it, and the smoky streamers of soft sounds were not coming from behind its wooden barrier.

A feeling of betrayal overwhelmed her. Tears slid down her cheeks, huge and wet, leaving great sticky tracks. She wanted to turn away, to seek her mother's arms, but then she felt herself vibrating like a tuning fork to a sustained, rising keening.

Looking about, she saw the lighted room again, trying to skip away down the hall. Determined not to let it escape her, she staggered after it, her hands clutching at the wall to hold it back. Then she was at the door, and the lighted room was alive with noises. Metal cried in shrill protest; fabric rustled with a dry, powdery sound; and the air was filled with gasps and cries and whimpers.

For a moment the room was a kaleidoscope of convulsing shapes and colors, painful against her eyes. She closed them to shut out the sight, and when she reopened them, the scene was steadying. Abruptly it sharpened into crystal-clear focus.

She crept forward until she could see the whole room. The only light was from a small fixture attached to the head of the bed, but it was quite enough. The floor before her was strewn with clothing and lingerie. Sprawled on the bed, naked, was Molly, the pretty young brown-haired girl she had seen earlier at the nurses' station. Leaning over her, supported by one hip on the edge of the bed, was the nurse with the disturbing eyes, Shane. She was also nude.

She was kissing the prone girl. One hand clutched the smaller girl behind the neck, and the other, its painted nails like bright drops of blood, traced its way over the white flesh of the girl's thigh, molded her hip, and slithered over the smooth, faintly rounded stomach. The hand slid and shaped, teased and caressed—the sound, to Elizabeth's terribly sensitive ears, a silken susurrus.

Their lips would part with a wet sound that exploded through Elizabeth's head and then the blond's mouth would fasten again on the tender lips with a devouring hunger. Molly seized the probing hand which kneaded and stroked her soft flesh, staying its course a moment until her fingers appeared to weaken, freeing the pillaging intruder to continue its search, then she stiffened as the stroking, seeking hand found what it sought. Molly tried to strike Shane's face, but her hand was knocked away, falling limply beside her own hip.

Elizabeth, with her hawk's vision, saw the two mouths come apart, the moist pink lips barely touching, while Shane's tongue, like a swollen, angry serpent, struck time and time again through the open lips that were clinging in mute surrender. Suddenly, she shifted her position, and she hungrily sucked Molly's breasts. Her hand was moving rhythmically now. One of the younger girl's arms lay like a rag doll's across Shane's back and the other by her own side, both hands clenching and unclenching spasmodically.

Molly's mouth was open, and her tongue licked at her lips. She was shaking her head slowly from side to side, as if to deny the body that was betraying her. She was beginning to pant, her breathing broken only by soft wails of pleasure.

Her knees weak, Elizabeth clutched at the door frame. She could feel what the girl on the bed was feeling, and her own loins were afire.

With a swift movement, Shane turned on the bed, settling between the slack legs of her conquest. She fell atop her aroused prey in a frenzied assault, her mouth devouring the pulpy red lips beneath her own, her hands clasping the yielding white flesh on which she was feeding.

Elizabeth was bewildered by the sudden shift of scene. She remembered. *The Lansford gardener was atop the girl, his hard, muscled body driving into her, using her—and she was letting him.* An intense sweetness shot through Elizabeth. She was unable to look away, helpless to move, as unaware as the two women writhing on the bed that a toneless wailing was issuing from her throat.

The image before her eyes altered, changing shape and color until she could see the blond's golden skin rippling over her muscular back and firm buttocks as she rocked in ever faster thrusts against the soft flesh imprisoned beneath her. Abruptly Molly pulled her mouth free and buried her lips in the neck of her ravisher. Her arms flashed around the straining body atop her, trying to draw Shane closer still, and she cried out in her pleasure as the two bodies twisted in the final uncontrollable spasm.

In her heated confusion, Elizabeth clutched at herself, trying to slake her own desires. She stumbled out into the hall, desperate to get over the edge. An ear-bursting shout thundered through the corridor. "My God! Mrs. Shea, what are you doing out of bed?"

A dark-haired woman in a nurse's uniform and pink cardigan was running toward her. It was the woman who had stood, silent, earlier in the treatment room. Elizabeth tried to escape from her, still concerned only with getting her hand under her gown.

The woman seized her in her strong arms. "There, there, dear. It's Mrs. Eddy. I'm here to help you. What are you doing out here?"

She looked at Elizabeth, who was sobbing in her unrelieved excitement, her eyes dull and unfocused. The nurse laughed. "You don't even know where you are. Let me put you back to bed."

She tried to resist, but she was like a child in the woman's grasp. It was all very confusing for a moment, but then she was back in her bed with the covers over her and the room dark save for the sliver of light from the door left ajar.

She yanked at the hem of her gown, desperate for fulfillment, and as she did, the room brightened and she was in her bedroom in California. Jack was at her, like a crazed stallion, and she was almost there. But the glow began to fade, and she heard herself calling to him, "No, please, please! Don't stop now."

It was dark again, and she was lying there, miserable, ashamed of where she had her hand. She jerked it away, rolled over onto her side, and cried.

The tears passed quickly, and a dark warmth crept insidiously through her body. She fought it for a second, then gave in and slipped beneath the surface.

CHAPTER 5

Somewhere in the distance Elizabeth could hear voices. She opened her eyes to a darkness marred only by the narrow vertical bar of light beyond her shoulder.

Puzzlement quickened to fear before she remembered that she was in the hospital, lying in bed with a sheet tangled around her body. She was sweaty and had a pounding headache.

She heard the voices again, closer and quite distinct, and tried to raise up on one elbow. She was not dizzy, but her limbs felt leaden. The approaching footsteps halted right outside her door. One of the voices stirred vague memories of the wreck. Its owner was trying to speak softly, but she could hear every word.

"Doctor, I want to thank you for seeing me. I'm sorry that you had to walk all the way down to the gate, but it couldn't wait until morning. I thought you had an automatic system on your gate. Our responsible sheet at the office shows that you do."

She recognized the second voice, more jovial and louder, as that of Dr. Mainwaring. "Oh, we do, but the darned thing went out yesterday morning. Wouldn't you know it! Normally that gate is only opened a couple of times a week to let supply trucks pass, and here we have needed it several times tonight. Now, why do you think we can help you with your missing ambulance, Sergeant Kendall?"

"Maybe we should go to the office to talk, sir. God knows, I wouldn't want to disturb your patients."

The doctor laughed loudly. "No problems there, officer. At Skystone the rooms are soundproof. After all, it's expected at our level of operation. But if it will make you more comfortable, let's step into the visitors' lounge."

When the doctor spoke again, his voice was almost as loud as it had been in the hall. She decided the lounge must be directly across from her room.

"Now, Sergeant, about the ambulance."

"Well, after it left here, it flat-out disappeared. As a matter of fact, the county dispatcher never received a ten-eight from them. That's a radio designation that indicates they're back in service and ready to receive calls. It should have been sent within a minute or so after they walked out of your emergency room. It's been a busy night. The phone has been ringing off the hook all night . . . flooded roads that need barricades, calls for the fire department to pump out basements, fender-benders. The county doesn't have the resources to handle this sort of thing. The dispatcher was running so far behind on calls, it was over an hour after the ambulance left Skystone before she realized she had not heard from them. To tell you the honest-to-God's truth, I don't know when she would have noticed if we hadn't had another accident call. We spent about thirty minutes trying to contact them, and then put out an APB. So far, none of our units or any other police agency has spotted them."

"Ah, that's why you wanted us to run a bed check. You're wondering if perhaps one of our more active guests might have commandeered your ambulance."

There was a brief pause before the sergeant replied. "Well, with all due respect, Dr. Mainwaring, we have to check every possibility."

"Here's the night supervisor, Mrs. Eddy. She must have finished the bed check."

Elizabeth recognized the voice as that of the nurse who had discovered her in the corridor. "Doctor, all the patients are accounted for, although I'm afraid we may have brought a bit of work on ourselves. Two or three of the old dears have managed to upset themselves at being awakened."

She laughed, and Mainwaring joined her. "Well, after all, nurse, the day-shift people claim that you night folks have it too easy anyway."

"By the way, doctor, I woke the orderly that let the ambulance out the gate. I assumed the sergeant would want to talk to him."

"Thank you, ma'am," the sergeant said. "That's very thoughtful of you."

Elizabeth heard the nurse's footsteps fading away in the corridor. She had been so intent on the conversation that her headache was forgotten. The doctor started to chatter to pass the time, but the sergeant interrupted him.

"How is the badly injured man, Mr. Thorne?"

"Sergeant, to be honest with you, he's not going to make it. It's a matter of time—a day or two, at most. Maybe any moment. That's why we're shorthanded tonight, why I'm staying up all night, and why you don't see our usual staff. We've set up an intensive-care unit for him. A nurse will remain by his bedside all night."

"Hmmm. I wondered why I didn't see your cardiac monitors going at the nurses' station. Perhaps, doctor, we can consider moving him tomorrow."

"I certainly wouldn't recommend it. The expense would be enormous and needless. Mr. Thorne has irreversible brain damage. If he were surrounded at this moment by the finest neurosurgeons in the United States, it would do him no good. Believe me, I know. Of course, when Miss Thorne is capable of making a decision, it's her say, but until then we won't release him because we don't think it's wise."

"How about the others? Any problems there?"

"Well, a physician hates to venture an opinion this early after a trauma, but I rather think not. Miss Thorne caught a terrific wallop on the head. There's no question she has a moderate concussion, but if there are no complications, she should be ready for discharge in four or five days. The young man, Mr. Sutherlin, has a badly fractured bone in his left arm, but Dr. Caudill is an excellent man at that sort of thing. We have quite a bit of experience with broken bones here, as you might imagine. He's healthy, and he's young. I foresee no problems—just time."

"How about the other girl, doctor? Elizabeth Shea? She didn't look as if she was hurt beyond being a little shaken up."

"Darn it, what's keeping that orderly? Oh . . . Elizabeth Shea? They are the tricky ones, Sergeant. The medical profession used to release people like her after a cursory examination. On occasion—rare, I'll grant—the patient would drop dead in a day or two with a massive hematoma. After all, the girl has no idea how long she was unconscious. I'm going to recommend we keep her for observation at least seventy-two hours. If there is a problem, it should show up by then. Oh, I hear the orderly coming."

Elizabeth also heard the slow, heavy tread approaching the door.

The heavily accented voice complained, "Jesus Christ, man, I'm dead on my feet. I need sleep. What do you want now?"

"I'm sorry to have to awaken you, but the officer here has a problem."

"You mean that stupid ambulance? The nurse said something about it. It didn't make any sense. Why did you wake me up?"

Dr. Mainwaring sounded as if he was getting a bit annoyed with his sleepy employee. "Joe, their ambulance is missing. According to the sergeant, they have had no contact with it since it left Skystone. This is a serious concern to these people. I told the deputy he has our full cooperation. I know you would want to lend him every assistance possible. Isn't that right?"

Elizabeth heard a noncommittal "Yeah" that was more a grunt than a word.

"May I have your name for my report?" asked the deputy.

"Hey, why have you gotta have my name?"

Mainwaring's voice was sharp. "Give him your name, Joe."

"Okay, okay. My name's Joe Rogers. . . . Satisfied?"

Cobb Kendall choked back a retort. He wanted to ask

Mainwaring why a snooty place like this had such a sullen bastard working for it. It was the thought of Mainwaring's complaining to Sheriff Toby Mears or Judge Lynch that stopped him. Instead, his voice became monotonic, devoid of nuances.

"Mr. Rogers, the doctor has told you why we wanted to see you. It seems you're the last known person to see our ambulance."

"Well, what does that make me, copper?"

Mainwaring's voice developed a distinct chill. "Mr. Rogers, I would suggest that you adopt a more reasonable tone. I told you Skystone intends to cooperate with the local authorities in every way we can."

In the lounge, the orderly assumed a smile that was more sickly than acceptable. "I'm sorry, sir. Guess I'm tired— didn't get a lot of sleep last night, either. What can I tell you?"

Cobb opened his notebook. "The ambulance left here at about twelve forty-five—right?"

Rogers smiled again. It was a better effort, if not totally convincing. "Why, I couldn't rightly say. I know it was long enough before one o'clock for me to get back inside by then."

Cobb nodded. "You went outside to assist them backing out of the porte cochere and then followed them down the drive to take care of the gate. Is that correct?"

"Yes, sir. It's what Dr. Mainwaring told me to do, and I did it."

"I don't suppose they mentioned what they intended to do?"

The heavyset Rogers shook his head. "No. The one guy was a real sourhead. He started acting pissed while he was still inside. He wouldn't say a word to me. The other guy talked on the way down to the gate."

Cobb looked up in surprise. "Down to the gate? You rode down to the gate with them?"

"Yeah. I asked them for a ride. I didn't see any reason to take a two-way hike on a wet night when I didn't have to."

"Did they use the radio while you were with them?"

He shook his head again. "No. The one fellow—the

pleasant one—talked with me the whole time. He was asking about Skystone. That sullen bastard driving the ambulance didn't say a word."

Cobb drummed his pen against the notebook. "Hmmm. I guess that explains why we didn't get an immediate ten-eight from them, but"—he was lost for a moment in thought—"why didn't we get the ten-eight after they reached the road? Say ... did you notice which way they turned?"

The heavyset man stared at Cobb as if he had not heard the question, and Cobb repeated it. Rogers shot a look at Mainwaring before facing the sergeant again. "Why ... by God, I'm not sure. I think it was ... yeah ... he turned left."

Cobb's voice was incredulous. "Left! But five more miles in that direction would have taken them out of the county."

Mainwaring intruded. "Joe, you told me they turned right. Don't you remember?"

The orderly nodded, staring at the doctor. "Uh ... yeah. By God, that's true. It was right. I'm sorry, officer. They turned right."

Cobb was puzzled. "Dr. Mainwaring, I don't understand. Why were you and Mr. Rogers talking about which way the ambulance turned?"

Mainwaring chuckled. "No big deal. It's just that when he came back into the treatment room last night, he mentioned it. I believe Joe's exact words were, 'Man, that son of a bitch drives like a maniac. He did a sharp right onto the highway and took off like a' ... I believe his rather eloquent phrase was 'a scalded jackrabbit.'"

He peered at the orderly. "Am I right, Mr. Rogers?"

The man grinned. "By God, you're a wonder, doc."

Cobb closed his notebook. "Huh! That doesn't quite sound like the Johnson boys. Well, thank you, Mr. Rogers. If I need to talk to you again, I know where to find you."

The man's heavy shoulders sagged. He nodded, gave Mainwaring a last look, and shuffled from the room.

Cobb waited until the footsteps had faded away before saying, "Mr. Rogers is not quite the type I would picture working here, doctor."

"How right you are, Sergeant, but I don't hire them and I

don't fire them. I'm one of the lackeys here myself. But I will tell you this. It would really amaze you to see how gentle that man can be with the elderly. Now, it's rather late. Is there anything else I can do for you?"

Cobb Kendall was not going anywhere for a moment. "Dr. Mainwaring, just how effective is your security system . . . considering the difficulties you're having with your front gate?"

"As I'm sure you know, we have extensive grounds here. There is a twelve-feet-high stone wall running the length of the front footage and a ten-feet electrified fence enclosing the rest of the estate perimeter. They say you would have to dig down four feet to get under the thing. It's like everything else around here—first-class.

"The yardman has a trail bike and responds to any alarms. There must be two or three a month. Usually it's a large bird or something like that which has enough bulk to disrupt the circuit, setting off the alarms. To answer your question, the gate is normally opened by remote control from a panel in the office. Codes are punched in both to release the gate and to deactivate the horn alarms. If the control malfunctions, there is an override that allows the gate to be opened manually. The silent alarms operate anytime the gates are open and can't be deactivated.

"The silent alarms, large red globes, flash at the nurses' stations. We use a visual device because it does not disturb the patients, and of course nurses are always on duty in those areas. There are two horn alarms, one in the business office and one in the yardman's quarters. At Skystone, what's in stays in and what's out stays out. Why your sudden interest in our security system, Sergeant?"

"Oh, I was wondering if someone could have commandeered the ambulance and then sneaked back in later."

Mainwaring laughed. "I can promise you that would have been absolutely impossible. I'll guarantee it."

As the men moved into the hall, Cobb said, "This is shaping up to be quite a puzzle. There must be a rational explanation, but it has me stumped. I want to thank you for your time. We'll be over about nine o'clock in the morning to take statements from the accident victims."

They moved out of Elizabeth's hearing. Her head had grown so heavy while she listened, propped on one arm, that she could no longer support it. She sank down on the pillow to rest a moment.

Elizabeth lolled like a limp doll under the vigorous shaking. Forcing her eyes open, she found the exotic face of Mrs. Eddy hovering above her. There was enough outside light from the window that she could make out the woman's features.

"Wake up, Mrs. Shea. Wake up. Dr. Caudill is coming in to look you over. He's been busy all night with Mr. Thorne."

Elizabeth struggled to a sitting position. "Oh, my God, how is he? Is he okay?"

Before the nurse could answer, the door swung open to reveal Caudill's craggy face. Behind him, for a split second, the sloe-eyed blond nurse was visible, peering into the room. When the doctor came close, she could see that his face was gaunt and strained.

"Well, Mrs. Shea," he said. "Did you sleep well? How do you feel?"

"Doctor, how is he? How is Mr. Thorne?"

The doctor looked at her gravely. "I understand he was your employer, Mrs. Shea. Is that right?"

She nodded, straining toward the word *was*.

When he spoke again, his voice was low, as if he intended it for her alone. "I'm afraid that Mr. Thorne is dead."

He glanced at his watch. "He passed away about thirty-five minutes ago. Nothing could have saved him, even if he had been in the finest neurosurgical center in the country. I want his daughter and the rest of you to understand that he never had a chance. Now . . . how about you?"

Elizabeth sank back on the pillow, fighting against crying. She was in the best physical condition of the three of them to do what had to be done. She looked up at the doctor, who was viewing her with some concern as the silent tears escaped, tracing tear tracks down her cheeks.

"Excuse me, doctor. I don't know why I'm crying this way. I didn't know Gavin Thorne all that well. It's just that, somehow, this doesn't seem the right place for him to have died."

The doctor patted her hand. "But you, Mrs. Shea. How are you?"

She told him about waking during the night and the odd tricks that her mind had played on her—her sight, her hearing, her sense of smell, and her distorted sense of dimension. She made no mention, though, of what she had seen across the hall.

"You were out of bed?" he interrupted. "And in that condition?"

"Yes. I went out . . ."

He interrupted her, turning to the nurse, demanding in a harsh voice, "What was it?"

She shrugged. "Ask Mainwaring."

CHAPTER 6 _____

*H*e wheeled about without another word and left the room. The nurse seemed uncertain about whether to follow him. She shrugged and reached for Elizabeth's wrist. Dr. Caudill returned as the nurse finished taking her pulse.

Using a small penlight, he peered into Elizabeth's eyes, tersely commanding her to look in first one direction and then another. Then he had her move her neck and arms while he scrutinized her carefully. Satisfied, he straightened up.

"Mrs. Shea, here is a tranquilizer. It should be sufficient to make you quite relaxed. I want you to stay in this room —in bed—all day. Your problem last evening was that you were hallucinating. It's a normal reaction to the drug you were given."

"But, doctor, I know what happened. It was strange. I heard them talking, so I followed them, and—"

His voice was harsh. "Mrs. Shea, I'm busy. I have no time to listen to your drug-induced fantasies. I would certainly advise you to keep them to yourself because that's all they are—hallucinations."

He left the room before she could protest further. Elizabeth looked after him in bewilderment. Tears trickled from her eyes. She wondered why she was bursting into tears with each slight provocation; it was totally unlike her.

Mrs. Eddy sat down on the bed and took Elizabeth's hand between hers, patting it. "Now, now, Mrs. Shea, there's no point in upsetting yourself. The doctor doesn't mean to be gruff. He's busy . . . he's been up all night because of the accident. I want you to tell me what you think you saw."

Elizabeth protested, "It isn't what I think I saw . . . it's what happened. My senses may be all screwed up, but I know what I saw."

The nurse plucked a Kleenex from the table and wiped Elizabeth's eyes as she would a child's. "Okay, tell me what you did see."

"But I shouldn't. I . . . I don't want to get anyone in trouble. It's just that they . . . they shouldn't do that here."

The woman chuckled. "My dear, you're making quite a mystery of this. Go ahead and tell me."

A reluctant Elizabeth, her voice little more than a whisper, related what she had seen and heard during the night, beginning with the struggle in the hall and ending with her last glimpse of the entangled bodies of the lovers. By the time she finished, the smile had vanished from Mrs. Eddy's face and she was looking at Elizabeth very thoughtfully.

"I'm afraid Dr. Caudill is right. It was a hallucination, pure and simple. If you think about it, you will realize how absurd your story is. After all, things like that couldn't go on in a hospital without people being aware of it."

"But I heard Dr. Mainwaring say the rooms are sound-proof."

The nurse smiled again. "That's very true, but you said yourself the two doors were open. Besides, both nurses were on duty with me during the night. Don't you think I would have missed them? One or the other was in view almost constantly."

A stubborn note invaded Elizabeth's voice. "But I know what I saw. It happened just as I told you."

Mrs. Eddy slipped off the bed. "Mrs. Shea, we might as well settle this, embarrassing though it is. I'll be back in a few minutes."

Five minutes passed before the supervisor stepped back

into the room. Elizabeth's eyes widened in disbelief. The two lovers, clad in their nurses' uniforms, trailed behind their superior. Her face flaming with embarrassment, Elizabeth flung herself around so that she faced the window, refusing to acknowledge them.

"Mrs. Shea, look at me!"

She wanted to crawl under the mattress and die.

"Mrs. Shea, I'm asking you to look at these young ladies face-to-face. You have made accusations against them that are quite serious—that could terminate their careers. The least you can do is face them and repeat your charges."

The woman's grip on her arm was strong. Reluctantly, she turned toward the waiting nurses.

The two girls were a study in contrast. The younger, shorter girl was as red and confused as Elizabeth, looking down at the floor. The blond, the one with the unearthly jade eyes, was staring straight at Elizabeth, at ease and amused.

Mrs. Eddy's voice was unrelenting. "Mrs. Shea, this is Shane—Shane Covington."

The exotic blond jerked her head around, staring at the supervisor in surprise.

Mrs. Eddy ignored her and nodded toward the younger girl. "This pretty young lady, our student nurse, is Molly Hatcher. Girls, Mrs. Shea was wandering about in the corridor last night, and she says she observed you committing a homosexual act."

The supervising nurse was eyeing the younger nurse as she spoke. Molly again blushed furiously and stared at her feet, nervously interlacing her hands. Mrs. Eddy smiled. "Look at Molly. She's a good Southern Baptist girl. I'm not sure she knows what I mean. Molly, were you loving and kissing Shane last night?"

Molly shot a quick look at her questioner. "No, ma'am. That's a terrible thing to say."

The supervisor turned to the grinning Shane. "And, Shane, how about you? What's your answer?"

"I would suggest that Mrs. Shea talk to my boyfriend the next time he's here if she has any doubts."

The head nurse faced Elizabeth. "Well? You heard the

girls deny your charges. I assure you there was probably no interval longer than three or four minutes all night long when one or the other of them was out of my sight. I hate to mention this, but you force me to. Quite frankly, you were rubbing your pubic area through your gown when I found you in the hall. That could explain the erotic nature of your hallucination."

She turned to the two young women, now listening avidly. "Very well, ladies, get back to your stations. That will be all."

The nurses filed solemnly from the room.

Elizabeth lay with her eyes closed, her lips trembling, dying with shame at the knowledge that the woman had seen what she was doing.

The supervisor gripped her shoulder. "Mrs. Shea—Elizabeth—I'm not trying to embarrass you. Hospital employees have to be above suspicion. We must make a patient understand when she is confusing reality with hallucination. We cannot allow innocent women to be maligned. If, for example, you were to mention this to the police when they come to see you, it would be painful to two innocent girls and end up making you look like a fool, or worse. Now, let's take your Valium and let you rest for a while."

Despite the Valium, Elizabeth could not go to sleep. She lay, deeply relaxed, lids heavy, but still awake, watching the curtains brighten as the sun angle slowly changed.

She remembered that she had not yet been fed and reached lazily for the call button. As she was about to press it, the door swung open and the sloe-eyed Shane slipped into the room, carrying a breakfast tray.

"I was about to buzz. I wondered when breakfast was going to be served."

Without bothering to acknowledge the greeting, Shane yanked up the folding table leaf on the console and slammed down the tray.

Elizabeth's anticipation of a breakfast in keeping with her luxurious room vanished in a twinkling. The tray held a bowl of cornflakes, burnt toast, and a carton of milk. She looked at Shane in bewilderment.

"Is this it? This isn't much of a breakfast, and besides, I don't like cold cereal."

The nurse's face flushed with anger, but as quickly her features relaxed. "I'm sorry, but everything is going wrong. There is no gas pressure in the lines. We're having to serve everyone a cold breakfast this morning, and everyone's griping, just like you."

"I didn't mean to gripe. It's just that I figured Skystone would serve elaborate meals. I'm a little woozy from the Valium. Would you mind moving the table over me and cranking the bed up?"

The girl snapped the leaf on its pivot to where it was across the bed, but her face darkened again. "I ought to let you fix your own damned bed, princess," she snarled. "Maybe you wouldn't have so much time to be shooting your mouth off."

Shane placed a long, red-tipped finger on one of a row of buttons built into the side of the bed console, and with a low hum, the upper part of the bed rose. She released the button and stepped back before it was high enough for Elizabeth to sit up comfortably. She favored Elizabeth with an indecipherable look.

"There, you know how to adjust your bed now. Enjoy your breakfast." She marched out of the room.

Feeling a bit better after the food, Elizabeth decided to explore the other mysteries of the bedside console. In the first drawer she found a folded sheet of heavy cardboard. It was the week's menu for the hospital. It took but a moment's browsing to make her regret the kitchen difficulties.

As she read, the menu kept falling across her face, and she laughed lazily. The effects of the Valium were not gone, after all. She started to replace the menu and blushed.

Standing in the doorway, observing her, were two men. One was short with sparse gray hair and a face like an owl: flat and round, with big eyes, and the strangest little beak of a nose she had ever seen. His tiny mouth was stretched in a grin.

Behind him was a taller man dressed in a deputy's uniform and a western hat. He was a bit over six feet tall and in his mid-thirties. His dark brown hair was cut unfashionably short. He had an intelligent face with regular features. Despite his smile, she could sense an intensity in the way he held himself.

The older man removed his pearl-gray hat and advanced into the room. "Mrs. Shea, I'm the local sheriff, Toby Mears, and this is Sergeant Cobb Kendall. He serves as county detective when we need one."

The tall, intense man nodded, and when he spoke, she recognized him as the policeman who had talked to the doctor during the night about the missing ambulance. He had also been in charge at the crash scene.

The sheriff crossed to the bed and extended his hand.

Elizabeth was embarrassed. Her coordination was so bad that she grabbed his thumb and then walked her fingers across his palm until she could grasp his entire hand. She wondered what he must think of her.

He laughed. "I'd say you are feeling no pain, young lady. I'm sorry to hear about Mr. Thorne. I'm sure all was done for him that could be done. As a matter of fact, the Skystone people went out of their way to try to help him. Usually they don't allow outsiders on their grounds.

"If you don't mind, I'd like to ask a few questions about you folks . . . Mr. Thorne's next of kin, and things like that."

Elizabeth nodded, trying to shake off the effects of the drug. "I know. I'll try to help all I can, Sheriff. His daughter Meredith and Scott Sutherlin were injured worse than I was."

"Don't you worry about them, Mrs. Shea. As a matter of fact, when I talked to the doctor, he said Miss Thorne was much better this morning. At first they thought she had a severe head injury, but they have decided it was probably psychological shock as much as anything—what they call disassociation. She does have quite a bump on her head. And the gentleman, Mr. Sutherlin—he's as big as a mule and twice as strong. He's hurt, all right, but they may have to tie him to the bed to keep him in it. Now, don't you worry about your friends.

"By the way, Mrs. Shea, when Mr. Sutherlin was brought in, he was carrying a weapon in a shoulder holster. In his wallet there was a permit for it issued in Cook County, Illinois. Do you know why he would be carrying a concealed firearm?"

Elizabeth sensed that she needed to be as exact as possible with her answer. "Scott—Mr. Sutherlin—was Mr. Thorne's personal assistant . . . I suppose you might say, in some instances, his bodyguard. Normally he didn't carry a gun, but Mr. Thorne was extraordinarily afraid of his daughter being kidnapped. I don't know the story, but something happened in his own family when he was quite young. Oftentimes he had Scott arm himself when he accompanied Meredith, even on shopping trips. Many times, on trips, Mr. Thorne carried a good deal of expensive jewelry, and he insisted that Scott carry a weapon then."

She looked up expectantly at the sheriff.

He nodded. "Don't you worry none, young lady, but we are going to take that gun into town and hold it until Mr. Sutherlin is ready to leave the county. Unfortunately, we can't honor a county license from Illinois."

Then he started asking her about the accident. As he plied her with questions, the younger man took notes in his notebook. When the sheriff asked her if she had been watching the road prior to the wreck and she said no, he glanced at the sergeant. The younger man shrugged.

When the sheriff finished, he nodded. "Okay, young lady. Just one thing . . . Before you leave the county, I want you to drop by the office and sign your statement. Okay?"

Elizabeth nodded, and he turned toward the sergeant. "Well, Cobb, do you have any more questions?"

Approaching the bed, the younger man smiled. The intensity she sensed in him earlier had vanished. The smile grew warmer as Cobb Kendall slipped on one of his interrogation faces. "I'd like to call you Elizabeth, if you don't mind."

She nodded wordlessly.

"Elizabeth, we seem to have lost, misplaced, or thrown away the ambulance that brought your friends here last night. I don't suppose you know anything that might help us, do you?"

Before she could stop herself, she said, "You can call me Liz."

He favored her with an even broader smile.

There was little she could tell him. She related what she remembered of the hectic hour after they arrived at Skystone. The sheriff looked rather uninterested, but the sergeant listened gravely as she described how upset the medic had become when Dr. Mainwaring insisted that he write a summary of the incident.

When she finished, the younger man gave her a long, searching look and frowned. Elizabeth was flabbergasted at the change in him. His face had that tense, determined look once more. There was no warmth or obsequiousness in the manner in which he addressed his superior.

"Okay, Toby, that's all the questions I have. I need to go find an ambulance."

The sheriff clapped him on the back and winked at Elizabeth. "I've got a real bloodhound here, Mrs. Shea, a real bloodhound."

He tipped his hat to her as he disappeared into the corridor.

Elizabeth's lassitude vanished with the interview, and soon she was sitting up in bed, increasingly restless. One feature of luxury convalescent hospitals was most disconcerting—the incredible silence. She had not been a patient in a hospital since she was sixteen, but she remembered the hustle and bustle, the voices, the clatter of equipment—noises that lasted far into the night and made it difficult to sleep. She was tempted to sneak out and try to find Meredith's room, but the thought of another encounter with the formidable Mrs. Eddy deterred her.

She had never been much of a television viewer, but restlessness drove her to explore the TV controls. Dr. Mainwaring appeared as she was trying to figure them out.

CHAPTER 7

"Well, I know it."

Louise raised her head, squinting at Elizabeth. "Huh?"

Elizabeth blushed. "That was strange. I thought I heard someone say I was fourteen. It was like they were talking in my head."

"Honestly, Liz, if you had brain one you . . . sssh! Did you hear that? I think someone is in the cabanas. Come on!"

Louise scrambled to her feet. Elizabeth, uncertain whether her friend had actually heard something, hesitantly followed the redhead as they tiptoed over the tiles around the Lansford pool, tiles reflecting the fierce August heat. Louise first stopped outside the men's and then the women's cabana and put her ear to the doors. They heard nothing.

Elizabeth was about to protest the game they were playing when the sound of a woman giggling filtered through the heavy door. The confirmation of Louise's suspicions caused Elizabeth a moment of fear, and she reached for Louise's arm to pull her back. She was too late.

Louise stepped into the room, followed by Elizabeth. In the dim light, they saw a man and a woman—the woman with her skirt up around her waist and the man nude—lying on a low bench, making love. The woman, one of the Lansfords' maids, became aware of their presence at the same moment Louise shouted, "Theresa!"

With a twist of her supple body, the woman sent her lover crashing to the floor. She came upright in one fluid move and ran past the girls.

Louise whirled to confront the man, whom she recognized as a transient hired two weeks earlier as an assistant gardener. As he came to his feet, Elizabeth saw that he was still aroused, his organ glistening in the reflected light from the pool.

Louise yelled, "How dare you do this! I'm going to tell my father."

The man seemed beside himself with lust, paying no attention to her. Elizabeth knew instinctively that he was aware of nothing but their bodies, almost nude in the tiny bikinis. Panic welling in her, she fled from the cabana, followed by the deserted Louise.

As Elizabeth ran, she could hear the man's bare feet slapping against the tiles. Running behind her, Louise shouted a warning, but it was too late.

Two paths opened through the tall shrubbery border at the far end of the pool. The right-hand path climbed the slope to the house, while the other one ran past the gardener's shed into the Lansfords' extensive gardens.

With stoic resignation, Louise followed Elizabeth along the left-hand path, moving farther from help with each stride.

Gasping for breath, Elizabeth knew she could not go much farther. Topping a rise in the path, she saw, to her left, the gardener's shed, its door open. She swerved through the opening, hoping that she could find something inside with which to wedge the door shut.

Louise started to follow but, glancing over her shoulder, saw their pursuer a bare ten feet behind her. She stayed on the descending path through the trees. The sounds of pursuit vanished, and she glanced back to find the path empty.

Elizabeth slammed the shed door and threw her weight against it, but as she sought something to wedge against the door, it crashed open, flinging her across the narrow room.

Before she could raise her hands to defend herself, he had his arms around her, driving her against the wall. His arms tightened, and his body crushed hers against the rough planks. She tried futilely to push him away, but he was a stocky man, his muscles hard and thick. Her struggling served to excite him further.

Elizabeth became aware of his penis, hard and wet, moving against the bare flesh of her stomach. She tried a last, desperate attempt to slip under his arms. It allowed him to slide his hands around her buttocks, cupping them and lifting her. He made no attempt to remove her bikini bottom, content to hold her tight against his loins. He thrust rhythmically against her, grunting.

She surrendered, near to fainting. She was aware of little but his sweat-slick, rock-hard torso pounding, like one vast muscle, into her soft, defenseless body. Elizabeth was vaguely aware of yelling behind him. Louise had raced back to the gardener's shed and launched herself, with fearless abandon, at the man's back, futilely pounding him with her fists.

Her attacker gasped, and a hot, thick liquid splashed over Elizabeth's stomach. For several moments he was motionless, leaning against her. Then he released her, and she sagged to the ground, betrayed by nerveless legs. He spun around, sent Louise reeling across the shed, and disappeared out the door. Louise rushed after him, returning only when she was satisfied that he was long gone. She found Elizabeth still huddled where she had fallen, crying.

When she showed no signs of stopping, the impatient Louise pulled her to her feet. Elizabeth's tears continued, and Louise shook her, none too gently.

"Stop it, Liz. Are you hurt?"

Elizabeth stared at her, bewildered at Louise's lack of sympathy.

When she still did not react, Louise asked with growing concern, "What is wrong with you? He is gone. That son of a bitch won't dare show his face around here again."

"Oh, God, Lou, don't you understand?"

"Understand what? He didn't hurt you. Nothing really

happened. Nobody will ever know about it. Now, come on, Liz, quit acting like a baby."

Elizabeth started to cry again, her words barely intelligible through her sobs. "Please, listen to me. I let him do it to me. I let him."

Awkwardly Louise embraced her friend. "What are you saying? That guy was as strong as an ox. You couldn't have stopped him with a two-by-four."

No, she couldn't have stopped him with a two-by-four. She didn't even know he was still in the house.

The morning was no different from any other. When Jack Rundstedt, Ted's obnoxious buddy arrived, she retreated to her bedroom. Elizabeth always used her enforced confinement to complete a leisurely toilet. She lingered longer than usual in her shower. When she came out, she discovered she had forgotten to put the fresh toothpaste in the bathroom when she unloaded the groceries the day before. Quickly she pulled a short, mid-thigh-length robe over her nude body and opened the bedroom door, listening, although she was sure that Ted and Jack had long since gone. The house was silent. She ran down the hall to the kitchen.

Because of the noise of the shower, Elizabeth didn't hear the phone. It was Ted's office, telling him that a client was arriving unexpectedly early. Having just poured Jack a cup of coffee, Ted insisted that he stay to finish it.

As Jack raised the cup for a last swallow, Ted's Jaguar was disappearing up the hill. He was rising to carry the cup to the sink when he heard Elizabeth running barefoot along the hall.

She ran past him—standing in the corner by the table—without seeing him, opened a cupboard, and reached high on to the shelf where she had stowed the toilet articles. Standing on tiptoes, she stretched, the short green robe riding high in the back, sliding up to reveal the shapely rounds of her buttocks. The rustling of the paper bag hid the sound of the three quick steps. The first she knew Jack was there was when his calloused hands closed on her hips.

Fear surged through her, and she turned her head, unable to twist her body around in his viselike grip. She saw that it was Jack, but a different Jack from the crude but jovial neighbor she knew. His face bore a dull, expressionless look, and his eyes were half closed. As he pulled her against his hard-muscled body, terror swept through her. She remembered where she had seen that same look before.

Panic gave her strength to break free of his hands, and she ran from the room, thinking only of the sanctuary of her bedroom.

She veered into her room, eyes rolling in fright, gasping for breath. Confused and terrified, she tried to think—to know what to do. She could hear him in the hall, moving toward the bedroom. She thought of the door and its lock. Turning, she lunged for the door, pushing against it with the palms of her hands.

Jack slammed into it with his shoulder, sending her reeling toward the bed. She turned her back toward him, holding her face in her hands. She thought of dashing across the room and out the patio door but knew she would never make it. She could sense him behind her, watching her. Her legs were so weak she very nearly sank to the floor. There was movement behind her and the sounds of clothing rustling.

Jack, his voice husky, commanded, "Turn around."

He took a step toward her, and unable to stop herself, Elizabeth turned to face him. He was standing only a couple of feet from her, his nudity revealing the thick ridges of muscles across his stomach. Slowly he raised his hands and grasped the zipper of her robe.

"Jack, don't. Oh, God, please don't."

She caught at his thick wrists with her hands but had no strength to resist. As her powerless arms fell to her sides, he lowered the zipper until it parted. Jack slipped the robe from her shoulders, and it fell around her ankles in a soft whisper. She felt his eyes feasting on her flesh and watched him growing erect. It was how she expected him to be.

She stammered, almost beyond coherency, "Are you crazy? This is rape. Oh, Jesus, you're going to rape me."

He surged forward, his strong arms gathering her soft, vulnerable body against him. It was against her stomach, powerful, the way it was in the shed. Clutching her hair, he pulled her head back and brought his mouth down against her tender lips, kissing her hard. She jerked her head away, struggling against him for a moment, but his arms tightened and she was helpless. He was going to finish what had been started at Lansfords'. She had to let him. Let him? God, she wanted him to finish it.

He stepped forward, pushing her before him, and they tumbled onto the bed. For a moment they were side by side, one of his hands on her back and the other fondling her buttocks while she embraced his thick, brawny body. He sensed her excitement, and in one violent motion, rolled her onto her back and entered her. She gasped at the fury of the assault as Jack, beyond control, crushed her beneath him. She closed her eyes tightly, staring at the walls of the garden shed, feeling the hard, sinewy body, like one great muscle, pistoning against her.

She was being borne away in a building tidal wave of unbearable pleasure. Sobbing wildly, she clutched at the iron-hard buttocks, trying to impale herself still deeper, and exploded into an ecstatic chaos, vaguely conscious of his loud groans.

Elizabeth lay there for long moments, desperate to remain safely in the shed.

Growing impatient, Jack struggled free of her embrace and climbed from the bed. He stood, looking down at her body. She was too sated to cover herself or turn away.

Jack shook his head in disbelief, pulled on his cutoffs and T-shirt, and clumped down the hall without as much as a good-bye.

The days passed, three of them, days filled with guilt, anger, and disgust, days with no sign of Jack. On the fourth morning, she heard a knock at the sliding glass door in the master bedroom. She hurried into the room, a bit frightened that there might be an intruder on the deck, to discover Jack standing outside on the patio. Her rage at the sight of her violator swept caution from her mind. She charged across to the door and yanked it open.

Her voice was far louder than she intended. "You dirty, miserable son of a bitch! You have a lot of nerve! What in—"

He walked straight into her, knocking her backwards, and once inside the bedroom, slid the door closed behind him.

Elizabeth sputtered, trying to maintain her outrage. "Bastard! Where is Adele? Where is your wife?"

Jack's hand clasped the back of her neck and drew her close. "She works in her studio until noon every day. She won't bother us."

She tried to pull away from him, but his grip tightened. Holding her powerless, he unbuttoned her blouse and slipped it off. Then he reached around her and unhooked her brassiere. As it dropped away, he stepped back to look at her breasts.

She knew she could be away from him and out the patio door before he could stop her, but she looked up into his face. Already it wore the dull, heavy-lidded look she had seen the first time.

She whispered her absurd question. "What do you want?"

"The same as you," he growled.

Pleasure arced through her loins, and she could not have moved had her life depended on it. She stood stock still while he unbuttoned and then drew off her shorts and panties. Quickly he stripped, stepped forward, and wrapped her in his embrace.

They stumbled to the bed, their tongues coiling around each other within their locked mouths. She rolled under him.

It was as it had been the first day—no words of love, no endearments—just a quick, violent coupling, with her hands digging at the hard, thrusting body, shrieking at the end with a pleasure beyond anything she had known.

His only words came as he reclothed himself. "Don't waste time tomorrow wearing all that crap."

The next morning she kept her nightgown on, ignoring Ted's question about whether she was feeling well. After Jack arrived, she stood apart from him and slowly, teasingly, pulled the gown over her head. Her excitement at the lasciviousness of the act was thrilling. As he came toward her, she looked past him at the mirror. She barely recognized her own face, transformed by the same dulled look she had seen on Jack's.

After that, their coupling was a daily thing. The fever of

their lovemaking did not diminish in her. In fact, it grew and with it her loathing of both Jack and herself.

She saw Jack's leering face looming above her and lashed out at it with her hand. As she struggled against the arms holding her down, the face began to change. It was someone in a white coat . . . a doctor.

"Where am I? What's wrong with me? Help! . . . Oh, Dr. Mainwaring."

Her vision had come into focus, and she recognized Mainwaring standing by the bed, glasses askew, eyeing her warily. Cautiously he extended his arm and patted her foot. "Relax, Elizabeth, everything is fine."

It came back to her in a rush. He had come into the room shortly after the sheriff left to announce, "Well, Mrs. Shea, time for your medication."

She looked at him in surprise. "Medication? I don't understand. Dr. Caudill said that I was okay. He told me to stay in bed and get plenty of rest, but there was no mention of shots."

"Elizabeth, we are a bit concerned about the hallucinations you experienced last night."

He raised his hand when he saw the sudden fear in her eyes. "No, no, no. It has nothing to do with your injury. In maybe one case in a thousand, the drug you received last night produces this phenomenon. Normally it is not a problem. The attending physician simply discontinues its use. However, there is the rare case where there are flashbacks— the sort of thing that is popularly ascribed to LSD. You see, what happens is that some of the drug is absorbed into the brain tissue. With most people, it breaks down so quickly that there are no post-hallucinatory episodes. Still, better safe than sorry. I would like to inject an antidote and be one-hundred-percent positive that it doesn't occur in your case. It will allow us to release you a day or two earlier, too. What do you say?"

"No, wait! I don't know what to . . . you people should know. You're doctors. Yes . . . go ahead. God, I wouldn't want that to happen to me again. It's just that it didn't seem like a hallucination."

"I'm sure it didn't. This type of event is quite vivid. I'll be right back."

He returned with a small metal cart on which two bottles were suspended together with some lengths of rubber tubing.

She looked warily at the tubing and glass pipes. "Doctor, what is the drug you are going to give me?"

"The name is quite a mouthful, and you have never heard of it."

Finding her vein was not such a simple job. It took four electric pinpricks of pain before his "Ahhh" indicated success. "Sorry, my dear. An old man shouldn't be trying to find a difficult vein after being up all night. I hope I didn't hurt you too much."

She watched as the first drop tumbled into the lower part of the clear tubing past the valve, and a moment later felt a stinging as it entered her arm. Elizabeth felt the drug invading her senses and found it extremely relaxing. It was an effect that went far beyond that of the Valium. The doctor was talking to her, and she struggled to concentrate on his words. It was fantastic. Within moments, she was aware of nothing but his voice, and her own as she effortlessly answered his questions.

With memory came indignation and then anger. She glared at the doctor. "What did you give me? It was some sort of truth serum, wasn't it? How dare you!"

"Please, Elizabeth, calm down. Yes, it was a form of truth serum, something newer and more sophisticated. But I did it for your own good. . . . I swear to you."

She yanked the covers down, forgetting the inadequacy of her gown. "My own good? I am getting my clothes and getting out of here. And I'm coming back with the sheriff to get the others."

"Shut up! Shut up and listen to me."

Their gazes dueled for several seconds and then she looked away.

He sat down on the edge of the bed and seized her hand. She struggled to free it. "Elizabeth, look at me. Do you think I want to hurt you? My God, I didn't know you had had such problems. You're lucky you are not a patient in . . . a mental hospital."

She wanted to stay angry, but she could see into his eyes. The deep concern in them was genuine. Her anger gone, the effect of the drug returned and she slumped back, barely awake.

"Elizabeth, I want to help you, but I need to know more. How did you become acquainted with this Rundstedt?"

She tried to resist, but it was hopeless. She found herself telling Mainwaring everything. She had met Jack during the sixth year of her marriage to Ted Shea, a successful young architect in Carmel, California. Elizabeth enjoyed life as a young wife in the upper echelons of Carmel society. The marriage had not been physically satisfying for her, but it was sufficient compensation that her husband needed her.

Jack and Adele Rundstedt had moved into the home next door to the Sheas. Adele had the money and Jack had the youth, some fifteen years of it over Adele. Adele had bought herself what she considered a noble savage. Elizabeth found him uneducated, vulgar in every sense of the word, and able to converse only in schoolboy obscenities. At first she could not see that he favored the gardener's assistant in looks and body type and that his foul mouth was how she had imagined the assistant would talk.

She found him intolerable, but Ted seemed fascinated by the man. Jack, with nothing but time on his hands, started every day with a long run on the beach. Ted began inviting him in each morning for coffee before Ted left for work. That was how he came to be in the house on the morning he attacked her.

Thomas Mainwaring patted her hand. "My dear, one thing puzzles me. You keep referring to what happened that first day as rape, yet you told neither the authorities or your husband. Why was that?"

"I was so confused—not about him, about me. During the three days until he came the second time, I went from recrimination to self-justification because Ted had invited him over. I tried to convince myself that I had been raped, powerless to stop what had happened. I would ask myself why it had brought such unbelievable pleasure if it was rape. I kept thinking about Ridgeview and my behavior there. I wondered if I was a tramp who gave off signals to every man passing by. I was so afraid Ted would find out. I watched his every word, his every expression."

Long seconds dragged by before Mainwaring asked, "And how did you finally come to end it, Elizabeth?"

Her laugh was harsh. "Me end it? I didn't have the courage to do that. It was Adele Rundstedt who ended it. One early evening while Ted was at a meeting, Adele showed up, unannounced, well along in her cups.

"It wasn't the abuse that bothered me. It was what I saw in Adele as she began to wind down. God, the pain and humiliation in her eyes! It was like she had finally realized that money alone couldn't hold a man. She finally broke down then and started to cry. The last thing she said to me was, 'What have I ever done to any of you? I want to die.'

"The next morning, I left for San Francisco. A week later, I wrote Ted from San Francisco. I knew it would hurt him, but I couldn't lie. I told him everything.

"I decided to go to Chicago and stay with my aunt. Three weeks after I arrived, I went to work for Gavin Thorne."

Mainwaring arose, walked over to the window, and stood for a minute staring out, before returning to look down at Elizabeth. "My dear, over and over again you kept referring to Ridgecrest, almost as if it were the lair of monsters. What is Ridgecrest?"

"It was the school where my parents sent me when I was fourteen after what happened at Louise's. You know, I never would have been sent there if Mother hadn't caught me coming in that day. I started crying and blurted out the whole story. Daddy said all the kids would find out about it and start teasing me, so he decided to send me to a private school.

"Daddy thought I might be traumatized by what had happened at Lansfords' and insisted I have special help from the school psychologist, Eunice Blakely. God, I hated her. Every day she would meet me in her office, and she would make me tell every detail of what had happened in the shed. Then she told me I had to think about it every night before I went to bed. She said I would get it out of my system. But I began to masturbate at night, thinking about it. When I told Miss Blakely this, she said I was repressed and tried to make me use filthy words. Oh God, I hardly knew some of those words, much less used them. I thought I was turning into a sex fiend. I ran away the next day, and Mother and Daddy let me go back to regular school." Elizabeth's voice broke. "Please help me, Dr. Mainwaring. I don't know what I am."

The room was filled with the sounds of Elizabeth's sobbing while he stood, watching helplessly. When she subsided at last, Thomas Mainwaring spoke quietly. "Elizabeth, I don't know how to help you. Promise me you will see a psychiatrist when you leave here. You should have long ago. Elizabeth, I'm sorry about what I did to you. I didn't know."

He turned away from her and moved toward the door. He stopped abruptly and faced her. Thomas Mainwaring had undergone an amazing metamorphosis in a few seconds. "Elizabeth, about your hallucination last night. It was just that—a hallucination. To lessen your guilt in thinking about your ex-lover, your mind cast the roles in your erotic fantasy as female. You talked of seeing the muscles flexing under the skin of Shane's back and buttocks as she made love to Molly. You sensed Shane as the more aggressive, so you cast her as the male figure. Your description confirms that. In the final consummating act, her figure was turned in such a way that the feminine characteristics lost their shapes and appeared male.

"You have found gratification in being mastered by a dominant male figure. You equate pampering, the manners of your social group, with being effete. The men in your social class ask rather than take. Your conflict is within yourself. Recognize that you need aggressive sexual partners, or you will be forever in conflict with your own perceptions of sexuality. Elizabeth, you saw nothing. Your hallucination can have a therapeutic effect if you will only accept the reality of your sexual needs.

"If I hadn't made you understand, you would have added another thorn to the crown you wear. You would have begun to wonder if you were homosexual. You have enough problems, Elizabeth Shea, without that. Never speak of this fantasy again. It will only hurt you and others."

He started to roll the cart out of the room.

Upset at the anger she had displayed toward him, she called, "Dr. Mainwaring."

"It's okay, Elizabeth. I'll see you later."

He disappeared into the corridor.

CHAPTER 8

A fter the doctor left, Elizabeth lay there for a long time. After her experience with Eunice Blakely, she did not put much stock in pyschoanalysis and was able to put out of her mind much of what he had said. She noticed the telephone, mounted low on the side of the console. There was no dial, which meant it was routed through a switchboard. She would call Meredith! Surely they would not object to her talking to Meredith and trying to console her.

The phone was dead—not even a hum. Jiggling the hook brought no response. She tried a dozen times during the next half hour, finally putting the receiver down in disgust.

As she lowered the phone, the door opened and a woman leaned in. It was no one that Elizabeth had seen before. She was about sixty-five, with gray hair that tumbled about her head in wild disarray. She was wearing an unadorned blue dress that looked institutional. She appeared ready to flee at the slightest provocation and did when Elizabeth ventured a tentative greeting.

She smiled when the door closed behind the woman. At least she had met one of the patients. She decided she was part of a game when the woman went through the same routine twice more.

74

A considerable time passed before the door opened a fourth time, and the woman slipped through. The disheveled crone closed it behind her and stood with her ear pressed against the wood panel. Turning toward Elizabeth, she made a moist hushing sound. Then, ignoring Elizabeth, she toured the room, running her hands over the paneling, looking at the paintings, and sitting briefly in one of the leather chairs. On her feet again, she opened the bathroom door, looked in, and whistled. Then she grinned at Elizabeth. It was not a pleasant grin, for she was without her dentures.

"Pretty spiffy," she lisped.

Elizabeth smiled. "You mean they are not all like this?"

The woman rolled her eyes. "Oh, no, dear. Not hardly. Not very likely."

The woman moved to the window with an odd, scurrying step and pulled the heavy curtain aside. "Oooh, it's so pretty out there. You know, I often think about being outside, feeling the sun on me and smelling the flowers. I want to feel the wind against my face one more time. I dream of it so."

Elizabeth's reservations about her visitor disappeared, and she felt sorry for the poor creature, who must know that part of her world was gone forever.

Elizabeth found herself mouthing the usual comforting falsehoods. "I'm sure things will get better. You'll soon be out of here. You have many years ahead to walk in the sunshine."

The woman shook her head vigorously and, releasing the curtain, asked, "What's your name?"

"Elizabeth Shea."

Her visitor nodded thoughtfully, as though it was somehow important that she remember the name. She turned toward the bed. "You . . . you sound different." Peering at Elizabeth, she squinted. "Why, you're young. Are . . . are you one of us?"

Elizabeth chuckled. "Oh, no. I came in last night. We were in a bad automobile accident, and the doctors agreed to let us come here to be treated."

"It was a mistake, all a mistake. I remember . . . I heard them talking about it . . . about the accident and about you coming here . . . but it's all so unfortunate."

Elizabeth, not knowing how to answer, decided to change the subject. "Where do you stay?"

The woman's expression changed quickly from one of inquisitiveness to one of infinite sadness. "Where do I stay? Why . . . I stay in hell."

A sense of disquietude stirred in Elizabeth. She had accepted the intruder as a lonely older patient who had sneaked out of her room unobserved, curious about the newcomer. It wasn't that the woman was threatening, but her replies went farther than idle prattling. Elizabeth knew that some patients, sinking into senility, became delusional and dangerous.

As unobtrusively as possible, she edged toward the call button. She knew it was important that she keep talking and not upset her guest. "Oh, surely it isn't that bad. I don't know your name yet. I told you mine."

The woman grinned, brushing her hand across her untidy hair, trying to smooth it into some semblance of order, a feminine gesture that disarmed Elizabeth's concern. In a soft, whispery voice, she said, "I'm Carrie Dalton, but I don't suppose you'd know about us."

"I . . . I'm afraid not. You see, until about midnight last night, I didn't know there was a Skystone."

The sad look returned to her odd companion's face. "I know, dear. Not many people know about Skystone. That's why it's here . . . so not many people will know. It's like a treasure chest. Treasure is buried . . . only here, they bury people. Don't you think it's a disgrace?"

Elizabeth knew she was in over her head again. "I . . . I don't understand you, Mrs. Dalton—Carrie. A disgrace?"

"Oh, we're a disgrace . . . this place . . . this Skystone is a disgrace. All we do here—for whatever reason we're here —is to sleep and eat and wait. Many of us sleep very little. When we're awake, we sit and while the hours away until we can sleep again. We cast away the remaining days of our lives. You're so young, so pretty. It's a shame you had to come. Skystone has an easy way in—doors, pretty lady, like any other building—so easy to walk in, but only one way out: death. This is a place for dying, for sitting and rotting. You sit here and think, 'If only I could get away from them.

If only I could be where they couldn't watch me, then I could leave. I could escape.' But, no. Even you, you poor child . . ."

The elderly woman moved toward her, and Elizabeth's hand closed on the buzzer, frantically pressing it.

Elizabeth held her breath, trying to tell herself she had nothing to fear. Physically she was stronger than Carrie Dalton, but there was a vehemence, a burning in the woman. That was what frightened Elizabeth.

Without warning, the woman reached for her, but the heavily veined, tissue-skinned hand did no more than briefly pat her calf.

"I know I'm frightening you, dear. Don't worry. It will be quick. You will not have to sit, staring at the walls day after day, as I have. Look."

She took three wooden matches from the single pocket of the blue garment. "We can find our salvation, our cleansing . . . the end of our wait. Fire, the glorious, God-given cleansing of fire. And the old and the weak, the useless, the demented, the vicious, and the evil shall be redeemed in the destruction of the flesh and the purification of the soul."

Elizabeth, uncertain of what to do, stared in fascination at Carrie Dalton's face. It had been transformed as she spoke. There was a radiance in it. Her eyes were aglow, and her voice was vibrant with a strength that had not been there before.

The door crashed open, and a young man in an orderly's uniform raced into the room. In a split second, Carrie Dalton reverted to the timorous, frightened creature that had first entered Elizabeth's quarters. She backed a couple of steps toward the bathroom before the orderly caught her, locking his arms around her. She struggled for a moment and then, abruptly, hung limp in his grasp.

He peered toward Elizabeth, who had come to her feet. "I'm sorry, ma'am. Carrie tricked me. I wasn't supposed to let her out of my sight. She's as slick as pond ice on a cold day. Come on, Carrie, let's go."

Carrie, struggling again, begged, "Please . . . please . . . please," but her threshing about availed her nothing.

As they staggered through the door, Elizabeth, hating it

but knowing it was necessary, called, "She has matches in her pocket. She said she was going to burn something."

The orderly roughly pinioned the elderly woman against the wall, her face flattened against the paneling, while he searched her pocket.

Producing the matches, he chuckled. "God, Carrie, you do love fire, don't you?"

Her resistance vanished, and she hung limply against him as he paused at the door.

"I'll be back in a few moments, ma'am, after I take care of Carrie."

It was a quarter of an hour before she looked up, startled, to see the same orderly standing in the door. The television had masked his approach. He was in his late twenties, of medium height and medium build. His eyes, too close together, and his mouth, in a perpetual pout, gave him a ferret look. His receding mousy brown hair was too thin to be worn as long as he had it, looking stringy and unkempt.

"Sorry, I didn't mean to startle you. I . . . I hope Carrie didn't cause you any problems. It won't happen again . . . I guarantee it."

She resisted the urge to tell him it was plenty uncomfortable, seeing Carrie Dalton evolve from a forlorn old lady to a wild-eyed fanatic, but it would do nothing but alienate the attendant, who, no doubt, was feeling bad enough about his poor supervision.

"Oh, that's all right. It's just that she startled me the way she changed right before my eyes."

"Oh? What did she do?"

"You know . . . she was raving a bit."

The orderly grew attentive. "Raving? Mrs. Dalton usually doesn't do that. What did she say? I'm sure her doctor will want to know."

"Well, she said that this place should be burned—that it was full of the old and the demented and the evil . . . that sort of thing. Just ranting . . . almost like a hell-and-brimstone preacher."

The attendant laughed. "Well, I guess I can't dispute that, not after you saw Carrie. She's living proof of the demented, and God knows this place has plenty of old people lying around. Oh, well, I promise you've seen the last of her."

He started to leave, but she stopped him.

"Listen, I wonder if you would tell the nurses that I haven't had my lunch yet. I hate to ask you, but the call button doesn't seem to work."

He looked annoyed. "Nobody's brought you lunch? I'll go check on it myself. I don't know why they would have forgotten you . . . probably because you aren't a regular patient."

"I thought maybe it was because of the problem with the gas in the kitchen."

"The gas in the kitchen? Oh, yeah, that's probably it. I'll check and be back."

He was almost out the door when she stopped him again. "Say, could I ask you about the other lady who was brought in with me—Meredith Thorne?"

He grinned. "Sure. What about Meredith?"

"Oh, you must have met her already."

"Yeah, you got it."

"I wonder if I could see her."

He laughed, and the formality slid off him as easily as a silk shirt. "Hey, old Meredith is swacked right out of her living mind. I'll bet she wouldn't know you from the Queen of England."

Concern surged through Elizabeth. "You mean she's worse?"

"Hey, don't you worry about that, honey. You know . . . she's great, but she's got a few aches, so doc gave her something to make her comfortable. I'll tell you what. I'll guarantee you see her later, and that's a promise. Okay? Now, I'll go check on your lunch. We've got to keep you in prime shape."

Before she could question him further, he was gone.

CHAPTER 9

It was over an hour before the balding attendant reappeared. He paused at the door and winked at her.

"Hey—you're sure enough going to hate us, but I want you to remember, mama, before you start throwing things, that it ain't Johnny's fault."

Despite her annoyance at the way she had been neglected, Elizabeth appreciated the orderly's friendliness. He was the first member of the hospital staff that did not appear to resent her being there. "No promises, Johnny. What's the problem?"

"I don't know how they overlooked a good-looking chick like you, but honest to God, they forgot you when they delivered lunches. Man, everything's shut down and the cooks are out of the building. But I didn't fail you. I have two peanut-butter-and-jelly sandwiches and a glass of milk for you. Just like school days, huh?"

He looked at her like a puppy waiting to be petted. Elizabeth tried to rekindle her anger. She knew that when Skystone presented the bill to her insurance company, it would be astronomical, but it was not the orderly's fault. He was doing the best he could.

Grudgingly, she yielded to his charm. "Okay, Johnny, but

you tell those idiots in the kitchen that I want double helpings at dinner. My brains may be scrambled, but there's nothing wrong with my stomach."

He pulled the table leaf up and swung it over the bed. Unfolding a paper napkin with a ridiculous flourish, he laid it across her.

"Wait just one minute," he said. "I forgot dessert."

The orderly Johnny dashed out into the corridor, only to return a minute later bearing a candy bar in one hand and a soft drink in the other. "Hey, the management aims to please."

His gaiety was infectious, and she laughed, her worries forgotten for the moment.

"Uh-oh, I'd better get out of here before they think I'm having my way with you. I don't get you as a present. Oh, by the way, later in the afternoon, one of the nurses will take you out onto the patio for a little air. Bye-bye, now."

She thought of Meredith again, but he was gone before she could ask about seeing her.

The sandwiches tasted awful, but her stomach demanded food. At least the soft drink washed away most of the taste. Elizabeth pushed the tray aside and slumped down in bed. Her eyelids grew heavy, and soon she was asleep.

She awoke to find Mrs. Eddy beside her bed. The nurse was looking somewhat the worse for wear. There were bags under her eyes, and fatigue had eroded her carefully made-up face.

"Hi," Elizabeth said. "I didn't expect to see you. I thought you were the night-shift supervisor."

Nurse Eddy grimaced. "Well, as you see, dear, the consensus is that I can do without sleep."

"Gee. I hope our coming here this way hasn't caused you a lot of extra work."

"Well it certainly hasn't made it any easier, Mrs. Shea. But I find that everything has its compensations, doesn't it? I understand you've been getting a little antsy, closed off by yourself. Dr. Mainwaring thought you might like a bit of fresh air on the patio. It's a little late, but some of the old ones may still be outside."

As Elizabeth sat up, she saw the wheelchair. "What's this? I'm perfectly capable of walking."

"Sorry, Mrs. Shea, but the doctor's orders are that you be treated like any other patient. You ride in the wheelchair, and you stay in it."

"But what do the patients do for exercise?"

Mrs. Eddy patted the wheelchair, looking a little annoyed. "You certainly are an inquisitive young woman, but for your information, there is a gymnasium for patients able to use it. Now, if I've satisfied your curiosity, I suggest we go."

Mrs. Eddy stopped the wheelchair in mid-hall to readjust the footrest. While she bent to her task, Elizabeth stole a quick glance toward the room where she thought she had seen the two nurses. The door, closed now, bore the numeral 13. She wondered how she could have imagined such a scene. She had never entertained a fantasy like that. Dr. Mainwaring must be right. In a way she hoped he was. It would explain so much that she did not understand about herself.

Mrs. Eddy rolled Elizabeth into a large room filled with sofas, chairs, and several coffee tables burdened with an assortment of magazines. One end of the room was dominated by a large-screen television. Directly across from them were double steel doors, each with a foot-square glass pane reinforced with wire mesh.

Mrs. Eddy pivoted the wheelchair so Elizabeth could view the entire room. "Since you are so curious, Mrs. Shea, this is the lounge. It's where ambulatory patients come to socialize and where visitors wait to be conducted to the patient's rooms. Dr. Mainwaring thought it best we not expose our more active patients to you. They become excited, and then they don't sleep well. Most of the poor dears out on the patio now are semi-comatose. They show little response to stimuli. I thought I should warn you."

The patio was a large concrete slab tucked into the angle of the L-shaped building. The two open sides, girded with a waist-high wrought-iron railing, overlooked a strip of well-tended lawn. Beyond the grass strip lay the driveway leading to the porte cochere.

As she was pushed out onto the patio, she saw the orderly

Johnny standing behind another wheelchair, waving to her. She gasped when she saw the chair's occupant. It was Carrie Dalton, but her appearance was so altered it was hard to recognize her. On the side of her face was a vast purple bruise running from her cheek, high onto her forehead, and back into her temple. One eye was swollen shut. She looked ghastly.

Startled, Elizabeth looked at Mrs. Eddy, who was setting the brake on her wheelchair. "My God, I . . . I know that woman. She was in my room. What happened to her?"

"I am aware you met her, Mrs. Shea. I heard all about Carrie's visit. When Mrs. Dalton was returned to her room, she had a temper tantrum—not an unknown thing with the dear lady. Only this time, she fell out of bed and struck the side of her head against the console."

"Please, push me over there. I want to see how she is. She may be a little unhinged, but I feel so sorry for the poor thing."

Mrs. Eddy motioned to Johnny, who, after a quick glance at Mrs. Dalton, joined them.

"Johnny, our Mrs. Shea is concerned about Mrs. Dalton. Is she still sulking?"

When he nodded, she continued, "Come back in five minutes and take her in. She's going to be quite uncomfortable when her shot wears off."

Johnny laughed. "Hey, you're talking bad times now. Okay, I'll be back in five, darling."

As he vanished through the double doors, Mrs. Eddy glared after him. "Impudent little . . ."

She caught herself. "I'm afraid you're stuck with me, Mrs. Shea. I don't think our other two sun worshipers are going to do any socializing."

She nodded toward the two huddled figures in their wheelchairs at the far end of the patio. Elizabeth followed her glance.

One was an elderly gray-haired man with weather-cured skin like brown leather. He slumped in his wheelchair with his head thrown far back. He had a bandanna knotted around his neck and a hat pulled down over his eyes to shade his face from the afternoon sun.

The other chair was occupied by a middle-aged woman whose plump body sagged sideways in the seat, her head lolling forward on her chest. The most extraordinary thing about her was her flaming red hair, glowing with the rays of the sun.

Elizabeth stared at her, then at Mrs. Eddy. "Why, she really doesn't seem old enough to be here . . . certainly not in that condition."

"Oh, Mrs. Mueller isn't here because of her age. She suffered brain damage. It was an accident . . . a sad case."

That said, Mrs. Eddy walked across the patio and leaned back, resting her hips against the wrought-iron railing, glancing first at one and the other of her comatose charges. She closed her eyes, arched her body, and stood, breathing deeply. Elizabeth sensed that the woman, despite her words, was not interested in conversation.

Johnny popped through the double doors and approached Elizabeth. "Hi, chickie. Anything old Johnny can get for you? Something from the bar or the grill? Maybe another soda pop? Another candy bar? Hmmm?"

Elizabeth basked in his good-natured bantering and had started to thank him for cheering her up when he whistled softly. As she turned to follow his glance, he muttered, "Not too shabby for an old broad . . . not shabby at all."

Mrs. Eddy had removed her nurse's cap, and her raven-black shoulder-length hair was loose. She stood, her body bowed back over the rail, breasts outthrust, legs wide apart. The steady wind had plastered her uniform like a second skin against her lush body. Elizabeth thought of her husband for the first time in weeks. Ted would have sized up Mrs. Eddy as a rose in its fullest bloom before the first falling petal signaled disintegration.

Johnny shook himself free of whatever spell the pagan imagery had evoked. "Hey, chickie, I'd better get old Carrie in before the power starts going to Tina's head again. See you later."

As he wheeled Mrs. Dalton past Elizabeth, she saw the woman watching her with her one good eye. Softly, Elizabeth called, "I'm sorry you're hurt, Mrs. Dalton. I hope you'll be better soon."

A sudden tear appeared in the corner of Carrie Dalton's undamaged eye as she passed from Elizabeth's sight.

Across the patio, Mrs. Eddy stirred, trying to recapture her windblown coils of hair to confine them under the white cap. When she finally succeeded, she rejoined Elizabeth.

"Okay, Mrs. Shea, time to get you back in."

Elizabeth looked at the two inert forms remaining on the patio. "If you like, Mrs. Eddy, you can take them in first. I'm comfortable, and there is quite a wind coming up."

A tight little smile did nothing to soften the sarcasm of the nurse's answer. "Oh, I don't think they will complain. Do you, Mrs. Shea?"

The woman said no more until Elizabeth was back in her bed. Mrs. Eddy stopped in the act of pushing the wheelchair into the hall.

"By the way, I understand that you are having difficulty being served. We are having trouble in the kitchen. Your dinner may be late, but you will get your meal. Bye-bye."

Elizabeth had a miserable time the rest of the afternoon, tossing and turning on the bed. She wished the nurse had not said anything about dinner. All she could think of was food.

At five o'clock the door swung open, revealing Johnny, smiling infectiously, a finger across his lips. With exaggerated stealth, he crept across the room, slid a soft drink and a couple of candy bars onto the console, blew her a kiss, and departed.

Elizabeth had never been a big candy eater, but she devoured the sweets with dispatch, if not appreciation.

The curtains lost their snowy-white light, became gray, and finally were a vague ghostly lightness in the dark. The digital display on the small console clock read 8:15 when Elizabeth gave up all hope of dinner. But as she slid off the bed, determined to find someone who could explain why she wasn't being fed, a small figure darted into the room.

Her heart sank. It was all she needed—starving to death, and another old loony to deal with.

Without ceremony, her visitor plopped down on the bed, illuminated by a shaft of light from the corridor. Elizabeth was overjoyed. It was Meredith.

Meredith kissed her on the cheek. "Liz, darling. I'm so glad to see you. I've been so worried."

Elizabeth blinked in astonishment. This was a Meredith she didn't know. Meredith Thorne had never called her Liz —always the more formal Elizabeth—and had never displayed an iota of affection toward her. Certainly she had never kissed Elizabeth on the cheek before. Elizabeth wondered if Meredith, left alone by the death of her father, was trying to use affection as a lure to buy sympathy.

Awkwardly she patted Meredith's knee through the thin hospital gown. "Oh, God, Meredith, I'm so terribly sorry about Gavin. He was a fine man, and I know he was a good father to you. I am going to miss him.

"When you're feeling better, we'll talk over what you want to do about the funeral, and I will start calling people. But take your time. Everyone understands what a shock it is."

"Hey, now, Liz, let's don't get all maudlin. Gavin's gone, you know? So, we all gotta go. God, did you see his head? He would have been a total vegetable if he had lived. Listen, I want you to make all the arrangements. I mean . . . what do I know about funerals? You know where I'm coming from?"

Elizabeth stirred uneasily, uncertain of how to reply. It was not at all the response that she had anticipated from a grieving daughter. "Yes, Meredith, but . . . I mean . . . you're the only family he had. You should decide."

Meredith yawned. "Come on, Liz, help me out. I'm asking you. I've always treated you right, haven't I?"

Elizabeth did not think it was the time to discuss their relationship. There was nothing she could do but agree.

Meredith industriously patted the bed for a moment and then, realizing her mistake, shifted her hand to Elizabeth's thigh. "Good girl! And now my public calls. I wonder where old Scottie, my overgrown lapdog, is."

Elizabeth told her what Dr. Mainwaring had said about Scott. "I know you want to see him, Meredith. Why don't you ask one of the nurses where his room is? Maybe you'll have better luck with them than I did."

Meredith laughed—a slow, dark laugh. "Hey, I can relate

to that. You have to use the old barter system around here, Liz baby. It's been working for several thousand years now."

Elizabeth realized what was different about Meredith. She was talking so slowly, and her words were slurred. Elizabeth started to worry about her, wondering if it was a residual effect from her concussion or if they still had her on pain-killers.

"Meredith, you . . . you sound funny . . . the way you talk. Maybe you should ask the doctor to check you again."

Meredith laughed again, peals of brittle, excited laughter. "Poor little Liz—such a worrywart. Not to worry, honey. Old Meredith is just a bit spaced out, courtesy of the joy chest. You know how it is. Nobody wants the patients to be hurting, and, honey, I'm not hurting. Hey, I'd better go. Little Meredith has to be a regular Boy Scout. You know, 'Always ready.' Take care, Lizzie. And, you know, take care of Gavin's funeral—something real nice. Okay? Bye-bye."

She was outlined for a brief second against the lighted doorway and then disappeared before Elizabeth could stop her. There were male orderlies around, and in the thin hospital gown Meredith might as well have been nude.

Meredith was right. She was a worrywart. Still, she thought she would mention Meredith's odd behavior to Dr. Mainwaring or Dr. Caudill.

Five minutes later, the light came on and Dr. Mainwaring entered. As with Mrs. Eddy, fatigue had taken its toll on his distinguished face. Still, he greeted her with the same hearty manner as earlier.

"Hi, Elizabeth. How are you doing?"

"Hungry."

He tweaked her toe. "Yes, I know you've been mis-treated, young lady. Well, don't worry. I left a nasty little note with the cooks. I expect they will be along, within a half hour or so, with a meal that will knock your eyes out. But first we need to take our shot."

Elizabeth shrank back. "Shot? What shot is this?"

The doctor chuckled. "I'll swear to God, Nurse Eddy is right. If all our patients were as curious as you, we wouldn't have enough time in the day."

He lowered the tray bearing the syringe and vial to the

console and, leaning over Elizabeth, fumbled in his coat pocket. He brought out a penlight and examined her eyes. When he was through he returned the penlight to his pocket and looked thoughtful.

"Elizabeth, you still have a slight contraction of your pupils. Dr. Caudill and I both think that may be caused from the blows you received when the car rolled. The effects of a mild concussion usually disappear within forty-eight to seventy-two hours. These shots are intended to lessen the irritation to your brain tissue. I haven't killed you yet, have I?"

He winked at her.

Embarrassment swept over her. She knew she was acting like a baby. "I'm sorry. Go ahead. I'll try to quit being such a pain in the neck."

But as Dr. Mainwaring picked up the syringe, she sat up in bed. "Doctor, I want to talk to you about Meredith."

He lowered the syringe, and she could tell he was fighting to keep the exasperation out of his voice.

"What about Miss Thorne?"

"When she was in the room a few minutes ago . . ."

"In the room! She came in here?"

Elizabeth nodded, startled at his vehemence. Mainwaring chewed his lip in vexation.

"Damn it! She wasn't to be allowed out of that room."

He shot a glance at Elizabeth and blushed. "I'm sorry, my dear. I'm afraid our staff hasn't been exposed to people as active as your crew. You folks are running around like a Chinese fire drill. But you said you were worried. Why? What did Miss Thorne say?"

"It wasn't what she said. It was the way she acted. She appeared as if she was high on drugs, doctor. When I said something to her about it, she said it was painkillers."

He picked up the hypodermic syringe. "Well, that is true. Miss Thorne is unusually sensitive to medication. As a matter of fact, that's why I was so insistent that she be watched closely. Was that all that happened?"

"Yes. She wasn't here over two minutes. I tried to talk to her about arrangements for her father, but it was useless."

He nodded in satisfaction. "Well, that's good. At least she

seems to have no side effects except a high good humor and the will to roam. Don't worry. She'll be fine."

"What room is she in, doctor? I thought I would talk to her in the morning."

He rubbed the alcohol-soaked cotton over her arm and slipped the slender silver needle into her yielding flesh. "Let's get this shot into you, Elizabeth, and I'll go make a note for the nurse to admit you. Okay?"

He withdrew the needle, dabbed her arm again, picked up his tray, and left the room. He left the door ajar.

She sank back onto the pillow as a wave of intensely pleasurable relaxation swept through her. There was a moment's fear at the unexpected reaction, and she started to reach for the buzzer; but before her hand could complete its journey, she wanted nothing to disturb the effect. She rolled onto her back and surrendered to it, sinking down and down until there was nothing.

CHAPTER 10

*E*lizabeth struggled awake, trying to shake free of the delicious darkness drawing her back into unconsciousness. A scream hammered at her eardrums and she tried to turn her head, but her body was not the servant of her mind. Her nose twitched to the acrid smell of smoke. Fear jolted her, but she couldn't move, even knowing there must be a fire nearby.

A second scream sliced into the confusion of her mind, coming from somewhere down the hall. She tried again to rise, clutching at the edge of the mattress. There was no strength in her, and her body rebelled at being roused from its reverie.

The smoke grew heavier, and she heard an excited male voice shout, "Get another extinguisher, damn it!"

A woman's voice, near hysteria, shouted, "Finish it, you son of a bitch!"

There was another scream, and then another, sabers of sound slashing through the darkness.

In the distance, someone shouted, "Okay, I got it out, thank God."

The same voice rose in a second cry. "For God's sake, Howie, do it!"

Another horrible cry shattered the silence, but ceased as abruptly as if a knife had severed it.

There was a moment of quiet before a faint, disturbingly familiar voice cried, "What in the hell is going on . . . ?"

The sounds of a violent struggle stilled the voice. Elizabeth heard a woman call, "Get Mainwaring!"

The struggle subsided, except for an occasional flurry. Elizabeth heard someone running, and then Mainwaring shouted, "Shut up! All of you! I'll take care of it."

There was one last scuffle . . . and then silence. Elizabeth could struggle no longer against her body's demand for oblivion. The bar of light, coming in past the slightly ajar door, wavered and then disappeared.

Some time later, Elizabeth awoke again. This time she managed to raise herself on her elbow, ignoring the sweet bonds that still held her.

Somewhere far off, someone was crying. The sobs would grow louder and then fade in volume until they ceased. Soon she could hear, barely audible, the single syllable "No" repeated again and again, building slowly into more sobs. Struggling mightily, she came to an upright position. She was dizzy, throwing out her arm to avoid pitching over backwards.

The strange sorrows continued for a long time and then ended abruptly with cries of "Please!" that rose to a scream.

After that, all she could hear was an ill-definable far-off sound that sounded vaguely like chanting. She strained, but she could not be sure of what she heard. There was an odd clunk, and the sound ceased.

Elizabeth huddled in the dark, frightened, wondering what to do, trying to regain control of her body. The room light flared before her unfocused eyes, revealing a vaguely distorted Dr. Mainwaring standing in the doorway.

Aware that she was practically naked in the thin gown pulled up to mid-thigh, Elizabeth clawed at the sheet upon which she sat, unable to understand why she could not pull it free.

The doctor muttered, "Just what I thought," and walked out, leaving the room light on.

Elizabeth tumbled backwards onto the bed, puzzled by

why the sheet was suddenly free. Fumbling with its intricate folds, she drew it over her.

Dr. Mainwaring returned, but it was only when he leaned over her that she realized he had a syringe.

"Please, Dr. Mainwaring," she begged. "Don't. I don't want to be like this."

She tried to pull free, but was far too weak. She felt the cool brush of alcohol against her skin and then the sting of the needle. After he had discarded the syringe, he brushed the light brown hair away from her eyes. "My child, don't you understand why I'm doing this?" He patted her cheek. "Maybe someday you will."

Thomas Mainwaring looked down at her again with affection and said something that Elizabeth couldn't understand. She was whirling down into a deep, blissful tunnel, watching him grow ever smaller and finally disappear.

CHAPTER 11 _____

*E*lizabeth opened her eyes and sought the clock. It read 10:18. The warm morning sunlight was backlighting the white curtains. Her mouth was dry, and her stomach was so empty that she felt slightly nauseated.

A long shower did wonders for her, and by the time she finished, she felt halfway normal but still hungry. Back in the bedroom, she punched the call button. She was determined to have a good breakfast if she had to cook it herself.

For ten long minutes she worried the button without results. She grabbed the telephone and jiggled the hook, but there was that same disturbing deadness to the phone that she had noticed the day before. It was strange that the phones had not been fixed. They had had at least a full day to effect repairs.

It was the last straw for Elizabeth. She was mad. She had endured indignities that the worst hospitals didn't force on their patients. The phones didn't work; neither did the call buttons; no one had asked about the disposition of Gavin Thorne's body; she had received no cooked food.

She had been drugged without reason. She suffered headaches and dizziness only after being injected with drugs. She had examined her eyes in the bathroom mirror. The pupils appeared normal to her.

It was time for a confrontation. While on the patio, she had noticed a sign reading Office, with an arrow pointing toward the front of the wing in which her room was located. It would get their attention when she appeared there clad in nothing but a hospital gown. She wanted the right to use the telephone; to see Meredith and Scott; to be fed.

Cautiously, she peeked into the corridor. It was empty, but for some reason the night-lights along the baseboard were still burning. The only thing that disturbed the silence was the soft rush of air through the ventilating system. That a hospital could be so quiet defied belief. It was well along in the morning, but no rooms were being cleaned; no nurses were hurrying about their rounds; no staff members were gathered around the nurses' station, chattering.

She took a deep breath and stepped out into the corridor. The air was warm, but the tiles were cold against her bare feet. The closet in her room had been empty—no clothes, no shoes. That was one thing she was going to see about. Even her purse was gone.

Elizabeth started for the office at a brisk pace, but her determination was eroded by each step she took down the too-quiet corridor. Her senses thrilled in anticipation of a shout marking her discovery. The Exit sign above the double doors filled the darkness at the end of the hall with a sinister crimson glow. The silence of the place was getting on her nerves. Could the staff be in conference? They surely needed it, the way the hospital was being run. But would they have dared leave the nurses' station unattended?

Growing more uneasy by the moment, she slowed her pace. A film of dust felt gritty beneath her bare feet. The corridor had not been swept for several days.

Elizabeth pushed through the swinging doors into the short entry hall beyond. The outside walls and the entry doors were fashioned of thick, clear glass. Through the glass wall, she could see the driveway curving past the building. Beyond the drive was a parklike setting of bare-limbed hardwood trees.

She glanced nervously back into the corridor behind her. It

was a long, dark tunnel—too quiet, too empty, and scary. Panicking, she bolted for the outer door, desperate to be away from the place. The unyielding door brought her to an abrupt stop. Grasping the push bar with both hands, she lunged against it several times. Near the edge of hysteria, she backed away a step and rammed her shoulder into the door. It was as unyielding as a solid steel plate. As she turned away, frightened at the prospect of retracing her steps down that corridor, she remembered why she had entered this part of the building. She had forgotten all about the office when she saw the outdoors beckoning through the glass walls.

The business office was to her right. Its wall was, like the outer one, of glass, and she could see the entire area at a glance. It was surprisingly small, housing two desks and a row of file cabinets. The front third of the office contained an enclosure of wood and frosted glass panels, obviously the director's office. The lights were off, and both sections appeared vacant.

She stared at the empty office in dismay, her plan shattered. For a moment Elizabeth was close to giving up and returning docilely to her bed. But she was too much like her father— stubborn and determined. Mainwaring might be right about how screwed up she was sexually, but still he and his lackeys were going to find out that she couldn't be mistreated.

Burning with righteous indignation, she turned back to face the dark passage. Why not try to locate one of the patients? Surely one of them was coherent enough to explain the hospital routine. There must be more patients like Carrie Dalton than the two unfortunates on the patio yesterday.

She glanced at the number on the door immediately to her right. It was room 8, she realized, so there were only thirteen rooms.

Elizabeth tapped at the door. There was no response. She knocked again, a bit harder. Still there was no reply. She was afraid to knock any harder. As it was, the light blows seemed to reverberate throughout the vacant hallway. She grasped the doorknob and tried to turn it, but the door was locked. Why would a patient be locked in?

The darkness, unabated except for the ghastly red of the Exit sign staining the walls of the corridor, gave the shadowed doorways a sinister quality. She forced herself to try one more room.

Uncertain whether she might find all the doors locked, she stepped across the hall to room 9 and gripped the knob. The door opened with quiet precision, revealing a room like hers, except that the carpets were a different color, the chairs of another style, and the drapes a dissimilar pattern. The hospital bed was like hers, with one difference: it was empty and the bedding was rumpled, as though someone had just left it. She crept hesitantly into the room and, crossing to the closed bathroom door, tapped gently on it. There was no answer. The door opened into an empty bathroom.

She shivered. Room 9 suddenly was unpleasant, and she fled into the hall. She started to close the door behind her, but the corridor looked more comforting with the natural light spilling into it.

Desperate now to find someone—anyone—to be with, Elizabeth crossed to room 10 and rapped on the door, which swung open at the blow. This room's layout was reversed, with the bed at the far end, but this was not what had her attention. She was staring, transfixed, at the bed. The bed linens were strewn around the foot of the empty bed.

Knowing it was useless, Elizabeth looked into the bathroom. Retracing her steps, she spotted the call buzzer looped around the bed's side rail and jabbed at it. She hurried to the door to wait. The tiny blue call light was on above the door.

She was so scared that she was close to losing control. Her fear was all the more terrible because it was so unfocused.

Elizabeth broke from the doorway, moving with timorous haste along the corridor, opening doors, glancing into empty rooms with bedding scattered across the beds. Her heart was beating furiously. Reaching her room, she paused, trying to catch her breath. It was so hard to breathe.

Ahead of her, the lights of the nurses' station beckoned. It didn't matter what they thought of her. She had to know what was going on. She rushed toward the lights.

There was no one there. The cold illumination from the fluorescent panels glittered off a cheerless expanse of stainless steel. But there was something peculiar. A heavy scent permeated the air—a smoky smell with a sour, caustic overtone that made her eyes water. Her memories of the night—of the screams and of the smoke—exploded into her mind.

Elizabeth clutched at the counter, her mind reeling. Oh, God! Was she hallucinating again? She wondered if she any longer knew what was dream and what was reality.

Caution forgotten, she yelled, "Hey . . . where is everybody?"

There was an eerie echo to her words, bouncing off the corridor walls. Instantly, she was terrorized by her thoughtless indiscretion. A fearful idea hit her. Pushing against the counter, she raised herself to where she could see behind it. There was no one on the floor. A single water glass, halffilled with an orange liquid, sat next to the blank-screened heart monitors. On the back wall, between the cabinets and under the clock, two blue lights glowed in futile summons on the call board. One was hers, and the other was the one for room 10.

An electric motor came on, and Elizabeth jumped. Whirling around, she identified it as coming from the ice machine sitting in the corner at the junction of the corridors. It was a low affair shaped like a home freezer, and long enough for a person to stretch out in. The ice machine failed to mask a steady dripping from somewhere down the connecting passageway. These familiar sounds seemed so lonely—tiny mementos of familiarity in a terrible silence.

She peered around the corner into the shorter corridor. It was brighter, thanks to a large frosted skylight illuminated by the morning sun. On the right-hand side of the hall was the gleaming red steel door she had noticed the night she arrived.

Eyeing the opening at the rear of the nurses' station, she slipped behind the counter and stepped into a medication supply room.

Whatever hopes she had retained of finding a reasonable explanation vanished when she looked about her. The room was in disarray, with cabinet doors open and counter drawers pulled out. Several glass bottles lay, broken, on the countertops. A large floor safe, with NARCOTICS CHEST stenciled across its gray steel door, was at one end of the narrow room. It was closed and locked, but the door was badly dented, as if it had been battered with a heavy object. Her nose led her to peer into the corner beside the safe. The walls were stained, and the tiles were covered with a foul-smelling mixture of powders, encrusted with a colorful topping of capsules and pills. Sprays of glass fragments from countless broken bottles were mixed with the chemical debris.

A destructive rampage had taken place in the storage room, and a feeble effort had been made to conceal it.

As Elizabeth stared about at the destruction, her thoughts flashed back to last night. The screams, the smell of smoke, and the piteous begging were again vivid in her mind. Something awful must have happened during the wee hours.

She stepped out into the hall and glanced up, surprised at the skylight. A grid of heavy iron bars was suspended under the glass panel. The hospital was making certain that no interlopers gained entry that way. The bright light lent an alien quality to a hospital hallway that should have been bustling with activity. Her passage had stirred up dust, and she could see the tiny motes dancing in the glare from the skylight. There was a feeling of disuse, of abandonment, about the hospital, of a place that had not been inhabited for a long time. Absentmindedly, she bit her lip, not wanting to think about it.

The dripping was louder—a slow, measured sound that never varied, liquid landing with a muted, mushy sound. It was coming from the next room. She had to know.

Reluctantly she headed toward the sound. It was coming from a smaller room furnished as a lounge. The dripping was at the side of the room, blocked from her view by the door.

As Elizabeth stepped into the room, her nose was assailed by a harsh, acrid odor. Her eyes were drawn to the sofa against the far wall, a sodden, fire-gutted wreck. The charred remains of the fabric and the ugly black mass of melted plastic padding were covered with white powder. The wall behind the sofa was blistered and discolored all the way to the ceiling. Her skin crawled with the knowledge that behind her the steady drip demanded her attention. Slowly she turned to confront it.

A small counter attached to the wall held a large coffee

urn. A stainless steel sink was built into the countertop, and from its faucet water was dripping with monotonous regularity onto a sponge. Pegs on the wall held at least twenty coffee mugs marked with first names or illustrations. There was a sizable cork board on the wall, crowded with a miscellany of cartoons, short articles, and pictures. A quick glance at some of them confirmed that this was not an area open to visitors.

A thought struck her, and she reached for the coffee urn. Its sides were cold. Though it was still morning, no coffee had been heated in the appliance for quite a while.

Elizabeth grabbed the faucet handle and slammed it shut with far more strength than necessary. The sudden cessation of sound was as bad as the dripping had been. She fled from the room with its burned sofa and bitter stench.

The lounge door was directly opposite the strange fire door. Up close, it looked more like the door to a bank vault than an emergency exit.

Elizabeth tapped its flat metal surface. It conveyed a feeling of massive solidity. There was a heavy handgrip on the door, and immediately below it a bright steel locking mechanism was affixed to the surface of the door.

She grabbed the handgrip with both hands and pulled at it, at first easily, and then as hard as she could, but it was as solid as the wall.

A movable steel plate sliding on tracks was set into the door at eye level. She gripped the knob on the plate and pulled. At last she would see what was beyond the red door. It slid easily.

She groaned in disappointment. The plate covered a four-inch-square opening that pierced the door, but there was a similar sliding plate on the other side. Her curiosity aroused, Elizabeth pressed her fingers against the plate, trying to work it free. The plate started to slide. But after a half inch it stopped, as though it was jammed or something was holding it. She turned away, unaware that the plate had slid gently back into place.

The last room off the corridor was the kitchen. A large commercial stove and ovens lined one wall. Opposite it were three upright frozen-food lockers standing higher than her head, their stainless steel fronts gleaming moistly in the dim light. A trickle of water ran from the base of one of the lockers to the drain in the middle of the concrete floor. At the far end were sinks, dishwashers, a large steam table, and several rolling carts for food trays.

Only the treatment room—the one where they had been received—remained to be searched. There was nowhere else to look.

She saw three vending machines near the end of the hall and hurried toward them, forgetting her anxiety at the memory of Johnny's kidding around yesterday.

She froze in midstride. Her eyes widened, and she felt weak-kneed.

The glass had been broken out of the cigarette machine and two candy machines. A carpet of glass fragments littered the hall in front of the dispensers. Much of the candy and all of the cigarettes were missing.

Elizabeth found herself biting her finger, trying to stifle a scream. She was trembling uncontrollably. Staring back at the horrible emptiness of the corridor, she knew she had to get out of the building. Beyond thinking, she whirled and lunged through the double doors into the treatment room.

Slumping against the wall of the empty room, she fought to regain her composure. She started for the doors leading to the porte cochere, but stopped abruptly, unable to credit her eyes.

The treatment room had not been cleaned since they were brought in. The sheeting on top of the nearer table was rumpled and smeared with mud. On the far table, bloodstains remained where Gavin Thorne's head had rested. Against the far wall, in the shadow beneath the windows with their heavy steel mesh covering, she could see Gavin's crumpled clothes lying where they had been thrown.

Elizabeth averted her eyes, sick of finding nothing but more puzzles, and pushed through the doors into the tiny hall that she remembered from the first night. Caution was forgotten. She would lose her mind if she didn't get out of the place.

With a sigh of relief she hit the push bars of the windowless outside doors. Her hands slipped off the unyielding bars, and her shoulder hit the door. She pushed again with all her strength, but they wouldn't budge. She moaned, terrified now. She was locked in the deserted building.

She reentered the treatment room, trying to gather her wits, to find some rational answer. What had happened? Why had everyone in the hospital—patients, doctors, and nurses—disappeared? Had there been a nuclear war? Had some natural disaster forced them to flee? Maybe something even more horrible had come to the hospital.

She shuddered as she glanced about her refuge . . . seeing Gavin Thorne's clothes and the rumpled examination tables.

She hated the Goddamned silence. Elizabeth wanted laughter, talk, people moving around—the sounds a hospital should have. It was horrible. She slumped onto a chair and started to cry, very close to cracking.

She sat there for five minutes, her defenses down, before her sobs subsided, leaving her numb. The sound of an electric motor switching on caused her to jump.

It came from the shadowy far corner of the room, from something that looked like a low, overlong file cabinet. The metal box was about eight feet long and had two pull-out drawers, one above the other. At the rear were vents, emitting the busy hum of an electric motor.

For a moment Elizabeth was puzzled, and then she knew what it was. It was a body cabinet, like the movies showed in morgues. Skystone would certainly be no stranger to death. The cabinet must have been used more than a few times.

She turned away from it, but as she did, she heard a noise—a brief metallic ping from somewhere behind her. She spun around, the flesh of her neck crawling. There was nothing behind her.

The only sound was the humming. Her imagination was running wild. She started to relax. The noise came again, not loud—a sort of metallic drumming. She cried out in alarm. All was quiet for a moment, and then the drumming came back, so faint she would have missed it had she not been straining to hear. She was close to screaming. She knew where it was coming from.

Something was alive in the body case.

CHAPTER 12

*E*lizabeth leapt to her feet. She pushed her fist hard against her lips, trying to stifle the screams, knowing that if she started she would never stop. Not wanting to but unable to control herself, she started toward the case, past the examination table on which Gavin had spilled his life's blood, unaware that she was whimpering. She halted before the metal container, trying to control the tremors racking her body.

The sound came again—a sort of metallic squeaking.

Her hand, moving with a will of its own, grasped the icy-cold handle of the lower drawer and pulled it open. Staring up at her were the dead eyes of Gavin Thorne. The mangled side of his head was exposed, and his face was distorted in the hideous smile of the death rictus.

She put her foot against the drawer and pushed it shut. The cabinet came alive with thumps and thuds. She screeched, "Oh, God!"

Beyond coherent thought, she seized the upper handle and pulled it with all her strength. The drawer shot out. The sight of motionless bare legs greeted her, but then the feet, taped together above the ankles, started wigwagging. She pulled aside the cloth covering the upper part of the body.

Looking up at her, his eyes wild, was Scott Sutherlin, clad in shorts and a T-shirt. His mouth was taped shut. One arm was in a cast, but the entire upper part of his body was wrapped in elastic bandages, pinning both arms against his sides. He shivered violently and looked up at her with pleading eyes. He was trying to talk, mumbling behind the tape.

Elizabeth spotted a pair of scissors lying atop Gavin's clothes. Quickly she cut the tape from around Scott's feet. Grasping his shoulders, she helped him into an upright position, still sitting in the cabinet.

She set to work on the tape around his mouth. It was not an easy job, and she had to cut away great swatches of hair to clear it from the back of his head. Once the tape was away from his mouth, he began to gag. Scott opened his mouth, revealing a glob of white inside. Gritting her teeth in distaste, she pulled out a sodden wad of gauze.

He tried several times before he could say, "Water."

After he downed several swallows, he was able to talk, his voice little more than a scratchy whisper.

While he was struggling to find his voice, she unwrapped the elastic from his body and helped him out of the cabinet. She had to support him to a chair.

Scott's problems were as much emotional as physical. He had been lying too long in that frigid, claustrophobic chamber, just above Gavin Thorne's body.

For a short, giddy time Elizabeth forgot she had any problems. She was not alone anymore, and that was all that counted.

When Scott was able to tell his story, it did not turn out to be much different from hers. He had been confined, apparently next door to her, in room 1. Like Elizabeth, he had been checked a couple of times by Dr. Caudill but had not seen him since yesterday morning. Dr. Mainwaring had plied him with the same strong drugs that Elizabeth had been forced to take. Last night everything had changed.

"I . . . don't remember . . . honestly don't remember much of what has happened. I remember our being brought here, and I remember Dr. Caudill putting the cast on my arm; but once they put me to bed, I slept all night. Dr. Mainwaring —is that the short doctor's name?—gave me a shot of something yesterday morning, and I went back to sleep. It was after I saw the other doctor.

"God, I'm hungry. I was so wasted that I didn't think much about food yesterday. A nurse—an older, black-haired lady—brought me a tray yesterday morning. I remember thinking how odd it was because all that was on the tray was a bowl of canned peaches. I ate a few spoonfuls, but I didn't want them.

"I kept drifting off to sleep, I would wake up briefly, but I would soon be asleep again. Before I knew it, it was dark outside. The best I can recall, the black-haired nurse came in a couple of times during the day, and Dr. Mainwaring came in once and gave me another shot. Then, sometime last night, all hell broke loose. I was awakened by those screams.

"I panicked and crawled from the bed. My God, that was a job! I couldn't get my arms and legs to do what I wanted. When I stood, I was so dizzy that I was afraid to let go of the bed. Finally I was able to stagger to the door.

"It was weird. There was smoke in the corridor, so thick near the ceiling it formed a blue haze. Several people were coughing. When I stuck my head out the door, they acted paralyzed, staring at me. One of the orderlies—the heavyset guy who was in the treatment room—was holding an elderly woman in a headlock. Her face was red, and she was drooling. There were several nurses in the hall. The older nurse was there—the black-haired one—and there were some nice-looking young gals. They were all watching the orderly holding the old lady. Two of the nurses looked plenty scared, but the others didn't seem to give a damn. The heavyset dude released the woman, and she just slithered down his leg to the floor. Before I understood what he was after, he had grabbed me. If my arm had been okay, I would have dropped that clown on the spot, but I was as weak as a baby. He clamped me in a bear hug. And that was it.

"Toward this end of the corridor, another guy was carrying a fire extinguisher. They started yelling for Mainwaring, and he rushed out of a doorway near where the fellow was with the fire extinguisher. When Mainwaring saw me, he shouted, 'Howie, don't let him go!'

"Mainwaring looked mad as hell. He yelled at the black-haired nurse, 'Why in the hell didn't you watch her? This never would have happened if you had done as I told you.'

"Then he told the guy holding me to put me back to bed. A few moments later, Mainwaring came in, carrying his trusty hypodermic syringe. I tried to stay away from him, but it was useless. I couldn't move a muscle with that dude holding me. It wasn't thirty seconds before I passed out.

"The next thing I knew I was cold as hell, lying on icy metal. I tried to raise up, but I hit my head. I could sense the closeness around me and went bananas. At first I was unaware that I was tied hand and foot. I must have thrashed about for ten minutes before calming down. I never understood until now what claustrophobia is like. Jesus! It was terrible!"

Scott closed his eyes, fighting his memories. "My God, Elizabeth, if I had known where I was . . . if I had known that Gavin was just a few inches away . . . I swear to God I believe I would have gone crazy."

He whirled toward Elizabeth. "Meredith! Where is Meredith? Tell me. They . . . haven't hurt her, have they?"

Elizabeth struggled to organize her thoughts, to try to explain about Meredith's odd behavior. Scott mistook her silence for bad news. His fingers dug into her shoulder.

"God in heaven! She'd dead, isn't she? Something has happened to her. Damn you, Elizabeth! Tell me!"

Pulling herself free of his painful grip, she gave him a judiciously censored account of Meredith's nocturnal visit and of Mainwaring's remarks. After she finished, Scott continued to stare at her, silently demanding a more satisfactory conclusion to her story.

"We've got to find her. I'll take this damned place apart brick by brick if I have to. If any bastard has hurt her . . . Come on, Elizabeth, we are wasting time."

"Scott, listen to me. Listen!"

The wild look faded from his eyes as the vehemence of her voice found its way through his churning emotions.

"The hospital isn't that big. I've searched it from one end to the other. There is no one here—no Meredith, no living soul. They have all gone . . . somewhere. We need help . . .

for Meredith and for us. We have to get out of here and find somebody. We're locked in the building."

Scott's shoulders sagged in sudden surrender. He looked very young and very vulnerable as the intensity faded from his face, replaced by etched lines of pain from his broken arm.

"What are we going to do, Elizabeth?"

"Something is terribly wrong here. At first I thought maybe there had been a nuclear war or something like that, but that doesn't explain the way things have been vandalized. It doesn't explain why you were treated the way you were."

It dawned on her that she was talking to a man clad only in boxer shorts. She glanced down at herself, embarrassed to see how clearly her breasts were outlined beneath the hospital gown's thin material.

"The first thing we need to do is find suitable clothing."

Scott looked bewildered at her sudden change of topic.

They searched the treatment room. Scott rummaged through Gavin's discarded clothes. Beneath the pile, he found his unfortunate employer's shoes, which proved to be uncomfortably small but wearable. Meanwhile, in a metal locker, Elizabeth discovered three uniforms of white pants and tunics as well as a pair of badly worn sandals that would fit her. The garments were all too large for her and too small for Scott. However, they managed to struggle into the clothing. Since she had no panties or bra, she pulled the garments on over her gown.

Feeling less vulnerable now they were together, they reentered the corridor and headed for the shelter of Elizabeth's room.

They paused at the nurses' station while Scott examined the cabinets. He pointed to a panel on the wall that Elizabeth had overlooked. There were numbers on the panel, and above each one a small, unlit red bulb.

Scott whistled. "Jesus! They have quite a security system here! I don't know whether this is intended to keep people out or in. It looks far too elaborate for the building alone. There must be a fence around the place that is tied into this board."

"But what does it mean, Scott?"

"Christ, don't ask me. But I'll tell you one thing. This place is guarded like Fort Knox."

Again, an unpleasantly cold sensation played along her spine. "Please, Scott, let's go. We have to make some plans."

Once in Elizabeth's room, Scott checked the windows. Outside they could see a well-tended lawn, its edge marked by a low border of concrete blocks. Beyond that were thick stands of young hardwood trees. In its way, it was a landscape as lifeless as the inside of the hospital.

He tapped at the window. "These windows sure are odd. There is another piece of glass on the outside—like a storm window, only it doesn't have a frame. These things aren't intended to open."

He pulled the curtain back. "Look, Elizabeth. Both panels are fitted into a metal plate. Apparently, it is fixed this way to muffle sound as well as for insulation."

A puzzled Scott tapped the panel as Elizabeth looked on. "This doesn't sound like glass. It must be that acrylic stuff that's supposed to be unbreakable."

She joined him at the window, suddenly interested in the outer pane. "Look, Scott, see those metal strips on the top and bottom of the glass. See—with the tiny wires running into the frame. What are those for?"

Scott whistled. "Like I said, this place is another Fort Knox. These windows are wired into the security system. It's a wonder I didn't set it off banging on the glass. Say, that's an idea. Why don't we set off the alarms? That should bring somebody on the double."

Elizabeth stopped him as he was pulling off his shoe. "Wait, Scott. I'm not sure we should call attention to ourselves yet."

When Scott looked at her questioningly, she stared back, defiant. "Okay, I'll say it. Maybe we were overlooked. Maybe it's a good thing we were. Look around us—the medication room ransacked, the vending machines robbed. I'm afraid something bad happened to them—the staff, the patients. We must get away from this place. Then we can seek help."

Scott blushed. "You're right, Elizabeth. Damn it, I can't think about anything but Meredith. Anyway, we couldn't batter our way through this plastic with a sledgehammer."

Elizabeth sank onto the bed, her head in her hands, while Scott remained at the window, staring morosely at the unattainable outdoors. They remained that way for several minutes before he whirled around, animated again.

"I wonder about the garbage."

"What?"

"I said I wonder about the garbage. How do they get the garbage out of the kitchen? Surely they don't roll it down the corridors. Did you notice an outside door in there?"

She tried to visualize the kitchen but could only remember the stainless steel cabinets and food lockers gleaming in the shadows.

"I'm almost sure there wasn't."

Scott pulled her toward the door. "Come on. I have an idea how we can get out. I worked in a place like this once."

They surveyed the outside wall of the kitchen. Most of the wall next to them was taken up by the freezers. The motors were running, as they had been during Elizabeth's first exploration. She tugged at Scott's sleeve, pointing.

"Look. One of the freezer doors is ajar. No wonder it's running so much."

Not only was the door open, but the liquid which Elizabeth had noticed earlier running into the floor drain was dripping from the open door. She started over to close the freezer, and as she did, her nose was assailed by the odor of putrification.

CHAPTER 13 _____

Scott saw that there was something wrong with Elizabeth. Her extended arm hovered in midair, not touching the handle, and her face was blanched. She backed away a couple of steps, her eyes wide, staring at the freezer.

"For God's sake, Elizabeth, what's wrong?"

She didn't acknowledge his question. He tugged at her arm.

"I . . . I smell something funny in there." Her voice broke, growing shrill. "I think something's dead."

Roughly, he pushed her aside and yanked the door open. The sickening odor billowed out around them, and Elizabeth fought to keep from vomiting. The compartment was crammed full, with mounds of thawed packets standing in a shallow film of water. The worst of the odor was emanating from the plastic-wrapped trays of hamburger stacked along the side of the compartment.

"It's all right, Elizabeth. Some of the food is spoiled, especially the meat. That's what you smell."

She still was not reassured. "But why was the door left open? Why didn't someone notice it? This must've happened a couple of days ago for it to be in this condition."

Refusing to meet her gaze, he shrugged and closed the freezer door. He pulled her past the frozen-food lockers.

Elizabeth scanned the far wall, knowing as she did that it was all so hopeless. She could not stifle the absurd accusation: "You said there would be a door. God, we're never going to get out of here."

"Wait a minute. Help me move those tray carts and that steam table."

They cleared the corner, working as quietly as possible. When the last cart was out of the way, Scott pointed into the shadows. There was a hinged steel door, perhaps four feet high and three feet across, secured with a heavy padlock.

He squatted before it, examining the edges of the frame. He rose with a sigh. "Thank God it's not wired. Now all we have to do is find the key for the padlock.

"The only people using this hatch would be the kitchen staff. I can't see them going to a doctor or nurse every time they need to take a garbage can out. The medical staff wouldn't want to waste time on that. The key has to be in here somewhere."

"There must be a thousand places here to hide a small key."

Scott ignored her comment, studying the area around the garbage port. "They wouldn't make any big deal out of it. The key to the cutlery drawer—I can see that on somebody's key ring—but not the garbage key. Now . . . where would it be?"

Elizabeth pointed to the wall above the sink. "Well, I would put it about where that key is on the hook above the sink. You know . . . hide it in plain view."

The job proved too difficult for Scott—trying to hold the padlock and unlock it with one hand. He smiled apologetically as he surrendered the key to her.

After the padlock was freed, Elizabeth slowly opened the steel door. It swung easily on heavy, well-oiled hinges.

A head-high enclosure of concrete blocks faced them across a small concrete apron. The narrow gap in the concrete wall revealed at least a dozen large garbage cans in its interior.

Elizabeth peeked around the edge of the metal door and then jerked her head back. "Oh, no!"

"What's wrong? Who is out there? Did they see you?"

She shook her head. "No . . . at least I don't think so. It's the patio. Those same elderly people . . . you know . . . the ones I told you were on the patio yesterday. They're out there again."

"Who is with them?"

She leaned through the port again and then stepped out into the open. A moment later, she ducked back inside.

"I don't see anybody—just the two of them sitting there. But that can't be! Who could have rolled them out there when the hospital is deserted? Scott, we had better go—"

Scott pulled her back. "Stop it, Elizabeth . . . we have to get out while we can. If you aren't confused about what you saw when the cops brought you here the other night, all we have to do is slip past the office, and the driveway will lead us to the gate. Right?"

She nodded.

"Okay, let me take a look. When I give the word, go."

Thinking about the two pathetic figures on the patio, she started to object but bit her tongue, sensing Scott's need to assert himself.

Groaning as his cast brushed against the hatchway, he squirmed past her, peeked toward the patio, and then motioned for her to follow. Ducking her head, she dived through the door after him.

Walking fast, they moved along the side of the building, feeling uncomfortable as they passed the windows. Soon they stood at the front corner of the hospital. Behind them, the comatose sunbathers sat, unmoving, on the patio.

Scott's voice was strained. "I think we'd better stay off the driveway. It looks like easy going through the woods. Head for the trees across the driveway."

"What if there's somebody in the office?"

"Hell, it's too late to worry about that now. Let's go."

Grunting painfully with each jarring step, Scott dashed across the graveled strip. Elizabeth followed him into the grove of trees, running easily despite the floppy sandals.

He was breathing hard, sweating, his face white. He

gasped, "Okay so far. I'm going to have to take it easy. I think we got away . . . I don't hear anything. It shouldn't be too far to the gate."

As they moved slowly through the trees, conscious of the crackling leaves beneath their feet, she glanced at the sun. It was directly overhead.

As she looked down, she spotted something moving among the trees ahead of them. Startled, she clutched at Scott's injured arm, pulling him up short.

"Elizabeth, for God's sake . . . my arm. What are you—"

"Sssh! I saw something through the trees. See . . . there it is again—that flash of white. It is near the gate. It must be one of the orderlies."

"You're right! I see it, too. Quick! Duck back farther into the woods."

"No. He might hear us moving in these leaves. Get behind a tree trunk."

Faintly, they could hear movement through the carpet of dry leaves. The sounds died away, and after waiting a short while longer, they started toward the gate again, moving at a snail's pace, taking a few steps and then stopping to listen. Before they had traversed twenty yards, Scott stopped, pointing. "Look, there it is—the gate. See? Past that tree."

They began to walk faster, keenly aware that they were clad in the same brilliant white as whomever they had seen near the gate. The trees thinned, and they no longer had any cover.

They ran the last few yards to the gate, with Scott beginning to limp noticeably in the pinched confines of Gavin's shoes. He halted a few feet away, but Elizabeth ran past him, arms extended, reaching for the gate latch.

"Watch out!" he shouted, grabbing her with his good arm, stopping her bare inches short of the wrought-iron gate.

She looked at him with offended dignity. "Damn you, Scott. What is wrong with you?"

He pointed toward the gate. "Jesus Christ, Elizabeth, you're a walking disaster. Didn't you see those insulators?"

She looked at him, puzzled. "Insulators? So what? What are insulators?"

"The damned gate is electrified. God knows what the voltage is. There's no telling what you might have done to yourself."

She jumped back, her eyes growing wide. "Oh God, Scott. I owe you one. I forgot it might be electrified."

Her face brightened. "Maybe it isn't on."

He turned aside to search the grass. Locating a small branch, he flipped it against the wrought-iron bars. There was a sun-white flash, and the branch exploded into smoking bits of wood. His one-word expletive "Jesus!" was eloquent enough for Elizabeth.

"God, I'll bet you set off the alarm," she complained.

"Nope . . . there wouldn't be that sensitive an alarm on the live wires. Small animals, branches, and things like that must brush against it all the time. An alarm would sound only if the circuit was broken. Come on. Let's check along the wall."

They walked about fifty yards back into the woods before Scott stopped, looking up into a small, many-branched tree. He grinned at Elizabeth. "What kind of tree climber are you, kiddo?"

"When I was a kid, I could climb a pretty mean tree. Why?"

"That stone wall is too tall for us to see the top, and I can't climb with this arm. You'll have to shimmy up and see if it's wired."

Discarding the clumsy sandals, she ascended the tree with surprising agility. When she had climbed high enough to see over the wall, her "Oh, no!" told Scott all he needed to know. She descended from her perch, not bothering to hide her disappointment.

"I'm sorry, Scott. There is glass embedded in the crown, and steel posts set in the top, angled outward. They have three strands of barbed wire strung along them and two other wires with those insulators on them."

He looked thoughtfully at the stone enclosure. "They can't have a wall like that all the way around this place. It would cost a fortune. Let's keep looking."

They turned back toward the hospital, moving through the

woods. Just as they caught sight of the building, they encountered a narrow gravel lane badly overgrown with weeds. It turned off the driveway to the right. The lane ran straight for a bit before curving to the left as if to circle the building. After a moment's hesitation, they turned into the lane.

They lingered among the trees a couple of minutes, watching the woods ahead of them. By the time they resumed their exploration, they were shivering. There was a sharp, steady wind blowing, and in the shade of the trees, the air was chilly. The light cotton uniforms provided little defense against the cold.

The lane curved in an ever-wider arc away from the hospital. Soon it left the trees altogether, running through an open field. A high chain-link fence loomed up ahead of them, across a stretch of rank weeds.

The fence was topped with an angled rack of barbed wire. From the lane they could see the white insulators glistening in the sun. The entire perimeter of the hospital grounds was electrified.

"Maybe we could crawl under the fence," Elizabeth offered hopefully.

They left the dust of the lane, wading through a sea of knee-high weeds. Before they had gone very far, her feet and legs were a mess, scratched and itching. She was moving so slowly that Scott ordered her to wait while he went ahead to inspect the fence.

She looked back toward the hospital and was surprised to discover that across the intervening treetops she could see part of its flat roof. Her gaze sharpened. She was having trouble understanding what she was seeing. The roof was not the L-shape it should have been. It looked like a T.

Confused, she lowered her gaze to scan the woods between the lane and the hospital. Her heart skipped a beat. In the woods, perhaps a hundred yards to the rear of the hospital, she saw a flash of white. She found it a second time, and realized it was not moving. It was not the sort of brilliant white that the uniforms were.

When Scott rejoined her, his expression was so forlorn that she didn't have the heart to question him.

"It's bad news. That fence is built right into the ground to prevent anyone's burrowing under it. It's no use—we have nothing to dig with. Besides, I'll bet there are alarm sensors underground."

She pointed toward the distant hospital. "Scott, do you see the roof?"

"Yeah, sure. Why?"

"What shape is that building?"

"Why, it's an L-shape. It's . . ." He fell silent, then he whistled. "Hell, that baby is T-shaped. That means there's a section we didn't know existed. I'll bet that is where Meredith is. By God, that has to be it! Let's go, Elizabeth. I should have looked closer. This is a wild-goose chase."

He dragged Elizabeth several steps before she could stop him. She tugged several times at his tunic before he became aware of her.

"Scott, calm down. We have to find out what is going on if we are to help Meredith."

Turning him around, she pointed her finger where she had seen the flash of white in the woods. "Look there."

"Where?"

"There. See—something white, but not like these uniforms. It looks shiny."

"Yeah, I see it. I wonder what it could be."

"Let's cut through the woods. We need to take a look at the other wing of Skystone. Besides, I think we should find out what the white thing is behind the hospital."

They crossed the gravel lane and plunged into the grove. The woods on this side of the hospital was thick and unkempt, unlike the front where the brush was kept cleared to create a parklike setting.

Elizabeth's feet were growing more uncomfortable all the time. Blood droplets showed on several of the scratches. It was colder with the woods—heavier here—shielding them from the sun. Her toes were beginning to ache with the cold.

The brush-choked woodland seemed endless. When they reached the building, they were so exhausted, hungry, and cold that they blundered out into the open. They dived back out of sight behind a clump of bushes.

Directly before them, the part of the hospital with which they were familiar—the part constructed of concrete panels —was joined with an older wing, one built of brick. The second part was single story and appeared of equal length to the newer wing. Here were no acrylic window panels, but heavy steel mesh painted a dark green that blended with the ivy growing rampant up the walls. It was a dismal-looking place in the lengthening shadows—dark-windowed and silent.

Elizabeth glanced at Scott and saw that their discovery had only deepened the mystery for him, as it had for her. He touched her shoulder. "Hey, we're not going to figure it out standing here. Come on—let's try to find what it was we saw back of the building."

"Scott, I'm getting cold."

A more confident Scott grinned at her. "So, what else is new?"

They retraced their arduous journey through the heavy underbrush to the gravel lane. By the time they stumbled onto the lane, Elizabeth longed for the warmth of the sinister building behind them. Her strength fast diminishing, she followed the limping Scott along the graveled ruts.

They were about ready to give up when he cried, "Hey, look. A car has been driven off into the woods here. See how these seedlings are flattened? And here are the tire tracks. Come on."

They were about forty paces into the timber when she tugged at his tunic.

"Scott, look!"

The sun was reflected off a shiny white object ahead of them. Cautious now, they crept forward, and then, as they moved past a clump of trees, they saw glittering red glass catching brilliant highlights from the afternoon sun. A few more steps, and they saw the white object in its entirety.

The front of the ambulance was wedged between two trees. Limbs and small bushes were piled atop it and along the sides.

Elizabeth's voice was barely audible. "Oh, my God! It's the ambulance! What on earth is it doing here?"

Scott shook his head, speechless.

She took a step to her left for a clearer view. She jumped backward, almost falling as she stumbled over his feet.

"Oh, Scott! I think they spotted me. The medics... they're sitting in the ambulance!"

CHAPTER 14 _____

When there was no outcry, Scott peeked around the tree trunk toward the vehicle. He started to say something, then stepped into the open, looking toward the ambulance.

"Wait here," he said. "Something is wrong."

She went with him.

When they were still ten feet away, they could clearly see the lattice of dried blood decorating the driver's face, like a bizarre mask. He sat with his hands on the steering wheel, his eyes open, staring straight ahead. Across the seat, slumped against the door as if he were asleep, was the second medic. His face was battered beyond recognition. His mouth gaped open, a red wound without teeth. His nose was badly smashed, with a long shard of bone jutting through the bridge. One eye rested against his cheek below the empty socket, from which a river of blood had flowed. The ruined face was alive with a moving mask of flies—feeding on it.

Scott spun away from Elizabeth, vomiting, while she struggled to stay on her feet in a world that threatened to go black.

This time she waited, as he ordered, while the pale Scott limped over to the ambulance and peered inside. From where she stood, she could hear the incessant buzzing of the flies. She watched as Scott opened the rear doors of the ambulance. He trudged back to her and stood with his eyes closed. She knew she would have to ask.

"Scott, tell me! I have to know."

"They were beaten to death with something heavy. The one called Otis was beaten until he is like pulp. God, he doesn't have a face anymore. The back of the ambulance is a mess . . . there is blood all over the place. The key is still in the ignition. I'll swear to God, I believe that—"

He stopped and swallowed noisily, looking around at the quiet, waiting woods. "I believe they were dumped in the back and driven here and then propped up like that. I swear it's the work of a madman!"

"But why?" She was struggling to control herself, her voice breaking. "Oh, please, dear God! What kind of place is this? What in the name of God has happened here?"

Scott shook her. "Shut up! You're getting hysterical. Forget about them. We have to find a way to turn the power off to the fence. We can't stay out here indefinitely, anyway. It feels as if it will get down to freezing tonight."

"You mean . . . you want to go back in there? Back in that building?"

He nodded. "It's the only way. Besides, I have to find how to get into the other wing of that building. I'm not leaving Meredith. If she's here, I'll find her."

"Maybe we can attract attention some other way, Scott. Listen, maybe we can set the woods on fire. Surely someone would see that."

He shook his head. "Do you have any matches? I don't. Besides, we don't know which way the fire would burn. What if it burned the building? We can't just destroy someone's property. And what about Meredith? Damn you, Elizabeth! Don't you care about Meredith?"

She turned her back, ignoring his emotional outburst, and made her way back to the lane. Scott was limping so badly that she soon outdistanced him.

As they neared the junction of the lane and the driveway, the lagging Scott called to her. "Elizabeth, wait up. I'm sorry. I spoke out of turn. Please stop. They'll see you."

She waited until he caught up. She couldn't control herself. Her voice was scornful. "Who, Scott? Who will see me? Those poor men in the ambulance? The nurses and doctors that have disappeared? Just who is it that will see me?"

Elizabeth Shea had grown up believing that she owned her share of the world. She had been urged to treat people with dignity and respect, to understand that she would receive equal measure. Her family had indoctrinated her with the belief that people of class persevered in the knowledge that everything would always be all right in the end. There had been no lessons that men could be beaten to death and stuffed into the front seat of an ambulance or that hospitals —hospitals for gentlefolk—could suddenly turn into unfathomable, silent prisons. Whatever she did, she would not cower.

Elizabeth marched out into the open, past the front door of Skystone Institute. Scott, awed by her bravado, mutely followed her. They paused by the corner housing the office.

"Wait a minute," Elizabeth commanded. "Let me check."

She pulled her head back quickly. "Scott, how long have we been out here?"

He shrugged. "At least two hours. Why?"

"Those . . . those old people are still sitting on the patio. Do you guess they were forgotten when the building was evacuated?"

"I don't know, and I don't plan on finding out."

"We have to do something. This wind is cold. They could catch pneumonia."

"For God's sake, Elizabeth, I don't believe you. Don't you remember? We saw somebody checking the gate, and then we found those poor bastards in the ambulance. There is a killer loose out here. Look at me! I'm not chicken, but I only have one good arm, and my feet are a mess. We have to stay out of sight."

She yielded reluctantly. "I feel so funny about it. They are people. They are somebody's relatives."

"Can't you understand? We don't know what in the hell is going on. We can't take chances. We have to keep going for her . . . our own sakes."

Elizabeth's nose twitched, and she brushed by him, her

face contorted. "God, that garbage smells terrible. I didn't notice it when we left the building."

"It's the wind—it's changed. It's blowing this way now. Jesus, you're right. It really smells rotten."

"I don't like this. Come on—quick!"

When they reached the garbage hatch, Scott realized that Elizabeth was looking toward the patio again.

"What's wrong?"

"Scott, that dead smell—it's worse here, and we're past the garbage enclosure."

Choking back his irritation at her obstinacy, he sniffed the air. She was right. It was a different smell. Before, there had been the complex odors of garbage with the overtone of decay. Here, the pungent odor of garbage was missing, but the trenchant smell of decay—death—choked the air.

They looked at each other, their eyes wide with fear, before Elizabeth spoke. "Come on, Scott. We have to find out. You know we do."

She had taken three or four steps before he understood what she was doing. He called after her to stop, but she gave no sign she had heard. Elizabeth slowly crossed the strip of lawn.

Scott caught up with her as she reached the edge of the patio. She stopped, looking at the two silent figures in their wheelchairs.

The woman with the bright red hair sat exactly as she had yesterday, with her plump body slumped sideways and her head against her chest. The breeze gently moved strands of her red hair across her forehead and ruffled the light scarf around her neck. Her eyes were closed, and her mouth was open. Her parted lips looked dry and cracked.

The elderly man in the other wheelchair was several yards away. His body sprawled backwards in the chair, with his head thrown back as it had been yesterday. A hat was pulled low over his eyes, its brim fluttering in the wind, threatening to blow off. A strong gust hit the hat, and it lifted enough to let the sunshine fall full on his face, and they could see his open eyes.

Elizabeth looked at Scott, her eyes pleading with him. He felt angry at her for what she was asking, but he climbed over the wrought-iron railing onto the patio. The smell was ghastly, and his stomach churned. Biting his lower lip, he leaned forward and touched the woman on the shoulder, calling, "Ma'am."

Even the gentle touch was enough to upset her balance in the chair, and her body pitched forward, tumbling headfirst onto the flagstones. Elizabeth's shriek frightened a covey of quail feeding along the far side of the driveway; with a great fluttering of wings, they rose into the air.

Scott stared at the body in disbelief. When he glanced toward Elizabeth, she had her knuckles pressed against her lips, shaking her head. He walked quickly to the other wheelchair.

The smell of death was even stronger here. He lifted the stained fedora from the man's head. The eyes gazed directly into the sunlight without flinching, the pupils huge. Scott put the man's hat back over his face.

He refused to look again at the corpses, gazing across the drive into the woods climbing toward the crest of the small hill. He stiffened. Above the distant tree line, a roof was visible.

The bodies forgotten for the moment, he turned toward Elizabeth. Before he could say anything, she said, "Scott, put her back in her chair."

A look of disbelief spread across his face. "Are you crazy? God, she's been dead for days. She smells terrible."

"Put her back in her chair. We can't leave her out here."

He was angry again. "Take her in? How? Through the garbage hatch? Where do I put her? Do you want me to walk down the corridor pushing a Goddamned rotting corpse?"

Elizabeth burst into tears, and Scott, ashamed of himself, slipped his good arm around her.

She looked up through tear-blurred eyes. "It's my fault, Scott. I was talking nonsense. God, I am so scared."

A mute pact made, they bent to the loathsome remains of the poor creature at their feet and reseated her corpse in the chair. It was the most terrible task Elizabeth had ever undertaken.

Leaning over the railing, trying to ease the queasiness in her stomach, she did not hear Scott until he called a second time. He was pointing toward the steeply pitched roof visible along the hilltop.

"Look. There is a house over there. Maybe we can get someone's attention if it's near the boundary fence."

She nodded in silent assent and followed him as he vaulted the wrought-iron railing onto the lawn.

"Scott, wait a minute!"

He stiffened in anticipation of a fresh disaster.

"Let's circle around toward the front to climb the hill."

"Why? What difference does it make?"

"I think I've figured out what the old section of this hospital is used for. Look—there's no parking area here, is there?"

He shook his head.

"It's obvious that these people don't commute to work, so there have to be living quarters for them. That's what the old section is—dormitories for the employees."

He whistled. "By God, that has got to be the answer. Why don't we go back there—"

"No, we still don't know what happened to them. It doesn't explain where the patients are. We need help. The authorities must be informed about this. To be on the safe side, let's stay out of sight until we figure out how to attract somebody's attention."

Soon they were climbing the slope in the direction of the distant roof. As they came out into a tiny clearing, Scott pointed back downslope.

"The driveway doesn't end at the porte cochere. It comes out the rear and then disappears into the trees."

The brush was thicker on the slope, and their progress slowed. Gradually, Elizabeth left the sore-footed Scott behind.

He was about forty feet behind when she stopped and cried, "Oh, no!"

He joined her. "What's wrong?"

"Look."

The woods ended abruptly a few yards ahead of them, revealing a large three-story house that looked to be an authentic Victorian. Its symmetry was marred by a new single-story addition to the rear. The long, many-windowed structure made no attempt to imitate the architecture of the main structure. A paved driveway passed on their right, opening onto a concrete apron before an attached five-car garage. Beyond the garage, alongside the barracks-like addition, were two tennis courts.

Scott, his arm throbbing from the climb, looked questioningly at Elizabeth.

"Look beyond the house, Scott—across the lawn. Isn't that the fence?"

"Yeah, it sure is."

"Don't you see? That means this house is on Skystone property. It's part of the hospital. That must be a dormitory at the back . . . and with the tennis courts . . . this is . . . Oh, God, this is where the employees live—not down there. That's what the cop said when we arrived here. I had forgotten."

Nearby, a squirrel was working in a tree, and his angry chatter at their presence was the only sign of life. There were wind chimes somewhere around the place, and each chilly gust of wind set them to their tinkling clatter. The windows of the silent house revealed nothing of its shadowed interior.

"Well?" Elizabeth asked.

"Let's go back in the bushes for a while."

She giggled, a lopsided smile on her face. "Why, Scott Sutherlin, do you think this is the time for that sort of thing?"

The tension broke in him, and they stood there for a moment, red-faced, hands over their mouths, laughing like children until the tears ran down their cheeks.

Their hilarity vanished all too soon. Scott hustled her back down the slope to a thick clump of brush.

"Elizabeth, you stay here. I'm going in there. Jesus, I am scared to death!

"I shouldn't tell you, Elizabeth, but I will. The old man on the patio—his neck was badly bruised. I think he was strangled. We have to find a weapon with which we can defend ourselves, and we need shelter until we figure out how to short out the fence. If I'm not back in thirty minutes, it means I'm not coming back. I can't tell you what you should do because I don't know, but for God's sake, don't come after me."

He stepped out into plain view on the lawn and hobbled slowly across the grass. His heart was beating far too fast, and he had a metallic taste in his mouth like when he broke his nose. At any moment he expected to be discovered.

He reached the foot of the steps that led onto the high porch fronting the house. There was no movement behind the dark windows. Slowly, he mounted the stairs.

The front door failed to yield to his hand, but at the end of the porch, where it was shadowed by a vine-covered trellis, there was another door. He saw, with a start, that it was standing open. He paused outside the screen door, listening.

From somewhere inside, a radio was playing. It sounded muffled and far off. Quickly, he stepped through the doorway.

The room in which he stood, an old-fashioned area with a twelve-foot ceiling, had been made into an office. In one corner was a large gun cabinet, its glass door standing open. There were no guns in the cabinet racks. Nothing else in the room appeared disturbed.

Scott crossed the room and found himself in a narrow cross passage that led into the main hall. In the large, dimly lit entry, the hollow ticking of a clock supplied a rhythm for the distant radio. A few steps into the hall revealed the source of the ticking. A magnificent grandfather's clock stood along the wall, its brass pendulum gleaming dully in the limited light.

Quickly, he peered into the four large rooms that opened onto the entry hall. A cursory glance was enough to convince him that he was not in an ordinary residence. The first room, entered through an open arch, held a large-screen television similar to those in the lounge at the hospital. It was obviously used as a living room, furnished with several sofas in the room and a Ping-Pong table, which was pushed against the back wall.

Across the hall the partition had been removed between two smaller rooms to make one large chamber. It contained two long dining tables with an ornate chandelier above the far one. He counted the chairs. There were twenty-six. The windows were narrow and tall, reaching almost from floor to ceiling, typically Victorian in style. Without lights, the dining hall had a dark, forbidding aspect.

The fourth room contained several painted tables with overhead lights. A small pile of books was on one of the tables. Obviously, the area had been used as a study.

He turned toward the closed green door at the rear of the broad hall. It concealed a short hallway with a door to each side. The hall's limit was marked by a glass-paned door. He could see through the pane into a low-ceilinged corridor beyond. It was the new addition at the rear of the old house.

Letting the green door swing shut, he returned to the main hall and an ornate staircase that led to the second floor. The sense of terror had not diminished since he entered the house, but its effect had changed. There was an inevitability about it. As he mounted the first step he was overwhelmed by a terrible premonition. Revulsion swept over him as he turned his gaze toward the gloom at the top of the stairs. Scott knew, somehow, that he would never descend those steps as the same person who climbed them. He was entering hell.

Grimly, he mounted the stairs and paused at the top, knowing now what he would find. The upstairs was heavy with the putrid odor of decaying flesh, of blood, of human excrement.

The hallway was dim, illuminated only by open doors from which the sun was spilling its chilly light. Somewhere above him on the third floor, violins cried in the anguished discords of Prokofiev. Scott turned toward the front of the house, with the floorboards betraying his every step. The door to one of the front rooms was not quite shut, and he pushed it open with his foot.

He had found the first of them: a tall redheaded man lying stiffly in the middle of the room, his stained hands gripping the blood-sodden midriff of his pajamas, his face frozen in surprised terror.

Scott edged around the body. The man's quarters, fixed up as a small apartment, showed no signs of a struggle.

He closed the door behind him and renewed his search. There were two other apartments opening off the front hall, but these were mercifully empty. Nothing had been disturbed.

In the first of the single bedrooms he found the body of an older woman. The covers were still drawn about her, and across the foot of the bed lay a blue robe with the name Opal embroidered on it. Her throat had been cut with a single long slash. She had died with perhaps no more awareness than a single terrible moment of strangulation.

In the next bedroom, a man lay facedown in the bed, the covers down to his waist. There were two deep stab wounds in his uncovered back, and the blood-soaked pillow gave evidence of a severed throat.

In shock, feeling nothing, Scott went from room to room. The killer had been remarkably successful in his silent pursuit of death. Only two of the eight dead gave any indication of having struggled.

The last victim was out of bed, lying near the window, apparently overtaken as she prepared to dive headfirst from the second floor to escape the horror pursuing her. In her room, as in those of several of the other women, was a gift-wrapped package. The attached tag read, HAPPY BIRTHDAY, OPAL, FROM YOUR LOVING SISTER.

Like a robot, Scott came back down the stairs, paused for a moment near the front door, and then turned toward the green door leading to the new addition.

Passing the kitchen, he saw, from the corner of his eye, a form crouched behind one of the refrigerators, between it and the side wall. Scott cried out in sudden terror, crashing backwards into the corridor wall. He stood there, helpless, but the form never moved. He peered across the kitchen and then relaxed.

The young girl would never move again.

CHAPTER 15

*H*e stared down at the young girl, perhaps eighteen, who had tried so hard to make herself invisible in that cranny before the slashing steel found her.

The murders in the upper floor were aesthetic masterpieces compared to what Scott found in the dormitory. Small monastic cubicles, holding little more than a bed and chair with a tiny closet, opened off each side of the passageway. No knives had been used in the dormitory. Immediately inside the building, he began to encounter them, bright red, their brass glittering in the sunlight: spent shotgun shells by the dozens littering the corridor. The floor was marred with rivulets and pools of blood dried to a rusty brown. Seven male bodies lay strewn along the corridor, flesh ravaged by steely storms of birdshot.

There was no way to avoid the blood. It was dry, and yet there was a stickiness, a smacking sound, as Scott's soles pulled free of it with each step. The dead were in a bewildering array of postures. Some had seen that blinding flash of sun fire as they prayed, others while clawing desperately at the walls or trying to crawl under their bunks. There had been no real resistance, unless it had been by the males sprawled in the hallway, who had perhaps made some mad, chivalrous gesture to protect the women in the dorm. The expenditure of ammunition had been prodigious, for the walls of the corridor had been shredded where blast after blast of birdshot ripped into them.

No one person could have done it, but several, reloading as they made their inexorable and deadly sweep through the dormitory.

In the large room at the end of the hall—a commons room with a table, cheap sofas, and a coffee machine— death wore a more puzzling face. There were five bodies, all young women and all nude. The five of them had been severely beaten about the body and the face. Two of the girls had broken necks, their heads at grotesque angles to their bodies. Two others had hemorrhaged badly from their vaginas. A blood-caked softball bat—lying across the stomach of one girl—spoke its own grim story of how this had happened.

Scott's stomach was rumbling, threatening to erupt again, and he knew he was losing his emotional isolation. The area was more confined than the main house had been, and the stench of death was heavy. He wanted to take the baseball bat with him as a weapon, but knowing how it had been used, he could not bring himself to touch it. He turned away, dry-heaving.

Leaping over the bodies of those who had sacrificed themselves in futile heroics, he hurried back into the older part of the house. Here he stopped, weakened, dizzy, leaning against the wall and gasping for breath. He was staring at a fireplace, and there was a poker by it. Scott had found his weapon.

He grabbed the iron bar and slumped wearily onto a chair, groaning as the pain from his arm flared into his body. He tried to remember what he had seen, to count the bodies. There were twenty-six—twenty-six people dead in the house, an old man and old woman dead on the patio, and the two murdered medics. Thirty people were dead—all murdered.

The distant music drew his attention again. It served as a reminder that the third floor had not been searched. For a second he considered mounting the stairs again and seeking the source of the radio. He was not likely to find a maniacal killer calmly listening to music. The radio played for those who would never again hear it.

Had he climbed those gloomy flights of stairs to the third floor with its spacious but dingy rooms, he would have found six more bodies. If he had walked into the room where the radio played he would have found a pretty nineteen-year-old, her face calm and tranquil, the breeze—coming through the crack in the window she had opened to the night air—gently moving her soft brown hair across her smooth but far too pale forehead. Kari Burnett had possessed a sense of humor and, had she not carried that angry red slash across her throat, might have appreciated the irony of Rachmaninoff's ISLE OF THE DEAD floating through the high-ceilinged mausoleum.

Scott came to his feet, knowing that he had exhausted the time limit he had given Elizabeth. He shot a quick glance out the window. Directly below him was the roof of the garage addition. The oddly placed door in the corner of the dining room must lead down to the garage.

Scott had an idea—a lifesaver of an idea. There had to be cars in the garage; and with a car, they could crash through the electrified gate and be on their way to freedom. He hurried across the dining room, never thinking of the food or the coats that they needed so badly. The poker lay forgotten where he had put it on the floor by the chair.

Stumbling down the narrow stairway, he grunted as his cast-laden arm bounced against the sidewall of the confined passage. He stepped out into the large, well-lit garage, confronted by four vehicles: two large luxury cars, a panel truck, and a pickup truck.

His hopes crashed to earth. The hoods of all four vehicles were up, and he could see into the engine compartment of the nearest car. A rat's nest of wiring lay across the engine, and the carburetor and air cleaner were battered into shapeless metal. A large steel maul was propped against the front fender.

He forced himself to walk along the line of vehicles, looking at the destruction wrought on each by the heavy maul. The panel truck was last in line. He glanced into the motor compartment and then, raising his eyes, looked beyond it into the empty fifth space. The sense of detachment that had sustained him vanished.

There, piled in a grotesque heap, was a collection of dead bodies. The gowns of many of them were twisted around their bodies, unmercifully exposing matchstick limbs and wasted bodies. Opened eyes, set in dead, wrinkled faces framed in scraggly gray hair—with deeply sunken mouths agape—stared owlishly at Scott.

He had found the patients of Skystone Institute.

He remembered nothing of the next few seconds, unaware that he had lurched through the garage and out the side door. Only when he saw Elizabeth step out into the open, her eyes wide with fear, did he manage to control himself. He grabbed her, unable to breathe, and clung weakly to her. Only vaguely did he hear her cry, "What is it, Scott? What is it?"

As Elizabeth stared at him, her gaze never leaving his face, he told her in devastating detail of the horrors of the old Victorian structure looming above them, sheltering its butchered dead from the cruel, capricious winds. While he talked, trying to maintain a monotone that threatened at times to splinter like glass into a shrill-toned hysteria, his hands, always moving, had pulled the keys from his pocket. He thrust his finger through the key ring, slowly turning it with his other hand.

He finished his story to find Elizabeth no longer watching his face but staring at his hand, twisting the shiny metal ring. The ghastly scene at the ambulance had profoundly affected her. The cataloguing of the terrors felt by another had little effect on her.

"The keys, Scott. Where did you get them?"

He stared at them in surprise. "Why . . . I don't know . . . I must have . . . that's right. There's a side door on the porch. The first room I entered was an office. I remember seeing a ring of keys on the desk. I must have picked them up without thinking and put them in my pocket."

She pulled the keys from his hand and examined them.

Talking about the horrors of the house had purged Scott of a burden that threatened to explode within him. Much calmer, he raised his eyes to look at the old mansion. Shuddering at what he would never forget, he slipped his arm over Elizabeth's shoulder, as much for his own comfort as hers. Thinking only of the keys, she shrugged his arm away. Scott blushed, embarrassed by the unthinking rejection.

Elizabeth was growing excited. "Look at these keys—all shapes and sizes. The house wouldn't have that many locks. They must belong to one of the doctors. I think we've hit the jackpot. I believe they are for the hospital. Come on . . . let's go."

"Wait a minute. Go and do what?"

"Look, one man couldn't have done this. A gang, maybe bikers, came in here and killed them all. God knows why. Maybe robbery. We must get into the office. There has to be a master switch for the fence. They would have to have a way of turning it on and off, and there has to be a telephone."

"But how do you know they're not still here?"

"Where, Scott?"

"I don't know. Maybe they're in the other part of the hospital—the older part."

"Why would they hide? There are only two of us left alive. They certainly have nothing to fear from us—especially if they have shotguns. You said it yourself. We can't stay outdoors, doing nothing."

"Listen, Elizabeth, let's sneak back in and get food, blankets, and . . ."

She frowned. "No! We have to get out of here and contact the police. Scott, you can come with me or not, but I'm taking these keys. Now, I'm going back to the hospital. God, yes, I want to stay here, out in the open, clear of the buildings, but I'm hungry and I'm cold and I'm not doing a thing standing here to change that."

She started down the slope the way they had come. Scott watched her passing through the sharp shadows drawn by a cheerless winter sun on the dormant earth, never glancing back to see if he was coming. He hesitated and then followed.

The newer part of Skystone glared brightly in the afternoon sunlight. The older portion crouched darkly behind its screen of vines and meshed windows. Only the trees moved in the gusts of chilly wind. The hospital remained lifeless.

Scott pointed. "Look!"

The door of the garbage hatch stood open. They could see it swinging to and fro in the building wind.

"Elizabeth, did you leave the hatch open?"

"I . . . I don't remember."

Scott choked back his irritation.

They came out on the driveway to be confronted by the two silent figures sitting without complaint in the cold sunlight. When they reached the garbage hatch, they paused, reluctant to face whatever awaited them in the kitchen.

Elizabeth took a deep breath, dodged past Scott, and disappeared through the opening before he could object. She blinked, trying to see clearly in the dim kitchen after coming out of the bright sunlight. Scott bumped into her as he followed.

While he rearranged the food carts around the hatch, she stared idly at the small pool remaining on the floor beneath the freezer they had found open. She thought again of the food crammed into the locker, and then she understood why so much food was in the one freezer. A chill arced down her spine.

"Scott, we won't be using food from the other freezers. You know that, don't you?"

His eyes widened as he understood, but his voice denied it. "Oh, shut up, Elizabeth! You don't know what you're talking about."

"Open the door."

When he failed to move, she said, her tone shrill with a tremolo to it, "Go ahead, damn it! Open it, or I will!"

Crossing the room quickly, he yanked open the heavy door of the second locker.

Elizabeth's first impression was that a large bundle of clothes had fallen from the locker, but the solid weight with which it hit the floor told her what it was.

Scott's voice broke. "Christ, that's the woman that was in the hall last night—the one that was screaming."

"God, yes, I knew her. She was the old lady that came to

my room to talk to me. She was so sad, so unhappy. Her name was Carrie."

He looked into the open freezer. "My God! There's another one stuffed in the back."

He slammed the door shut.

Her voice was trembling. "Do you want to open the third locker? Do we have enough bodies yet?"

"Shut up, Elizabeth! Damn it, shut up!"

Averting their eyes, they stepped past the solidly frozen corpse of Carrie Dalton and out into the corridor. She threw her arms around his waist.

"I'm sorry, Scott. I shouldn't have acted like that."

Scott, looking pale and desperately tired, patted her arm.

The sun, rapidly sliding down the western sky, was striking the skylight at an acute angle, and the interior was much darker than when they had left the building.

Elizabeth stopped before the red steel door, her voice a whisper. "Scott, this can't be a fire door. It must lead into the other part of the hospital. But why is it painted red . . . and why is it so massive? Why does it have the viewing panel and the heavy lock?"

Without waiting for the answer that she knew he couldn't give, she moved on past the door. At the nurses' station the two blue lights still silently pleaded for nurses that were not here. All the doors along the corridor remained open. Everything seemed exactly as it had been, but it wasn't. Their innocence had been taken from them, and nothing was the same.

The quiet, dusty halls, the empty rooms with pools of sunlight spilling onto the floors were components of a waking nightmare, a silent stage that awaited its actors.

Scott slipped behind the counter of the nurses' station to try the keys from the house in the lock of a gray steel box suspended on the wall. He had tried most of them before he grunted in satisfaction and swung the cover open.

"Just what I thought. This is one of the security control stations, but damn it, there aren't enough switches in here. This must be an interior system for this wing only. There are no diagrams, so I'll just turn them all off."

She watched as he flipped the toggles and closed the box with a flourish. There was a bit of the old Scott in his grin.

"Okay, let's go open that office."

She stood behind him as he squatted before the office door, trying the keys. Within the office, the venetian blinds to the west had been left open, and the sun was sending long streamers of yellowish light across the dark green carpeting. The bright light spilling across the desktops brought into bold illumination the light film of dust on their surfaces, giving the whole office an air of neglect.

The bolt slid back with a click.

"At last!" Scott said. "I think things are beginning to go our way."

Inside the office, Scott waved in the direction of the desks.

"Check the file cabinets, Liz. Try to find out something about this place. I'll go into the inner office and call the cops. No point in being overheard."

Elizabeth watched as he closed the door behind him. She opened a file drawer, but before she could examine its files, Scott stuck his head out of the small room.

"Jesus, everything is against us. I found the control panel for the front gate, but it operates on codes that have to be punched in. We can't do anything with it. Incidentally, you'll have to call from out there. Ask the operator for the sheriff's number. I'll search through the desk here."

She pushed the file drawer shut, turning to find the phone. The near desk had very little on it and certainly no phone. She switched her attention to the second desk. It was more cluttered, but there was no phone. Despair overwhelmed her. There wouldn't be a phone. She raced about the room in a futile search. She was right. There were no telephones.

As she backed across the office, she noticed loose coils of white cord partially hidden under one of the desks. The cord terminated in a bare phone plug.

She stepped into the inner office where Scott was examining one of the open file drawers. His face brightened.

"What did they say? How long is it going to be?"

She shook her head, not wanting to put it into words. She did not need to.

His shoulders sagged. "Like in here, huh? The phones have been taken away."

He slammed his fist down onto the metal cabinet. "They are smarter than we are, aren't they? One step ahead of us in everything."

He pointed at the files. "Most of these files are full of patients' histories, but there's one with building blueprints in it. We have to find out how to unplug the perimeter circuits. You look through it. Maybe you can find the answer. After all, your husband was an architect."

"But, Scott, I didn't know anything about his business—absolutely nothing."

"Damn it, do what the hell I ask you. My God, we've got to get out of here."

She choked off an angry reply when she saw how close he was to going over the edge. He watched her for a moment before disappearing into the outer room.

Fifteen minutes later, she was sitting at the desk, staring forlornly at an incomprehensible wiring plan, acutely aware that the room was growing darker and that the sunlight streaming into the office was a bright orange.

She looked up, startled to see Scott standing in the doorway, holding a colorful brochure in his hand. She waited for him to speak, but he seemed beyond words.

"What's wrong? What is it?"

He flipped the pamphlet onto the desk, took a deep breath, and blurted out, "Elizabeth, we're in an insane asylum!"

CHAPTER 16

S tunned, she looked at him, shaking her head, begging, "No, Scott. Oh, please, no. It can't be."

He slapped the pamphlet down on the desk. "It's true. Read it."

The brochure was a slick professional production suggesting money and stability and loaded with euphemistic language, beginning with a sprightly tale of how Dr. Caudill had named the institute after a meteorite that fell in the area in 1923. The rest of the text hammered home the themes of anonymity and security. The interior panel of the brochure proclaimed Skystone ready to enfold all those who chose "in their golden years to seek the sylvan glades of privacy where they can meditate upon life's great lessons, untroubled by trivial family demands."

She read it over a second time before glancing sharply at Scott, puzzled at how he could find such sinister meaning in the words. He yanked the pamphlet from her hands and, turning it to the last fold, tapped the single paragraph. She read, "Skystone maintains a counseling staff for those that struggle to cope with the extraordinary demands in life. The staff is trained to provide comfort and safety for psychiatric participants. The most modern technological devices are employed to ensure the inviolability of our guests."

She closed the pamphlet, laid it on the desk, and stared at it. "No, Scott. We're reading too much into this. How could it be? These rooms aren't designed for that kind of patient. Maybe it means some sort of counseling for the elderly."

"Elizabeth, beyond the red door—that is what's beyond the red door. The other wing of the building—it's a madhouse."

She refused to meet his gaze. "Don't use that word. Many people see psychiatrists. It sounds horrible. You must be wrong . . . you have to be wrong."

"Look at me, Elizabeth. Why do you think this place is in an isolated area like this? Why does it have such elaborate security? We wondered why that door is built like a bank vault. Well, now we know."

He unfolded the pamphlet and, pointing to it, said, "The cost averages four thousand dollars a month. That's forty-eight thousand a year. This place is for the rich. It's where they hide family members that embarrass them—that are old and senile or that are raving mad. Oh, yes, this is a madhouse!"

Roughly, he pulled her to her feet, and she protested, "Scott, for God's sake, calm down! This isn't helping."

"Damn it. Can't you see now what happened? Somebody with a grudge—maybe an ex-patient—came in here and killed everybody, patients and staff. Or . . . or maybe one of the maniacs got loose and killed them. It doesn't matter. They are dead either way."

"But why not us? Why weren't we killed?"

"Maybe they didn't know we were here. Maybe they knew we were outsiders."

"But that doesn't make sense. Why . . ."

He struck his open palm against the side of his head several times. "Please quit asking so Goddamned many questions. I don't know the answers. Just do what I tell you. Go to your room while I try to find some food. I'm going to bring Meredith to your room. We'll hole up there. Sooner or later, somebody will get curious and come. There are grocery orders not being placed, phone calls not being made. It can't be too long before somebody comes to check."

She stared at him in bewilderment. "Meredith? You know where Meredith is? But why didn't you tell—"

"There's just one place she can be. Damn it, she has to be there."

"Where, Scott?"

Reaching past her, he snapped off the light in the office. The sun was below the horizon now, and it was growing quite dark.

He leaned close to her ear. "It's obvious where she is, Elizabeth. She's in the locked room you found at the end of this hall—room eight. Meredith is a lot sharper than you or I. She must have suspected right away that something was wrong, locked herself in, and plugged the keyhole."

"Then why don't we just get her?"

By now they were out of the office and standing in the corridor. His voice was a fierce whisper. "No! Listen to me. I want you safely in your room with enough food for us to wait it out. Then I'll go for her."

"But why get her last?"

"Because Meredith isn't going to open the door until she knows it's me, so I'll have to raise my voice. Maybe the killer is still lurking around here somewhere. Remember the guy in white we saw by the gate this afternoon? We may have to make a run for it. You have the door ready, and as soon as we are inside your room, we'll barricade it."

They stopped by the double doors that led into the inner corridor and peered through the glass panes. The distant glow of fluorescent light from the nurses' station revealed a hall still deserted. Elizabeth paused in the red glow of the exit light by room 8, but Scott pulled her past the door. He led her into her room, but as he turned to go, she reached for him.

She threw her arms around his waist, frightened by a sudden premonition. "Please . . . don't leave me alone . . . I don't like it. We'll have a better chance if we stick together."

Awkwardly, he struggled out of her embrace. "My God, Liz, don't you understand? I love her."

She could see his face in the dim light, his lips trembling

as he tried to suppress his emotions. "I . . . I can't live without her . . . I don't want to. It's for me to find Meredith and bring her back here safely. Now do what I ask . . . I beg you."

Her eyes teared at the sight of his naked emotion. "Good luck, Scott. Be careful."

He was not gone long, but in the short interval, the twilight had vanished and it had become difficult to see the stand of trees beyond the lawn. She drew the curtains and was debating whether to turn on the light when Scott reentered the room, limping badly, struggling to hold a large cardboard box with his one good arm. He did his best to sound cheerful.

"Hey, Santa Claus is here. There wasn't a lot of canned stuff, but I found some processed meat and canned fruit. What bread I located was as hard as a rock, so I brought some crackers. Here are some big bottles of cola, too. We can ice down the lavatory with ice from the ice machine."

Quickly, they ate some of the processed meat and crackers. There was the temptation to keep eating, but they knew the food might have to last for several days.

After they finished, not wanting to ask the question, she said, "Scott, did you hear anything . . . notice anything different?"

In the faint light, she saw him shake his head.

He slumped against the wall, saying nothing. The one brief flash of the old Scott, youthful and exuberant, was gone. When he spoke, hopelessness clung to each word.

"Elizabeth, you know why I put off looking for Meredith, don't you?"

It was not a question that sought an answer.

"It's because I'm afraid I'll find her dead, like the others. Oh, God, I can't stand the thought of that. I keep telling myself that she's locked in that room, scared, hoping one of us will come for her. I'm so afraid."

She knew that what she was saying was madness. "Go ahead, Scott. Go look for her. You have to know, don't you?"

He pushed away from the wall, and she caught at his arm.

"Leave the key to the room with me. I . . . I think I'd better lock myself in."

"I can't do that. I may need it if we get trapped on the way back. There's just the one master key for the patients' rooms. I know because I checked the other keys on some of the locks when I went for food. I don't think I'd better lock you in because if . . . if something happens to me, you wouldn't be able to get out. Just keep the door closed. If Meredith is in here, it won't take long to bring her back."

Elizabeth clutched at him as he started for the door. "Scott, maybe you—"

"No, I've got to do it my way."

He was out the door before she could remonstrate further. She closed it softly behind him.

It was full dark outside when Elizabeth sank down on the hospital bed and looked at the console clock: it was 7:22.

For a while she sat, staring bleakly into the darkness, willing the door to open on Scott and Meredith. She fought against the awareness that too much time was passing. Unwillingly, she turned to look at the clock again. It read 7:43. Scott had been gone twenty-one minutes.

Eight o'clock found Elizabeth twisting the sheet back and forth in her damp hands, her mind in turmoil. A terrifying feeling that Scott was dead was overwhelming her. She wanted to believe that he had found some clue in room 8 that had led him outside into the night. Dear God, how she wanted to believe that, but she knew it wasn't so. He would have come back and told her what he planned. No, poor Scott was dead like all the others. She was the only one left.

Finally, at 8:40, she knew she had to do something before she went crazy. She thought of the bottles of cola. Quickly, she emptied the meager food supplies from the cardboard box so she could use it to carry ice from the ice machine to the lavatory. Irrationality was the child of fear. If she iced the cola for Scott and Meredith, then surely they would have to come back to drink it.

Elizabeth leaned out into the hall, looking toward room 8. It was impossible to see if the door was open. She looked in the other direction. The stainless steel of the ice machine gleamed softly in the corner of the hall.

When she reached the ice machine, she placed the flimsy pasteboard box on the floor and squatted next to it to load the ice. From the corner of her eye, she could see down the other hallway. Something seemed odd. For a moment she was puzzled. Then she saw what it was.

The red door was open, perhaps no more than an inch, but it was open. Whatever it imprisoned was loose.

Terrified, she remained on her knees, feeling for the lid of the ice machine, afraid now to show that she had noticed the door but unwilling to turn away. She tried to tell herself she would be safe if she refused to recognize that it was ajar. She wanted to turn her back—to ignore it—but it was as if she was paralyzed. She remained on her haunches, covertly watching the red door. She raised her arm, feeling for the lid of the ice machine.

Reaching over the rim, she fumbled for the ice. Gathering a handful of small icy cubes, she put them, as quietly as possible, into the box. Her gaze never left the red door. She could swear it was moving ever so slightly, even as she watched. She reached into the ice machine again, burrowing into the packed ice. Before she could react, her hand had slipped across stiff fingers and was gripping a cold hand.

It seemed to clutch at her own hand as she shot to her feet. She stared down at the corpse of Scott Sutherlin under a scattering of ice cubes. She shrieked and pushed her clenched fist hard against her mouth, trying to stifle her screams.

Scott had been crammed into the narrow confines of his icy tomb, his distorted face with its protruding eyes glaring at Elizabeth. Around his neck, tightly twisted, was a cotton hospital gown like the one she wore under the uniform. She whirled away to shield herself from the machine's terrible burden.

Dr. Mainwaring was standing a few yards away, his hand lifted to placate her. She felt another scream welling up into her throat and fought against it, realizing instinctively the need to be quiet.

He begged, "Please . . . don't make that noise. I'm not going to hurt you. I've had chances, haven't I? Have I hurt you? You must be quiet . . . listen to me."

He took another step toward her, and Elizabeth recoiled against the cold side of the dreadful ice machine.

Watching her, Mainwaring coaxed, "No, my dear, no. I just want to talk. You must understand me—believe in me. I'm sure you realize by now what has happened here. These people around us are insane. If I am to keep the two of us alive, you must do as I say. You must keep out of harm's way."

"You . . . you're a doctor? You're not one of them?"

He shook his head slowly, almost sadly, and continued to move closer, so close now that he could touch her. She found herself relaxing despite her terror.

"No, I'm not one of them. But they have the power of life and death here. You mustn't provoke them before we can get away. Let me take you to your room . . . please. You must not attract their attention. I'll tell you everything that has happened and what we have to do to stay alive."

He slid his arm around her shoulders, and though her flesh cringed under his touch, she accepted it.

"Good girl! You poor child, look at me. It's going to be all right. The young man in the icebox did a very stupid thing, but it's going to be all right. Now, let's get out of sight before they see us."

Elizabeth yielded to the insistent pressure of his arm, wanting to believe that she had found a protector.

They moved down the hallway. Behind them, beyond their line of sight, the red door stirred.

CHAPTER 17

obb Kendall stared across the sergeant's desk at the dingy wall, the telephone receiver tight against his ear. He could see Emmaline, the daytime county radio dispatcher, smiling at him from her cubicle as she always did when Margaret called. His attention snapped back to his wife's soft voice. It held that inflection, the combination of pleading and hope, that tore him apart.

"I know I should have reminded you earlier, honey. It's just that I was afraid I would be like a little girl asking Santa Claus if he was coming to visit on Christmas Day and him saying no." She laughed nervously. "Now, isn't that silly? I . . . I just finished decorating your cake, but Wilhelmina says that she isn't going to prepare a big dinner unless she's sure you are coming home. . . ."

"Margaret, I've told you this a dozen times. I have to know beforehand when I need time off. This is a small department. Every time I take off, it puts the monkey on somebody else's back. It isn't fair."

She was silent for a moment, and then the pleading grew more abject. "But, darling, your birthday! You know I always have something for your birthday. I've been talking about it for two weeks. I didn't even intend to call you until

Wilhelmina started grumbling. Please, I'm sure the sheriff and the other men will understand. I wanted this to be something special with us."

Emmaline was watching him again. He spoke as quietly as he could. "Margaret, I'm sorry. I don't mean to hurt your feelings, but it's impossible. I can't afford to take the time off. We have something important going on here."

"Oh, Cobb. Is it anything to do with those poor women?"

"We haven't found a trace of Madeleine Turner or her car, and Toby is raising holy hell about it. My theory is that she got tired of Benton being away so much and took off, but Toby won't bother to check it out. We have bigger problems than Madeleine Turner. There's something fishy going on out at Skystone, and I can't get Toby to move off his rear end about it. I have to go, Margaret. I'm sorry about tonight."

He heard her sigh. "It's not your fault, baby. It's mine for taking it for granted. Listen . . . the cake's fixed, so I'll leave it out on the table. When you get home—I don't care what time of night it is—you wake me, and we'll cut it. Okay?"

"We'll see, Margaret. I have to get off the phone."

"I love you, Cobb . . . always."

He lowered the receiver and felt the rage flare through him. He couldn't understand how life could be so damned unfair. He rested his head against his forearms, his eyes closed, unaware that the inquisitive Emmaline was watching him, her brows showing her perplexity.

Cobb did not know how much longer he could take it. He was being torn apart—emotionally and mentally.

He and Margaret had been married for ten years. They had been childhood sweethearts who grew up together in Stoneville. Cobb had spent three years on the New Orleans police force in what amounted to an apprenticeship before they were married. Margaret had insisted that they live in their hometown, and since Toby Mears was her uncle, Cobb was quickly offered a job by the Sheriff Department.

It had been a good if not ideal marriage. Margaret was very social, very outgoing, while Cobb tended to be introspective, caught up in his police work—which he saw as a never-ending struggle of good against evil with no compromises. Though he would not have admitted it, he had been enormously pleased with his wife's popularity. It seemed to him that Margaret was active in every social activity in town.

When they found themselves with just each other for company, she would look at him with a degree of unrest, wishing that he could be more unbending. Still, the community found them to be a most acceptable young couple; and the marriage settled, as all good marriages do, into an unstrained relationship.

When disaster struck, it had been complete and without warning. Cobb had gone to Mobile, Alabama, to pick up a prisoner. He was awakened in his motel room that morning at two-thirty with the news that Margaret had been severely injured in an automobile accident. He rushed home in open defiance of the speed limits, arriving the next afternoon to find her condition stabilized, though she was paralyzed below the waist.

It was a bizarre accident. The Kendall car had come around a curve to find a loose cow standing in the middle of the road. Margaret swerved, but the car struck the rear of the cow. The impact had sent the vehicle tumbling down a steep, brush-covered embankment, out of sight of the road.

The first week had been a nightmare for Cobb as Margaret fought for her life. The second week was no better. He had watched helplessly as it dawned on her that she was paralyzed for life. It was thirteen days before he read the police report on the incident and ingested the first dram of the suspicion that was to poison his life.

The county road where the accident had occurred was so lightly traveled at night that it was likely it would have been some time in the morning before the accident was discovered, had not a peculiar incident occurred. Margaret might well have been dead by that time. It was as fortunate for her as it was unfortunate for her marriage that the Sheriff's Department had received an anonymous phone call about the wreck soon after it occurred. A male adult had called, giving not only the specific location of the accident but adding that the victim had been thrown clear and was unconscious. The call must have been made within minutes of the accident, for when the police and ambulance arrived, the car's engine was still warm.

The odd call disturbed Cobb enough that he had asked the other deputies if they had any idea who made it. He was tempted to talk to Margaret about it, even though she had been unconscious after the crash.

The seed took root about a week and a half later. It was a slow, hot day in town, with only an occasional pedestrian wandering down the walks under the porches of the old-fashioned stores. Cobb was standing in the shaded doorway of the sheriff's office, shirttail out, trying to catch any stray air current that might pass. Outside, sitting on a bench on the sidewalk, shaded by the huge maple tree overhead, was Tip Crable, a young deputy.

Guiltily, Cobb began to stuff his shirt into his pants when he heard someone addressing Tip. It was Mace Bellman, the local barber.

"Well, Tip, is it hot enough for you today?"

"It sure as hell is. What are you doing out of the shop, Mace? Closed for the day?"

"Yep. When it gets this hot, people don't come in to get their hair cut—don't matter how shabby it is. By the way, how's Cobb doing?"

"Cobb?"

"Yeah, Cobb. I mean . . . it must have been an awful big shock to that boy."

"Well, I guess he's doing all right. It hasn't been easy, though, I guarantee you."

There was a pause in the conversation, and though he couldn't see Mace, Cobb knew what he was doing. The barber was lighting the corncob pipe that he always puffed while he was walking along Main Street.

"Well, it's a real shame. Margaret sure is a pretty little thing. Of course, I think the town believes it was as much his doing as hers."

"His doing? What in the hell are you talking about?"

Mace chuckled nastily. "Well, I always say, when you turn a young mare out to pasture, somebody is going to ride her if you don't watch out. You don't think Margaret Kendall was out there that time of night by herself, do you, Tip?"

Cobb's ears rang with the words, and before he knew what he was doing he was out on the walk, grabbing Mace Bellman by his shirtfront. "You miserable son of a bitch! If you ever open your mouth about my wife again, I'll beat you to death."

The pipe had fallen from Mace's mouth, leaving a trail of ashes and glowing bits of tobacco down the front of his white shirt. He was deadly pale, and Tip was on his feet, trying to pull Cobb away. The old man was repeating himself, his voice quavering. "I'm sorry . . . I'm sorry."

Finally, Tip wrestled Cobb away from him, shouting, "For God's sake, Mace, get out of here!"

The fury left Cobb at the sight of the frightened old man lurching down the sidewalk in headlong flight.

Cobb's voice was icy cold. "Get your hands off me, Tip. I'm okay."

Without another word, he walked back into the station and never spoke about the incident again.

The next day, Tip tried to talk to him about it, but he had no more than opened his mouth when Cobb looked up, his eyes glittering, and said, "Shut up!"

He never confronted Margaret with his doubts. From time to time over the next two years, he would ask her with studied casualness why she had been out that night. The question came at unexpected moments, asked in different ways, but always it was the same question. Why had she been out that night? The answer was as consistent as the question. She had been unable to sleep, had felt strangely restless, and had decided to go for a late-night drive. It was something she had never felt the need to do before.

During the first months of her recovery, he fought the urge to lay his suspicions before her, to relieve the growing pain bottled within him, yet he couldn't. He was not insensitive to the terrible demons with which she struggled. Despite the brutal finality of the doctor's words, she clung for a while to the foolish hope that she would walk again. As that hope vanished, she tried to convince herself that there was a place for a Margaret Kendall who would always be dependent on others and who would never again move through her little world with that bouncy walk of hers.

The intensity of his anguish could not be maintained, and with time it had dwindled. Cobb, a puritan at heart, was beginning to look at Margaret with a smug satisfaction that she was paying, and paying dearly, for what she had done. But as quickly as these thoughts would bloom in his mind, remorse would engulf him, a shame that he could convict her in his mind with evidence that would be laughed out of any court of law.

Now, four years later, he did his best not to think of those things that prompted the pain—the need to hurt, the remorse. He had built a wall between them against which she beat futilely. Cobb vented his anger against the world that conducted itself in such a way that he could have his doubts. It was a wall built of frustration and had grown to the point that it threatened his sanity. When it seemed he would crack, he had found some process within his mind that served as a safety valve to the pressure. He had no idea of how it worked, but for the past two years he had ridden a roller coaster of ups and downs with which he could cope.

Cobb lifted his head as the telephone buzzer sounded. Looking up, he saw Emmaline mouth the words, "For you."

It was Tip Crable, the same young deputy who had heard Mace Bellman's accusation four years ago. "Cobb, this is Tip. Is Toby around?"

"Nope. I don't expect him in before noon. Why, Tip?"

"I've got a man with me I believe you'd like to chat with. I don't think you'd want Toby to overhear him, though."

"What in hell are you talking about?"

"I was visiting my brother this morning—the one that's a cop over in Ducktown. He responded to a prowler call last night at old lady Barkley's place. They found a fellow—a vagrant—up in the hayloft of her barn. They threw him in jail overnight just to roust him up a little. They were going to turn him loose about eleven.

"It seems he was over near Skystone Monday night. The reason Jimmy knew that was because this bum asked him what all the excitement was about. He saw our patrol car turn into Skystone. It might not be a bad idea to talk to him about that ambulance, Cobb."

"You say they have him there right now?"

"Well, they must have released him by now, but that dude couldn't have gotten far walking, and nobody around here would give him a ride. I can have him here in thirty minutes. What do you say?"

Cobb hesitated. "I don't know. We don't have a charge against him."

"Hell, this ain't going to take no charge. This sucker will do anything you tell him to."

Forty minutes later, Cobb, figuring it was about time for Tip and the vagrant to arrive, went into Emmaline's cubicle. After asking her a couple of short questions, he ducked out, closing the door behind him. He was under no illusions about her loyalty to Toby.

The transient was an emaciated man in his early thirties, with long, unkempt black hair falling to his shoulders. His eyes, under the heavy black brows, had burned out, and his face had the lines of a much older man's. He made no effort to hide the old needle tracks that dotted his arms. When he saw Cobb looking, he said, "I'm clean now, copper."

The vagrant started on his story without much prompting. His name was Bertram Cutts. On Monday morning, driven to shelter by the hard rain, he had ducked into an abandoned barn several miles beyond Skystone. He had found little warmth and many leaks. Finally, shivering violently and disgusted, he had packed his gear and left, determined to walk through the night until he found a decent shelter.

Whatever else he was, Bertram was a good witness. He had been less than two miles from Skystone when the big Cadillac thundered past him like "a black bat out of hell." He was within a few hundred feet of Skystone's gates when he saw the flashing emergency lights of a vehicle coming toward him at high speed. Bertram's life had been such that he headed for cover when he saw flashing lights. He had been close enough to see clearly as the ambulance pulled into the drive, sat there for perhaps a minute before the gates were opened, and then disappeared inside.

Bertram, despite the cold and the lingering mist, had felt a need to answer a call of nature at that moment. By the time he was again on the road and walking, the second vehicle with a flashing red dome light that spelled *cop* to Bertram was approaching. Hunkered down in the wet, clinging weeds, he watched the police car disappear through the gate.

Bertram knew he had the deputies' interest and decided to play his trump card. He smiled at Cobb. "Gentlemen, all this talk has made me so dry I can hardly go on. I don't suppose there's a bit of . . . er . . . spirits about that might alleviate my thirst."

After regarding him steadily for a moment, Cobb left the room. He grabbed a paper cup from the bottled-water dispenser and entered Toby's office. From the lower desk drawer, he extracted the always present bottle of bourbon and poured a hefty double jigger into the cup. Back in the sergeants' office, he watched as the aromatic Bertram belted down the three ounces of whiskey in two swallows.

Cobb's tone was as grim as his look. "Okay, buddy-boy, that's your pay. Now get on with your story."

Bertram nodded and flashed him a smile as big as it was insincere.

"Somewhat piqued with curiosity, I walked up to the gates. I tried to make out the name over the gates, but it was too dark. Then I noted an odd construction to the stone pillars supporting the gates. Each of them had a squarish niche in its front that runs all the way from the capstone to the bottom. It was wide enough to sit down in if you kinda rolled in a ball, and it provided a blessed relief from the wind. I must have dozed off, because I didn't hear the one car coming back down the driveway. The sound of somebody opening the gate awoke me. I wanted to run, but it was too late. Besides, I didn't think they would notice me, tucked into that niche. Actually, somebody did point a flashlight in that direction, but I was out of sight. A police car—one painted like the one you brought me here in—drove out, and I heard the gates being locked again.

"The scare I got did wake me up, though. I must have stayed awake for at least an hour. Then, just as I was dozing off, another cop car drove in, stayed maybe twenty minutes, and left."

Cobb nodded. "Right—that was me."

The vagrant ignored the interruption. "Finally, I went to sleep, and the next thing I knew the cold light of dawn—and I do mean cold—was breaking."

Cobb was watching him closely. "How about the third vehicle—the ambulance."

"Ambulance?"

"Are you saying that no ambulance came out?"

"That's right. Nothing else came out. What's the big deal? I thought ambulances stay at hospitals."

"Maybe it came out after you went to sleep."

Bertram grinned slyly. "My friend, when you live the life I do, you soon learn to sleep lightly. I guarantee you I would have heard anything coming out that gate."

Tip leaned forward. "You mean you didn't hear any vehicle except the two sheriff's cars?"

"Officer, I didn't say that. The wind was blowing from that direction. I said no other vehicles came out. Yes, I heard another car. It started, backed up, and then drove forward. As a matter of fact, the headlights swung in my direction. Then it stopped. It must have stayed there ten minutes or so—maybe more—with the lights on and the engine running. Then it backed up again and went off in some other direction. The lights disappeared, but I heard the motor running for a while, growing fainter. Then I heard nothing but the wind until the second cop car came."

"And you will swear that the ambulance never came out that gate."

Bertram, relaxed by the hefty shot of whiskey, laughed happily. "What's the matter? Has the local heat misplaced its ambulance?"

Cobb looked at Tip. "Toby will never stand still for holding this creep as a material witness. The best we can do is get his statement on tape. When you get through, give him the rest of the whiskey from Toby's desk, and replace it with a fresh bottle. He keeps several in the closet. Then run this bird up the road a couple of miles and dump him . . . okay?"

When Tip returned, he found Cobb sitting on the bench before the office. After rolling down the car windows to rid the car of the olfactory evidence that Bertram had left behind, Tip stopped in front of the bench.

"What in the hell are you doing out here in the cold, Cobb?"

"Thinking."

Cobb continued to stare at the cirrus clouds high over Stoneville, while Tip shuffled his feet nervously. When this produced no effect, he cleared his throat several times and dropped onto the bench beside Cobb.

"Well, what did you make of his story, Cobb?"

"It confirms what I've thought all along. The ambulance never left. God, what do we have to do before we can get Toby to act? Who really knows what goes on at Skystone? They're immune to the law. Did the Johnsons see something they shouldn't? Toby should be on his way out there this minute."

"You're damned right, Cobb. Six women have been killed around Stoneville here in the last two years without a clue. Now the Turner woman disappears, and the Johnson boys are missing. But what can you do about it?"

Cobb rose. "Forget about the Turner woman until we check for a boyfriend. I'll tell you what I'm going to do: when Toby gets here, I'm going to get this ambulance thing settled."

Tip bounced to his feet. "Damn it, you can count on me. I'll go in with you to back up what that bum said."

"I appreciate that. I really do."

Toby Mears had dominated county politics for so long that he no longer bothered to make excuses for the mornings he took off to go squirrel hunting. When he arrived an hour later, Cobb gave him fifteen minutes to settle down before he rapped on the office door.

The double-barreled Remington stood in the corner, and Toby was seated at his desk, comfortable in his camouflaged hunting gear and L. L. Bean boots. He gave Tip no more than a cursory glance before he transfixed Cobb with a baleful look.

"Okay, Cobb, spill it. I can tell you have a hair up your ass. I want to get out to the house and wash up. I knew damned good and well I shouldn't have stopped by here on the way home. Go on, boy. Speak up!"

Cobb had suffered through too many encounters with Toby to be disturbed by his opening thrust. He grimaced at Tip and settled down in the chair facing Toby. He looked at the sheriff without a trace of a smile.

"Bad day, huh? What was it—no squirrels, or shaky hands?"

Toby tried to stop himself from frowning. He did not care for the shaky-hands remark. He wondered what the surly, self-righteous son of a bitch was trying to tell him—that he thought he was too old or drinking too much? He had never cared much for Cobb, but the boy had two things going for him. He was married to Margaret, for whom Toby would have done anything, and second, he was the best lawman Toby had ever seen. He saw right through the bullshit the local punks tried to put out. He was like a bulldog when he got on a case. Still, they were going to have a private chat soon about his mouth.

Toby grinned weakly. "No, I was worrying about what was happening with the people I left in charge here. Now, what's your problem?"

Cobb looked at Tip. "You tell him. He always accuses me of dramatizing."

A stolid Toby sat without interruption and heard Tip through. When he finished, Toby looked at Cobb.

"So you're still dancing to that tune, eh, Cobb? The mad doctors at Skystone made off with our ambulance and the Johnson boys. Well, let me tell you something. I just had a call from that one doctor—not the guy who owns the place, but one of the others, that...ah...Mainwaring—the one we talked to yesterday. He did some checking with the staff.

"If you ask me, them damned Johnsons were acting peculiar last night. He said they were getting kinda high-spirited out there. As a matter of fact, the head doctor, Caudill, finally asked them to leave. Mainwaring said they were disturbing the accident victims. One of them Johnsons came out with a smart-ass remark. He said something about the only thing that kept them in business were Yankees that didn't know how to drive. They started laughing so hard that he had the orderly put them out.

"Let me give you a little something to think about. You know Orville Johnson is kin to them, and he's the biggest bootlegger in this county. Maybe them boys got themselves mixed up with something back in the hills that they couldn't handle. Well, Cobb? What have you got to say about that?"

"Toby, you know as well as I do that neither of those boys has ever had a drop to drink. They haven't been in any worse scrapes than other boys growing up in this town. I'm telling you, that ambulance never left Skystone. What we need is a search warrant."

Toby turned red. "You listen to me, Cobb, and you listen well. You, too, Tip. In the last two years, six defenseless women have been killed in this jurisdiction. The press treated the first two as insignificant local cases. They were nice women—fine little ladies—and nothing was made of it. But after the third murder, a reporter showed up from Little Rock. Last January, after the fourth one, reporters came from Memphis, Saint Louis, and New Orleans. After Elaine Ritchey was murdered in August, we had four television crews here. Now you say Mrs. Turner has run off from her husband. You find me the boyfriend. You find me one person that can say she and Benton were on the outs."

"Listen, I—"

"You shut up while I'm talking. You started to get a burr under your saddle regarding Skystone about a year and a half ago. Just sly little digs, but I noticed. So did a lot of other people in town. Judge Lynch got wind of it, and so did the county commissioners. Now, with no evidence whatsoever beyond the ramblings of a drunk vagrant you want me to search a hospital full of elderly and emotionally disturbed people, looking for an ambulance that could be anywhere."

"I don't think that's very—"

"In the meanwhile, what are you doing about this maniac that has Beauregard County petrified with fear—that is giving this county a black eye on national TV? You haven't come up with one solid lead yet. Your only contribution has been an unauthorized crime-prevention scheme that has made the county look ridiculous. You have stopped nineteen women driving alone on county roads at night and ordered them—not suggested, but ordered them—to go home; in some cases, even followed them home. That's nineteen you entered on your log sheets. God knows if there are more. Of those nineteen, seven have complained. They want to know what constitutional authority you have to do that, and, Cobb Kendall, I didn't have an answer.

"But maybe I'm being unfair. Tell me. Just what have you found out about this sick bastard?"

He whirled toward Tip. "*What*, Tip? The cat has Cobb's tongue. Everybody in the department receives briefings."

"But it's not my case, Toby. I—"

"It doesn't matter whose case it is. You know as much as anybody else. Tell me what we know about this maniac."

"Shoot, Sheriff! I feel silly telling you what you already know."

When Cobb saw the storm clouds gathering on Toby's brows, he intervened: "We know that these women were beaten—savagely beaten. They were struck so often it is obvious the killer was possessed by a maniacal rage. Some of the bodies bore evidence of strangulation, but there was no indication of sexual molestation on any of them. They all drove away with the killer, abandoning their cars. They were all killed where their bodies were found. The first one was located out in Blake's Woods on Mill Valley Road. Three others were found in isolated barns or outbuildings. Two of them were taken back to their own houses. All were younger women. In each case, the victim's car was found abandoned alongside the road. There were no signs of a struggle around the vehicles, so they must have entered the killer's car willingly.

"We questioned the folks living around where the cars were found, but we haven't had any luck. We questioned most of the husbands of the victims and they had alibis—at least, we couldn't place them on the scene. We dug up a couple of boyfriends, but we didn't have any better luck there. The only common denominator among these women was that they were alone, making them easy pickings for the killer. It takes time, Sheriff. Someday we'll get a break and—"

"Takes time, hell!" the sheriff cut in. "You damned right it takes time when you have people lollygagging around trying to make tigers out of pussycats.

"You listen to me, Cobb! You ought to thank your lucky stars Judge Lynch is in Europe on vacation. The Judge has done a damn fine job of making sure Skystone and the people of Stoneville get along together. If the businessmen in this town found out that you're trying to stir up trouble with Skystone, they'd be after your ass. Don't fool yourself! Just because you don't see the Skystone people on our streets, don't think they're not important economically to this town."

Cobb looked at him, his face hard. "What does that mean, Toby? We have to sacrifice victims to them?"

"Don't interrupt me, Cobb. This is a poor county, and Skystone puts more money into the county than any other single business. They order special foods through our grocers. Most folks in this town never even heard of some of them foods. Our local merchants make a mint off of it. We special-order fancy sheets for them. Hell, they buy hundreds of sheets and blankets and towels. They are rich people out there, and they spend like rich people. All they ask in return is not to be bothered. Hell, there are even a couple of local people working out there: Gladys Mueller—she's a cook— and Ike Brown. You've known Ike's family all your life. Do you think he would put up with working at Skystone if there was anything wrong with it? Answer me!"

"Maybe he doesn't know what's going on," Cobb mumbled.

"Maybe, maybe, maybe! Hell, you live here. Open your ears. Women in this town are afraid to go out at night. These are people you grew up with. They want help. They need your protection. Now, you quit chasing straws." Abruptly, Toby shot upright out of his chair. "I'm going home!" The sheriff, looking annoyed, grabbed his shotgun from the corner and stormed out the door.

The two deputies remained seated, with Cobb trying to rid

himself of his anger and Tip wondering about his job security.

The silence was broken by an ancient voice. "Cobb?"

Alex Knox was standing in the doorway.

Alex surely had some claim to being the world's oldest deputy. He was a white-haired man with rimless glasses perched on his hawklike nose. His dentures, ill-fitting on his shrinking gums, provided their own rhythmic accompaniment as he spoke. His voluminous pants were suspended from his frail shoulders by wide red suspenders from another era. Toby, a sympathetic man, had retained Alex decades past his usefulness.

"Cobb, I couldn't help hearing you and Toby. To tell the truth, a man could have stood out in the middle of the street and heard what you two were saying. Maybe you ought to have a chat with Dr. Witherspoon."

Tip looked impatiently at the elderly man. "Just who in the hell is Dr. Witherspoon? I've never heard of him."

"He worked at Skystone until about two weeks ago. Andy Witherspoon was born and raised here."

Cobb's eyes were bright with interest. "How could he help us, Alex?"

"I heard someone say that Doc Witherspoon and that Caudill fellow got into a scrap, and Doc flat-out quit. He had been out there since Caudill opened the place about twelve years ago."

Alex Knox had Cobb's complete attention now.

"I knew the Witherspoons to speak to them, Alex. They kind of kept to themselves, but I didn't know there was a doctor in the family."

"He's quite a bit older than you, Cobb, but he's not as old as me. He never did practice medicine here. He did his doctoring down in Fort Smith. I heard folks say that Caudill wanted somebody known in these parts to help him get started smoothly when he opened Skystone. I never saw Andy in town but two or three times. Of course, his mama and daddy are dead. He was an only child."

"You're damned right I'd like to talk to him. Where is he living, Alex?"

"He's staying at his mama and daddy's farm. He leased

the land, but there's another house on the place. I hear he moved in and is fixing it up."

His last words were addressed at Cobb's back, as the lawman was disappearing through the door.

Tip shrugged, and tapped the ancient deputy on the shoulder. "Alex, if I were you, I'd forget about this conversation when I talked to Toby."

CHAPTER 18_____

T he small white house glistened under a fresh coat of paint. It was the centerpiece in a tranquil setting of plowed fields, but the hammering issuing from inside the house was at odds with the quiet Arkansas morning. Cobb waited for a moment beside the car, wondering if the house's occupant had heard him. The hammering ceased, only to be followed by the whine of a power saw.

Cobb climbed the porch steps and paused at the open door. "Hey, is anybody here?"

The power saw wound down as if it were embarrassed to be caught in such a shrill mood, and a masculine voice called, "Just a minute . . . be right there."

Dr. Andrew Witherspoon was as short as any of the diminutive Witherspoon clan. He could not have been more than five-five, with a slender build. His thick hair, mostly white now—save for a last outpost of dark brown on top—was combed back from his forehead. He wore work jeans and a T-shirt. The doctor lent some credence to the aphorism that people, like wine, grow better with age. He exuded an air of youthful dynamism.

Appearing in the doorway, he cocked his head to the side. "I don't know what it is, officer, but I didn't do it."

Cobb, somewhat intimidated by an energy he had not expected in a man of Witherspoon's years, formally extended his hand. "Dr. Witherspoon? I'm Cobb Kendall. I don't think we've ever met."

"You must be Larry Kendall's boy. I remember Larry well."

Cobb and the doctor meandered through a few minutes of polite conversation until Witherspoon stopped in mid-sentence. "Sergeant, I don't think you came out here in uniform to chitchat. Come on into my study. At least I have that fixed up. It's the first room a doctor puts to order when he moves into new quarters. Let's hear what your problem is."

Seated across the desk from Andy Witherspoon, Cobb told the story of the missing ambulance, the circumstances that had brought it to Skystone, and Bertram Cutt's claim that it never left.

When he finished, the doctor eyed him shrewdly, sizing him up. "You don't care very much for Skystone, do you, Sergeant?"

Cobb shrugged.

Witherspoon nodded thoughtfully. "I suspect it bothers you that it's an inviolable sanctuary, doesn't it? It more or less defies the territorial imperative that every policeman feels toward his beat."

"Doctor, I don't care for a lesson in psychology. There is more to it than a matter of jurisdiction. As you must have heard, we have had six unsolved murders here in the past year and a half. Because of the nature of the crimes, I don't think it unreasonable to wonder if all the patients at Skystone were home on those nights."

"Carleton Lynch doesn't know you're out here talking to me, does he? Why? Where is the old bastard? Isn't he still the man Caudill deals with in Stoneville?"

Cobb made a futile attempt to stare the doctor into silence, but he was already learning that Andy Witherspoon was a hard man to discourage.

"Where is the sheriff? I would have thought that old asslicker Mears would have been Lynch's errand boy. Why you, Sergeant?"

Cobb struggled to keep the hostility out of his voice. "Sir,

I'm out here to ask for your cooperation, not to discuss the internal politics of Stoneville or the sheriff's office."

The petite Witherspoon laughed. "Don't get upset, Sergeant. I know Al Caudill has Lynch on a leash. He has convinced him that Skystone is too important to the local merchants to be hassled. I want to make it clear that I don't give a damn about them . . . or Al Caudill."

The little doctor had found the words that unlocked Cobb. "Judge Lynch is in Europe, and I don't think Toby knows how to get hold of him. He's scared shitless without the judge around to tell him what to do."

Nodding, Andy Witherspoon reached into the desk drawer, brought out a pipe, and went through the ritual of filling and lighting it. Cobb squirmed uncomfortably, wondering where it was gong to lead—if he had come on a wild-goose chase.

The doctor squinted at him through the curling smoke. "I find your story about the ambulance interesting, but I can sit here and say in all honesty that I am not convinced you are on the right track.

"There's a matter of ethics involved in talking with you—a doctor's ethics toward his fellow professionals. Ordinarily, I'd dismiss you right out of hand, but you see, Sergeant, I left a job that was the most important thing in my life because I developed concerns about the operation of Skystone. I'm going to tell you what I know, and then I want you to leave me alone.

"When Al Caudill approached me about Skystone twelve years ago, I thought he had a hell of a good idea. Certain people with money and power are so mercilessly exposed to the public eye that they need a place to put family members who can no longer maintain a public image. That was what Dr. Caudill proposed—a so-called convalescent facility with luxurious surroundings commensurate with the financial status of the families involved—a place of absolute privacy. At first, the facilities were intended for elderly people whose bodies were so eroded by age that they could no longer function properly, yet still had mind enough to appreciate the amenities of the good life. Skystone was also intended for patients who developed mild mental aberrations—such as kleptomania—that made them an embarrassment to themselves and their families."

"That's not how the place has been described to me," Cobb interrupted.

"Unfortunately, there's more than a grain of truth in what you've heard. Things went well until four years ago. Then Al changed. Our fees went up at an astronomical rate, and Al, who exercises the prerogative on who would be accepted at the facility, began to admit patients in a state of advanced senility. In some cases the patients were comatose. Of more concern, younger patients with violent histories were being accepted in our mental ward. Homicidal behavior became a common denominator in our patients' profiles, behavior in many cases known to the families but not the authorities. On occasion, Skystone would accept a patient sent to us as a result of negotiations between the authorities and influential families, patients whose acts are never publicized nor likely to be successfully prosecuted."

"Are you telling me, Doctor, that a bunch of homicidal maniacs are locked up at that place?"

The doctor allowed himself a slight smile at the dramatics of Cobb's question. "Let's say that we reached the point where most of our ward population, were they adjudged sane, would be tried for capital crimes."

"And that's why you left?"

"I left for two reasons . . . first, because the institution no longer functioned with its original intent. Second, I left because Skystone had neither the staff skills nor physical facilities to deal with violent patients.

"Skystone has an excellent electronic security system. It was designed to keep intruders out of the grounds, but it functions equally well in keeping people in. Still, the facility has become a dangerous place for both the staff and our elderly patients."

Cobb was on point now like a bird dog, following the man's words. "Then you're saying it is possible—just possible—that one of the patients is responsible for the disappearance of the ambulance. Is that right?"

"Skystone is actually two buildings joined together, one much older than the other. The older part is used as the mental ward. The two parts have but one common connection, a massive steel door painted red. It was our defense in case the population of the mental wing went beyond our control. That was a nightmare that haunted me with increasing frequency. What would happen if they got beyond the red door?

"I knew they would quickly seize control of the whole building. I'm sure you know that the entire staff lives in the old Albritton mansion on the property. If the hospital was seized, that would have to be our rallying point. If I asked Al Caudill once, I asked him twenty times to install a security system in the house and to get that damned collection of shotguns out of the glass case in his office. Unfortunately, Dr. Caudill has reached the point where he's willing to spend money only to make more money, not for safety."

He dropped the pipe carelessly into the ashtray and leaned back. Cobb could feel the bitterness spilling from him like a physical thing.

"Doctor, do you think that could have happened?"

"Why do you suggest it has? . . . That is, beyond your missing ambulance."

"I've run several patrols by there today. We have seen no activity, and they haven't answered our phone calls."

"But I thought you said you were out there after the ambulance disappeared, and everything appeared normal. It's certainly not unusual for them not to answer the phone. You don't phone Skystone about admitting a relative. That's not the way it works. Besides, why do you think the two sheriff's deputies were allowed to leave and not the medics?"

Cobb tried to find the right words. He knew he had to say the right thing or else he was gong to lose Witherspoon's interest. "Maybe something was wrong in the treatment room . . . you know—some procedure. The Johnsons might have noticed it where our deputies wouldn't have."

The doctor nodded.

"When we went out to the hospital the next morning, it didn't cross our minds that anything could be wrong. For all I know, the doctor could have been covered from a doorway by a shotgun."

"Whom did you talk to? Caudill or Fischer?"

"No, that doesn't sound right. His name was . . . ah . . . oh, what was his name? . . . yeah . . . Mainwaring."

Cobb happened to be looking into Andy Witherspoon's face at that moment and saw him go white.

"What . . . what name did you say?" the doctor sputtered.

"Mainwaring. That was the name, for sure. Why?"

The doctor's small hands clenched into fists. "Because, Sergeant, he's one of the patients, a man under the delusion that he's a medical doctor. Oh, God! It's not just a nightmare anymore. They must have seized the hospital."

"Doctor, I would appreciate it if you'd tell me a little something about the mental-ward patients and what we're up against." Cobb's voice was controlled.

It was a different Andy Witherspoon before him now, the energy drained, ashen-faced, his voice a monotone. "Mainwaring—his first name is Thomas—has practiced medicine illegally. He has an excellent mind, abnormal though it is. He's like a blotter. He listens and learns the jargon. He watches, and he can mimic the technique. He believes he's being held at Skystone because he's discovered a cancer cure and the drug companies had him locked up to keep from being deprived of vast profits. Without question, Mainwaring is responsible for the deaths of three people in his bogus role as a surgeon. One of them was his own daughter, Ruth. He will not accept the fact of her death.

"Then there's Shane Covington, a beautiful woman in her late twenties with the most unusual eyes you'll ever see. She's an aggressive lesbian who will not tolerate rejection by her lovers. She has killed one girl and sliced another to pieces—scarred her for life.

"Sergeant, do you want a professional analysis of their illnesses or the sort of anecdotal record I'm giving you?"

Cobb looked up from his writing. "You're giving me just what I want. Is there any chance this girl would attack the young ladies from the accident if they refused her advances?"

"Oh, no. I think she is vicious enough to kill as an expedient, perhaps even in a murderous orgy, but her violence to date has been directed toward once accepting lovers who later rejected her."

He paused a moment before continuing. "Carrie Dalton is in her mid-sixties. She became a pyromaniac—an arsonist—about ten years ago. Mrs. Dalton set at least six fires before she was identified. After that, she set two more, for which her family paid the damages. But then she got away from them and fired a rooming house. Six people died in that house."

"Are you saying that she sets fire to commit murder?"

"No, she has been a building burner. Unfortunately, people live in buildings. I'll guarantee you she would have burned Skystone a thousand times over if she weren't under close supervision. There have been some disturbing changes in Carrie. Before I left she added a certain Old Testament fervor to her interviews, speaking of fire as an agent of purification.

"We have a man in his late twenties, John Hughes. John is the most personable man you'll ever see. He's a heroin addict, but unfortunately, he also takes PCP, 'angel dust.' When he is on PCP, he becomes a killing machine. John Hughes has killed one time, for sure, and probably on three other occasions."

Cobb looked up from his notes again. "Would there be any PCP obtainable at Skystone?"

"No, thank God. John will do a lot to get heroin, but I'm not sure he would kill to obtain it. Incidentally, he is the only addict I've ever seen who has not lost his sexual desires after becoming addicted. I can't promise that he wouldn't be a danger to your young ladies."

"All we can do is hope that they are decent girls and won't encourage him."

The doctor looked surprised at Cobb's puritanical statement, then asked, "Did you ever hear of Duchin Chemicals, one of the two or three biggest chemical companies in the United States? Well, we have the owner's wife with us—Tina Duchin. Somewhere along the line, Tina converted from Christianity or paganism or whatever the hell it was to Satanism. It became a big number on the West Coast, really popular in weirdo circles. The popularity disappeared in the wake of a lot of bad publicity after three girls were kidnapped. They were used as living altars and raped. The diehards went underground and became more violent. Human sacrifice became part of their rituals. Tina Duchin surfaced as a high priestess in the cult. She presided at three murders."

Cobb whistled softly. "Holy smoke! She's a walking time bomb, isn't she?"

"Yes and no. Most of the time, Mrs. Duchin will strike you as a socially acceptable woman of wealth. Her dress and makeup are a bit garish, if not bizarre, but her manners are impeccable. But I don't believe that she could be free twenty-four hours without doing that Black Mass mumbo-jumbo, and I think most of the others would join her just for the hell of it. She is one of your big worries, especially with the girls you brought into the hospital.

"The most dangerous of our wards is a young man who, unless my memory fails me, is thirty-two years old. His name is Howie Delgado. Howie is a stocky bruiser, sullen and pushy. He is constantly seeking sexual outlets. Unfortunately, he can only achieve sexual arousal by inflicting pain on whatever hapless soul happens to be nearby. His response to this stimuli seems inexhaustible. He's an absolutely frightening individual.

"Skystone gained a new patient the day I quit, Paul St. Denis. I think I may say he is the straw that broke this camel's back. St. Denis is afflicted with a homicidal paranoia. His records indicate that his is a classic case of this disorder. He is what popular literature calls a homicidal maniac. St. Denis is the sort of man who can move easily through society with all the attributes of a normal personality. This type of individual, depending on what his triggers are, can be moved to violence a half-dozen times a day or, just as likely, go a year or ten years without any sign of aberrant conduct. These patients do much better in isolated situations where they don't have a lot of stress—particularly the stress from other disturbed personalities. The day Caudill agreed to accept him was the day I resigned. As far as I know, those are all the mental patients at Skystone."

"My Lord, this St. Denis sounds like something out of a horror movie."

Witherspoon was picking up his pipe again. "Not really,

as long as he's identified. He is a menace because of his protective coloration. Delgado is the most dangerous person in there—if you can keep Carrie Dalton away from the matches, that is."

His eyes narrowed. "If, Kendall, in some way that I cannot imagine, one of our wards found a way to leave Skystone unobserved and kill your six women, I think it must have been Howie Delgado."

Cobb came out of the chair, but the doctor raised his hand to stop him.

"Let me finish. If there is, in truth, an escape route, there's the danger that Delgado has shared the information with others. God help the countryside if that's so." The doctor climbed wearily to his feet. "You want me to go in with you and talk to your sheriff, don't you?"

Without waiting for an answer, the little man, stoop-shouldered and somehow older now, walked past Cobb.

CHAPTER 19

*E*lizabeth's flesh cringed under Dr. Mainwaring's hands as he gently pushed her through the door into her room. He stepped through after her and eased the door shut. The panic surged into her again, and she backed across the room. He remained by the door, his arms by his sides, a solicitous look on his face.

"Please, my dear, you're overwrought. There's nothing to be afraid of. I won't let anything happen to you."

She stopped, wanting desperately to believe him.

Seeing her hesitate, he continued. "You know I would never hurt you. You're upset over finding that poor boy. God knows, I can't blame you. It was terrible. He was so foolish —so brave but so foolish. You can't use threats against people as violent as these."

Fighting to hold back the sobs, she begged for an answer that would give some rationale to the horrors around her. "But . . . what happened? Why did they have to do that to poor Scott?"

Carefully he came forward, reached into his pocket, and brought out a vial of pills, which he laid on the bed. "I think you should take two of these. They are Valium. That's why I left them in the vial—so you could tell. Take them. Then

I'll tell you what happened. It's very important, because you and I must do the things necessary for us to get out of here alive. Please, I promise you it'll be all right."

His soft words wove a hypnotic net around Elizabeth. She wanted so desperately to believe him, to believe she was safe, especially with Scott gone. She forced herself to reach for the pills.

"Please, doctor, don't hurt me."

"You're the last person that I would hurt. Do what I ask you."

Still watching him, she took two pills from the tube and reached for the water from the bedside console. Quickly, she swallowed the pills.

"Sit on the bed while they're taking effect. I'll sit in a chair so I won't be between you and the door. Perhaps that will make you feel safer."

"Thank you," she mumbled.

Twenty minutes later, the Valium had done its work and Elizabeth was stretched out on the bed. That horrible moment of finding Scott had been drained of its emotional residue. It didn't really seem to matter. Elizabeth knew she should be grieving for him, but she could find no tears. It was as if she were dead inside. The only thing that seemed important was to keep the doctor talking. She asked the first thing that came to mind.

"Doctor, what's happened here? I know that some of the patients have seized control of the hospital."

"Yes, they have, Elizabeth. Let me caution you again. The only way we can stay alive is to cooperate with them.

"It happened Monday morning, about three A.M. It started with the new patient in the mental ward—Paul St. Denis, a terrifying creature. Dr. Fischer, the new staff psychiatrist, worked with him in the wee hours because he was so easily disturbed by the other inmates. Mrs. Dalton, a rather harmless old creature except when she has matches in her hand, is allowed to wander around the ward, unsecured, at night. She has claustrophobia. The doctor, being new, didn't know this. He and the orderly had just placed St. Denis back in his cell when Carrie—that's Mrs. Dalton—appeared. Apparently, it rattled Dr. Fischer. He told the orderly to lock her in her room. Carrie started screaming and ran down the corridor, with the orderly after her.

"Dr. Fischer had forgotten to lock St. Denis' door when he stepped back outside to confront Carrie. St. Denis followed him out, and the doctor, without thinking, yelled at him to get back in his room. It's not a safe thing to alarm Paul St. Denis. Somehow, St. Denis killed Fischer without much outcry and pulled the doctor's body back into his room with him.

"Meanwhile, Carrie had fled to the nurses' station, which is located just inside the red door. The nurse understood the situation at once and realized that Fischer did not know about Carrie. She knew Carrie would require sedation and sent the orderly into the convalescent wing to the drug room. To calm Carrie, she promised the old gal that she would accompany her back to locate the doctor and explain to him. The nurse violated one of the cardinal rules of Skystone.

"There is a button at the nurses' station—a panic button—that, when pressed, will automatically lock the door between the two wings. Once locked, it cannot be opened except from the other side. Staff rules are that a staff member is always at the nurses' station. If the duty nurse must leave that station, she is required to use the panic button.

"When the nurse turned into the corridor, she saw it empty and decided that Dr. Fischer must have gone on back into the therapy room to clean up. She told Carrie to wait in her room, and she would find the doctor.

"Unfortunately, she went by St. Denis' room, and he stepped out into the passageway after her. When she saw him, she made no attempt to reason with him, but simply tried to shove him back in his room. Of course, that was her last mistake.

"Everyone else awoke during St. Denis' struggle with the nurse. When things quieted down, they asked Carrie to get the keys from the nurse's body, which St. Denis had left in the hall. Carrie is a stubborn old woman and somewhat of a tease, and it was several minutes before she did. Finally, she let everybody out.

"Of course, the first thing they did was to lock the door on

St. Denis, who was back in his room. Even Howie finds him more than he wants to deal with.

"Believe it or not, I slept through the whole thing. I hadn't been sleeping well and had saved up four sleeping pills—"

"Saved? Why did you have to save pills?"

He seemed puzzled for a moment. "Oh, that ... that's the quota I have for myself. Anyway, I slept through all of it, unfortunately.

"I think Tina—that's Mrs. Duchin—organized the group well enough that when they went through the red door, no one had a chance in the convalescent wing. Howie was the one who thought of the staff sleeping up at the large house and realized they had to be disposed of, too. Shane Covington, John Hughes, and Howie went up to the house. They carried knives from the kitchen, but once they got into the house, John and Howie found the shotguns. They used those on the staff, while Shane used her carving knife. They butchered all the staff in just a few minutes.

"By then, the blood lust was up in Howie. He drove one of the panel trucks down from the big house and went from room to room, killing those poor convalescent patients with his bare hands.

"Because of one circumstance or the other, six of the staff were not killed. Dr. Caudill and two of the nurses, Lena Farmington and Valerie Boulanger, together with one little student nurse, Molly Hatcher, managed to survive. The early cook, a woman named Gladys who had just come on duty, was spared, as was Ike Brown, the man who works on the grounds."

"Doctor, is ... is Meredith Thorne still alive?"

He smiled for the first time. "Yes, I've been able to keep your friend alive. It isn't easy."

His face reddened and, bounding to his feet, he started to pace back and forth. When he looked at Elizabeth again, she was frightened at the change in him.

"I'm going to say it. I don't like your associating with her."

"Associating with whom? What do you mean?"

"Did you know your friend is a narcotics addict—a stoner?"

"A stoner? I . . . I don't believe it."

"Oh, you can believe it, all right, and a little slut in the bargain. She'll do anything to get drugs."

Elizabeth's rejoinder died with Mainwaring's sharp order. "Shut up! We will not talk about her anymore."

He stared angrily at Elizabeth for a moment before relaxing. "Oh, you youngster—so naive. She's not worth your concern."

"Where are the others—the ones that were left alive?"

His face underwent another of its mercurial transformations. There was bitterness and disappointment in his eyes. "They're . . . they're dead now, all but Molly Hatcher."

"Oh, my God! They killed Dr. Caudill?"

Looking down dejectedly at his hands, meshed together across his knees, Mainwaring muttered, "No. Yesterday morning after I talked to the sheriff, Caudill managed to slip into the medication storeroom for a few moments. Later, after he and Mrs. Farmington were locked into a room in the mental wing, they took an overdose of something. Mrs. Duchin found them dead. Howie caught the yardman and the cook in the garage at the house. The old man was trying to repair one of the cars. We put the bodies in the wheelchairs on the patio so you wouldn't be suspicious about the absence of patients."

She blinked and looked at him, a chill creeping over her. "We? You helped?"

Awkwardly, he reached for her foot and patted it. "Don't be alarmed. Don't you see? With these unstable people around, I couldn't let you become hysterical. It would have triggered an outburst among them. I did it for you."

She searched his face, seeking the truth.

He looked at her blandly. "You know, I'd often wondered how they would act—the inmates of Skystone—if they were allowed freedom. Now I know." He chuckled softly. "They're like the rest of the world—greedy, violent, lustful. The insane are as corrupt as the sane, but they didn't corrupt me."

Again Elizabeth felt a coldness envelop her. She stared at

Thomas Mainwaring's smiling, innocuous face and saw the truth. She said what she had intended not to say. "You . . . you were a patient in the mental ward, weren't you?"

He looked at her, lifting his eyebrows in surprise. "Why, of course I was. Didn't your mother admit what she and the big drug companies did to me? . . . that they had me locked up?"

Elizabeth's voice was barely audible. "My mother?"

Mainwaring gave no indication he had heard her. "They would have lost their unholy millions—taken from the unfortunate—if news of my cure had leaked out to the world. Didn't I . . ."

His face collapsed, and he lunged forward, clapping his arms around her legs. Elizabeth struggled to free herself of his embrace, barely aware of his words muffled against the sheet.

"Oh, God, Ruth, I didn't hurt you—not my own daughter. They said I hurt you, but I didn't. I cured you. Don't you understand? I cured you. That's why I must get out of here. I must be free. I'll cure you again. You didn't die. I knew you didn't. They lied."

He released her and jumped up. She stared at him in horrified fascination. He looked toward the door and then back to her, his voice so low she could barely hear it.

"Ruthie, I called Harvey Figuroa yesterday morning. There is a private airstrip here, and he is going to fly his plane in late tomorrow afternoon. He will fly us out—take us to Mexico where they can't find us. All we have to do is to stall this bunch and divert their attention from you. They listen to me because they know I'm a medical man, the only one who can get them out. They think I'm taking all of them to Mexico. Stay out of sight until tomorrow, Ruthie, and we shall be free."

There was a sudden crash in the hall, followed by a shrill female curse.

"Oh, Christ!" he exclaimed. "The animals are at it again. At least there is one that is dependable, John Hughes. He's a drug addict, and I'm the only one who has the combination to the narcotics safe. I own him, body and soul. If, for some reason, I can't come to you, I'll send John. You can depend on him. Do you understand?"

When she remained silent, he returned to the bed, took her hand, and looked down at her. It was a look of such loving solicitude that Elizabeth sensed that, even though he was as mad as a hatter, he would give his life for her, somehow convinced that she was his daughter. She forced herself to meet his eyes.

"Thank you," she said. Taking a deep breath, she added, "Father."

Thomas Mainwaring left the room with a sprightly step.

CHAPTER 20_____

The cigar in Toby Mears' mouth was rapidly being chewed into a sodden ruin. He glanced from Andy Witherspoon to Cobb and back again.

"So, doctor, you believe the lunatics have taken over Skystone, killed the ambulance crew, and put the lives of everyone at the hospital in jeopardy. Right?"

Andy gave as good as he had received. "I didn't say that, damn it! I said that it may have happened. This affair with Mainwaring needs looking into immediately."

The sheriff smirked. "Doctor, I thought you said there were times that this Mainwaring was allowed into the convalescent wing—that the staff found it good therapy to let him do menial tasks normally done by orderlies. I believe you said Mainwaring is not considered violent—right?"

"Now, listen here . . ."

"Doctor, I asked you a question, and I want a yes or no answer."

"Yes, but he would never have been unsupervised. He certainly would not have been allowed to represent himself as a doctor."

The sheriff continued, "Now, Cobb thinks it highly significant that we haven't been able to contact Skystone by telephone. Are the phones usually manned out there?"

Witherspoon glanced at Cobb before replying, some of the fire gone out of him. "I have already admitted they aren't, Sheriff. The office is not operated in a conventional manner. Al used it mainly as a storage area to keep his files secure from staff and patients and as window dressing when state officials came for inspections. Actually, he used an accounting firm in New Orleans to handle Skystone's books. He feels it helps preserve privacy."

Toby glanced across the room to where the county commissioner sat, silently taking in the drama. "Well, Commissioner, do you have anything you want to ask these fellows?"

The grizzled, rotund man sitting in the chair, wearing a brown suit whose shiny seat indicated far too many years of service, allowed himself a brief guffaw. "Hell, Toby, it looks to me like you're doing pretty good by yourself. The judge would be proud of you."

Nodding in satisfaction, the sheriff renewed his assault. "Now, that being the case, Dr. Witherspoon, just why did you bother to come in here with the sergeant?"

For a moment Andy Witherspoon was close to storming out of the office. All he could see was a stupid political hack putting on a show for one of his bosses, but he thought of Cobb's concern and yielded. "I guess because of the ambulance, Sheriff. Those boys have seen enough ER treatment to recognize if anything was wrong. I like Sergeant Kendall's rationale. I think the medics may have spotted patients masquerading as staff members."

The sheriff's smile was triumphant. Coming to his feet, he opened the door and yelled toward the radio room. "Emmaline, do you have my call on the line from Memphis?"

When she replied in the affirmative, he picked up the phone. "Lieutenant Crabb? This is Sheriff Mears again from Stoneville, Arkansas. I appreciate your calling me about our ambulance. I hate to bother you again, but I wish you'd tell Sergeant Kendall what you found this morning. Just a minute." He thrust the phone toward Cobb. "Here!"

"This is Kendall."

"Sergeant, we received your APB yesterday and alerted our patrol units. This morning about four A.M., we logged a call from an RP who claimed he heard a car being driven into the river south of the city limits. We sent a unit out to check. They found tire tracks leading into the river, but it certainly wasn't an accident. The car went in at very low speed. This sort of thing happens on occasion. Car strippers will dump them in the river. We usually pinpoint the locations of obvious dumps and send a diver down about twice a month to check them. We remembered your APB and decided to have our man check the vehicle this morning.

"The water's quite murky in that area, and the current is a son of a bitch. The diver was working solo, and it was too dangerous to take chances without a second swimmer in the boat. But he did see that the vehicle's top was white and thought it was the right length for your ambulance. More to the point, Sergeant, it had a Decton light bar on it. Decton just made two hundred of those things altogether before they went out of business. They must be scattered all over the eastern United States."

Cobb was stunned, and when the lieutenant realized that he had no comments, he added, "I'm sorry to say that our man didn't get a look into the cab to see if your men were there. We're going to pull it out the first thing in the morning. I'll phone you people as soon as I know anything."

Again, there was an awkward silence, and the lieutenant asked, "Well . . . any questions, Sergeant?"

"No, I don't suppose there are, Lieutenant. Thank you a lot for your call."

He raised his eyes to find Toby staring at him, his face all business now. "I hope to God, Kendall, that answers your questions about the ambulance. I would just as soon not hear any more about it until it's raised and we find out if the Johnsons are in it."

The sheriff turned back toward the doctor. "Dr. Witherspoon, the mental ward of Skystone is quite old, isn't it?"

"Yes, it is. I think it was built in 1923. It was originally a tuberculosis sanitarium."

"Then I assume, sir, that you people installed modern heating and air conditioning when you assumed ownership. Is that correct?"

Andy Witherspoon nodded.

"Where did you place the ducting for these systems?"

Too late, Andy saw what was coming. "I think you know the answer, Sheriff. We installed false ceilings and placed the ducting in the space we created there."

"There's a vent in each room—right? How often do you inspect those vents to see if they've been loosened?"

The doctor shrugged.

"And how many times do you run a bed check during the night?"

Andy Witherspoon's face reddened. "Not at all, Sheriff. Why should we? The rooms are secure. Even if a patient could climb into the ducting, where could he go?"

Toby Mears ignored the question. Cobb had known him long enough to know that he was like a bloodhound on the trail now.

"Doctor, are there roof hatches over the mental ward?"

"Yes, one, but it is locked from the outside. When we remodeled the mental ward, we ran the wing's wiring through the attic. There are a lot of heavy cables in there. Some of the machines take a tremendous amount of electricity."

"If someone entered the ducts and found a way to loosen a section of it from within, he could climb out through the hatch and be free. Isn't that correct? How long since that hatch lock has been checked?"

The doctor sat up straight, and Cobb knew he had found a loophole in the sheriff's case. "It's never been checked that I know of, but you are forgetting one thing. The hospital grounds are surrounded by an electrified fence. There's no way a patient could crawl over or tunnel under that fence. So you see, Sheriff, your whole theory is, to put it quite bluntly, a crock of shit."

A look of glee flitted across Toby's visage. "I suppose that the fence is controlled from the convalescent wing, and the circuit breakers are there. Right?"

Witherspoon shook his head. "No, the control panels are there, but the circuit breakers are up in the attic where the—"

Carefully, the sheriff placed the shredded remnant of his cigar in the foul ashtray and leaned back. "In other words, if an inmate climbed into ducts which are never checked, flipped a circuit breaker which is in the attic, and climbed through a hatch that is never inspected, he could go from here to China and back without a worry on earth."

He turned away from a chagrined Witherspoon and fixed Cobb with his baleful stare. "Well, Mr. Cobb Kendall, they say that you're the hotshot in this department. They say that Toby Mears is too old to do anything except keep winning elections. Now, Mr. Hotshot, I've given you one lead in investigating these murders. In a couple of days when Judge Lynch gets home, we will go out there and talk to Doc Caudill—maybe check out that roof hatch. Until then, you forget about Skystone. That's an order. Now if you will excuse me, we have wasted enough time talking about inmate takeovers. Doctor, I want to thank you for coming in."

With a spryness that Cobb hadn't witnessed in years, Toby came to his feet and shook the hand of the embarrassed doctor. Andy looked apologetically at Cobb.

As Cobb started to follow him out of the office, the sheriff called, "Just a minute, Cobb," and motioned him back into his seat.

He looked toward the commissioner and then at Cobb. "Cobb, I hated like hell to do that to you. You've been a good man, but damn it, boy, you've gotten so uppity you won't listen to old Toby. Not only are you getting this town nervous, but you're at a dead end. Remember what I said . . . no freelancing. You don't have any excuse to go out to that hospital.

"Ignore what I said in front of Witherspoon. I want you to start getting the fingerprints of Skystone's mental patients, but get them through their hometowns, not here. The doctor already gave you their names and addresses. The day we're sure who is sneaking out of that place at night, we'll go out there and bring him in. I'll guarantee you Caudill will not object. He will be grateful because we'll handle it discreetly, and he will make sure it never happens again. The judge says he is a reasonable man.

"The citizenry will be safe, yet nothing will have happened to threaten the existence of Skystone. The families of the victims will be happy. They will have their privacy. And I'll be happy, Cobb, because we did it the right way."

He looked toward the commissioner. "Anything to add, Commissioner?"

The fat man guffawed. "Cobb, you're damned lucky to have an old warhorse here to help you out. By God, Toby, you're something else."

Cobb closed the door after him, muffling the volleys of compliments ricocheting off the walls.

Tip Crable was standing by the sergeants' room. He rolled his eyes upward, giving Cobb a sympathetic slap on the back as he walked past.

The doctor waited at the front door, his hands balled into fists. He wasted no time on gratuitous statements. "Well, what are you going to do now?"

Cobb shrugged. "What can I do? He sure as hell shot holes in our case, plus making me look like a stupid ass. I have been ranting about our killer coming from Skystone, yet I never bothered to formulate a theory of how it could be done."

Cobb's comments did not satisfy the little gamecock of a physician. He stomped his foot against the boards of the walk. "Goddamn it, I thought you had more balls than that, Kendall. I never thought you would let an old fart like that fuck around with you. When do you get off work?"

"I'm off work now. The shift was over an hour and a half ago."

"Then I'm going to haul that worthless ass of yours out to my place and get you stoked up on some good whiskey. Then you and I are going to figure a way to check on Skystone. I have the feeling in my bones that we don't have any time to waste, and crotchety old sons of a bitch like me are right more often than we are wrong."

Cobb grinned. Men like Andy Witherspoon were a new experience in his life. "Listen, if you don't mind, I'm going to ask Tip to come with us. He's a damned good cop."

Twenty-five minutes later, the three of them were trooping through the unfinished living room of Witherspoon's house into the study.

CHAPTER 21 _____

*T*he tranquilizer (what was it her husband had once called it?—Prince Valium, because it demanded tribute from a great part of American society) had done its work well with Elizabeth. The hospital room seemed a safe haven from the rapacious inmates of Skystone. She found herself comfortable with Mainwaring's reassurances that nothing would happen to her.

The door opened abruptly and closed as quickly. The light came on, revealing a grinning John Hughes standing before her.

"Hey, mama, how's it going?"

With the explosion of light in the room, she had yelped and shot up into a sitting position, the sheet drawn tightly around her. Remembering what Mainwaring had said, she tried to be flippant, to mask her fear of him. "Johnny, you scared me to death!"

"Hey, not to worry, pretty thing. The main man told me to keep an eye on you. As a matter of fact, he laid a little bit of heaven on Johnny as a bonus. I'm here to tell you, mama, this dude is flying high."

As Elizabeth watched him swaying slightly, his eyes unfocused, whatever satisfaction she had gained from Mainwaring's promise that Johnny would help protect her faded. He was so stoned he could barely walk. Oddly enough, he sensed her concern and winked.

"Hey, not to worry, doll. Johnny comes down in a hurry. I'll be real cool in a few ticks. Can you dig that? Hey, I can't stay. Some of those creeps will be wondering what I'm doing in here. It wouldn't be good for little Elizabeth if old Tina got to thinking about you."

His laugh became a cackle and lasted and lasted.

"Tina? What about Tina?"

He stepped away from the door for the first time and came nearer. She eased backwards across the bed. When he saw what she was doing, he raised his hands above his head.

"Hey, chickie, I'm not gonna hurt you—promise. Let's don't talk about the Dragon Lady. I don't want that broad to hex old John."

"Hex you!"

"Yeah, Tina claims she is an honest-to-God priestess of Satan. I used to think the old bitch was just fucking off at the mouth, but after last night, no shit. I mean . . . Jesus Christ! I've got a strong stomach, but it was too much for me. It started out great—horny as hell—but, oh, brother!"

"What do you mean? What happened last night?"

"Swear to God you won't tell?"

She nodded.

"We kind of jived around last night, all of us on a natural high after creaming the fuzz. About midnight Tina said she had to give thanks to almighty Satan for her deliverance. I mean, nobody started dropping cookies over it, if you get my meaning. But then Howie got kinda interested. You could tell Doc Mainwaring didn't like the idea worth a shit, but, hell, he was trying to do the same as me—keep them crazy bastards happy so we can get our asses out of here in one piece.

"Tina dug up some candles from the kitchen and got one of those rolling tables they put you on to examine you. By that time, everybody was getting tuned. I mean, Shane was getting to where she was all for it. That little bull-dyke bitch is ready for anything. Nobody was paying much attention to old Carrie, so she copped some of Tina's matches and split.

All at once, we smelled smoke. Of course, that scared the shit out of everybody. Apparently, somebody had been fucking around and trashed the smoke alarm.

"We hauled ass out of there and found old Carrie in the staff lounge, trying to burn one of the sofas. I thought, 'fuck this shit.' I grabbed an extinguisher and started to put the fire out, and that son of a bitch Delgado grabbed her. Hell, I mean he stood right there in front of us in the hall and broke her neck—literally broke her neck and was laughing about it. I thought that was probably the end of the Satan crap. The doc had me put Carrie's body into the same freezer locker we had stuffed Caudill's nurse in. By the time I finished and got back, I heard that slinky blond chick Valerie screaming her fucking head off."

Elizabeth knew she should be denying any interest in his story, but she couldn't help asking, "Valerie? Who's she?"

"She was the nicest little old nursie here—really sweet, you know. Always made me feel like I was somebody, not a locked-up crazy. Good-looking chick, too—tall, silvery blond hair.

"I hurried back into our ward. By then, they were all in the therapy room and all the lights were out. The candles were burning, and Valerie was tied down on the table, stripped naked. Old Tina was standing there in front of her, stripped down to her panties and chanting some kind of damned gibberish. I'll tell you something, Tina's a little plump and smears a ton of makeup on her face, but she's still a prime piece of ass. She was chanting like hell, and Shane and Howie were both trying to join in . . . you know, sing along time. All at once Tina signals to Howie. I hadn't been noticing him. Looking at Valerie lying there and seeing Tina in next to nothing was enough to give a statue a hard-on. All at once, Howie stepped in between Valerie's legs and threw the meat to her.

"Well, that was all Mainwaring could stand. He cut out. Hell, I had a bone-on. Who wouldn't? Old Howie was just humping away. Tina and Shane were chanting, and damn if Molly didn't join in!"

Elizabeth had her face in her hands now, willing him to shut up. She managed to moan, "Stop!"

But the memory and the poison in his blood had deafened John Hughes to such remonstrations. "Christ, I'll tell you I was thinking about joining Tina's religion—or whatever the hell it is—so I would get the next crack at Valerie, but no way. When Howie got off her, Tina tied her, spread-eagle, against those weight machines at the far end of the room. Do you know where I mean?"

He peered at her, blinking. The silence grew.

"Ah . . . yeah," she finally said. "Yeah, I know where you mean."

He grinned. "You're a damned liar, baby, you know that? I mean, do you think I'm stoned out of my fucking mind? I know you've never been in there. Now what—?"

"Please, I'm sorry. I . . . I wasn't thinking."

He nodded. "Jesus, I've never seen anything like it. Tina must have had old Howie collect leather belts from up at the house. She took off her panties, and she and Howie stood there naked, whipping the hide off Valerie. She was screaming. God damn, she looked sexy, writhing around like that, but I knew they were killing her. Christ! I liked Valerie, but I was afraid to say anything. I looked over at Shane, and she and Molly were all wrapped up in each other's arms, kissing and panting. A week ago Molly wouldn't have said shit if she had a mouthful, and now she's a Goddamn les-nympho-maniac. I couldn't take it, and I left.

"After a while it was quiet, and I came back in. Poor Valerie was already dead—I'm sure of it—and that bitch Shane and Molly weren't in sight. I heard this grunting noise, and I walked around the examination table. Old Howie and Tina were lying on the floor, screwing their brains out. Hell, it was a freakout . . . you know what I mean?"

As he asked the question, his hand closed on Elizabeth's ankle. She was so upset by the horror of his story that her voice held a note of menace that she had never heard in herself.

"You get your damned hand off me, or I'll kill you!"

John Hughes jerked his hand away from her ankle as if it were red hot. A fatuous grin spread across his face as he backed away. "Hey, sweet thing, don't get excited. I mean,

John's cool—not making a pass at you. I know you're a high-class broad. I mean, don't go telling Doc Mainwaring that I'm trying to hit on you. You dig it?"

"You just remember that."

Elizabeth thrilled to the realization that John Hughes was afraid of her. The thrill disappeared when she realized it was the loss of his drug supply that he really feared.

He paused at the door. "Hey, baby, gotta split. Like I say, you be cool around Tina. Better watch that Howie, too. Man, he's got a cock like a bar of iron—it never wears out. See you later, 'gater."

Elizabeth rolled over, buried her face in her pillows, and cried. She was going to die. She did not know which one would kill her or how terrible it would be, but she knew she would never leave Skystone alive.

CHAPTER 22

The study had an unreal quality in the stark light of the Coleman lantern. The power company had not finished stringing a line to the house, and so the three men sat around a table in the middle of the study, staring owlishly at the cloud of light bugs circling the lantern's glass globe. Well into their cups, they sat in morose silence broken by occasional flurries of conversation. An empty bottle of Tennessee sipping whiskey lay on its side atop the table. A second bottle, half full, was lifted with reverence from time to time by one of the trio. They had long since eschewed the use of glasses.

Andy Whitherspoon roused himself and took a wild swing at the light bugs, his hand precariously near the glass chimney. "If one of you bastards hadn't left the door open, we wouldn't have the damned bug problem."

This remark produced gales of laughter from his companions.

Tip drew himself up with alcoholic dignity. "Just one damned minute, Witherspoon. We're here to talk about the fucking Bluestone, or whatever the hell it's—"

"It's Skystone, you bastard," the doctor shouted.

"Well, whatever the hell it is. Now, Cobb has an idea."

They leaned forward with exaggerated emphasis, looking at Cobb who sat peering fixedly into the glowing brilliance of the lantern's mantle.

"Listen, Crable, I don't mind talking about Skyspot, but—"

Andy smashed his palm against the table, causing the gas lantern to teeter. "Damn it to hell, it's Skystone!"

"Okay . . . Skystone. But I'm not going to talk about any damned woman killer."

He lunged upright. "By God, you people keep harping on the wonderful Madeleine Turner and those other women. If you are so all-fired smart, you find the damned bastard. My wife—good old Margaret—is at home right now waiting for me. Do you know that this is my birthday? She's sitting there waiting for my rear end, and I haven't even called her. Everybody talks about brave, adorable Margaret. She sure as hell sits, I guarantee that. You don't know a damned thing about Margaret." Tears glistened in his eyes. "Goddamn her, anyway."

Tip stumbled drunkenly to his feet. "Okay . . . okay . . . I'm sorry. Christ, am I sorry! I don't know what in the hell I've done to your wife, but whatever it is, I'm sorry as hell. I'll swear to you, I just want to figure a way to get the Johnson boys out of Skystone. Now please sit down, Cobb. You know you're the best friend I have."

The diminutive Witherspoon jumped up, grabbed the whiskey bottle, and poured three generous dollops into the empty glasses. Lifting his glass, he cried, "A toast. A toast to whatever the hell Cobb wants to do. I sure as hell don't know what to say."

The three glasses shot aloft, sending whiskey sloshing onto the table. They collapsed into their seats, with Tip and Andy looking expectantly at Cobb.

Cobb motioned them closer. He whispered, "Gentlemen, if this rathole of a house had a telephone—"

"Whoa," Andy shouted. "I won't have my damned house slandered. This rathole of a shack has a frigging telephone. No doctor worth shit does without a phone. It might not have light . . . it might not have water . . . but, by God, this doctor's house sure as hell has a telephone."

"Okay, then. I'm going to call that guy again in Memphis —that Lieutenant Crabb. I have an idea."

Tip clapped his hands. "What is it?"

Andy suddenly seemed more sober. He was looking speculatively at Cobb. "You'll have to sound a hell of a lot less drunk than you are if you're going to get anywhere."

Cobb ruefully nodded.

Andy and Tip stood by the phone, listening. Cobb was talking very slowly, trying not to slur his words.

"Yes, Sergeant, I'm aware the lieutenant needs time away from his job. We feel the same way here. But this is important. It's a matter of life and death."

The connection wasn't a good one, and the distant voice came and went. "I'm going to put you through to Lieutenant Roper. He'll have to decide about going against department regulations."

Again Cobb related the circumstances of the APB and Crabb's call. The Memphis lieutenant seemed more uninterested with every word. Finally a desperate Cobb told him what they believed the situation might be at Skystone.

There was a long pause before the lieutenant said, "I can't understand why Sheriff Mears hasn't called for mutual aid from all over this area."

The wall broke on Cobb's frustration and, his voice badly slurred, he shouted into the phone: "Because, by God, there may be thirty or forty people out there that will die if we make the wrong move. We have a political hack for a sheriff who doesn't know what the hell to do."

There was a longer pause. Cobb was certain that he had not only ruined his chances of contacting Crabb, but that this Memphis officer would be on the phone to Toby within five minutes.

"By God, I'm going to do it, Kendall. If Crabb complains, I'll be up there looking for a job with you, but I'm going to do it." He rattled off a telephone number and slammed down the phone without bothering to say goodbye.

Lieutenant Crabb answered on the second ring.

"Lieutenant, I apologize for calling you at this time of night, but there's one thing I need to know. Are you aware of any other theft reports involving ambulances around Memphis—especially in the last year?"

Crabb's shrill whistle burst from the receiver. "By God, I hadn't thought of that. I remember . . . I believe . . . yes, I remember two being mentioned in briefings."

"Have they been found?"

"No, they haven't. You're suggesting that the ambulance in the river is one of ours."

It was a statement, not a question, and Cobb waited for the lieutenant to continue.

"Whoever had it may have found out about the APB and decided it was too hot to keep. You know, there's been a rash of ambulance thefts nationally the last couple of years. We suspect they've been used to haul aliens, dope—you name it. After all, if an ambulance isn't running Code Three, the patrol units usually won't question its being in the area—even one from quite a ways off. They figure it's a long-distance hospital transfer. It could be our ambulance. I'll call you in the morning. I hope I haven't screwed up your thinking on the case."

Cobb was jubilant. "Hell, no, you haven't. You may have gotten us back on the right track."

He put down the phone. "By God, I'm calling Toby."

Tip moaned. "Oh God, this is where the shit hits the fan."

The phone rang for so long that Cobb was about to hang up, deciding he was mistaken about Toby's having a dinner party. As he was lowering the receiver, there was a click, and Rose Mears' waspish voice stated importantly, "This is the Mears residence."

"Rose, this is Cobb. May I speak to Toby?"

Her voice immediately grew hostile. "Cobb, you aren't on duty. I have the roster right here. Besides, the sheriff and I are entertaining tonight, and he doesn't wish to be disturbed."

"True, ma'am, but this is important, or I wouldn't have called."

With a note of long-suffering tolerance, Rose relented. "Well, if you must, but I can guarantee that the sheriff will not be pleased."

The crash of the phone against the tabletop was enough to make Tip and Andy wince.

An interminable length of time went by—so long that Andy grumbled, "Where in the hell is the old fart? Sitting on the crapper?"

Toby's first words made it apparent that Rose had not overstated the case. His voice dripped ice water. "Cobb, this had better be good. A man with the responsibilities I have needs some recreation without being bothered about petty details. That's why we have sergeants. Now, what is it?"

Quickly, Cobb summarized his conversation with Lieutenant Crabb.

There was a long, painful sigh at the other end of the line. "Well, thanks for the information. I'm glad to hear that ours isn't the only ambulance ever stolen in the U.S.A."

Toby sounded as mean as Cobb had ever heard him. "Now let me refresh your memory. I told you this afternoon that I wanted you to hump your—" Apparently the fastidious Rose was lurking nearby. "Er—hurry up on these murders. I'm appalled that the fair ladies of this town have to live in fear of a madman."

Cobb heard someone talking to Toby, too low and too far off to be intelligible. There was a long pause, and then the sheriff snarled, "Now, you listen to me, you son of a bitch. I love Margaret. By God, she's a fine girl and I don't want to hurt her. But if I hear one more word about Skystone, by God, your ass is going to have a two-week suspension without pay. I told you I'll call you when I hear about the ambulance."

The crash that came through the receiver gave ample evidence that Rose's annoyance was no more than a pale imitation of her husband's.

Cobb stared morosely at the phone. "Well, what do we do now?"

Andy belched loudly, and Tip said, "I guess the doc summed up our whole evening."

Andy glared at him. "The hell it does. I'm going to make a pot of strong coffee and get this poison out of us. Then we'll sit down and form a vigilante committee to take action. Right, Cobb?"

Cobb, still disconsolate, shrugged.

The little man glared at him. "I said, right, Cobb?"

Cobb grinned. "Right, you little banty rooster."

With the lantern out, they sat in the coffee-scented darkness, talking, able to see one another only as vague shapes.

"Cobb, I can't understand why you say speed is more important than numbers. I mean . . . it seems to me what you need is to surround the grounds and burst in from all sides."

"Doc, in an operation like this, you have to establish your priorities. In other words, is our primary interest to ensure the safety of the hostages or simply to subdue and recapture the escapees?"

Tip broke in, "I don't think there's any question about that. How far could an inmate run, even if one or two slipped past? I'm not saying they're not dangerous or somebody might not get hurt, but we're balancing that risk against the lives of a lot of innocent people."

Cobb took another swallow of coffee. "Doc, you said you thought they were capable of organizing, particularly when they have somebody as sharp as Mainwaring. That's another reason why speed is more important. It would take time to recruit a large assault team."

"What do you mean?" Tip asked.

"If Mainwaring is bright, he won't stay holed up in there. He would have already made a break for it unless he has a plan that will take him a long way in a hurry."

The doctor grinned. "By God, I hadn't thought of that— the airstrip."

"Yes, that's one possibility. We need to be on top of them before they know we're there, and we can't wait much longer. We don't want them to have time to think about using the hostages."

Andy began to see what Cobb meant. "Cobb, if we crash the gate and cut through the trees, maybe using a four-wheel-drive vehicle, we should be on the porte cochere within thirty seconds. With the soundproofing, they won't know what is happening until we are on that last stretch of driveway."

It was the first plan Cobb had considered and discarded. He waited to see if Andy would see the obstacle.

The little doctor struck the table, sending the mugs into a clattering dance. "Damn! I forgot that electrified fence. The second the gate is breached, the alarm will go off. It will give them time to barricade the doors and do whatever they want with the hostages."

Tip moaned. "Another idea down the drain. We're getting nowhere fast."

"I keep thinking about what Andy said about the circuit breakers in the crawl space. If we could turn them off, our problems would be solved."

"Just how do you plan to do that?" Tip asked. "Do we phone and ask them if they would mind running up and disconnecting them?"

Andy became excited. "By God, you've got it! If we can get to the circuits, we have it made."

"The only problem is that's a mighty big if," Cobb said.

The doctor bounced out of his chair. "Wait a minute. I know how to reach the attic. We use a helicopter."

Tip was incredulous. "A helicopter! Are you out of your mind? Why, they would hear it coming a half-mile away and know something was up."

"Wait a minute, Tip," Cobb said. "I don't think they would. There is a high-voltage transmission line a little way north of Skystone's property boundary. A helicopter patrols that line, checking for trouble. Everybody at the hospital must have heard it a thousand times."

Andy whistled appreciatively. "You're right! I used to hear that chopper several times a week."

Cobb continued, "If the chopper barrels in low from the north, they shouldn't have over ten seconds' warning that something is wrong. Tip or I will drop onto the roof, go down the hatch, and turn off the power. After the juice is cut, we'll bust through the gate and that will be the end of it. Shoot! This should be as slick as that Israeli raid on Entebbe."

"Hold the phone," Andy protested. "Where do you get that Tip or I crap? I'm the man to drop to the roof. I've been in the attic and know the layout. You two guys can make like the cavalry riding to the rescue."

Sensing their resistance, he continued. "It's my idea.

And, besides, where are you planning to get the helicopter? Will the county pay for it?"

Tip answered before Cobb could. "It will be a cold day in hell before they do that. Well, it was a great idea, anyway."

"It's still a great idea. You miss my point, Tip. Somebody has to dig into his pocket to rent a helicopter, and you're looking at the guy that has the money for it. So what I'm saying is that I own the basketball. Do I get to play, or do I go home and take my ball with me?"

Tip chuckled. "By God, you're all right for a doctor. You're a feisty little son of a bitch."

Andy leaned over, feeling for the unlit lantern. "I know the man for the job. He has a chopper in Little Rock. The guy's name is Smitty Plunkett. We've used him two or three times to transport people to Skystone. He doesn't have any more sense than we do. Several times he's flown out there with a damned psychopath serving as copilot, sitting beside him. Let me at the phone."

CHAPTER 23

*T*he glowing red numbers of the digital clock blurred before her eyes. She blinked to clear the mist. It was 1:57. The Valium had long since worn off, leaving Elizabeth to toss fitfully on the bed.

Several times she thought she had heard the metallic whisper of the doorknob turning and had peered fearfully toward the corridor. Her many short naps had left her hot and sticky.

She sat up in bed, unbuttoned the hospital tunic, and pulled it off. She worked her gown out of her uniform slacks, yanked it over her head, and flung it across the room toward the window. Hurriedly she slipped back into the tunic, afraid that John Hughes would catch her bare-breasted.

She looked at the clock again and groaned in frustration. Time was at a standstill. Only two minutes had passed since her last glance.

Elizabeth slipped off the bed, glancing a last time at the clock—2:01 A.M. Dr. Mainwaring had warned her about wandering about the hospital. She thought again about building a barricade across the door. Could it hold if they really tried to get in? And what about Mainwaring? He seemed to be her only hope of escaping. A barricade would cut her off from his help. Thinking was getting her nowhere. She had to know what was happening.

Feeling her way across the dark room, she located the doorknob. The velvet-smooth hinges did not betray her. Cautiously, she peered out.

It was quiet in the dimly lit hallway. She wondered if Mainwaring's dangerous charges were herded safely into the mental wing for the night.

She was about to go back to the bed when she heard feminine laughter in the distance. Opening the door still more, she heard the rumble of a male voice and then peals of laughter.

A second male voice, higher in pitch, angry, intervened. She glanced first toward the nurses' station and then down the hall, and her eyes widened in surprise. Light spilled across the hall from room 8.

Again, the sound of giggling broke the silence. Recognition left her bewildered. She had heard that sound a thousand times. It was Meredith!

She had to know what was going on.

Elizabeth started down the hall, aware of the faint slap of her sandals, terribly afraid but determined to contact Meredith, whatever the cost. She slipped her sandals off, feeling the gritty tiles beneath her feet as she tiptoed from doorway to doorway. Her journey seemed endless.

When she reached the darkened room 7, she slipped inside. She strained to hear Meredith again, but in vain. Finally, frustrated and keenly aware of her vulnerability, she stepped back into the hall where she couldn't be trapped. Staying close to the wall, she crept to a spot beside room 8's door.

The room came alive. The sounds of soft moans and hard breathing floated through the door.

John Hughes snarled, "Goddamn you, Howie, get out of here! Mainwaring promised her to me. You hear?—to me!"

The other voice she recognized as the one who had called himself Joe Rogers the night they arrived. "Horseshit! You stashed this little piece away and kept her full of dope so that she would be your private stock, but Howie's taking over."

Even as he talked, Meredith's husky voice was imploring, "Hey, what's wrong? Don't stop. What's wrong?"

"Goddamn you, Howie! That's not so. Ask Mainwaring. She freaked out the night she got here. She's a real fricking junkhead."

Howie laughed, a low, caressing laugh, one full of confidence and contempt for the distraught Hughes. "Okay, you little prick, let the pretty lady decide."

There was a rustling, and the rapid breathing grew louder.

Elizabeth could not believe what she was hearing. She knew Meredith probably had done pot with her crowd, but she had far too much sense to become a drug addict. She would never allow these two lowlife types to touch her. Meredith might not be a virgin, but she sure had chosen men with money in Chicago. She must be scared to death—and yet she sounded so willing!

Elizabeth stepped across the hall to where she could peep into the room. Her eyes widened.

Meredith was on her knees atop the bed, her arms wrapped around Howie's thick-set body. They were feasting on each other's mouths, his hand molding her back and buttocks with heavy strokes. She pulled her mouth free, arched her body, and moaned. Howie released her, stepped back, and quickly pulled off his tunic and pants.

Elizabeth gaped in astonishment at his body. She had never seen a man so covered with hair. Meredith's eyes were devouring him, her tongue licking greedily over her lips. Elizabeth gasped as he turned, apparently to look at his unseen companion. He reached down to display himself and sneered at Hughes.

"Okay, you cocksucker, ask her what she wants—that shriveled-up tool of yours . . . or this."

He turned back to Meredith. "How about it, baby?"

Meredith came off her haunches and reached for him. He drew her close and slid his hand over her flat stomach. Suddenly, she shrieked in pain, pushing futilely against him with her arms. Elizabeth, her senses reeling, could see the sudden cruel thrust of his fingers. Then Meredith's arms were back around him, and she was shuddering against him. He took a step forward and, lifting her body, turned it in midair as though she weighed nothing.

Placing her on her hands and knees in one swift motion, he vaulted onto the bed behind her and, clasping her hips with his hands, entered her with one driving thrust. Her head reared and she shrieked again, struggling against him for a second, but to no more effect than a child. Within moments she was seconding his lunges with her own.

As Elizabeth watched, Howie's eyes glazed over with lust. Meredith dropped her head, her hair falling about her face, her moans timed to his thrusts.

Lifting her head, she looked toward John Hughes and screamed, "What are you waiting for, you bastard!"

John stepped into Elizabeth's view and stood, staring at the furious rhythm of their bodies. She screamed at him again. "Now, bastard! Now!"

He climbed onto the bed and grabbed her by the hair, sobbing in his excitement.

Elizabeth's last view was of Meredith, her pale body sandwiched between the two darker, muscular forms that struggled against her. Elizabeth fled back up the corridor, the noise of her feet against the gritty surface covered by the shuddering cries of the entwined trio.

She dashed into her room, sending the door crashing against the wall, and leaned over the corner of the bed, trying to drive the erotic memories from her mind. The darkness before her was filled with images of the interlocked bodies on Meredith's bed. She became aware that she was crouching over the mattress, rhythmically moving against its corner. With a cry of shame, she fell forward onto the bed, pounding the pillow with her fist. Long minutes went by before the lingering heat left her loins.

Elizabeth pushed herself upright, stung by the remembrance of one of Mainwaring's comments. He had said that people inside the mental ward were like those outside, only more transparent, concerned only with satisfying their lusts, their egos, and their thirst for violence. Anxious to shut off the memory of her own body's betrayal, she slid off the bed and closed the door, trying to ignore the building cries from the far end of the hall.

Elizabeth felt her way through the unlit room to the bathroom. Standing in the dark before the lavatory, she washed her face. She closed the door and turned on the lights, conscious of a sudden need to see herself. She stared at herself long in the mirror—at her hair, her skin, her eyes, and her lips—and wondered what the two men thought of her . . . if they wanted to use her as they used Meredith.

Her hand moved as if it had a life of its own, slowly unbuttoning her tunic. A part of her mind protested, shocked, and she was frightened because she could not stop herself. The warmth stirred in her as her hands opened the tunic and exposed her breasts. Her hands closed on them, cupping them, and the nipples swelled under the caress.

Something seemed to explode in her mind, and she cried aloud, "My God, what am I doing?"

Frantically drawing the tunic shut, she buttoned it.

Elizabeth extinguished the light and stood in the dark, trembling. She was beginning to fear for her sanity. She had grown up in a religious family, and until she was in college had believed that her body must be a sanctified temple for her husband. Even when she yielded to the clumsy temptations in college, there had been a shadow of shame, elusive but very real, in the far chambers of her mind.

The trouble was that, without her realizing it, her nicely ordered fantasy world had begun to come apart that day in the gardener's shack. Until that moment, a devoutly religious Elizabeth had believed the romanticized garbage she had read about sex as some unmentionable reward of the perfect marriage, some vague sort of touching that produced music like the sweep of one hundred violins, performed on marital couches with the fragrance and softness of a million rose petals. Despite the near rape and her fumbling failures in college, she had still expected a romantic fantasy in her marriage, not a husband who acted as though she were a complex piece of machinery that had to be primed and pampered before it could be used.

She left the bathroom and felt her way to a chair, aware that Skystone's atmosphere had changed abruptly and she was no longer afraid. The darkness seemed warm and inviting, alive with an electrifying energy. She laughed aloud.

She should have known her mother would have a fairy tale about sex, the same way mothers sugarcoated every unappealing need or want.

It was Jack who had shown her what sex could be. At first it seemed dirty because he had been so direct, caring for nothing but the sweet ecstasy of it. But that first morning she had discovered the animal in herself, had found she was no different from Jack and the man in the gardener's shed. She had loved it. She needed to wallow in it, to be treated like a bitch in heat. Without that, it was like doing push-ups.

Grinning, she came to her feet and moved across to the bed. She pulled off the confining slacks and began to caress herself. Eagerly she thought of Meredith and the two men ravishing her. All too soon, a keening, gasping cry escaped her lips and she shuddered deliciously. Looking down at her body, she thought of what John Hughes and the hairy one would do to her if they caught her that way. She groaned at the vivid imagery of her thoughts and opened herself again to her caressing hand.

Later, she pulled free of her sated reverie, stretched luxuriously, and drew the slacks back on. It had been more intense than anything she had known.

CHAPTER 24 _____

*T*he sounds of slamming drawers, the rustle of stacks of paper, and a recitation of innovative curses streamed from the study. With a groan, Cobb rose from the living room chair, sidestepped the dozing Tip's feet, and— groggy with fatigue—entered the lantern-lit study.

Andy looked up at him as though the whole thing was Cobb's fault. "Damn it! Of all the nights for the son of a bitch not to be at home! He gave me his girlfriend's phone number, and it's in this desk. I put all my files from Sky-stone into this damned thing. But, by God, I don't know where in the hell it is."

Cobb dug his knuckles into his bleary eyes. "Shut up for a minute, doc, and listen. There's no point in us sitting here taking catnaps while you're trying to find that phone number. We can run down to the sheriff's office and pick up the flare gun."

"What flare gun? You didn't say anything about a flare gun. Why in the hell do you want it?"

"How do you think we're going to know when the juice has been turned off—grab the gate and see if we electrocute ourselves? After you throw the circuit breakers, you will have to fire a flare to let us know."

"What good is a flare in the daytime? How can you see it?"

"Those things put out smoke as well as a ball of fire. We'll see it."

Back in the living room, Cobb kicked Tip's boot to awaken him. "Okay, old buddy, let's go commit a bit of petty larceny."

The farmhouses along the road lay dark and quiet, like sleeping beasts hunkered down in their night lairs. Cobb had never minded working the graveyard shift. It was a fresh, quiet world free of the inconsequential bickerings and frictions of his fellow beings. He always felt a sense of aloof power as he moved through the night guarding the hapless citizenry defenseless in their beds.

Parked along quiet country roads in the wee hours on stakeouts, he had been aware of the microcosm of life around him in the road weeds. He had heard the slithering rustle of the predators, sliding powerfully through the vegetation until a tiny scream of terror signified their success.

Cobb had grown to where he spent those long hours of solitude toying with the illusion that he, too, was a predator, stalking the lawbreakers that sought the shelter of the night for their deeds. The night world was his world. He punished and he rewarded. Soon Skystone would no longer be forbidden ground, immune to the retribution of the law.

As they came over the hill, passing through the pale bluish circle of the town's outermost street light, Cobb shook Tip. "Come on, sleepyhead. Wake up."

The deep breathing ceased abruptly. Tip sniffled, and wiped the back of his hand across his nose.

"God Almighty, I'm worn out." He yawned. "What time is it?"

"Two twenty-three."

"Jesus, I wish we hadn't drunk that whiskey. How do you figure on getting that flare gun out of the office?"

"Wipe your nose, for God's sake." Cobb pointed to the box of tissues posed precariously on the transmission hump.

"Listen to me, Tip. Either J.T. or Curtis will be in the office. The other one will be on patrol."

"I hope to hell J.T. ain't at the station. That son of a bitch is such a stickler he wouldn't let you borrow a match without getting an okay from Toby."

"Well, we'll just have to risk it."

It was quite dark on Main Street. There were only three street lights along its length—the old-fashioned incandescent types. Most of the storefronts were dimly lit by single low-wattage bulbs burning inside. Stoneville was safely tucked within its walls by ten o'clock each night, many miles away from the tourist traffic that was attracted to brightly lit store windows.

A single one-hundred-watt bulb lighted the doorway of the sheriff's office, barely illuminating the weather-beaten plaque reading *Beauregard County Sheriff's Department*.

The slamming of the car doors sounded startlingly loud in the deserted street. Their footsteps were hollow on the boardwalk before the office. As they turned into the doorway, J. T. Carruthers' head popped out of the doorway of the sergeants' room.

"It's just us, J.T.," Cobb called.

J.T. sounded petulant. "Well, shit! You startled me. You're not supposed to be around now."

Cobb, followed by Tip, pushed past J.T., catching a glimpse, as he did, of the tiny radio room. Millie, the night dispatcher, was sprawled forward over her desk, her head resting on her fat arms, sound asleep.

Cobb hurried around the desk and slipped into the chair. It was a game he and J.T. had played more than once, and losing it now didn't help J.T.'s mood.

"Damn it, Cobb, what do you and Tip want?"

Before answering, Cobb rose and offered the chair to J.T. He swallowed noisily, stalked with enormous dignity around the desk, and settled into the chair. He swung his feet on to the desk and smirked at Cobb.

"Well, Cobb, I understand you're walking on thin ice these days. Working overtime to try to get back into Toby's good graces?"

"No, not exactly, J.T. Tip and I were sitting around talking, and—"

J.T. laughed—a dry hacking more like a cough than a

laugh. "It appears to me you two have been doing more drinking than sitting."

The smugness of his voice matched the smugness of his expression. "Besides, big shot, your little wife called here twice tonight, wondering where you were."

"J.T., you've always been a pain in the ass. I was taking Tip home and remembered I was supposed to check the emergency equipment in the morning. I thought I'd just drop by and get things laid out."

"Check emergency equipment? Nobody told me anything about checking equipment. The sheriff would have told all of us about that. Listen here. You're not going to take anything out of the office until I check with Toby, and I sure the hell don't plan on calling him in the middle of the night."

Cobb turned to Tip. "Well, okay, Tip, I tried. Toby's not going to be happy about this."

They started toward the door, but Cobb stopped again. "By the way, why is Curtis back in the alley by the furniture store checking the windows?"

J.T. blinked. "You saw Curtis doing what? You're crazy! He's out on patrol."

Cobb nodded toward Tip. "Ask him."

"It kinda looked like him, J.T.," Tip said. "Besides, why would anybody else be fooling around at the furniture store this time of night?"

J.T. pushed past Tip, drawing his gun. "Come on, boys. Follow me. Someone's trying to rob the furniture store."

He ran out the front door.

Cobb looked at the grinning Tip. "Go with him and keep him busy. Stall him until you hear me getting in the car."

The various emergency kits had been picked up willy-nilly over the years and were stored under the shelving or in the closet of the sergeant's room. Cobb cursed silently. The kit, stored in a small metal suitcase, was not where he had last noticed it.

He got off his knees, knowing that he had very little time, and rushed to the closet, only to find the door locked. He turned back to the desk and, opening the top drawer, reached for the old iron key.

J.T.'s voice stopped him in mid-reach. It sounded as if he

was right outside, on the walk. He was shouting, "You stay there, Tip. I'm gonna have Millie call Curtis in. We're gonna need more help to search the woodlot behind the store."

Before Cobb could shut the desk drawer, Tip yelled from the distance, "Come here, J.T., quick! I thought I heard someone on the roof."

J.T. shuffled about the boardwalk in indecision before shouting, "Coming," and racing off to a volley of echoes from the loose boards.

Securing the key, Cobb unlocked the closet door. The air-sea rescue kit was in a white metal case sitting in the corner. Pulling the flare pistol from the case, he tucked it inside his uniform blouse. The flares took forever to free from the case. As he removed the last of them, he heard J.T. shouting, "I'm calling Curtis. If we don't watch out, he'll get away."

Cobb shoved the case back into the closet and crammed the cartridges into his bulging pants pockets. Just as he put the key back in the drawer, J.T. charged through the door.

"Damn you, Cobb! Toby's gonna hear about you sitting on your ass while we were trying to catch that sucker."

Cobb shrugged. "I'm not going to stay around here and be insulted. The hell with you!"

He started out the door. J.T. called after him, "I'm gonna tell Toby about you coming in here asking for equipment."

When Cobb and Tip reached the Witherspoon house, they found Andy on the phone. He was not happy.

"Hold it a minute . . . my colleagues just walked in. Let me fill them in."

He put his hand over the mouthpiece. "We've got trouble. His chopper's out of service for its FAA inspection. Besides, he's not too happy with me for calling him at this hour. He must have been pouring the old pork to the little lady when I called. Any suggestions?"

"If we could find another helicopter, maybe we could rent it and let him fly it," Cobb said.

Andy thought for a moment. "That's not a bad idea. Let me try it on."

"Smitty, is there any chance of you renting a chopper?"

He listened in silence.

"Hell, no, I don't want another helicopter service. I want

you. Listen. I need a tough son of a bitch like you to fly this job. I told you it's a matter of life and death."

He paused again.

"No, I can't guarantee that. They may have a couple of shotguns."

This time his face relaxed as he listened.

"Hell, the damned thing would have to have insurance on it—right? Listen, Smitty, there's an extra five hundred for you and an extra five hundred to the chopper owner if we do it."

He nodded toward the two deputies.

"Yeah, I know it's a hell of a time to be calling, but I told you what we're up against. That's why I'm offering extra money."

He massaged his temple as he listened.

"Okay, call me back the minute you hear. Listen, buddy, there may be a hell of a lot of lives riding on this—mine included. That's why I want you. Understand?"

There was a last pause before he said, "I know you will," and lowered the receiver.

He looked at Cobb and Tip. "I'm going to make some coffee. What some?"

Cobb grabbed him by the arm. "Wait a minute. What did he say?"

"It's a bad season to rent a helicopter on short notice. Everybody wants work done before winter sets in. He heard a guy talking last Friday—griping—something about having a job canceled for the middle of this week. Smitty's going to call him."

He shook his head, and Cobb knew the little man had lost most of the emotional surge that carried him through the night.

"I'm sorry, fellows. It was my best bet. We tried, damn it, we tried. Now we're going to need some luck."

The two deputies settled into living room chairs, listening to Andy stirring in the kitchen. Soon the aroma of frying eggs reached Cobb, and he remembered that he hadn't eaten for hours.

CHAPTER 25 _____

With the curtain drawn back, the stars, smeared by the double panes of glass, filled the frame of the window. Elizabeth sat in the heavy chair she had pulled to the window, staring out. The shame and self-loathing, which overwhelmed her in the aftermath of her masturbation orgy, had receded, leaving her empty, stunned at the enormity of her disgusting passion. The question raced through her mind in unanswered repetition. Why had she so abjectly surrendered her values after the disgusting spectacle she had witnessed?

She remembered a book she had read, a suspense novel about an American couple in England. They had moved into an ancient monastery that had been used, at some earlier date, as an insane asylum. The couple had invited several American friends to join them for a week. Soon the group was acting strangely, and as the days went by, they plunged into licentiousness and brutality. The novel ended with hosts and guests being destroyed by a fire that engulfed the old monastery. The author's premise had been that the evil in the minds of the lunatics had lingered to infect the vulnerable group with vile and thwarted desires.

She wondered if the same thing could be happening to

her, remembering her reaction to the encounter between the nurses, as well as the debasement of Meredith. In the past, such sights—even hearing of them—would have filled her with revulsion. That must be it. The deranged degenerates in Skystone were emanating such vile thoughts that they were infecting her like some foul contagion.

It had grown chilly in the room, and she was ready to return to the bed when the door flew open and the light came on. Startled, she came out of the chair.

Shane stood in the doorway, smiling, one arm behind her back. She had changed since Elizabeth last saw her. The nurse's cap was gone, and the golden hair, so neatly arranged on Tuesday morning, hung loose and unkempt around her face. Even her magnificent jade eyes seemed dull. Her uniform was badly rumpled and unbuttoned to the waist.

Without speaking, she glided toward Elizabeth, the smile slowly fading. Elizabeth was so frightened that she couldn't move until it was too late. Cut off from the refuge of the bathroom, she backed toward the corner until the converging walls brought her to a halt. Shane stopped within arm's reach.

Her voice was mocking. "Well, if it isn't Dr. Mainwaring's long-lost Ruthie."

Elizabeth stammered, "My name is Elizabeth."

"I don't give a shit what your name is."

Slowly she brought her left arm from behind her back. It held a carving knife, which gleamed dully in the overhead light. She slid her other hand caressingly along its cutting edge as her gaze roamed over Elizabeth's body.

"So wholesome looking—the all-American girl," Shane murmured.

She took a quick step, and the blade was touching Elizabeth's stomach. "How would you like to have that luscious, all-American body slashed into bloody ribbons? Hmmm?"

Elizabeth shook her head, too terrified to answer.

Shane whipped the knife upward, and Elizabeth, shrieking, threw her hands over her face. The crazed girl's free hand struck with blinding speed, seizing Elizabeth's uplifted arm and jerking her off balance. Quick as a cat, Shane was behind her, gripping her around the waist with one arm, the other holding the knife against the side of her neck.

Gleefully, she whispered in Elizabeth's ear, "Put those pretty arms down, my dear. We wouldn't want to cut you, would we?"

Elizabeth froze, her skin crawling in revulsion at the contact. The girl's body pressed hard against her.

"I'm not going to hurt you, you stupid bitch. Relax. I have a very special invitation for you . . . to a party."

In an awkward lockstep, they left the room. Just before they reached the red door, Shane jerked her to a stop, with the deadly edge of the carving knife hungry against Elizabeth's throat.

"Just one moment, my dear. You are the guest of honor tonight—a very special guest of honor. Dear Tina didn't forget you, you lucky little devil."

The red door swung open, and Howie Delgado stepped out into the hall. He wore a bed sheet that had been fashioned into a sort of robe.

"Here the stupid bitch is, Howie. I guess Tina's little party can start now."

Howie grabbed Elizabeth by her hair, twisting it in his hand, and pulled her away from Shane. She groaned with the pain.

He spoke sharply to Shane. "We're not ready yet. Tina wants you to find John. The wimp's been sulking since I kicked his ass."

"I'm nobody's errand girl. I—"

Howie looked at her, anger blazing into his face. "You're not gonna be anybody's nothing if you don't do what I tell you. Don't fuck with me, dyke."

Reluctantly, she backed away and stalked down the hall.

Howie pulled Elizabeth forward, controlling her by her hair.

She gasped, "Oh, God! Please. You're pulling my hair out."

They were inside the red door now in an unlit corridor. He pulled her against him, his lips near her ear. "That ain't all I'm gonna pull out of you before it's over, baby."

He released her, sending her reeling down the hall with a

hard shove. The reflected light of candles coming through a doorway illuminated the hall. "In there!" he ordered.

She stepped into the room, instantly recognizing the scene from John Hughes' description. Terror flooded through her as the meaning of Shane's words became all too clear.

In panic, she turned to run at the same moment that Howie appeared in the doorway. Arms grabbed her from behind and pulled her aside. She struggled vainly until she recognized Mainwaring's soft voice.

"Relax. It will be okay. They're not going to hurt you."

Her gaze sought the top of the table. It was bare, but beyond the table stood the woman she had known as Mrs. Eddy, Tina Duchin.

Tina was stroking a long length of leather and looking down. Elizabeth took a step past Dr. Mainwaring to see what the Duchin woman was looking at. She couldn't suppress a cry.

Molly Hatcher was on the floor, nude, resting on her knees with her forehead pressed against the floor. Her hands were bound with nylon stockings. The pale perfection of her milky white hips and buttocks was marred by several dark, glistening threads that Elizabeth knew were blood.

Tina Duchin placed a bare foot atop the arched back for a moment, rocking the lovely body. Then she removed it and, in a blur of motion, brought the length of leather whistling across the girl's buttocks. Molly screamed, a sound that coursed through Elizabeth like an electric shock.

She heard Mainwaring groan. From the corner of her eye she could see Howie, his eyes glazed as they had been in Meredith's room.

Moments passed with no sound except Molly's choking sobs. Then her tormentor bent forward and ran her hand along the flaring curves of the girl's hip. The hand moved slowly, stroking the soft flesh, and Elizabeth couldn't turn her eyes away. It slipped down under the trembling flanks to caress the smooth stomach. Elizabeth grasped the edge of the table, her knees suddenly weak, as Tina's bejeweled hand glided across the rib cage to cup the heavy, swaying mound of a lovely breast.

She heard Tina sigh, "God, you're a luscious little piece. I can understand what Shane sees in you. What a bride you'll make for the Horned One."

As Tina's hand continued to weigh the heavy breast, Elizabeth chewed on her lower lip, trying to stifle the sudden sensation flashing through her loins. She felt all rational control slipping away from her.

A scream from the doorway startled her, and John Hughes reeled in, propelled by a hard shove.

Shane charged past him, the carving knife raised, shouting, "No, you old slut! Not her! I'll kill you!"

Tina tried to leap away, stumbling, a look of terror on her face. Shane had almost reached her when Howie's fist, with all of his two hundred pounds behind it, thundered into the side of her face. It lifted her off her feet, and she crashed to the floor, the carving knife skittering into the corner. She rolled up on all fours, crawling toward the knife. Howie sent his foot whistling into her ribs. She screamed in pain as he leaped over her to retrieve the weapon. Still, she didn't stop. She pushed herself up on one hand, shaking her head, begging, "No . . . no . . . no."

Tina, her composure recovered, returned to her improvised altar. She eyed the fallen Shane, her face distorted with hatred. "Why, Shane, how ungrateful. I thought you'd want to be present when we offered your lovely Molly to the Master."

Shane got her knees under her and crawled to where Molly lay. She left a trail of blood from her ruined mouth. When she reached the girl, she patted the naked shoulder with her bloody hand.

Elizabeth could barely hear Shane's voice. "I'm sorry, Molly. I'm sorry. I really love you. At last, it is real."

She looked up, her eyes directly on Elizabeth. "And it's too late. Far too late for us."

Tina's sharp voice cut through Shane's words. "Howie, get her out of here."

Grabbing Shane by her hair, Howie pulled her up to her knees and dragged her across the room and out through the doorway. In the corridor, he released her, and she collapsed to the floor, semiconscious.

Tina and Howie, working together, lifted Molly onto the

table and tied her down. Elizabeth turned her head aside. She could sense the overpowering temptation to yield to the ecstatic excitement of evil drawing her toward the crazed circle.

Tina began a chant, a recitation that slowly grew in volume, answered, syllable for syllable, by Howie's husky voice.

Elizabeth looked at Mainwaring. He was unaware of her presence, his eyes fixed on the table, his hands clenching and unclenching.

She leaned toward him and whispered, "Please take me out of here. I can't stand this."

Mainwaring, the muscles of his face rigid, his breathing quick and hard, ignored her.

Tina ceased her chanting and cried, "Oh, great Lord Satan, to this man, thy surrogate, show the lustful pleasure thou find in this, our gift."

Elizabeth heard Howie's animal howl and the sounds of the table protesting the surges of his weight.

"Give forth thy homage, Lord Satan," Tina screamed.

Howie's howl rose in volume with his lust, and then all was quiet. Mainwaring slumped against the wall, releasing his breath in a long shudder.

Tina called out again, panting. "Oh, Master of Lust, oh, Prince of Pleasure, we send thy handmaiden to join thee."

Elizabeth, hearing the clatter of the table, opened her eyes. Tina, stripped of her panties, was tugging at the limp Molly. Her big breasts, with their dark aureoles, bounced in the candlelight as she and Howie dragged the unresisting girl to the exercise machine against the wall and quickly suspended her to its steel arms.

As Tina stepped away, the burly Howie caught her from behind, his hands clutching her breasts, his mouth buried against her neck. She arched against him, groaning, but then her eyes opened wide. She struggled to free herself, and, breaking free, swung the leather strap into her companion's face. It curled across his forehead with a loud splat. He staggered backward, but was so crazed with lust, the blow had little effect.

"Damn it, Howie!" Tina shouted. "She's gone. Shane's gone! Quick!"

She dodged under his lunging embrace, shoved John Hughes from her path, and raced out the door. From the passageway, she shrieked, "Oh, God, she's coming back! Quick, Howie, she must have the knife. Stop her!"

Howie lumbered past Elizabeth, and she was borne after him by Mainwaring's shove.

In the dim hallway, she could see the white of Shane's uniform as she moved slowly and erratically toward them, illuminated by the narrow bar of light lancing through the gap in the red door.

"Shane?" Tina called.

There was no answer.

They could hear her labored breathing. Tina clutched Howie's thick bicep, pulling at him. "Howie, what's wrong with her? Make her answer."

He jerked himself free as Shane came even with the red door. She swayed, and put out an arm to brace herself against the ponderous door that opened more so that the light from the other hallway shone on her.

John Hughes whistled. "What the hell is that on her? It's all red."

Shane spoke, slowly, with effort. There was a gurgling to her words. "Tina, I let . . . Paul . . . out. I . . ."

She coughed, a horrible, hacking cough, and red liquid spilled from her mouth. "Told him . . . you wanted . . . to hurt him."

Tina moaned, "Oh, God, where is her knife? She gave him her knife."

"No, she didn't," Howie shouted. "I kicked it away after she dropped it. She didn't have anything to give him."

"The hell she didn't!" cried John Hughes. "Remember the straight razor she found at the house?"

Shane was gurgling now with each word. "Yes . . . razor . . . for . . . you, Tina."

Failing to brace herself against the wall, she slid noiselessly to the floor, sat upright a moment, and then slumped over, rolling onto her back.

Howie whirled, knocking Elizabeth and Mainwaring out

of his way. He rushed back into the therapy room. He found the knife lying by the feet of Molly Hatcher, whose limp body hung bonelessly from its bindings, still lovely in the flickering candlelight.

Flipping on the electric lights, Howie and Tina rushed down the hall and disappeared around the corner. Elizabeth, Mainwaring, and John Hughes remained huddled together outside the therapy room.

Elizabeth thought of trying to sneak back and free the injured Molly, but her fear of Howie was too great.

They heard someone running toward them, and John Hughes grasped Elizabeth, holding her in front of him as a shield.

Howie rounded the corner and raced toward them. Tina was far behind him, running unsteadily, gasping for breath.

"Howie, wait!" Tina pleaded.

He paid no attention. Elizabeth jumped out of his way as he ran past her into the therapy room. Tina skidded to a stop in front of them, breathing so hard she could hardly talk.

"He must have taken off after he attacked Shane. He got away."

She looked back at Shane, lying in a spreading pool of blood. "Is she dead?"

Mainwaring, his complexion an ashen gray, muttered, "I don't know. I haven't examined her."

He took a couple of steps, staring at the gap in the red door. Then he whirled, glaring wild-eyed at Tina.

"You bitch! This wouldn't have happened if you hadn't done all this—if you had waited until we were out of here!" He waved his hand vaguely toward the therapy room.

Anger flared in Tina's flushed face. "Why didn't you ask me to stop, old man? Why don't you tell the truth?"

She looked at Elizabeth. "Why don't you tell your little Ruthie the truth? Nobody made you attend our invocations. You stood there, quivering with lust, wanting to take Howie's place. You horny old bastard, tell her about today. Tell her what happened when I stuck my tit in your face—that you slobbered all over it."

"Stop it!" he shouted. "Damn you, stop it!"

He turned to Elizabeth, who was staring at him in disbelief. "Don't listen to her, Ruthie. Please don't. She's lying. I...I was there to try to keep them from killing Molly. I..."

Howie, back in his uniform, hurried out of the therapy room and, grabbing John Hughes by the arm, pulled him through the open door.

"Wait, Howie!" Tina shouted. "Don't leave me here!"

As she reached the red door, it slammed shut in her face. While she struggled with the heavy door, Thomas Mainwaring bent over Shane.

A straining Tina shouldered the door open and peeked into the corridor, ignoring Mainwaring's muttered, "She's dead."

"They've disappeared! I can't see them. He has killed them both."

Mainwaring came to his feet, eyeing Shane's body in horror. "God, he slashed her to pieces—at least twenty deep cuts. How on earth did she get this far?"

His face changed as he turned to Tina. "My dear, her hatred must have been beyond comprehension. I wonder if she managed to convey it to St. Denis."

"Shut up! Goddamn you, shut up, you old man!"

The three of them froze when they heard someone running in the convalescent-wing corridor. The heavy door swung open, revealing Howie and John Hughes. They carried shotguns.

"We're going after the bastard," Howie said. "It's every son of a bitch for himself."

"No, don't leave me like this," Tina cried.

Howie pulled the carving knife from his waistband and slapped it into her hand. "Here, Tina. Like I said, it's every son of a bitch for himself now."

Without another word, he disappeared through the door. John Hughes looked as if he wanted to say something to Mainwaring, but shrugged and followed Howie, calling, "Wait for me, you asshole!"

"Don't leave me behind," Tina screamed. She vanished into the other corridor.

Mainwaring and Elizabeth heard the clash of the treatment room doors being flung open, and then it was quiet.

"Dr. Mainwaring."

He ignored her, still staring at Shane's body.

"Dr. Mainwaring, please! Let's cut Molly down and do something to help her."

He blinked and became aware of her for the first time. "Didn't you hear, Ruthie? Howie said it's every man for himself. They went outside. St. Denis may still be in the building. I must save you. You're all I have. Quick!"

She resisted, but he was stronger than she. He pulled her past the red door into the convalescent wing and dragged her, still resisting, toward the treatment room.

She clutched at his coat lapel. "Listen to me! We can't go out that way. They may be waiting outside with those shotguns. They will shoot anything that moves."

His hysteria passed, and he stopped to think. "Come on! The kitchen! I'll let you out through the garbage hatch."

"No!" she cried. "I don't want to be alone."

He wrapped his arms around her and drew her to him. "Ruthie, you have to get into the woods and hide. Find a spot and lie low. They won't find you. When the plane arrives tomorrow, head northward past the rear of the building. The airstrip is near the north fence. If I don't show up, tell Harvey to take off without me. Now, hurry!"

Despite the persistent image of his avid face as he watched Molly Hatcher's humiliation, she wanted to be around him—anything but be alone. He was insane, but he was different from the others.

"No, please, let me stay with you."

He pushed her away. "No, I am sick, Ruthie. Your father is doomed. I've been corrupted by their evil. I didn't realize the immensity of it. I . . . Oh, God, I don't want to say it. I want to wallow with them in their degradation. Now go!"

He shoved her hard, and she staggered across the room. Forgetting the need for caution, he shouted, "Go, for God's sake, go! Go before I use you myself."

With sickening comprehension, she understood that he meant what he said. Some last bit of goodness in his mad brain was giving her a chance. She pushed against the iron panel. It swung open, and she crept out into the cold night air. She pushed the door shut and listened fearfully.

All was quiet.

Slowly Elizabeth worked her way toward the front of the building, cringing as she passed under the pools of light from the globes along the outside walls.

CHAPTER 26

T he first two rings of the telephone failed to arouse the
sleeping men at the table in the study. The third ring
dragged Andy Witherspoon from a troubled nap. Tip
and Cobb remained asleep, their heads resting on their
folded arms.

Andy, aware that the phone could have been ringing for a
long time, lunged to his feet and rushed into the living room.

It was Smitty, sounding much more cheerful than he had
during their first conversation. Andy was so exhausted that
Smitty's good news had little immediate impact.

The pilot had located an available helicopter at the Little
Rock airport. It slowly dawned on the sleep-dulled Andy
that their luck had changed. Smitty's news, however, was
not all good. It would be past 9:30 before he could have the
helicopter—much later than they wanted to make the assault.

Plunkett, while a daredevil on the job, was a careful man
in such mundane things as maintenance and having safe
landing zones. On several occasions, Andy had heard him
say that he didn't mind getting killed in the chopper doing
something dangerous but possible. What he didn't want was
to be killed through simple carelessness.

This prompted a discussion of a landing site at Stoneville. Smitty rejected Andy's first three suggestions before they agreed on the parking lot at the county fairgrounds. The pilot, still ebullient, was ready to hang up when the doctor interrupted him.

"Smitty, did you understand what I told you earlier? This is a dangerous job. We may be facing deranged patients that are armed with shotguns. I want you to realize what we are going up against."

Smitty giggled as he answered, and Andy realized he was not alone. "I wish you'd say that again, doc; that I'm going to be flying into the jaws of death."

Then he was talking away from the receiver. "You hear that, Ada? These may be my last hours, woman. You'd better pleasure this old boy to death with the time you have left. There may not be any seconds."

The sounds of a struggle, accompanied by gales of laughter, floated through the receiver. Smitty's voice, so loud that Andy winced, exploded through the phone. "Doc, I've gotta go. You can call the police and tell them old Smitty Plunkett is being sexually assaulted."

There was another burst of feminine laughter, and the phone went dead. The doctor put the receiver down with mild regrets that he wasn't a younger man and in Smitty's shoes.

He walked back into the den to find Cobb awake—pouring a cup of tepid coffee. When Andy told him the news, Cobb mumbled, "Good."

He said nothing else until he had drunk his coffee. Placing the empty cup on the table, he looked at Andy.

"Doc, are you still hell-bent on going with us?"

Andy nodded.

"You have a gun?"

"Yep. I have a thirty-two . . . just bought it. Several doctors advised me that I should. You know, nowadays drug addicts will try to hit on a doctor. Al Caudill taught me a little bit about shooting. I'm not bad at it, to tell the truth."

Cobb stared moodily at him. "Are you sure you know where those circuit boxes are?"

The doctor bristled. "Hell, yes, I know where they are. I

was up in that crawl space four or five times while they were being installed. I wanted to make sure there was no half-assed workmanship."

"What do the circuit boards look like?"

Andy thought for a moment. "There's an upright panel. It's connected both to the roof beams and the ceiling joists. The circuit boxes are on one side of the panel, grouped together, with the wiring coming in from the other side."

"Then all you have to do is drop through the hatch, crawl across the attic to the circuit panel, and check the labels. When you find the box labeled 'FENCES,' you throw the circuit breakers. Maybe two minutes to reach the panel, half a minute to find the right box and throw the breakers . . . say, to be safe, three minutes from the time you climb through the roof hatch. Right?"

Cobb had closed his eyes as he talked. When there was no answer, his lids flew open. Andy's wizened face wore a startled look.

"What's wrong, Doc?"

Andy pressed his hands against his temples. "Hell! What a stupid son of a bitch I am!"

Cobb felt his own hopes sinking as he asked, "Why?"

"There . . . there are no labels on the circuit boxes, Cobb. We talked about that when we remodeled. Everybody agreed that if a patient did get in there to try to shut off the electrical circuits, labeling would make it easy for him. If they pulled circuit breakers at random, lights and machines would be going off. It would alert the staff that someone was up there."

"How many circuit boxes are there?"

"That's hard to say. I don't remember that well—probably fifteen or more. The panel is filled with them."

"What you are saying is that you have no more idea than I do which is the correct circuit box—right?"

No answer.

Cobb repeated his question. "I said you don't know which circuit breaker is for the fences, do you?"

The fiery little man jumped up, sending his chair crashing over backwards. The noise brought Tip upright, staring wildly about him.

The Witherspoon temper vented itself. "Don't you yell at me! I'm the one who came up with the plan to get us in that place, and I'm the one that came up with the means to get in. I'll let you damned well figure out how to identify which is the correct circuit breaker."

For a moment they stared angrily at each other. Tip groggily demanded some explanation for the shouting. When they told him the problem, he shrugged.

"I don't think that's such a hassle. I know what I would do." But even as he relieved himself of this startling information, Tip's head sagged toward his folded arms.

"Tip, wake up!" Cobb roared. "What in the hell would you do?"

Reluctantly, the sleepy Tip pulled himself upright again. "Hell, I'd call the contractor who remodeled the damned place. I think anybody with the brains of a piss-ant would know that's the person to call."

Having delivered his rebuke, he paused to see if he was going to be yelled at again before lowering his head.

Andy rubbed his chin thoughtfully. "By God, that's right. Oh, hell! I can't call at this time of night."

"Why not? This is an emergency. I can't believe a contractor would want to get a bad reputation with places like Skystone, especially if there is an emergency."

"You're right, Cobb. If he doesn't like it, the hell with him! He made a bundle off of us."

He marched into the living room, with Cobb following.

Andy Witherspoon had far more patience than Cobb. He sat there, counting the rings aloud, and had reached number twenty-two before a woman's voice, slurred by sleep or too many sleeping pills, came on the line.

"Who in the name of God is this? Do you realize it's four-thirty in the morning? If this is some kind of stupid prank—"

"Mrs. Conroy, this is Andrew Witherspoon. I'm a medical doctor, and it's urgent that I talk to your husband."

"Who's sick?"

Andy began to wonder if he was dealing with a lady too deeply engulfed in a chemical fog to be reasoned with. "Mrs. Conroy, your husband remodeled Skystone, a convalescent hospital in central Arkansas. We have a problem here that has to do with construction. It's a matter of life and death. I must talk to him. Now if . . ."

"I can't make any sense out of what you're saying. Just a minute . . . I'll get Barry."

Getting Barry was not a simple task, and more increasingly precious minutes fled by. Finally, Barry Conroy came to the phone. He sounded his usual noisy, affable self, if one discounted a note of irritation tinging his voice. Apparently, he had not joined his wife in whatever she had ingested.

"Okay, this is Barry. What in the hell is going on?"

The doctor carefully explained the situation to him, or at least, what they were claiming to be the situation. He and Cobb agreed to say that a patient had concealed himself in a crawl space, and they were afraid he might kill himself or start a fire if he damaged the wiring.

The contractor, uninterested but still affable, didn't have the answers they wanted. "Nope, I'm not the one you want to talk to, doctor. I don't keep any blueprints at home, and I do too many jobs to remember yours. The man I used as electrical subcontractor is named Mike Caulfield. His offices are here in Memphis. By God, you might be in luck if you can reach him. He stores his blueprints at home—something to do with tax write-offs. I'll give you his number."

The doctor copied down the number and thanked him.

While Mike Caulfield was much sleepier than the contractor had been, he was reached much more easily. It had seemed so simple to that point that Andy was disappointed when he encountered opposition.

"I'm sorry, doctor, I'd like to cooperate, but my plans are my living. I have a lot of wiring techniques that my competitors would love to have. I'll be glad to get dressed and drive up there to help you. I'll charge you no more than a normal consultant's fee for the day—probably three hundred and fifty dollars."

Andy and Cobb had been sharing the receiver, but the doctor suddenly found himself holding thin air. He understood why Cobb held a certain reputation among the criminal element of Beauregard County as a man not to be trifled with.

"Mr. Caulfield, this is Sergeant Cobb Kendall of the Beauregard County Sheriff's Department. You must not have heard Dr. Witherspoon when he said that this is a matter of life and death. . . . Don't interrupt me. You can either pull those plans out and tell the doctor what he wants to know, or I can have a unit of the Memphis police at your house in twenty minutes. I'll make sure they seize the plans of every job you've ever done in Arkansas. . . . I told you not to interrupt me. I'm going to put Dr. Witherspoon back on the line, and I want you to get those plans and start talking. He doesn't care a gnat's ass about how you wire things. He wants to know where one circuit breaker is located on a control panel—no more, no less."

The man muttered a sullen apology and promised to call back as soon as he located the plans.

He was as good as his word. Five minutes later, the phone rang. The information was not given with good grace, but when Andy broke the connection, he knew exactly what he had to do.

Cobb stuck out his hand for a handshake, and Andy took it solemnly. He patted the little doctor on his back.

"Well, doc, I don't like the idea of going in that late in the morning, but by George, unless Toby finds out what we're doing, I think we're on our way."

Andy looked at him, his eyes twinkling now, the fatigue gone. "Right, my man. As they say—keep a tight asshole and a low profile."

He went back into the den, but Cobb lingered in the dark, watching Andy's jaunty figure. For the first time, he felt fear for the doctor—for them all. No sensible police agency would attempt what they were about to try with fewer than fifteen or twenty men.

CHAPTER 27_____

*T*he distant lights of the porte cochere dimmed as the bone-chilling fog drew a misty cloak over Skystone. Elizabeth shivered uncontrollably, her teeth chattering as she crouched behind a tree in the parklike area in front of the hospital. Her hands and feet were so cold that they ached in the moist air. The temperature hovered near the freezing mark.

Her situation had become intolerable. Soon she would be unable to move if she was surprised. She had to get out of the cold or find some extra clothing.

She shuddered at the thought of returning to Skystone. The building held no safe hiding places. She thought of the grim house perched on the hill above the hospital and remembered Scott's description of its horrors. No doubt, sooner or later, they would search the old place; but a mansion that large and old must have a dozen cubbyholes in which to hide. She was deterred by the thought of the house's unburied and decomposing dead, but Skystone held its own cargo of death. Her skin crawled as she thought of the silent figures sitting on the patio, staring sightlessly into the night sky, forever unmindful of the cold.

Scott had said the bodies were upstairs or in the dormitory

at the rear. She would be some distance from them if she stayed in the downstairs front of the building. The chattering of her teeth served to warn her of the increasing danger of hypothermia. The threat was enough for her to make up her mind.

Painfully, she struggled to her feet, wincing at the pain in her nearly frozen feet. The climb up the slope would have to be made by a more circuitous route than the one she and Scott had taken. The white uniform she wore presented a real danger in the night light. She had to reach the house quickly. Her reserves of strength and determination were almost exhausted, and if she lost her way she was not sure that she would not simply lie down and die.

The three maniacs who had rushed outside an hour ago seeking Shane's killer had not reappeared on the porte cochere. She wanted to believe that they had retired to the hospital to escape the bitter cold, yet she dared not count on it.

The crackling of the dry forest debris underfoot made each step a fearful ordeal. Still, the journey seemed shorter than it had that morning when she and Scott climbed the slope. She clawed her way around a large bush to find herself exposed on the edge of the lawn. She ducked back out of sight.

She had stumbled into the open directly across from the front porch. The old residence was dark—a towering, sharp-angled shape blotting out a large portion of the night sky, milky now with the light fog. The empty lawn, in contrast to the woods and the dark building, was lighter in hue. When she looked at the porch, her heart sank.

There was light enough to faintly illuminate the front of the house—enough that she could count the windows and see the Victorian bric-a-brac—but the porch lay in an impenetrable blackness.

Elizabeth crouched behind the bush, unwilling to walk out onto the lawn. The exertion of climbing the slope had left a film of perspiration on her skin; now, immobile in her uncertainty, she was feeling colder. Despite the futility of it, Elizabeth was ready to return to Skystone, when somewhere behind her she heard a disturbance in the brush.

Wihout thinking, she burst out into the yard and ran for the house, her loose-fitting sandals slipping on the grass. There was no escape if they were watching from the many windows.

Once in the shadows on the porch, she moved toward the entry that Scott had used. It was ajar, perhaps an inch or two, allowing a rush of warm air that felt good against her uncovered arms. The faint current of air carried an unpleasant smell. She stopped, suddenly faint with the realization of what the odor was. She leaned against the doorjamb for a moment to recover her senses, but there was no turning back.

Elizabeth stepped inside. The room in which Scott had discovered the empty gun cabinet was rich with the aroma of death, yet she knew it must be mild compared to how it would be in the upper reaches of the place. She closed the door softly behind her and waited futilely for her eyes to adjust to the darkness. It did not take long to realize that the house was not truly warm; that the warmth was only relative to the penetrating icy fog outside.

With her arms extended before her like a blind person's, she groped around the room, seeking something of cloth that she could wrap around herself. The exploration yielded nothing but some heart-stopping moments when she bumped into pieces of furniture. The faint bumps and scrapes seemed terribly loud in the hostile darkness.

She began to cry, silently, without cause, on the edge of leaving the house and walking down the hill to degradation and death. The pride infused in Elizabeth from her earliest years, the self-control breached for the first time by Jack, was on the point of disintegration. She stood in the darkness, cruelly driving her nails into the palms of her hands, angrily biting her cold, numb lip, seeking the determination to go on.

Scott's description of how he reached the living room flashed into her mind, and her dying hopes flickered to life. If nothing else, she could pull the cushions from the sofas and pile them around her for warmth.

There was an opening somewhere in front of her in the darkness, Elizabeth knew from Scott's description, but she could not find it. Raising her arms, she moved slowly, stopping when she encountered the wall. She sidled along its length until, with a sigh of relief, she found the doorway.

The faint, chilling sounds of the radio still flowed through the shadows of the ancient house in its never-ending requiem for the dead. In the hall there was enough light to discern the black maw of the wide-arched opening to the living room. It felt colder in the hall, with a current of air moving gently down the stairwell. She tried to shut her ears to the eerie sound of the radio floating down the steps on the gentle breeze. It was such a grotesque adornment to the ambience of that charnel house.

Elizabeth crossed the entry, conscious of the dark menace of the shadows behind her. The living room was as black a void as the den had been. She crossed the uncharted space of the dark room, gingerly placing one foot before the other.

It seemed that she had moved a great distance, yet she encountered nothing. Behind her, the relative brightness of the hall had dimmed with distance. She was about to abandon her exploration when her questing foot encountered the leg of a sofa.

Blindly she examined it, letting her hand trail along the cushions. It was a long sofa upholstered in a soft material. Over the back, something made of wool—probably an afghan—was draped.

Elizabeth sank onto the soft cushions, letting her tense, exhausted muscles relax. She worked the afghan free and, tucking her legs under her, wrapped it tightly about herself.

Slowly she grew warmer, and her hands and feet stopped aching. The softness of the sofa and the warmth of the heavy afghan were relaxing her, and her eyelids were growing heavier. More than once her head sagged, but then there would be a sound from somewhere within the house and she would start upright, her stinging eyes open. She would again be aware of the faint, plaintive music floating through the dark house.

Elizabeth's chin came to rest one last time on her chest and remained there. Her soft, regular breathing was a faint whisper in the room. She slept, sitting up, for an hour before she awoke with a start.

Her first thought was one of anger that she had allowed herself to doze off. A second, more immediate, thought was to ask herself what had awakened her.

She strained to hear, but there was only the radio. Somehow, the room appeared a bit lighter than it had before she drifted off to sleep. The faintly illuminated face of her watch read 5:50. Dawn was coming to the Arkansas hills.

She shivered delicately, drawing the afghan tighter. The light would be bright enough in another half hour to search the house for a proper hiding place. She thought of going into the kitchen for food—until she remembered Scott's description of the dead girl huddled by the refrigerator.

Outside, an early morning wind was stirring, driving the thin mist away. The dawn light steadily grew stronger as the fog dissipated. When she next opened her eyes, it was bright enough in the living room for her to look around. She tried to determine what the dimly perceived shapes in the room were.

It seemed impossible that she had missed stumbling over the coffee table resting immediately before the sofa. To the side of the sofa, a large table lamp displayed itself in silhouette. Immediately opposite Elizabeth's sofa, perhaps fifteen feet away, was a second sofa. A dim white object lay across it. Focusing her attention on it, she decided that someone had tossed a shirt onto the sofa.

She closed her eyes again to relieve the stinging, and when she reopened them, she sought the white object.

He was sitting there, still as a statue, staring at her.

CHAPTER 28 _____

*E*lizabeth opened her mouth to scream, but her diaphragm was paralyzed. She wanted to shut her eyes —to look away—but she dared not.

So they sat, mute, unmoving, watching—always watching. She wanted to cry out to him, to beg him to speak, to assure her that he meant her no harm. She thought him inhuman that he could sit so still, never glancing away, unaware that she was emulating his posture.

The growing light revealed that he was a stranger to her— young, perhaps no more than twenty-two or twenty-three. His shirt was light blue, not white. He had on dark pants and was wearing tennis shoes.

For a moment Elizabeth grasped at the hope that rescue was at hand, but then she thought of the unknown escapee that she had never seen, the one that inspired terror even in Skystone's vicious denizens. She tried desperately to remember the man's name.

She could stand it no longer. She freed herself of the embrace of the afghan and scooted forward on the sofa cushion. To her horror, the quiet figure did the same thing—moving forward, gathering his weight under him. She couldn't stop what she was doing. She came to her feet, and so did the intruder.

He was tall and slender and quite good-looking. Still, his piercing eyes never left her face.

She took a cautious step toward the foyer, and opposite her, the terrifying figure did the same. She took a second step, and so did he. Her third stride brought her to the end of the coffee table. Again the man's movements were the mirror of her own, except this time she could see he had taken a diagonal step, a step that brought him nearer to her. She would never reach the entry.

Twice she tried to speak, making unintelligible sounds, while he watched her with those eyes, bright even in the dim light. On the third try, she managed to ask, "Who are you?"

He answered at once. "Don't be alarmed. Please, I won't hurt you."

"Who are you? What do you want?"

"I'm Billy. I'm the only one left."

"The . . . the only one left? What do you mean?"

He came toward her, each step slow and measured, the eyes never wavering. His slender figure towered over her. She had moved backwards step for step, as though they danced some macabre *pas de deux*. The back of her knees hit the sofa, and she sat down abruptly. With one graceful surge he was sitting beside her.

"Don't be frightened," he repeated. "I'm one of the hospital staff, a ward boy. They killed the rest—all of them—but they overlooked me. I've been hiding here since it happened."

She wanted so much to believe him. "But . . . but why didn't they find you?"

"I was outdoors. I'm interested in astronomy, and there was a meteor shower that night. They passed me without seeing me, but I saw them sneaking up the hill to the house. They're vicious . . . like a pack of mad dogs. They crept in here and killed all the staff. I heard the screams, but I couldn't do anything to stop it. Later, when they were gone, I found the bodies. But you're one of them, aren't you?"

Elizabeth was so shocked by the sudden accusation that she began to stutter. Lamely she tried to explain about the automobile accident that brought them to Skystone. She was badly confused, and she could tell he didn't believe her. Suddenly afraid, she tried to lunge away from him, but with lightning-like reflexes he seized her by the wrist. She struggled until he ordered, "Stop it!"

The strength of his voice cowed her into submission. She stopped, her breath quick and shallow like that of a frightened animal. He pulled her toward him to where she lost her balance and sprawled half across his lap, her breasts flattened against his thighs.

She could sense him recoiling from the contact. He pushed her away and shifted his hip clear of contact with her. For a moment Elizabeth thought he was going to rise, but he relaxed again and, watching her closely, began to talk. His voice had a wheedling quality about it.

"I could have hurt you, but I didn't. I want to trust you, and I want you to trust me. They're after me. They will kill me if I don't get away. Please don't try to run away."

She remembered the name of the other inmate now. She couldn't help herself. "Okay, Paul."

He stared at her blankly, blinking. "Paul? Who is Paul?"

She shook her head. "I . . . I'm sorry. I . . . I had to test you. I had to know. I know I can trust you, Billy."

"What's your name?"

"Elizabeth."

"Elizabeth, I think I know of a way out of here, but I can't do it without help. Can I count on you? You won't betray me, will you?"

"My God, no, Billy. I want out of here as much as you do. What's your plan?"

He shook his head. "Oh, no. I'll tell you when the time comes. They're after me, Elizabeth. They will grow more impatient by the hour, and then they'll make their mistakes."

The sole surviving staff member seemed unnaturally calm. Only when she tried to rise from the sofa had he become upset. Elizabeth could imagine how traumatic the catastrophe must have been to him. Many of the dead in the house must have been friends of his. He was in shock, sublimating all his emotions.

Impulsively, she patted him on the arm, but he twisted

away as if her hand were red hot. For a moment, the atmosphere was charged with fear. But then he awkwardly reached out and squeezed her wrist.

"I'm sorry, Elizabeth. I'm touchy because I'm scared to death. I usually function much better with people. Are you hungry? There's food in the kitchen."

The hope that had flared in her died. "Yes, I'm hungry, but I . . . I can't go in there."

He nodded. "You're softhearted, aren't you? I—" Suddenly he was rigid, every muscle spring-tight, his eyes bright. "How did you know there's a body in the kitchen?"

"A friend who was in the accident—Scott Sutherlin—searched the house and found the bodies. He was killed yesterday."

Abruptly he rose. "You wait here. It would never do for you to be wandering around in here. The dead are all around you. Besides, I might hear you and decide it was them. That wouldn't be good, would it, Elizabeth?" He smiled for the first time. "There's not much in the kitchen, but I did find some canned sausages and potato chips."

He stopped in the archway. "Remember, stay where you are. I'm very nervous. You can understand that, can't you?"

One moment he was there and the next he was gone, as silent as a night predator.

Five minutes later, Billy, moving with feline grace, reappeared in the doorway. He had a can of fruit cocktail, sausages, and a bag of potato chips. Indifferent to what he might think, she wolfed the food down as fast as she could.

Elizabeth muttered a soft "Thanks," and was piqued when he failed to respond. BIlly still radiated tension, and his restless eyes, cold and bottomless, were forever weighing, forever judging. He watched her the entire time she was eating.

"Elizabeth, why don't they leave me alone? Why are they after me?"

"They're not after you, Billy. All the time I was down there with them, I didn't hear them say one word about any staff members surviving. I don't think they know you're alive. You and I should begin searching for places to hide in here. They're irrational, and they will soon forget about us. In time, somebody will come to check on Skystone."

Her words did little to pacify him. He seemed puzzled by what she said. "But . . . who are they after, then? I watched them outside, moving around, searching. Are you the one they're after?"

"No, there's another patient." She brightened at the thought. "Of course, you would know who it is—Paul St. Denis. I didn't see him, but they are terrified of him. One of the group—the one named Shane—turned him loose."

He turned to her, placing his arm on the sofa back so that his fingers rested lightly against her neck. Elizabeth stirred uncomfortably. She was still far too frightened to want the touch of this strange youth, yet she didn't want to offend him.

She could barely hear the whispered words. "Maybe that's why you're here. Maybe you're hunting Paul, too."

She tried to shift about to where she could see him, but his fingers tightened around her neck, holding her against the sofa.

"Look at me," she protested. "You must know all the patients. Have you ever seen me before, Billy?"

His fingers on her neck were like steel bands. "Please— my neck—you're hurting me," she gasped.

His grip relaxed, and he looked away. "I'm sorry. I'm so tired. Let me rest for a few minutes, and then we'll find a hiding place to wait until we're ready."

"Ready for what?"

"Be quiet, Elizabeth, and let me rest."

His hand fell away from her neck and slipped free of her shoulder. Billy stretched his legs out in front of him, letting his head loll against the sofa. His eyes closed, and his body slumped into the softness of the sofa.

Gradually the lines on his forehead lost their definition, and he looked very young and vulnerable. Elizabeth felt a surge of tenderness flow through her. She wanted him to be out of this nightmare almost as much as she wanted it for herself. He was too young to be carrying memories of the carnage that had destroyed his world.

She became drowsy again and closed her eyes, listening to the far-off radio. The quick, faint squeal of metal against metal brought her upright. It had come from the direction of the garage.

She started to rise, only to be slammed down by Billy's hand on her shoulder. "Quiet!" he whispered fiercely.

They sat there, rigid, for a minute, listening, his hand digging into her shoulder. His grip was loosening when they heard the second noise, this time a faint thud, as if something soft but heavy had struck wood.

Instantly they were on their feet. "That sounded as if it came from the garage," she whispered. "Maybe it was the wind."

There was a faint smile on his face, and his eyes were alight with a cold fire. She thought she saw hatred in them, another legacy bequeathed by the savages who had altered all their lives.

"Quick! We have time to find a place to hide in case those . . ." She faltered under his gaze.

"I thought you were with me." His voice was a mere whisper.

"I am. I am, Billy."

"Then you stay here. Understand? I can only trust you if you do as I say."

"Please, don't go after them. They're armed. The two men have shotguns, and the woman has a carving knife. Don't try to protect me. Let's leave the house. We can stay in the woods."

"Elizabeth, are you going to wait like I asked you?"

Bewildered by his demeanor, she could only nod. Afraid and confused, she watched helplessly as he glided through the archway and disappeared.

She pulled the afghan around her in the morning chill, and when the minutes dragged by without any further sounds, closed her eyes. She started several times, almost asleep, despite the danger. Everything was so still that she was sure they had heard the early morning wind stirring or some animal drawn to the garage by the rotting bodies.

She was at the edge of sleep when she heard the soft sliding sounds of feet against the carpet. She looked up, ready to smile.

Her eyes bulged in fear.

Tina Duchin stood not six feet away, clad in clothing she must have found in the house. The blue jeans she wore were far too small for her. She had been unable to zip them shut, and the white of her belly gleamed in the opening of the fly. She was wearing a long-sleeve white dress shirt, unbuttoned, its hem reaching to mid-thigh.

The long blade of the carving knife in her hand looked alive as the silvery highlights wavered along its gleaming length.

Swiftly, the Satanist covered the distance between them. The sharp tip of the steel touched the soft skin of Elizabeth's neck like a tiny wet spot of pain. Tina, her hair a tangled mess and her face scratched, smiled triumphantly.

Her voice a silken snarl, she said, "Well, Mrs. Shea, we meet in the strangest places, don't we? I don't need to ask you if you've seen St. Denis, because if you had, you wouldn't be alive. Well? Cat got your tongue?"

Elizabeth was afraid to move with the razor-sharp blade against her throat—afraid to even talk for fear of cutting herself. She whispered, "No, I haven't seen anyone. I swear it. I was trying to stay out of the cold."

Tina nodded, apparently satisfied, and grinned—a hideous, meaningless gesture of domination. "The question is, dear Mrs. Shea, should I kill you now so you don't interfere with my search, or shall I take you back to the ward—for the pleasures you will offer?"

She closed her free hand over one of Elizabeth's breasts, lifting it. With an intense effort, Elizabeth kept her hands at her sides. Tina Duchin freed the soft mound of flesh.

"Yes, I think the Master would approve of you."

With a lightning-fast move, she clutched Elizabeth's hair, jerking her head back. Tina pushed forward, one knee resting on the sofa, looming over Elizabeth.

The tug on her hair had pulled Elizabeth's face to one side, and she could see into the hall. Billy was standing in the archway, but—realizing she had seen him—he started backing away.

"Help me, Billy!" she cried, unable to stop herself. "She's going to kill me."

Tina whirled around, sending the coffee table crashing

onto its side. She caught only a fleeting glimpse of Billy's back as he fled up the stairway. All thoughts of Elizabeth were gone. She ran heavily from the room, chasing him up the stairs.

Elizabeth raced out into the hall, down the short cross passage, and through Caudill's office. She stopped by the outside door, suddenly fearful of running out onto the lawn.

Overhead, feet pounded against the floor and weight crashed into walls, rattling the whole house. A scream so inhuman it was impossible to tell the sex knifed through the house. It ended suddenly.

Elizabeth yanked open the door and raced across the porch. She ran for the dark, dubious haven of the woods as the blood-red dawn sunlight found the old brick walls of the mansion.

CHAPTER 29 _____

*T*ip's snores were loud and regular, growling outbursts that trailed off into lingering flutters. He was lying on his back, fully clothed, atop the unmade bed in the bedroom.

Andy and Cobb sat in the living room across from each other as the dawn light grew.

The doctor cleared his throat, interrupting Cobb's moody reverie. "We still have four hours before we need to get ready. Why don't you go take a nap? Just roll Tip onto his side and he'll be quiet."

For a time he thought Cobb was not going to answer, but finally he looked up. "How about you, doc? I'm tired, but I'm too pumped up now. I can't sleep. Go on. You grab a little shut-eye."

"Nope. Old men don't need as much sleep as you youngsters. Besides, a doctor gets used to doing without sleep. Don't say I didn't offer."

"Doc, I hate to ask this in a man's own house, but would you mind letting me have a little privacy to make a phone call?"

When Andy didn't answer, he lamely added, "My wife."

"Do you really think it's going to be that rough a trip, Cobb?"

"Do I think . . . Oh, I see what you mean. No, I don't think it's a suicide mission. If I did, I wouldn't go. I'm not happy about you going, though. I'm not sure what we may have to do to stabilize the situation. But that's not why I want to talk to my wife in private. I need to tell her something."

Andy came to his feet with a groan. "I need some fresh air, anyway. I'll be out in the yard. Come out when you're finished."

Margaret answered on the second ring. He knew she had been asleep in her chair by the phone.

"Margaret, are you awake? Listen very carefully."

"Are you okay, darling? I've been so worried about you. I didn't mean to make you mad last night. Please come—"

"Shut up, Margaret, and listen. Don't ever repeat what I'm going to say. Promise me that?"

"But I don't understand. Please, Cobb, give me a chance. Just tell me what's wrong? I've begged you for four years. Tell me what's—"

"I asked if you promise."

Her silence was broken by a long, shuddering sigh. "I promise. What is it you want to say?"

"I'm going to do some police work this morning that may save the lives of a lot of innocent people. Your uncle has forbidden it, so I can't win, whatever happens. If I succeed, I will be guilty of insubordination—finished as a cop in this town. If I fail, it won't matter a damn. I'm afraid that may be what I really want. They are depending on me, and I may want to fail."

"Cobb, what do you mean? Oh, God, tell me. I'm your wife, and I love you."

"You haven't had much luck with your men, have you, Margaret?"

"My men?"

"Margaret, I—" He slammed the receiver back into its cradle. "I . . . Oh, Jesus, I . . ." The tears were pouring down his cheeks. "I loved you so much. I had nothing else in my life."

He stumbled back into the kitchen where he leaned over the sink, splashing water onto his face.

As Cobb stepped out into the chilly air of the Arkansas dawn, he saw the doctor hurrying toward him, trailing a slipstream of steamy exhalations.

"Cobb, we've got visitors. There's a car coming up the road. It's an odd time of day for anybody to be lost."

The sedan came into view and crossed the plank bridge, trailing a thin funnel of dust that rose sluggishly into the chilly air before collapsing back onto the road.

Cobb came off the porch. "It's a county car. I'm afraid old Toby's got the wind up. I wonder—"

"Doc, get in there and wake up Tip. Warn him about Toby."

"But—"

"Damn it, do what I tell you—and hurry!"

Cobb watched the sheriff's unit carrying three men stop before the house. The sheriff got out, followed by J. T. Carruthers and Curtis Toler, the night-shift deputies. Behind him, Cobb could hear a puffing Andy Witherspoon descending the porch steps.

Cobb eyed the sheriff stolidly, determined not to speak first.

Toby Mears stopped before him. This time there was no smirking, no smiling, no false camaraderie—just an angry old man who had gotten too little sleep.

"Well, gentlemen, you're up early, aren't you? Or is it late? Where's Tip?"

When they failed to answer, he turned to J.T. "Go see if he's inside, J.T."

"Wait a minute," Cobb protested. "You have no legal grounds for entering this man's house."

The sheriff nodded. "You're perfectly right, Sergeant."

He turned his attention to Andy. "Dr. Witherspoon, I'd like to do this as quietly as possible, in deference to your profession. If I have to go get a search warrant from Judge Hargrove, then you will spend a few hours in the county jail for questioning. I have something to say to the three of you. I'll ask you again to have Deputy Crable come out."

Cobb nodded. Andy started to protest, but did as Toby requested.

While J.T. and Curtis stood to the side, shifting uncomfortably, looking anywhere but at Cobb, he and the sheriff eyed each other silently. Only when Andy reappeared on the porch with a yawning Tip did Cobb ask, "Okay, Toby, what in the hell is this all about?"

"J.T. got worried and decided he'd better call me. He discovered that you had removed, without authorization, a flare gun and flares belonging to the county. I dressed and drove down to the office so I could confirm J.T.'s allegations.

"On my way in, I started thinking about how we could go about inspecting Skystone. You see, Sergeant, there are people besides you that want Skystone checked, only they want to do it in the proper way, using standard police procedures. I decided on a contingency plan, in case that isn't our ambulance in Memphis.

"It was my intention to set a deadline. I was going to keep trying to reach them by phone until ten this morning. If that didn't work, I intended to hire a helicopter to make an overflight. I thought I would use that new bullhorn to gain their attention and order them to open the gate so that we could check the well-being of the patients. I decided to check on the availability of a helicopter. The oddest thing happened when I called Little Rock. There was some mention of Dr. Witherspoon's name. As a matter of fact, I was told he had also been inquiring about hiring a helicopter this morning. I don't . . ."

Andy Witherspoon, bristling, asked, "And may I ask what the hell is wrong with a man hiring a chopper? Now that I'm retired, I want to learn the county. I thought an overflight was a good way to do it."

The sheriff paid no attention to the interruption, even though Andy was standing chest to chest with him, glowering up into his face.

"As I said," Toby continued, "I don't know if you hired a helicopter. The only man I couldn't check on was Smitty Plunkett. They say that he's shacked up with some woman.

But, Cobb, you've always found a way to get things done. I have a feeling that you men plan a little flight this morning."

Cobb pushed Andy aside. The little doctor was showing every intention of launching a physical attack upon the sheriff.

"Okay, Toby, cut the shit. What are you here for? That's one thing I know about you. You don't brag about how smart you are unless Lynch or one of the county commissioners is listening."

Even in the gray light, they could see the sheriff's face darken at the insult. "Okay, you asked for it. Until the matter of this improper use of county property can be cleared up, you, Cobb Kendall, and you, Tip Crable, are relieved from duty as sergeant and deputy in the Beauregard County Sheriff's Department. Second, there are reasonable grounds to believe you are interfering with a police action to ensure the safety of as many as fifty people at Skystone Institute. You are hereby placed in protective custody until such time as this operation can be completed. Your weapons are your personal property, but for the safety of your custodian, I am confiscating your firearms for the length of the protective custody. . . . Okay, Sergeant Kendall, where is your gun?"

"It's in the patrol unit—under the seat."

While Curtis hurried down to the unit and J.T. relieved Tip of his weapon, the sheriff stepped toward Andy Witherspoon.

"Doctor, how about your firearms?"

Cobb struggled to control his anger. "Who in the hell are you trying to kid, Toby? You have no grounds to confiscate this civilian's weapons as a probable danger to any law officer. Now, if you want—"

The doctor shouted, "That's right, damn it!. You mealy-mouthed son of a bitch, you get a search warrant. Until then, you get your second-rate ass off my property."

For the first time, Toby donned his familiar sneering smile. "Hardly, doctor. Sergeant Carruthers is staying here to supervise your custody; and Kendall here, with his awesome knowledge of the law, will tell you that any attempt to flee custody will make you a fugitive from the law. That is a criminal offense.

"Now, gentlemen, I've informed Sergeant Carruthers that you may call your attorneys at ten o'clock this morning—the usual time for law offices to open. Until then, I assure you there will be no attempt to question you."

He looked at Cobb, his eyes bitter. "And this is the thanks I get."

The three men watched the county car rumble across the plank bridge and disappear into the trees before they trooped into the house, followed by an uneasy J. T. Carruthers.

CHAPTER 30 _____

*B*y the time Elizabeth came in view of Skystone, the morning sun had found it. The sunlight reflected from the array of metal vents atop the slate-gray roof. Tall trees screened much of the sun's low-angled light from the older wing, and it looked more sinister than ever, with its somber brick walls enveloped in their dense coating of ivy and its windows masked by the green steel grating. The driveway and lawns around the building were deserted, save for the lifeless pair on the patio.

Somewhere on the slope above her, she could hear someone running uphill through the brush. It spurred her down-slope toward the waiting building.

She had gone only a few yards when a white-clad figure stepped out from behind one of the massive supports of the porte cochere. The figure almost fell, reeling backwards to lean against the pillar. She took two more steps and saw that it was Dr. Mainwaring.

He had his hand against his forehead, and there was a dark splotch staining the front of his smock. He looked different because he was not wearing his glasses.

Without stopping to consider the consequences, she ran the rest of the way down the steep grade. He didn't become aware of her presence until she reached the driveway. He backed away, raising his arm to shield his face. Only when she called, "Dr. Mainwaring, are you all right?" did he relax, peering nearsightedly at her.

"Ruthie, is that you? I . . . I thought you had deserted me."

Elizabeth was appalled at the change in him. It was more than the cut across his forehead and his missing glasses. His shoulders sagged, and his face had collapsed, with quavering jowls and pouches under his eyes. His hands trembled. Thomas Mainwaring had become an old man in the last few hours.

Impulsively, she reached for his shoulder. "Dr. Mainwaring, what happened to you?"

He seemed puzzled for a moment and dropped his hand, revealing the extent of the gash on his forehead.

"They . . . they hit me, Ruthie. They said I'd let someone named Elizabeth escape. I don't even know anyone by that name."

He caught her hands in his, and she shuddered at their stickiness. "I had so much to give the world, but they locked me away in here. Thomas Mainwaring has conquered cancer." His voice quavered. "Don't they know that I was willing to share this gift with the world? But they put people in here to corrupt me. They made me want to stay here, and then they turned on me."

Tears welled in his eyes, and Elizabeth felt a surge of pity, not wanting to watch what was happening to him. She pulled her hands free of his and gripped his shoulders.

"Listen to me, doctor. Maybe we can still get away. Are they inside the hospital?"

He raised his eyes to her, and they held the look that a dog bestows on its master. He had nothing left to give her.

She repeated the question.

"Howie and Tina are out looking for St. Denis."

The name reminded him of the menace around them, and he broke eye contact with her, looking sharply to the right and left. "Johnny's inside. He's fooling with that poor girl, Molly."

Elizabeth shook him hard. "Listen to me. Is she still alive?"

"I . . . I think so. Johnny said she was. Tina wouldn't like it if she caught him. He's playing with her, feeling her. He wouldn't let me do it."

Elizabeth choked back the complex emotions aroused by his comment: pity, revulsion, anger, sadness. She tried to consider her options. She wished she knew what had happened to Billy. Mainwaring could no longer help her, but if Billy had escaped Tina, they still had a chance.

She pulled the unresisting Mainwaring toward the doors. It was better to face John Hughes inside than to stay outside and attract the tender mercies of Howie and Tina or St. Denis.

They moved quickly through the treatment room. The first sunlight was touching the skylights, and the hall was quite bright. Leading the unresisting Mainwaring by the arm, she passed the red door without incident. Elizabeth headed for her room, like a hounded animal fleeing to a den that no longer offered sanctuary. She had no idea why she was bringing Mainwaring with her. If he couldn't maintain control of the others, there was no way she could help him.

Once inside the bedroom, Thomas Mainwaring planted his feet and refused to move farther. He closed his eyes and took a deep breath, obviously trying to get himself under control. When he opened them, it was not the old debonair fraud she had first encountered—with his sense of savoir-faire—but he had found the strength within himself for a last effort. He reached into the console, pulled out a pad, and wrote briefly on it. He tore out the sheet and handed it to her.

"Ruthie, the plane will be here at four this afternoon. Give this note to Harvey. Tell him that I didn't make it. We go back a long way together, so he'll fly you wherever you want to go. You must be there when he lands, for there will be very little time. To keep the others in line, I promised to take them all along. When they hear the plane they will head for the airstrip."

He frowned at her imminent protest. "Listen, we haven't much time before they'll be back. I don't know exactly where the airstrip is. I've heard planes taking off and landing there. It must be several hundred yards behind our . . . the mental wing."

"We'll go together," Elizabeth begged. "We can make it. We'll hide in the woods until time to leave."

He shook his head. "No, little Ruthie. You don't understand. They'll wonder where I am. If Tina and Howie kill St. Denis, then they won't rest until they find me. After that, they'll go back to amusing themselves with poor Molly Hatcher and with each other . . . and you, if it pleases them."

"But maybe they won't succeed. Maybe this man you're all afraid of will kill them."

"St. Denis? Caudill said that St. Denis has an excellent mind. When he realizes I'm missing, he'll come looking for me. He is sharp enough to know I have a plan to escape from here."

He struggled for a last shred of dignity, betraying his weakness only by a slight trembling. "It's all over. It's time for your daddy to . . ." he hesitated over the word, swallowed, and said softly, "die."

Blindly he tried to kiss her, but missed, barely touching her forehead, and then he was out the door before she could stop him.

Elizabeth slumped into a chair, dead tired, fighting against tears. Blinking them away, she looked at her watch: 6:33. If she could buy ten more hours, she would be safe. She tried her best not to think of poor Thomas Mainwaring. There was a dignity and courage about him that went far beyond the warped perception of reality that the world called insanity.

The doorknob turned and she looked up, her eyes widening with fear.

A laughing John Hughes literally leaped into the room, closing the door behind him. "Hmmm, live meat! Elizabeth, baby, glad to see you. I wouldn't have known you were here if that old asshole hadn't been muttering about it. You dig me? Hey . . . be right back . . . got a present for you."

Elizabeth searched for something to jam beneath the doorknob, but before she could do more than look, he popped back into the room carrying a tray with a syringe on it.

She watched him warily. He waggled the tray, causing the glass syringe to chatter on the metal surface.

"Look what I've got for you, mama. This is the best cure you'll ever have."

"You . . . you've got what for me?"

He lifted the syringe as if it were a precious gem. "Psilocybin, dolly. Man, this is pharmaceutical-grade stuff from Switzerland. There's damned little of this in the U.S. You're a lucky little twat, you know that?"

He set the syringe back on the tray and faced her, his fist doubled. He swayed back and forth, twisting his pelvis like a rock singer moving to heavy rhythm. His face was growing red, and he was unable to stand still.

She appreciated that he had just taken some sort of drug. She had to control him now or not at all. "Get out of here and take that syringe with you! If you don't, I'll tell Dr. Mainwaring. I swear I will. Now, get out!"

He lifted his arms above his head in mock surrender. "Hey, heavy. Old Johnny just wants mama to have a good time. Hey, just a sec."

He dug into his pocket. Cupping one hand over the other, he thrust them before her. "Okay, sweetie, now you see it and now you don't."

He choked in a gale of laughter. Elizabeth was becoming alarmed over his condition. His face was dangerously red.

"Open, sesame!" he cried and uncupped his hands.

Resting in the palm of one was a key like the master room key that Scott had found.

"Hey, mama, don't get mad at old Johnny. The doctor said for you to take this key and lock yourself in."

With an enormous feeling of relief, she reached for it, determined to get rid of him. As she touched the key, he grabbed her wrist and jerked her forward. Off balance, she tried to keep herself upright by clutching at his shoulders but missed and stumbled past him as he brought her arm up behind her back in a hammerlock. Using her own momentum, he drove her onto the bed, resting facedown on it with her legs still on the floor.

Struggling with a strength born of fear, she almost raised herself from its surface with her free hand before he drove her locked arm hard against her back, and she cried aloud in pain. He was lying atop her, and she could feel his erection as he squirmed against her hips.

"Lie still, bitch, or I'll break your arm off!"

With his free hand, he grabbed the elastic waistband of her trousers and yanked them down past her buttocks. Despite the agonizing pain in her arm, she continued to struggle against him, but sensed that her moving body was exciting him further.

In one smooth motion, he reached for the syringe and drove it deep into the white roundness of her bottom. She gasped at the shocking pinpoint of pain. Johnny was a veteran of a thousand hurried fixes, and in one continuing movement, he depressed the plunger of the syringe, forcing the psilocybin deep into her flesh, and pulled the hypo free, flinging it backwards across the room.

"Why are you doing this?" she moaned. "What do you want?"

He was moving rhythmically against her. "'Cause I'm gonna fuck your stuff, baby. That asshole Howie killed your old buddy Meredith, and that little piece tied up in the therapy room is like handling warm sausage. You and Johnny are gonna have a lot of fun. Sweet stuff, I've got a war chest of goodies now that you wouldn't believe."

He moaned and pulled himself away from her. "Damn! I've gotta save it for the real thing."

While his weight was off her body, she tried to rise, but he levered her arm up again and she shrieked in pain. He tumbled across her back, pinning her.

"Johnny," she gasped. "What was in that syringe?"

"Psilocybin, like I said, baby. It's gonna put you on easy street."

"But what is it?"

"Never you mind. You're gonna love what it does for you. I'm gonna turn you on to everything."

Elizabeth turned her head to where she could see his distorted features. Her voice held a new note. "Please, Johnny, not now. I go for you, but not now . . . not this way. Besides, Dr. Mainwaring might catch us."

He laughed and gave her a stinging slap across the buttocks. He tried to talk, but dissolved into uncontrollable laughter, saliva sliding down his chin. Finally, he managed to say, "Hey, mama, that old fart ain't gonna bother anybody again. When I heard him open the safe, I sneaked up behind him."

Suddenly he was looking at her intently, and Elizabeth realized his question was serious. "You know what he did? That dumb fucker gave himself a mainline of morphine that would have stiffed an elephant. Can you beat that?"

He stared at her, wide-eyed, and when she did not answer, he laughed again. "Hey, I would have let the old bastard die happy, but the son of a bitch tried to close the safe when he saw me, so it was tough titty."

"You . . . you killed him?"

"I hate to kiss a pig's ass if I didn't. So, sweetmeat, it's just you and me."

Her hands and feet were growing cold. It was so odd. The room felt quite warm, especially after being outdoors, but she could feel the strange chill creeping up into her calves and forearms, numbing them.

Alarmed, she cried, "Johnny, something's wrong with my arms and legs! They're turning ice-cold."

This set off a fresh gale of giggles. "Hey, imagine that. That's par for the course, baby."

The coldness continued to work its way up her limbs, and her stomach felt nauseated. All at once she was terrified at what was happening to her. Johnny must not understand what she was saying.

"Johnny, there's something wrong. I'm dying!"

His face, peering at her, looked enormous. "Not a chance. You're on your way, doll."

John Hughes eased off of her. He released her arm, and when it remained behind her back, pulled it down to her side. He slid off the bed.

Elizabeth rolled over and struggled to her feet. He was crouched, ready to grab her if she was faking. Her hands were so numb that she had trouble gripping the slacks to pull them over her hips. The floor heaved under her feet, and the walls of the room were pulsating.

She sagged back onto the bed and tried to crawl toward the pillow. It was so far away, like a distant snow-covered hill. Between her and the hill was a long, white bed . . . a . . . no, a field . . . a field of snow. The snow was hot, warming her cold arms and legs. She scrambled toward the distant hill, but the snow was deep and the trip long. Finally, exhausted, she pitched forward into the soft embrace of the white flakes.

She could hear music, the notes of an organ—at first sustained and low and then building with a counterpoint of trills to a sforzando. Huge icy arches reared from the snow, and the sun burst into view from over the distant hill. Its rays beat against her painful eyes, and she heard a voice—the voice of a god, filling the heavens.

"I like to see what I'm working on . . . on . . . on . . ."

CHAPTER 31 _____

*T*he *on*'s reverberated about her until she thought she would scream, drowning out the soaring arpeggios of the organ. Without warning, the world came apart with a tremendous crash, and she heard the angry howlings of beasts, and another god shouted, his cry ringing across the sterile white fields. The awesome cascade of sound grew, and the icy arches crumbled, rumbling downhill in avalanches. She thrilled to the roaring, rising columns of sound, for she found understanding in it, words. The god had spoken in her tongue.

"What did you give her, wimp?"

The icy arches and the snow fields melted away, and she lay pinioned on a sacrificial altar. The sun shone down on her, its heat a physical caress that flooded her being. Far beyond her on the dark plain, her subjects quarreled.

Lying serenely, the one bright, sun-blessed adornment of a dark, angry world, she smiled at the childish bickering.

"... wanted it for yourself."

"No, Howie, I ..."

"You killed him, you little creep."

"No, I ..."

"Asshole! He would have gotten me out."

"Honest, man, I . . ."

"And my women . . . you tried to take my women. They're mine!"

"Okay, Howie, okay. Howie . . . No! No! I'm begging you."

"I'm gonna kill you! Beat your . . . face off."

Somewhere in the distance she heard the creatures of the earth fighting, snarling, and screaming. It was all so far away, somewhere below the precipitous ledges of the ultimate altar on which she lay safely enshrined. Elizabeth could her the gaspings of her worshipers as they moved in frenzied rhythms to the soft, fleshly thuds of their drums. Then it was silent except for the cyclonic exhalations that filled the chamber.

Wearily she opened her eyes to see a vast white column, touched with the rays of morning light, rising past her altar, stretching to the dark sky. Even as she looked, it changed, the shape simmering, breaking apart and coming together, changing from white to pink. A strange, hollow voice, so near it seemed to be within her own head, asked, "Jack?"

From somewhere atop the towering pink edifice came a reply, dark and smooth, vibrant and exciting. "Yeah, baby, this is Jack."

She tried to shake her head, to deny the voice, but her head, the head of a goddess, was so massive. It seemed to move forever until it hit a soft white cushion of clouds, and then swung back on a long, long journey until it floated into another cloud. It was so dizzying that she couldn't hold her eyes open, but then a great weight settled upon her chest. Struggling to get her breath, she opened her eyes and saw a great pink crab on her chest, its thick pincers against her body.

It moved toward her face. She shrank away, trying to shield herself from its attack. The pincers plucked at her flesh, tearing at the white cloth of her holy robes. She knew then that it was harmless, that it had been sent from the pink tower to help her shed her outer skin, like a royal chrysalis ready to reveal its sacred flesh for all the world to see.

She pretended not to notice the tentacles as they worked their way down the length of her robes, separating them. A second great creature appeared, and the two of them seized the severed edges of her raiment and pulled it free. Then the rapacious crabs settled over the two white hillocks of flesh rising from her chest. They moved restlessly about on the mounds, never still. Under their worrying assault, small reddish columns raised themselves. She could feel the very essence of her being flowing into the tiny rising peaks. She yielded to the tantalizing sensation, her concentration narrowing to an incredible awareness of the distillation of all her being within those two precious adornments.

Abruptly the crabs were gone, and her body was being pulled about. She moaned in protest, but then she understood. The metamorphosis to beauty was being completed. The last of the garments were being stripped away.

A gigantic shadow plummeted out of the sky, blotting out the sun, and the god was feeding on her mouth. A great wet serpent slipped between her lips, gliding, seeking, setting points of vibration within her mouth. Her tongue rose to greet the visitor. Then it was gone, hungrily feeding on the tantalizing sensation from the tiny red peaks. The great crabs returned, scuttling across satin sweeps of her flesh.

Her hands clutched at the crabs, but could not deter them. The velvety serpent continued to swirl about the aching pinnacles of her chest. The great pink edifice shifted forward to share her altar with her, and she could hear a voice by her ear, thunderously loud, saying, "It's Jack. Treat me right."

She fought to worm free of the enormous weight that had her pinned. Struggling, she twisted around to face the unyielding mass, and her eyes widened in surprise. It was Jack.

She tried to tell him there was something wrong about her bedroom, but his lips closed upon hers and she couldn't talk. She struggled to free herself.

"No, Jack, no more. It's over and done with. I can't take it anymore."

His grasp was inescapable, and he continued to talk. "No, no, it's Jack. You want me, baby. You're crazy for me. You want it so bad. You'll do anything to have me. I'm gonna . . ."

She shrieked in agony at the blast of sound beside her ear,

yet she could understand the sounds, meaningless as they were. "Jesus Christ, that's a fucking whirlybird. It's the cocksucking cops, sure as hell. You stay here, cunt, and keep your mouth shut."

The ear-shattering burst of sound brought great earth-quakes to the land. She felt the ground beneath her rolling and jolting, and there was a great threshing about. The tremors ended as suddenly as they had started, and there was peace in the land. She ran her hands over the white mounds and shuddered at the memories of their pleasure. The gods had paid their homage and gone.

The minutes lengthened to hours, the hours to days, the days to years, and she could sense the change. At first it had been a mere swaying, but then she began to tumble end over end, sinking through clouds of brilliant Kelly green and vivid pinks as the tumbling notes of waves of violins, thousands of them, swept over her.

She struggled to remember. Elizabeth was floating in a warm green sea, gently rocking in its restless waves. Overhead, the sky was filled with great billowing masses of clouds that dilated and contracted to the rhythm of her heartbeat. Her heavy limbs relaxed, drifting away from her body, leaving her spread-eagle.

The sly, lascivious currents, warm and caressing, played about her loins, and she stirred in vaguely remembered pleasure. It was a quiet, lingering delight, and soon she was caught up in the contemplation of it. Even as she did, she dipped beneath the waves into a twilight world of clear green, drifting down through the warm waters. She moved downward through living clouds of fish in their neon shades of blues and reds and golds. As the sea darkened around her, the soft-furred sensation of sweet pleasure slid across the tingling flesh of her body. Ripples of delight softly plied her pale skin.

CHAPTER 32

T oby Mears lowered the phone and, pulling a red bandanna from his pocket, wiped his suddenly sweaty face. The crow's-feet in the corners of the sheriff's eyes were sharply etched, and his brow was furrowed with worry.

His mind made up, he leaned forward in his swivel chair and quickly dialed a number. "Commissioner? This is Toby. I'm afraid they have us by the short hairs on this Skystone thing. . . . What? . . . just got a call from the Memphis Police Department. It isn't our ambulance. . . . I'm afraid I haven't made myself very clear. Skystone hasn't answered our phone calls since Tuesday morning."

Toby held the suddenly squalling earpiece away from his ear and pulled at his tie. As the outburst from the other end began to subside, he interrupted, "Damn it, I'm not an idiot, Commissioner. I tried to get a helicopter."

Having decided to lie, Toby grimly plowed ahead. "They're all tied up today. I can't get one until tomorrow. . . . But, damn it, I can't wait. I placed Cobb and Tip in protective custody. They are with that Dr. Witherspoon—the guy that quit Skystone. That's the worst damned part. I had to put him under protective custody, too."

The receiver spewed an avalanche of garbled words. The sheriff's face flared red, and he shouted, "Damn it, don't you understand? That place is enclosed by an electrified fence. If we go in there, we're going to have to use force, and we'll have to back that up in court. . . . What? That's the damned trouble. Cobb is right. Any lawman worth his salt would have gone in there before now. . . . I'll be damned, Orville. You're my boss, by God! You make the decision. . . . You're the guys that said leave everything to Judge Lynch. Well, by God, I don't know how to get hold of him, and you don't either—so it's your baby."

This time the voice on the phone was quieter and more measured. The conversation dragged on, more ambiguous with each phrase until Toby ended it.

"Okay, Orville, I'm going in, but you remember one damned thing: I informed you what I intended to do, and if my ass gets in hot water, your ass is going to be cooking right beside mine."

Toby slammed down the phone, pale for a moment, stunned to realize that he had just told off one of the county's big shots. He shouted as loud as he could, "Willie Joe! Willie Joe, get your butt in here."

A medium-height young deputy, his too thin but almost handsome face showing as much intelligent concern as it could muster, rushed into the office. "Yessir, Sheriff."

"Willie Joe, is Curtis in there asleep on the cot?"

"He must be. He ain't moved for an hour."

The sheriff rolled his eyes skyward in recognition of the cretins that political expediency had brought into his department.

"Well, you shake him awake. I want you boys to run over to see Henry Meadows."

Willie Joe stopped in midstride, a puzzled look on his face. "What's the matter, Sheriff? Something wrong with the lights?"

Toby put his hand on Willie Joe's thin shoulder. "Willie, when you wake Curtis, tell him to ask Henry Meadows the safest and quickest way to get through an electrified gate."

Willie Joe tried to pull away, and Toby jerked him back.

"Damn it, listen to me, Willie Joe. You tell Curtis we're going into Skystone. It's okay for him to tell Henry that."

The young deputy blinked. "Well, Sheriff, why don't we just drive through the gate?"

Toby carefully pointed Willie Joe in the direction of the door and shoved. "Ask Curtis to explain it to you later. Now shake your asses up. I want you back here as soon as possible."

The sheriff walked wearily back to his desk, slumped into his chair, and buried his face in his hands. He hoped he got through the day without being sued.

He reached for the phone and dialed the Witherspoon number. When Andy Witherspoon answered, he asked for J.T.

"J.T., I'm not gonna be a poor loser. You tell Cobb that I heard from Memphis. It wasn't our ambulance. Tell him I think he's right. I'm going out to Skystone today and find out what's going on."

J.T. was suddenly very excited. "Dang, Sheriff, I'm ready to go. You want me to bring old Cobb and Tip? We'll get them ambulance boys out of there."

Toby could hear the sounds of a struggle, and the phone crashed against something. Cobb's voice exploded in his ear. "Hello? Hello?"

When Toby replied, Cobb shouted, "At last you've come to your senses. Get as many of the boys together as you can, and we'll get organized. I figure we're—"

"I don't give a damn what you figure, Cobb. This isn't going to take any fancy plans, especially since I couldn't get a chopper. I sent Curtis over to Henry Meadows to find out the best way to get through the gate. We're going to drive right through that son of a bitch and up to the hospital."

"Hold on, Toby. You will trigger the alarm if you break the circuit. Doc Witherspoon says so. Those maniacs can slaughter everybody in there before we reach them. We'll have to—"

"We! Where do you get this 'we'? I called you because I wanted to be man enough to admit I was wrong. You're not going any damned place, because you're still in protective custody. You have some charges to answer to. Now, you put J.T. back on the phone."

There was another brief scuffle. Breathing hard, J.T. spoke into the phone. "Yeah, Toby, what do you want me to do?"

"Stay there and watch those bastards, J.T. They're not to leave."

As they talked, Cobb was explaining to Tip and a howling-mad Andy what the sheriff had said. The little fire-brand of a doctor lunged toward J.T., only to be brought up short by Cobb's powerful arms.

"Calm down, doc. It's not J.T.'s fault. He's nothing but the sheriff's lackey."

J.T. glared at him. "Well, fuck you, Cobb."

J.T., more wary now, crossed to the door where he could watch all three men at once.

Several minutes of hostile silence ensued before Cobb looked up. "Doc. I'm so damned upset my stomach is killing me. Do you have something I can take?"

Andy looked at him in surprise.

"I need it real bad."

The doctor looked at J.T. and back to Cobb. "Well, I have some antacid tablets in my medical bag. I'll get them."

Cobb came to his feet. "I'll go with you. I think half the cure is not looking at J.T.'s ugly face."

Once out of sight, Cobb whispered, "Doc, where is your thirty-two?"

The doctor sputtered, "Uh . . . it's in the den. Why?"

"We're running out of time. If we're going to reach Sky-stone before that blundering bastard, we have to put J.T. out of commission."

"Well, shit, why didn't you say so? I have an old twenty-two target pistol in here that I use for plunking at cans and rabbits, but I don't guess that's enough gun."

Cobb grinned. "All I saw out there was a big rabbit."

He died a thousand deaths when Andy wasted precious minutes searching the kitchen. At last, with a grunt of satisfaction, he pulled an ancient steel-blue .22 out of a cardboard box stored beneath the sink. Cobb grabbed it and hurriedly broke it open. None too soon, he confirmed that it was loaded.

As he snapped the gun shut, J.T. yelled, "Hey, you two. Get the hell out here. I want you where I can see you—now!"

Cobb was beginning to know his companion. He grabbed Andy just as the pugnacious little physician was ready to charge out to deliver a volley of obscenities at J.T. Cobb shoved Andy aside and entered the living room, holding the pistol behind his leg.

"J.T."

"What the hell do you want, Cobb?"

"I wanted to ask you if you feel like dying this morning."

He brought the long-barrel .22 revolver up in line with J.T.'s sternum.

Tip grinned when he saw the revolver in Cobb's hand. "By God, when you get in trouble you don't go about it halfway."

Cobb called over his shoulder, "Doc, call Smitty and tell him to get up here as quickly as he can. The fat's in the fire."

While the doctor was on the phone, Cobb handcuffed J.T. and led him out to the patrol unit. He pulled the leg irons out of the trunk, fitted them on J.T.'s ankles, and shoved him into the caged, handleless rear seat of the patrol car. Reaching into the front seat, he yanked out the hand mike and turned to J.T.

"J.T., I'll crack the window to give you some air. I don't think you'll be here over three or four hours."

J.T. snarled at him. "You son of a bitch, I'll get you for this if it's the last thing I do."

Cobb regarded him steadily through the steel mesh of the cage. "I think you're wrong, J.T. Something tells me nobody's ever going to get me for this."

He slammed the door and hurried back into the house, J.T.'s service revolver in his hand.

CHAPTER 33

When they reached the fairgrounds, Cobb ordered Andy to park in the deep shade of the ramshackle old grandstand. Here they were screened from the road that ran past the fairgrounds. Only cars driving into the grounds could spot them. In the unlikely event someone should drive up Cobb was prepared to hold them at gunpoint. It couldn't be helped.

He spun around in the seat to face his comrades. Tip gawked at him. Cobb wore an expression of such bleak desperation that Tip scarcely knew him. Even the irrepressible and fiery Witherspoon was quelled by the ferocity that burned in Cobb.

He held their gaze, refusing to let them look away. "Tip, all you have is Doc's twenty-two. You're going to have a hell of a time stopping anyone coming at you, especially someone who doesn't react normally to pain. Don't get separated."

"Listen, Cobb, I—"

"I'm not trying to protect you. I . . . I'm going to need you as much as you need me. Believe me—it's selfish. I need you to stay alive."

He turned to Andy, who was watching him with a puzzled expression. "What's the matter, doc? Trying to figure out

your comrades in arms?" There was nothing light or bantering about the question.

"Witherspoon, you're a good man. You have guts, and you
stick up for what you believe. This town needs you, particularly if the worst happens. You are to land on the roof, turn off
the power, and return to the roof. Nothing else. Understand?"

Cobb exploded at the frowning Andy: "Damn you! If the
place is overrun, we're going to be shooting first and asking
questions later. Two men are trying to do the job of twenty. I
wouldn't want you to pop out of a doorway in front of me. I
wouldn't want to live with that."

He grabbed Andy's arm in a grip so powerful that the
small-boned doctor winced. "Stay on the roof."

Tip shouted, "I hear it, by God! I hear it coming."

Three minutes later, Andy was aboard and the helicopter
rose quickly from the parking lot, its motor laboring under full
throttle. Peering downward from the tiny cockpit, Andy could
see Cobb and Tip running toward the old green car, their
figures diminishing so quickly that he felt a surge of fear. It
was as if they were shrinking into nothingness and he would
never see them again.

The town slid slowly beneath the chopper as it crawled
across the sky. Andy glanced at his watch. It was 11:26,
better than two hours past the time they had planned to storm
Skystone. The bright November sun flooded the cockpit,
making him perspire in the nylon windbreaker. Patting the
comforting weight of the .32, he sighed and closed his eyes.

Smitty's voice intruded on his moment of silence. "Hey,
doc, are you sure you're okay?"

Andy realized that he was not okay. He was far too old to
be doing what he had to do. He had never before thought of
himself as old. He would be lucky if he left the helicopter
without breaking his neck, much less crawl around in the attic like a commando. He felt desperately tired from the night's
long vigil, and his eyes burned. The warmth in the sun-
filled cockpit and the rhythmic vibrations of the engine were
overwhelming the excitement that had sustained him.

He opened his lids and winked at Smitty. "I feel great,
Smitty. All us superheroes try to relax until we explode into
action."

Andy's feeble humor fell on deaf ears. Smitty continued to regard him with deep concern. Uncertain of what else he could do to help, he repeated his lecture about the technique for leaving the craft and using the flare gun. The chopper couldn't land on the roof of the building because of the forest of protruding vents. It would hover about six feet above the surface while Andy descended an aluminum-runged rope ladder. Since the helicopter would be drifting across the roof, he had to move quickly.

He fought to concentrate on Smitty's words. When the pilot appeared satisfied, Andy looked down and was startled to see how much ground they had covered.

Below them lay the rugged area of descending ravines that marked the edge of the small plateau atop which lay Skystone. The helicopter's shadow flitted over the S-curve where Gavin Thorne had made his fatal mistake. Just ahead, the land abruptly flattened out on to the plateau.

The chopper banked sharply into a ninety-degree turn and headed due north, leaving the road behind. Off to his right, Andy could see in the distance the one wooded hill that thrust out of the flat land. The old Albritton mansion in which he had lived for so many years was clearly visible.

Three minutes later, the hill was to the southwest of them; the chopper was descending slowly, with little forward movement.

Smitty grabbed the hand mike. "X-ray, X-ray, Skybird."

The small speaker poured static into the cockpit. Andy tried to will Cobb's voice through the speaker.

Smitty tried again, while the small craft drifted across the tree-dotted open fields. He looked toward Andy and frowned.

"Damn it, doc, they should be close enough for us to pick up that portable of the sergeant's."

Disappointment etched Andy's voice. "I guess it was too much to hope for. Mears must have caught them on the way out of town. We might as well—"

"Skybird, X-ray, X-ray."

Smitty almost dropped the mike in his excitement. "Skybird here."

"Sorry about the delay. This old portable started coming apart on me. We're in position and ready to go."

Smitty glanced toward Andy. Andy nodded and reached between his legs for the flare pistol.

"X-ray, Skybird will be down in two minutes. Good luck."

The helicopter was barely above the taller trees now. It lunged forward as Andy tucked the flare gun under his belt. Seconds later, they were over the chain-link fence with its formidable crown of barbed wire and electrified cables. As they skirted a small grove of trees bordering a primitive airstrip, Skystone came into view ahead of them.

It seemed to Andy that they were rushing toward the hospital at a tremendous speed. The grounds looked deserted. He turned to his right toward the old mansion. Something definitely looked wrong on the hill. Despite the chill, on a sunny morning like this some of the younger, off-duty staff members should be outside. Both the lawn and tennis courts were unoccupied.

He shouted at Smitty, "No question about it, something bad has happened here."

They roared over the parapet of the roof, and Smitty saw that he was going too fast. By the time he could control their momentum, the helicopter was over the convalescent wing. As he spun the chopper around to ease back over the hatch, Andy acted too quickly, kicking the ladder over the side.

Smitty yelled at him above the tumult of rushing air. "Oh, Christ, you blew it, doc. You've got to get out of here. I'm afraid of snagging the ladder on one of those vents."

Feeling clumsy, his aged limbs protesting the strain, Andy dangled his legs over the side, feeling for the top rung of the ladder. With his hands slipping, he was sure he was going to fall, but then his foot encountered the aluminum rod. Twisting his body around, he started down. The ladder began to swing wildly, and he fought against becoming disoriented. He quickly became dizzy, with his energy fading fast. He would have given it up, but he no longer had strength enough to climb back into the chopper. Clinging to the bottom rung, he pawed for the roof with one leg. Just as his trembling, exhausted arms gave out, his foot found a solid surface.

CHAPTER 34

T he ladder flew from his grasp as Smitty gunned the motor and the helicopter rose in a tight turn. Andy had landed at the very edge of the roof. A second more, and he would have plummeted twenty feet to the ground.

A heavyset man wearing nothing but a white uniform tunic ran into view from beneath the porte cochere, looking up at the chopper.

Andy dived out of sight as the watcher turned. He lay on the tarry surface, his heart pounding. There was no longer the slightest doubt: the mental patients had seized the place. He had seen Howie Delgado far too many times not to recognize him. He thanked God that Delgado had been looking toward the helicopter.

For a moment he was content to lie there, basking in his success, but seconds were precious. If Delgado climbed the slope, Andy would be in plain sight, or if any of the inmates had been watching from the house, they were surely on their way down to raise the alarm.

As he struggled to his feet, the flare gun almost slipped from his belt. Had it fallen the noise would have been enough to catch Delgado's attention. Crouched low, he ran, crablike, across the roof to the hatch.

Its only lock was a pin latch on the outside. The latch was rusted shut, and he tore the skin on his fingers trying to open it. They stung under the bite of the metal, and blood dripped from them as he freed the .32 from his pocket. He hammered at the latch with the gun butt, knowing the noise could be heard on the ground below. There was nothing to be done about it now except hope that Howie had returned to the building.

With a screech, the pin broke free of its rusty bed and slid open. Andy swung the hatch up and lowered himself into the darkness. His arms were trembling so badly from his exertions that he came close to tumbling over backwards into the hatch opening. He sighed with relief when his feet found the flat surface in the darkness beneath him.

He denounced himself with every choice obscenity he knew. He had forgotten a flashlight. The only light in the broad expanse of the attic was the sunlight spilling through the three-by-three hatch. He wanted to give up—to sit there in the darkness and let fate take its course. He was old—too damned old. He had folded up like a dishrag, starting with the moment Smitty began the final dash for the building.

Andy took a last look at the blue sky and began the long crawl through the darkness. At first he was careful about masking the sounds of his movements, but once he was immersed in the blackness, choking on the swirls of dust rising around him, he no longer gave a damn. He was determined to find the damned breakers. After that, he didn't care. His crawling became endless, timeless. He was the damned Flying Dutchman of Skystone. The farther he crawled on his hopeless task, the more conscious he became of the passage of time. Cobb and Tip must be waiting impatiently outside the gate, wondering what the hell had happened to him. His hands stung with a thousand splinters, and the pain in his knees had reached the point where he could barely force himself to put weight on them.

Andy stopped and looked back over his shoulder. The hatch opening was the tiniest point of light, far away across the black cavern of the attic. He tried to think. He was having trouble breathing in the dust clouds and felt vaguely nauseated. He must be near the front wall. He had paralleled the two circulation ducts that served the patients' rooms in the mental ward, so he was pointed in the right direction.

With a groan, he started crawling again and butted, head-first, into the electrical control panel.

Blindly, Andy felt about the board, trying to visualize its extent. He sighed with relief. The breaker boxes were exactly as they had been described by the contractor in Memphis. He counted down and across and opened the breaker box, cringing at the thought of touching a live wire. His hand closed on the grip of the circuit breaker, and with a deep breath he yanked it down.

There was a vague sense of disappointment. Somehow, he had expected something to happen to signify that the circuit was broken.

Andy, exhausted, wanted to sprawl next to the breaker and go to sleep. He forced himself to turn back into the darkness that led to that tiny pinpoint of light. He was near the hatch when one arm gave out and he pitched forward onto his face. It was a frightening moment. For a split second, he thought he was paralyzed. He lay, his face against the dusty surface, coughing. Finally, he forced his trembling arms to lever his body up and traversed the last painful yards until he could see blue sky overhead.

With his leg muscles cramping painfully, Andy stood upright in the hatch, grasping the flare pistol with his aching arm. He fitted one of the flares into the pistol, pointed it toward the sky, and pulled the trigger.

Hurriedly he reloaded and fired again, and then a third time. Only then did he look up into the sky to see the third flare etch a path across the blue, trailing a dense trail of smoke.

Tossing aside the now useless flare pistol, Andy hoisted himself through the hatch. As he did, he could hear the approaching helicopter, moving fast. From somewhere near the distant road, there was a metallic crash.

He moved toward the edge of the roof in order to be away from the vents. The helicopter was within a hundred feet of him, slowing, when, without warning, it veered away under full throttle.

Somewhere below Andy, an explosion rent the air. He raced to the edge of the parapet and looked down.

Howie stood beyond the porte cochere, a shotgun raised to his shoulder. He was so intent on the helicopter, tracking it down the barrel of the gun, that he failed to see Andy until the little doctor had the revolver free of his jacket.

Peering down its sight, Andy could see Howie become aware of him and swing the shotgun toward him. Andy's trembling arm betrayed him, and his shot was far wide of the mark. The barrel of the shotgun steadied on him and, too late, he dived for the parapet.

He felt himself being spun sideways even in the act of falling. The pain came a split second later, and it was awesome. He rolled back and forth on the gritty surface, the fires of hell coursing through his body.

Regaining control of himself, he stared fearfully down the length of his body. The shoulder of the windbreaker was a ripped, bloody mess, and he could feel his life's blood, warm against his arm and chest, running down his body. Andy rolled across the roof toward the hatch.

A car was racing up the driveway, but he was afraid to rise, uncertain of where Howie was. When he reached the hatch, he scrambled upright, aware that he still held the .32. He shoved it into his pocket. The helicopter was hovering in midair about a hundred yards away, but it might as well have been a hundred miles away. The act of standing was making him dizzy. There was no way he could climb back into the cockpit.

The blood continued to spread, staining his pants below his jacket. He had no choice. He would die unless he could get down into the hospital and stop the bleeding.

Andy lowered himself through the hatch, crashing heavily onto the attic floor. Crawling was impossible with one useless arm, so he rolled through the blackness until he slammed into the duct. Lying on his back, he kicked at it, but the metal stubbornly refused to give. He tried over and over again.

With time running out and his strength ebbing, Andy became furious at the unyielding metal, giving it one last savage kick. The whole section of the duct popped out and rolled away across the floor.

He inched into the duct and wormed his way along its length through the warm rushing air. Before he had gone ten feet, he saw light ahead and knew that he had reached the first room vent.

Andy peered through the vent grill. The room was empty. He smashed at the grill with his good arm, and it popped out, landing with a crash on the floor below.

He twisted around to where he could slide, feetfirst, through the opening. Unable to cushion his fall, he landed hard, luckily on the bed. For a moment, his world went dark.

Grabbing the pillow, he shook the pillowcase free and crammed it inside his jacket against the bleeding, lacerated flesh of his shoulder. He was so weak he couldn't get up. He fell onto the bed, helpless.

CHAPTER 35 _____

*E*lizabeth struggled back to consciousness, exhausted, confused at the abrupt disintegration of her dream. She couldn't understand what was wrong with her. She had been having the most terrible nightmare. She blushed at the memory, thinking again of the lascivious corruption that permeated the place, distorting her dreams into disgusting fantasies.

She became aware of a faint slapping sound and recognized it as a helicopter. She must get out of the building and signal to them.

Elizabeth raised up onto her elbow, staring in surprise at her nude body. She clawed at the sheet, trying to free it to cover her nakedness. The exertion made her dizzy, and her vision blurred. She sank back, incapable of doing anything.

The brief sunburst of hope disintegrated as she heard the helicopter moving away. She had lost her chance for rescue because of the strange lethargy that gripped her.

The door crashed open, and Howie Delgado, wearing only a tunic and carrying a shotgun, stumbled into the room. Too late, she thought of her nudity and tugged futilely at the twisted sheet.

"Oh God, please, not this, don't rape me," she moaned. "Don't do this to me. I can't stand it."

He pointed the gun at her. "Shut up, Goddamn it, or I'll blow your fucking head off, cunt. You're gonna be my ticket out of here."

Elizabeth cringed, afraid to move, but despite the gun, she knew she would fight if he tried to touch her. Her life meant less at this point than that final outrage.

He came closer, and she whimpered. The cold steel of the gun's barrel came to rest against her stomach.

Outside the room, she could hear running footsteps.

Tip had eased the automobile up against the gates, trying to spare Doc's car serious damage.

When the three flares traced their smoky path across the sky, Cobb yelled, "Go for it!"

The gate held, and the car sat there, spinning its wheels.

"Back off and floorboard it!" Cobb shouted.

Tip backed all the way to the highway and then slammed the accelerator to the floor. They roared through the gate with a rendering of metal. He drove the two hundred yards to the porte cochere through billowing clouds of steam from the punctured radiator.

They just missed seeing Howie, who had heard the crash. He disappeared through the doors of the porte cochere just before they rounded the corner of the hospital.

As Cobb came out of the car, he looked toward the chopper, puzzled by why it was hovering rather than moving in to pick up Andy, but he had no time to use the radio. Tip was racing for the door, holding Doc's miserable peashooter before him, and Cobb had no choice but to follow him.

They ran into the treatment room and found it empty. Cobb grabbed Tip before he could rush out into the corridor.

"Damn it, keep your head. Let's cover each other. We're cops—not cowboys."

With Tip covering, Cobb plunged through the doors and dived behind the smashed candy machine. Covering the hall, he pointed toward the kitchen door. Tip leaped into the hall and dived into the kitchen.

The only hiding place that Tip could see was in the

frozen-food lockers. He jerked one of them open. An elderly woman's body, board-stiff, fell out of the locker against him. For a split second his face was only inches from hers. It was bluish, with its bulging eyes and swollen black tongue protruding from between the toothless gums. Tip screeched in revulsion. The body slid free of him, and he screeched again.

Cobb plunged through the doorway. "Damn it, Tip, it's only a corpse. Get hold of yourself."

The young deputy, his back against the work counter, shivered, seeing nothing but the abomination on the floor before him. Cobb grabbed him by the front of his shirt and yanked him toward the door, watching him uneasily because Tip looked as if he was scared to death.

Again he ordered, "Snap out of it, Tip."

The young deputy nodded. He refused to meet Cobb's gaze, but the color came back into his face.

Moving quickly, they worked their way down the corridor, covering each other as they searched. When they reached the red door, Tip started through it, but Cobb pulled him back.

"We can't risk being locked in there. We have to clear this wing first."

As they came even with the nurses' station, Cobb whispered, "Tip, we're in hot water. Our best chance was to catch them in a group, and we sure the hell didn't do that. I have to call Toby. We need help."

Tip nodded, his heart pounding.

Cobb stepped behind the desk and plugged in an outside line. He listened for a moment before slamming down the headset. There was a strangeness about him that Tip had never seen before. "The switchboard's been wrecked. Come on. According to Andy, the offices are down this hall. I . . . I have the feeling they're still here—all around us. We have to get help, and damned fast."

Cobb's shoulders sagged as he looked through the glass wall into the office. "Christ, it's no use. Look, not a phone in sight. I guess those bastards aren't so crazy, after all. We have to secure this one building and go from there."

Back in the corridor, they spotted a nude body on the bed

in room 8. She was not a pretty sight. Her upper body was covered with great purple bruises, and her face was battered beyond recognition.

A door slammed somewhere ahead of them. They leaped into the hallway in time to see a burly man wearing only a white coat of some sort disappear around the corner by the nurses' station.

They raced after him. As they reached the corner, they caught a glimpse of the fugitive crashing through the doors into the treatment room.

Cobb's training asserted itself before he could stop himself. "Stop! Police officers!"

He and Tip pounded down the corridor in pursuit of the half-nude man.

Andy Witherspoon struggled out of the hazy world of semiconsciousness. Although he was at the far end of the mental ward, he had heard Cobb shouting in the distance. Good, Cobb and Tip were in the building.

He pushed himself upright, looked down at the mattress, and sighed in relief. There was only a splattering of blood on the sheets. He suspected he had been hit with birdshot and that the pressure of the pillowcase was allowing the small entry holes to clot over. Still, he had lost so much blood that he needed immediate help.

He was very weak, but he managed to stay on his feet, gritting his teeth against the pain in his shoulder. He wobbled toward the door.

Andy stepped into the corridor, expecting the agony of cold steel slicing into his flesh, but the hallway was empty. No, he had to take that back. It was filled with the appalling stench of death.

On the floor near the red door lay a woman clad in a blood-drenched nurse's uniform. He was having such trouble with his vision dimming that it took a moment to recognize her as Shane Covington.

He pawed feebly at the heavy red door, striving to open it, but was interrupted by a groan from the therapy room. He tried to shut his ears to it, but Andy Witherspoon had spent a lifetime responding to cries of distress, and he couldn't change now.

Reluctantly, he turned away from the red door and a chance to get help for his own injuries. He staggered down the hall, leaving smears of blood against the wall each time he lurched into it.

The therapy room was so dim with the candles long since burnt down that he didn't see the female body spread-eagle against the far wall until she groaned again. The woman was swaying to the rhythm of her soft cries.

The image abruptly faded to darkness, and he found himself on the floor, trying to hold back the numbness in his feet and hands.

Howie Delgado made the last mistake of his life. His first thought had been to reach the safety of the old mansion and ambush his pursuers, but he was gasping for breath and a tightness gripped his chest. He stopped at the far edge of the porte cochere and whirled toward the door as an overwhelming anger burst in him. Nobody was making Howie Delgado run.

He brought the shotgun to his shoulder and waited. He was going to end it for the cocksuckers chasing him.

The doors burst open, and Howie triggered the shotgun, sending the load of steel-jacketed pellets slamming into the wheeled treatment table.

Cobb and Tip, who had dived away at the last second as they gave the table a final push, scrambled back to their knees. Howie gaped at them for one foolish, lost second before he raised the shotgun back to his shoulder, but two .38 slugs crashed into his chest while a tiny .22 bullet drilled a neat hole through his forehead. Howie never knew he died.

As the two deputies rushed across the concrete to where the thick body lay in a spreading pool of blood, Cobb looked at Tip.

"Get the portable out of the car and see what the hell Smitty is doing up there."

Elizabeth, frantic in the aftermath of the fusillade of explosions in the distance, looked up as the door softly opened. She flipped over onto her stomach in the same motion to hide her nakedness.

Billy slipped into the room and closed the door after him. Relief overwhelmed her.

"Thank God it's you, Billy. You're safe. What's happening out there? Why are they shooting?"

He crossed quickly to the bed. "I don't know, Elizabeth. I think they're trying to kill each other. I came in here to try to protect you."

Embarrassed, she tried to rise, to free the sheet to cover herself. He grabbed it out of her hand and flung it across the room.

"I need that sheet," she protested. "I don't know what happened to my clothes."

"Shut up, Elizabeth! You have worse problems than being naked."

"But, Billy, it may be the police. I heard a helicopter outside, and people were running in the hall. Howie Delgado was in here hiding, but then he ran outside. I think they chased him. It must be the police."

"No, you're wrong. I saw them."

"I don't understand. What do you mean?"

He looked genuinely puzzled. "There is something wrong about them. There are just two of them. They can't be the police."

"What are we going to do, Billy? They will find us if we stay here."

He shook his head. "Don't worry. You see, Elizabeth, they don't know about us."

"Thank God you're safe. I saw that terrible woman going up the stairs after you, and then I heard a scream. God, it was awful! How did you get away?"

The question appeared to confuse him. She realized he must be in deep shock, his mind refusing to accept what was happening. He smiled a sad little smile and leaned toward her.

She was fascinated by his arms. They seemed different—darkish and off-color.

He saw her looking at them. "It's blood, Elizabeth. I couldn't find anything to wipe the blood off."

She shuddered. "Poor Billy. How did you get away from her?"

Looking at his face, she suddenly understood. "Oh, no—did you have to kill her?"

He nodded and, reaching into his pants pocket, pulled out a straight razor. With a deft motion he flipped it open; the cruel edge of its bright chrome surface glittered menacingly.

"I cut her throat with this. I didn't want to kill her. I had nothing against her, but she tried to hurt me. I can never rest—never trust anyone. One of them is always after me."

Gently he laid the cool flat edge of the razor against her throat.

Elizabeth shuddered. "Don't."

His unblinking eyes sought her face. "Elizabeth, why did you send her after me?"

She looked at him, wide-eyed. "Send her after you? I didn't send her after you. I was scared to death of her. When I saw you in the hall, I couldn't help myself. I called to you because I needed your help."

He shook his head sadly. "I thought you and I were friends. I thought we could trust each other."

The razor had turned from its flat position, and the keen edge lay against the throbbing whiteness of her throat.

Elizabeth looked into his face. His eyes looked huge, the pupils dilated. She thought him hysterical and unaware of his own actions.

She brought her hand up to his wrist and pushed. It was like pushing against a steel bar.

"Please, Billy, you're frightening me."

Even through the closed door they could hear someone running in their direction.

CHAPTER 36

Cobb looked up from the dead man as Tip leaped from the car, shouting at him. "Cobb, Smitty thinks Doc's in trouble. This bastard took a shot at him."

Cobb paused in the act of pulling shotgun shells from the dead man's pockets to shout, "Check the room this son of a bitch came out of and then meet me by the red door. I'll join you as soon as I load this shotgun. We have to find Andy."

As Tip raced through the doors, Cobb yanked the shotgun out from under the dead body and began to slip shells into it.

Andy struggled to his feet, vaguely aware that he had heard an outburst of gunfire somewhere nearby. He staggered toward the girl and placed his hand on her shoulder. She stiffened under his touch, and he knew she was conscious.

His eyes widened. It was the Hatcher girl. He tried to talk, but he was having a hard time.

"Molly...it's Dr. Witherspoon...with police...save you...understand?"

For a moment, there was no response, just the swaying to the rhythmic groans, but then she stopped. He wondered if he really heard her words.

"Thank God," she whispered.

He turned awkwardly as he heard somebody running along the convalescent-wing corridor.

Billy turned back toward Elizabeth and sat down on the bed, resting the flat edge of the razor against her forehead. Elizabeth stared in near-hypnotic wonder as he underwent some sort of metamorphosis. He was smiling, and his eyes glittered with a strange light. She tried to think of some way to snap him out of his hysteria.

The door crashed open behind them, and Billy's hand moved in a blur, concealing the razor beneath his palm next to her shoulder.

Tip Crable's voice was shrill with excitement. "Freeze, you son of a bitch, or I'll blow you away."

Elizabeth lifted herself onto one elbow, her nudity forgotten, shouting, "No, no, you don't understand. I'm Elizabeth Shea, and this is one of the orderlies. We've been held prisoner by these people. Help us."

Tip was confused, and in a bid for time, asked, "Where are your clothes, lady? Why are you naked?"

"Oh, God, I don't know. They kept me drugged. I don't know when they took my clothes away from me."

Billy slid off the bed as Tip entered. In rising, he had managed to conceal the open razor behind his buttock. Elizabeth was grateful for that. She could see that the deputy was so tense he would have shot first and asked questions later if he had seen the razor in Billy's hand.

Tip stared a moment more in indecision and then slipped the .22 back into his oversized holster. "Okay, but I have to ask you some questions. Fellow, I suggest you come outside with me while the little lady gets respectable."

Billy glided forward, slowly lifting his hand with the razor, talking as he moved. "Sure, Officer—glad to. As a matter of fact, I managed to kill two of them. There was Shane. She's inside the red door, and—"

In that terrible instant, Elizabeth knew who was in the room with her and what he intended to do. She screamed.

Tip Crable had always prided himself on his reflexes, and he had never met a man who could outdraw him in a quick-draw contest. He pulled the .22 from the clumsy holster and squeezed off a round that hit St. Denis in his left shoulder an instant before the glittering edge of the razor slashed through Tip's left eyeball and across his nose and cheek. His scream of pure agony rang through the malignant corridors of Skystone with crystalline purity. He staggered backwards through the open door, the .22 dropping from his nerveless hand.

Paul St. Denis, unfazed by the pinprick of the small slug, came after him, mincing on the balls of his feet, and brought the razor slashing into the juncture of his neck and shoulder. The blood lust was in him, and St. Denis, sure now of his prey, moved lazily, aware of nothing but the blood-soaked figure that still tried to squirm away from him along the corridor floor.

Cobb had been crossing the treatment room when he heard the short, flat report of the .22 and the screams. He crashed through the doors and raced down the hall.

The noise of Cobb's passage echoing through the hall snapped the madman out of his rapt concentration and he leaped back into Elizabeth's room. Her scream died in midnote. She was incoherent with terror.

Cobb rounded the corner and saw the sobbing figure huddled against the locked door of the visitors' lounge, his face an unrecognizable crimson ruin. Cobb's brain refused for a moment to acknowledge the deputy's uniform and accept that it was Tip who lay before him.

"Tip!" he cried. "My God, Tip!"

The keening stopped instantly, and Tip spoke slowly and carefully, forgetting his own pain in his need to warn Cobb. "Naked girl in that room . . . a maniac, too. Be careful."

Cobb looked up to see a slender blond man wearing a light blue shirt splotched with blood step into the hall, smiling. His bloody hand held a straight razor.

"God, I'm glad to see you, Officer. I'm Billy, an orderly. One of the patients just attacked your friend and then forced this razor on me. I wanted to give it to you."

He came forward, still smiling, raising the straight razor.

Cobb waited until he was no more than six feet away before he pulled the trigger twice.

The center of Paul St. Denis' chest collapsed into a puzzle of bone fragments, muscle, and blood.

Cobb stepped over the body and entered the room, the shotgun tucked under his arm.

When Elizabeth saw him, she started to cry. She lay in a fetal position, her body shaking with uncontrollable sobs, unaware that Cobb was standing motionless in the middle of the room, his gaze roaming relentlessly over her body. His eyes found her breasts—with the nipples swollen from the ravages of Howie's mouth—the teeth marks on her body, and the pulpiness of her badly bruised lips.

As her sobs subsided, she managed to speak. "Oh, thank God, you've come. It's been horrible. They're dead—everybody. Poor Scott and Meredith . . . that poor officer. He—"

She burst into tears again, unable to stop herself. The paroxysm of sobbing went on and on until she understood that the policeman had not moved, had offered no words of solace nor gesture of comfort. She recognized him as the officer who had come with the sheriff. Still crying, she managed to blurt out, "You remember me. I'm Elizabeth Shea. Oh, God, it's been—"

Cobb's voice was cold and hard. "You're married, aren't you?"

"Yes, but I—"

He stepped closer to the bed. Her elation was vanishing, and she was acutely aware of her nudity. Her hands, more coordinated with the psilocybin almost gone from her system, freed the mattress cover from beneath her body; she started to cover herself with it.

Cobb ripped it from her grasp, as St. Denis had done with the sheet. His voice was guttural with emotion. "Don't you know people have been dying here? Why have you been fucking the crazies?"

Rage roared through her raw nerves, sweeping the feeling of relief away. She yelled, "How dare you—"

His open palm lashed across her mouth. "Shut up, bitch!"

He was staring intently at her now, and suddenly she was

deadly afraid. She had never seen eyes like his, not even St. Denis' glittering eyes. She could not tear her gaze away. They remained like that for long seconds, and he said nothing.

Abruptly the anger left his face, and a look of weariness and acceptance came into it. He turned and walked out the door.

Tip, panting like a dog in his agony, called "Is that you, Cobb? I'm afraid to open my eye. I'm afraid it will fall out."

Cobb looked around, bewildered. He frowned when he saw Tip.

Despite the excruciating pain, Tip sensed that his injuries, though horrifying, were not fatal. It was shock that was going to kill him unless he reached the hospital. He could feel himself in its grip, being dragged down. His heart action was becoming erratic. He knew Cobb was standing over him, doing nothing.

"Please, Cobb, get me to the hospital, for God's sake. I'll be dead in a few minutes if you don't."

Cobb stooped and gripped Tip's arm. "Sure, old buddy. Just as soon as I take care of a little domestic problem."

He rose and walked back into the room, leaving the bewildered dying man to mutter, "Domestic problem?"

Tip heard the door shut and, with terrible certainty, knew it was closing on his life.

CHAPTER 37 _____

T he blasts of the shotgun brought a screech from Molly, and she jerked against her bonds.

Andy raised his head, opened his eyes, and stared blankly about him. For a moment he didn't know where he was. Then he remembered he was in Skystone.

He was leaning against the wall. It, alone, had kept him on his feet.

He pushed himself upright, knowing that there was something he wanted to do. Then it came into focus—the explosions, the deputies, the takeover of Skystone. Cobb and Tip were still fighting to wrest control from the patients, and he had to help.

He reached for Molly to assure her that he would be back. His hand missed, and he pitched forward, off balance. He grabbed her shoulder and saved himself from falling. Their combined weight on her wrists brought a cry from her.

He muttered, "Sorry, Molly. Friends . . . must help. I'll be back. I swear . . . be back."

He lurched into the corridor, plunging his sweaty hand into his jacket pocket. He gripped the revolver, but the flannel lining clung to his hand when he tried to free it. It took all his depleted strength to pull the .32 free of his pocket.

At the red door, he stepped blindly on Shane's hand. His stomach did a flipflop at the sharp snapping sound. Andy stepped out into the convalescent wing, empty except for the strong, acrid odor of cordite. He was conscious of a current of cold air rushing down the corridor from the doors onto the porte cochere, left gaping by the running Cobb. He paused a second to listen. The faint sound of sirens, far too distant, far too late, rode the chilly wind.

Holding the gun before him in his trembling hand, he made the long journey up the passage, concentrating on each step. As he passed the door of the medical supply room, he saw Thomas Mainwaring lying on the floor, his face ghastly pale under the fluorescent lights.

By the time he reached the nurses' station, his legs were so rubbery he swerved with each step. His shoulder felt stiff and on fire. But there was none of the warm wetness of fresh blood, and he knew he would survive his wound. Still, without medical attention, he could not stave off lapsing into unconsciousness much longer.

Andy reeled around the corner and lunged for the countertop. His vision dimmed, and the floor swayed in sickening jolts. Closing his lids, he laid his sweaty face against the coolness of the metal counter, trying to pump oxygen into his body. Finally, the room steadied and he risked opening his eyes. The pink haze was gone, and his legs felt stronger.

He peered down the hall. What at first seemed merely two dark patches on the shadowed floor became two bodies.

He tried to focus on the nearer one, the one by the visitors' lounge door. A cold feeling ran through him as he recognized the olive drab of the Beauregard County Sheriff Department. The other body, some two or three yards beyond, was clad in civvies and bore such a gaping wound that it looked like a parody of a human torso.

Andy inched toward the wounded deputy, clinging to the wall for support. His stomach tightened when he reached the deputy.

The face was a hideous mask. The wash of blood, diluted with the thick, viscous liquid that had been the interior of the eye, lay thick on his cheek and around his mouth.

Andy leaned over, catching himself before he pitched forward onto the wounded man. The deputy's chest was moving in quick, shallow heaves.

"Tip? Tip, for God's sake, can you hear me?"

The deputy was trying to say something. Andy could see his lips moving.

"What is it, Tip? What is it?"

He dropped to his knees, his hands in the pool of blood on the floor, straining to hear.

It was a mere whisper, said over and over. "In two . . . in two . . . in two . . . in."

The whispered words, with their sense of terrible urgency, stopped abruptly. Tip Crable was dead. Andy clawed at the edge of the door frame, pulling himself upright in a trail of bloody handprints. As he stood, a roaring thundered through his head. He pushed himself away from the wall, almost going down before he caught himself, legs far apart and bent. He brought the .32 up and staggered toward the closed door.

The roaring built toward a crescendo, and a rose haze filled the corridor. A wall of blackness rushed toward him as he opened the door to room 2.

Elizabeth was standing by the window when the door opened and closed again. The sergeant stood inside the closed door. She had noticed her missing uniform trousers wadded up under the window and had retrieved them. She had pulled them on and was looking for the tunic when he reentered the room.

The time by herself had restored a bit of her courage. She demanded, "Sergeant, where are the rest of your men?"

He was coming toward her, silent and menacing. Her newfound courage vanished, and she couldn't move. His eyes were different—resigned, filled with a terrible pain. But what emotion they displayed was beyond reach—inhuman.

"Tip died trying to save you."

His hand closed gently on her elbow, and he walked her to the bed.

She felt as though she were sleep-walking—as if it were unreal. There was no resistance left in Elizabeth. This last terrible shock had swept aside the will to live that had sustained her through three horrifying days.

He did not hurry her. Still holding her elbow, he eased her down onto the bed.

Elizabeth looked up at him. She could not speak, though her lips formed the word "Please," again and again.

What he said was delivered with such a measure of gentle irrationality that the maniacal ramblings seemed worthy of consideration. "I didn't know you would stoop to this, slaking your lust in the beds of maniacs. I've loved you so much. Everyone who knows you loves you. It's like you're ill—like a cancer of lasciviousness grows in you."

Elizabeth's mind was reeling. What did he mean? Did he know about the gardener and about Jack?

Tears were streaming down his cheeks as he reached into his back pocket and pulled out the black gloves. Slowly, meticulously, he worked the tight leathers onto his hands, all the while continuing to talk.

"I never knew, not until that night. No, not until the night that God touched you in your sin and marked you for it. You still haven't learned. Seven times you have found a body that tempted men, and for the seventh time I must destroy it. You must go back to that warped and broken body from which no man can find pleasure. I'm sorry, Margaret . . ."

The black-gloved hands settled lightly on her shoulders and slid up to her neck.

". . . but you must die once again."

The grip was sudden and crushing. She clawed futilely at the powerful wrists. Only because the pressure had turned her head did she see the door fly open and the small figure stagger into the room. Through the roaring in her ears she could hear the cry, "Cobb!"

The hands tightened their grip. The sound of an explosion rocketed through her head and then a second and a third. The grip lessened and the hands fell away.

On a chilly late fall afternoon at Skystone Institute, Elizabeth Shea received the gift of life, and the dead man sprawled atop her received the gift of peace.